The Best Day of
Someone Else's Life

By Kerry Reichs

The Best Day of Someone Else's Life

The Best Day of Someone Else's Life

Kerry Reichs

AVON

An Imprint of HarperCollins Publishers

HarperCollins books may be purchased for educational, business, or sales promotional use. For information please write: Special Markets Department, Harper-Collins Publishers, 10 East 53rd Street, New York, NY 10022.

FIRST EDITION

Designed by Elizabeth M. Glover

Library of Congress Cataloging-in-Publication Data
Reichs, Kerry.
   The best day of someone else's life / Kerry Reichs.—1st ed.
      p. cm.
   ISBN 978-0-06-143857-8
   1. Marriage—Fiction.   2. Man–woman relationships—Fiction.   I. Title.
   PS3618.E525B47 2008
   813'.6—dc22   2007045090

08 09 10 11 12 WBC/RRD 10 9 8 7 6 5 4 3 2 1

For Katie, Bert, and James, for picking up the pieces every time.
Humpty Dumpty should have been so lucky in his friends.

Acknowledgments

First and foremost I want to thank my parents, Kathy and Paul Reichs. This book would not have been possible without them. They provided unconditional support, or, at a minimum, maintained an inspired silence, over my decision to quit the practice of law and move to California to write a novel. I am grateful for the support of my entire extended family. If I don't single out my sister, Courtney, she'll never forgive me, and my brother, Brendan, kept me going with the right vote of confidence at the right time. Special thanks go to my aunt Renate Reichs, book lover, early reader, Kerry-enthusiast.

Unlimited thanks go to my brilliant literary agent, Lisa Grubka, and to Jennifer Rudolph Walsh for introducing us. Special thanks also go to my editor, Carrie Feron, and her assistant, Tessa Woodward. They all made me feel brilliant and special, even when I was doing something ordinary. Elizabeth Rapoport was an invaluable early editor who helped me write myself out of a corner.

Ted Robertson is, hands down, the most extraordinary reader

a writer could have. I am so grateful to have his counsel and for the color he adds to my work.

It took a lot of courage to quit practicing law after six years, and that would not have been possible without the encouragement of my mentor, Christopher Smith, and the wise counsel of Rev. Robert Hardies and Rachel Becker. It also took nagging. This book exists because David Williams insisted I could, and Kyle Robertson made sure I did. I am thankful for their unshakeable belief in my talents.

I arrived in California with nothing but two cats and a vague plan, but it became my home. That would not have happened without the amazing ladies of Venice beach: Kimberly Cayce, Jamie Lanfranco, Janelle Moody, Hiwa Bourne, Tricia Hale, Dawn Warmuth, and Tammi Chase. Thank you. I also want to give a shout-out to the Novel Café, the best novel-writing setting on the planet, where they let you sit all day on one cup of coffee, and are happy to see you again tomorrow.

I don't need to thank any technical advisers because this book is about weddings, and my personal knowledge is thorough. Couples innumerable provided excellent material with ceremonies original, emotional, and comedic. For that, I want to thank all the friends who honored me by including me in their big day. And beg their forgiveness if they are startled to see something they recognize in this book. In particular, Kim Linkner, Ann Baker, and Barbara Zeller gave me my first "blue dresses" and wedding experiences. Veronique Bardach, Leigh Sweet, Jen Paisner, Lisa Hopson, Lori Hodsoll, and Emily Reichs kept the momentum going. However, even I could not have come up with all this stuff on my own. I must thank Kathryn Chinnock, Christelle LaPolice, Andrea Lohse, Kristen Milhollin, Lisa McCabe, Ruth Fisher, Jane Braden, Rebecca Fry, Maya Kabat, Wendi Norris, Cass Sturkie, Gabriela Daniels, Kathryn Falk, Caren Braun, Kirsten Hencken, Mina Guli, Jennifer Lehmann-Weng, Lesley Malus

Reed, Kathy Prendergast, Page Faulk, Anne Kenney, Anna Spencer, Hillary Stewart, Jessica Murty, and Sabina Fogle for their friendship and their stories. Sunday nights at Clyde's couldn't have been written without you. To give credit to the men, they shared their stories too, and for that I thank Craig Davis, John Robinson, Matthew Griffin, Ben Summers, Adam Baron, Kasper Zeuthen, Peter Moore, Matt Gavin, Mark McLaughlin, and Stone Burnette.

And finally, even though he didn't like the ending and had to look up the big words, to Alastair, for teaching me the true meaning of the BDOYL, and giving me three.

Part One

MY FIRST, HER THIRD

CHAPTER ONE

My First, Her Third

The first wedding I ever went to was my aunt's third, and it wouldn't be her last.

My aunt Jackie was beautiful, and demanded attention like neon graffiti on a church. She gave me my first taste of schnapps, a delicious, minty syrup that I later learned was good when drunk sparingly and disastrous when guzzled. Most importantly, Jackie gave me my first taste of the BDOYL.

At age six I was too young to realize that Jackie's (third) wedding was the beginning of my indoctrination. That my participation in the wedding ritual was intended to sucker me down my own bridal path, ring on my finger as firmly as a bit between the teeth, to what the world would view as my greatest accomplishment: the Best Day Of Your Life. The BDOYL begs the question of why girls are so eager to get married if it's all downhill from there. After the vows, does life hold only lesser happinesses, the mildly unfulfilling expectation that today might be the *Second* Best Day Of Your Life—but only if it's really, really good? Like winning the lottery, having a baby, or bumping into the ninth grade bully Susan Bland and seeing that she'd gotten fat and had some sort of skin condition while you had your skinny pants on.

But, as my aunt was having one of the three greatest days of her life (thus far), my brainwashing commenced. I was oblivious, of course. I was never very bright that way. It was third grade before I figured out the bait-and-switch of the New Lunch Box. Each August, I'd happily trail my mother to pick out a new My Little Pony or Strawberry Shortcake lunch box, eager to strut the new model at school. Dazzled by my shiny object, I'd be unwrapping my cream cheese and jelly sandwich the first day before realizing I'd been duped into a classroom prison for the whole year. With my aunt's wedding, instead of a lunch box, I was given a basket of flower petals, and instead of school, I was sucked into an elaborate "marry" tale about the BDOYL.

My encoding would progress from merrily scattering rose petals to the doctrinal texts of *Cinderella*, *Snow White*, *Sleeping Beauty*, and *Sweet, Savage Love*. (What can I say? I was a precocious reader.) Then came the junior preparatory rituals. I staged weddings between Barbie and Ken, and between my Sea Wees mermaid dolls and my brother's G.I. Joes, blissfully ignoring the sticky I-live-on-land-you-live-underwater issue. No problemo. It's true love. I would later observe similar avoidance in many a Determined Bride, myopically focusing on her glorious BDOYL and railroading blindly past warning flares: Fiancé has never filed an income tax return, Fiancé spends more on cosmetics than you, or Fiancé drives an '82 El Camino and calls it a "venerable classic." Worry not. It's true love.

Eventually the BDOYL Story led to eleven trips down the aisle, nine one-wear-only dresses in colors to make the blind wince, seven pairs of dyed-to-match shoes, thirteen Very Humiliating Moments, six seriously regretted hook-ups, one sprained ankle, four allergic reactions, seven stitches, multiple hangovers, and a total cost exceeding $56,800. And that was just *other* people's weddings.

Not surprisingly, I developed a healthy skepticism about marriage. Which isn't fair, really, since I embrace Christmas wholeheartedly, turning a blind eye to the same corruptions there. But I did, so there you have it. They'd title The Movie Starring Me "The Grinch Who Stole First Corinthians." You may mist up at the first mention of "Love is patient, love is kind . . ." but trust me, by the fifth time they trot out this warhorse of wedding readings, you'll be looking to bury your lavender satin pump in the minister's eye socket.

But not at the beginning. At age six, at my aunt's wedding, I presaged none of this. I was solely interested in being the center of attention and annoying my cousin.

I couldn't be Barbie. I knew that. But when I saw Jackie in her gown, I saw a version of princessness within my reach. You got the billowy shiny white dress and the sparkly earrings and the delicate shiny shoes. An admitted sucker for shiny objects, I was enslaved. When it was my turn, I would glisten and smile and laugh charmingly at my own carefully selected audience, self-conscious of my lofty status and the attention pinned to me as I twirled gracefully on the arm of my prince, a crisply tuxedoed figure crowned with a blurry face befitting his lesser status in the affair. The marriage to follow had no traction with me, but the lure of the wedding was awesome.

I didn't remember much about Jackie's Husband Number One except that he looked like one of the bad guys in *Return from Witch Mountain* and swept me into a lap that smelled like garlic. Husband Number Two was pretty in the way of gleaming appliances or game show hosts. He called me "Littlekin" and gave me smooth round stones that he polished in a machine that made loud grinding noises. Jackie met him when she worked in her first husband's office. People didn't talk about it, so I knew something wasn't right. People didn't talk about *him* anymore because he was in jail.

Now Jackie was marrying Cub. I didn't know much about him except that Jackie was happy to be getting married and Cub was helping her. The whole time Jackie was dating Cub, the adults would ask, "When are they getting married, when are they getting married?" Getting married was what everyone wanted, you knew that from the way people talked, and that's why you had weddings, which were the best things ever.

Watching Jackie star in her big show, I was ready to be Princess by Proxy. My white-blond hair hung in curler-enforced ringlets that contrasted starkly with my stick-straight bangs and the occasional escapee curler-eluding strand. I wore a floor-length Holly Hobbie–style pinafore and clutched a basket of pink and yellow rose petals. My cousin Jared was seven, and wore one of those short pantsuits that distort a little boy into a mini-man in a way that emphasizes his childishness. Plaid, of course, because it was the 1970s.

"You look like a girl," Jared said scornfully. Boys are immune to wedding infection, not realizing that Something Important is happening. Jared was unhappy because he wanted to run around but had been threatened with a wallop if he didn't behave. Jackie would do it too, and we both knew it.

"I *am* a girl." I stepped in front of him and smiled beatifically at an arriving guest. No hiding in mother's skirts for me. I relished the attention.

"Oh, aren't you sweet . . ." cooed a grey-haired matron in a puckery lavender suit. She patted my head. "Now what's your name?"

"I'm Kevin," I said. "I'm the flower girl."

It's true. My name is Kevin. When my mother was pregnant, my parents were convinced they were having a boy. Apparently I was holding my fingers in *just* the right place during the sonogram. Thrilled, they picked the solidly Irish Kevin, after Saint Kevin of County Wicklow, near my father's ancestral home of Glendalough. Kevin nicely means beautiful, gentle, and lovable, not bad qualities for a kid. Also, legend has it the good Saint Kevin lived to the ripe old age of 120, harnessing hopes of longevity for his similarly dubbed progeny. Most importantly, Kevin was the only name my parents could agree upon. When I showed up, they were too surprised and worn-out to consider any alternatives. So, Kevin Adair Connelly it was. People mostly called me Vi, the best feminine derivative for Kevin, unless I was in trouble. Then my mother called me Kevin. Adair. Connelly. With menace in the pauses.

The woman in lavender looked confused. I smiled winningly.

"Well. Now. Isn't that nice?" She hesitated, decided against comment and escaped into the church.

No one else came to pet me. Bored, I kicked Jared. He tried to retaliate but I was too quick and leapt away. He reached out in time to yank a handful of my non-natural curls. I began to cry, not because it hurt but because I wanted to get him in trouble. My mother rustled toward us in a long, stiff, flowered gown.

"What's going on, you two? Jared, I told you to behave."

"She kicked me," he whined.

"I don't care who did what. This is Jackie's day, and I won't have you ruin it for her. If you don't behave, you're both going back to the hotel to stay with the babysitter and the baby. Is that what you want?" My mother was tall and willowy, and an expert at Looming.

Eyes on the floor, we shook our heads mutely. We did not want the shame of having to stay with the babysitter.

"Behave." My mother liked that word. She rustled away. I stuck my tongue out at Jared. He scowled at me. My mother shot us a look. I beamed at her. She resumed her conversation.

"You're such a tattletale," Jared accused, ignoring the fact that he had been the tattler.

I glared at him and huffed off, basket held high. In a room off a side hallway a gaggle of ladies were squawking around Jackie. They hovered like a gnat swarm, preening her, vying to be singled out, and basking in the runoff from the Bride.

"Do you have something blue, Jackie?" Maria was Jackie's friend with stern features. "You must have something blue or it's bad luck."

Jackie flipped up her gown to reveal a blue swatch pinned under her skirt.

"Jackie, you need more blush . . . your cheeks are so pale. Here, let me." My aunt Leigh attacked Jackie with a makeup brush.

"Close your eyes," ordered Aunt Rebecca, before dousing Jackie in a liberal application of Clairol Final Net, triggering a fit of coughing from Jackie and temporary dissipation of the gnats. The swarm quickly reconfigured.

"Oh God! You've got a spot on your dress!" One of her bridesmaids, Emily, dabbed at an invisible stain with a washcloth.

There are three types of women who flutter about the Bride. Type One tries to recapture her own moment in the sun. She takes wedding details personally. She cares what kinds of flowers are in her bouquet. Type Two has never been married, and craves her own chance in the sun. Longing to be Runner Up in the princess pageant, she cares about blocking and choreography. It matters where she stands in the altar lineup. Type Three wants to shine in her own way with the Bride as a foil. Type Three will impress the world with her skill, as she efficiently bustles the Bride's gown, or with her prescience, as she produces a safety pin and a Band-Aid from her purse and fashions a MacGyverlike repair to a torn train. She wants to be seen fluffing the Bride's train at the altar. Occasionally an attendant genuinely wants the Bride to be happy, and is there solely to support her.

This is rare. Most of us are seduced into craving a sliver of our own limelight.

I was all about limelight. Swatting through the gnat swarm, I planted myself in Jackie's line of vision. Her glance flicked in my direction, then away, stalling my mission.

"I need to stretch my legs," she said. There was a soft but audible intake of air. Then the gnats jockeyed to offer best insider knowledge of the Wedding Ritual, ignoring the reality of Jackie's thorough personal experience.

"Someone might see you!" Emily's voice radiated horror.

"It's bad luck!" Aunt Rebecca's tone raised Emily's a notch.

"No one can see the bride before the ceremony." The purple feather on a woman named Melanie's hat twitched with apprehension.

Jackie flapped an impatient hand. "I'll be careful." She wrestled herself upright in the confining gown, a swath of white satin beaded with tiny pearls rolling to the ground, shoulders and neck erect with stiff lace. "I just need a minute. Alone. Please."

Amidst disapproving clucking, the Bride took evasive action, leaving her ladies bereft. I hung around waiting to be noticed and petted but got bored because no one did. After a silence, Melanie pronounced Jackie the most beautiful Bride, and said that she, Melanie, had insisted on the long veil. Immediately, the gnats all buzzed, highlighting their own contributions, heady again with the excitement. Limelightless, I wandered out.

I followed the sound of a door down the hall to where Jackie was entering another room. Inside a man in a black suit with a flower on his lapel was reading a folded piece of paper. Jackie spotted him, smiled, and headed determinedly toward him.

"Nick." She giggled, tilting her head. He looked up and smiled wolfishly. I pressed against the door.

"Jackie." He leered. "Don't you know it's bad luck to be seen before the wedding?" Palpable vibrations radiated from them. Was this something else that happened to Brides? I didn't know who he was, but he wasn't Cub. His smirking at Jackie reminded me of Bluto, the villain from Popeye. As an adult I'd describe that look as salacious. Of course, at six, I didn't know what "salacious" meant. I did know what "trouble" meant. My aunt was feeling feisty and I was looking at Trouble.

"As a matter of fact," she flirted, "I've done this once or twice before, so I can't say that *not* being seen causes *good* luck." Jackie laughed. Bluto the Villain laughed too.

"Don't worry, babe. Third time's a charm. Cub's a lucky guy."

"He's a good alternative to what I truly desire," Jackie purred.

Bluto gleamed at her. "And what would that be . . . ?"

She leaned in. "That would be . . ." She drew out her pause. ". . . a cigarette. And a shot." She laughed. She was playing a funny game where she talked really quiet and stood close, like telephone. She tickled him too.

Bluto laughed. "The Dolphin Queen smokes? Well blow me down."

Jackie looked delighted with herself. Another sign of Trouble. She batted her eyelashes. "I don't know what you mean," she pouted.

"Well," drawled her willing victim, "I may be just what you need."

"Oh?" She raised her brows. "How's that?"

Winking, Bluto produced a flat silver object from his pocket.

"You've got to be kidding!" She pounced. "My hero." She opened the silver thing and knocked back a healthy gulp. She tilted her head and made a production of sighing as she swallowed. Then she looked at Bluto and licked her lips really, really slowly, like she had just eaten a cupcake with lots of icing.

Putting her palms against Bluto's chest, she leaned toward him. "For that," she breathed, "you get a reward."

"And what might that be?" He slid a hand over her bottom.

"Mmmm, I'm not sure. It should be something really good. Something *very* good . . . like that time at Jefferson Park."

"Yes," he said. "That was a good time." He put his other hand on her waist and slid it up. Jackie drew in a quick breath.

"Or that time in Walter's backyard." She leaned closer.

"That was a good one too." His hand slid higher.

"Or that time we parked at the end of the airport runway." Jackie's face was barely an inch from his face.

"That was definitely a good time." He growled, and covered her mouth with his. I gaped, witnessing my first passionate adult kiss.

My mother walked in.

"Oh Jesus," she said. Jackie and Bluto jumped apart. Jackie recovered quickly.

"What?" She assumed an innocent look.

"For God's sake," swore my mother.

"It's not like that." Jackie chose indignant. "I had a cigarette and Nick was checking my breath."

"How dumb do you think I am?" My mother was now Looming over Jackie. Bluto began backing away; the two women ignored him.

"Jackie, for Christ's sake! It's time for you to get *married*. To *Cub*." My mother ranted, lasering a look at Bluto, who froze and looked sheepish. "Remember *Cub*? Remember the *white dress*? Lots of *people*. A *priest*. Right here in this *house of God*. You are *getting married* in *five minutes*. *If* you don't *screw it up!*" You could hear audible italics.

Jackie looked petulant. "Yes, I suppose. But—"

My saddle shoes slipped, and banged the door against the wall. All eyes jumped to me.

"Vi," my mother started, "where did you come from?"

I looked mutely at them. Jackie didn't meet my eyes. My mother shifted quickly from Looming to view-blocking. Taking his chance, Bluto scuttled out the far door.

"Have you been there long, scooter?" My mother tried to sound as if it didn't matter. I shook my head. "I expect you've come looking for this pretty princess." She nodded toward Jackie. I nodded back. "All right then. Best that we head to our places," she said breezily.

In a lower tone to Jackie, "We'll finish *our* conversation later."

Back in the dressing room, the gnat swarm engulfed, until a pert woman in a blue suit popped in and announced "Five minutes."

Next thing I knew, the lady in blue gave me a push and all the people were smiling at me. I walked slowly toward the front of the church. The lady in blue motioned frantically, making a picking and throwing motion, and I remembered the rose petals. Nervous now, I grabbed a great gob of petals and threw it at the ground. People tittered. I started to relish the attention. I grabbed another handful of petals. At the front of the church I turned and faced a red carpet littered with clumps of rose petals at intervals, like piles of rabbit droppings, and Jared walking behind me with a satin pillow, looking scared and angry at the same time.

A few moments later, my mother and the other ladies walked unnaturally down the aisle like uncomfortable soldiers, elbows sticking out awkwardly, clutching their flowers and smiling too big. Then the music changed and everyone stood up. The door opened again, and Jackie came down the aisle in her big white dress. It sparkled when she walked. Everyone stared and smiled really hard. She walked slowly, smiling hard back. Limelight. I wanted to be Jackie so badly I could taste it. Just wait, I vowed. I would marry my dad or someone just like him. That would be me someday.

After the ceremony, the photographer grouped the family, long bright dresses in front of tuxedos with ruffled shirts. We faced the camera and smiled as though our faces would break. Jackie bore the widest smile of all, bright lipstick gleaming. The photographer snapped picture after picture and captured the happy event for all eternity.

I would remember how different my aunt looked when she arrived at our house one night a year later with a puffy face and red eyes, before I was sent out so the adults could be alone. I went to my room and opened my Barbie coloring book to one of the best pictures, where Barbie, in a long, sparkling gown, goes to the ball with Ken. Humming to myself, I picked a silver crayon and began to color, dreaming of heavy satin dresses and crowds of people smiling at me.

Part Two

THREE BLUE DRESSES

CHAPTER TWO

Oh What a Feeling

Technically, it was "day" when I cracked my eyes open because I could see "light." It offended me anyway because I'm *not* a morning person. But if I was late for brunch again, Imogen would plot something nasty. That threat got me moving, and earned me the Hateful look when I dislodged my cat Clementine. Her brother Nigel yawned and twisted on his back so I could rub his exposed belly. He stuck all four paws in the air and torqued in delight when I did. When I pushed out of bed, he opened an eye at the cessation of tummy-rubbing. Clementine gave him a look that said, "See, you cannot count on them."

I was forgiven as my two shadows raced me to the bathroom and jumped on the counter expectantly, Clementine slinky and dark, Nigel orange and puffy. I shoved them aside so I could brush my teeth. Then I left a trickle flowing from the faucet. They had an odd symbiosis for drinking from the tap. Nigel stuck his head directly under the flow and drank from the base of the sink, while Clementine delicately licked the runoff from the back of Nigel's head.

"Weirdoes," I muttered, turning on the shower. "What kinds

of cats like water?" I appraised my reflection in the mirror while waiting for the water to get hot. I have straight blond hair that will flip a bit at the ends with some effort, a hair dryer, and a round brush. I have to wash and blow it dry every day or I look like a Drowned Rat. Sadly, the mirror didn't show my legs, my best feature. I can say that if it is true, right? It's why I'm addicted to high heels. I rarely go out without about three inches strapped to the bottom of my feet. This makes me pretty tall.

On the whole, I like my looks. When I was a kid, I longed to be eighteen and legally free to dye my hair black and change my name to Diana. It's not clear why I thought you had to reach the age of majority to dye your hair, but I'm glad I did. Now I'm a happy blonde, and appreciate my quirky name.

I completed my morning ritual: shower (evaluate whether any-one might see or touch legs in decision over whether to shave), daily ablutions (lotion all over, slap on limited makeup, peer in-tently at eyebrows with tweezers in hand to ruthlessly pluck rogue hairs), hair (mind-numbingly tedious drying of the hair with round brush to achieve desired flip and avoid Drowned Rat ap-pearance). Then came the challenging selection of the outfit. In a nod to the crisp October weather, I settled on a sweater, Burberry jeans, and boots, and left my Dupont Circle apartment to walk the two blocks to Kramerbooks & Afterwards Café to meet my best friend, Imogen.

Imogen had picked the place. I detest the Kramerbooks brunch. First of all, they don't have normal menu items like scrambled eggs and bagels. They have Café Frittatas, Whole Grain Waffles and Imported Italian Prosciutto Benedicto, all served with "break-fast breads." Not ordinary muffins and biscuits, which they, in fact, are, but "breakfast breads." Second, I'd once gotten very, very ill after eating a Kramers' quesadilla. Coincidence? I don't think so. And, for Saturday brunch at Kramers you have to wait for a table, and the waiting area is an excellent bookstore. I hate this about Imogen. She knows I won't protest because I'm weak in the knees for books. I compulsively buy them at a rate that I could never read. I love to browse, trailing my finger on the spine of books I've already read and loved, like kissing the cheek of an old friend in greeting. It occasionally alarms the staff.

Kramers also has great greeting cards, which I collect. Like anything you'll need, it's better to buy a good one when you see it, rather than be forced to seek it under duress. I have extensive greeting card files. *Someday* my mother will turn seventy-five, and I have the perfect card. I did become concerned when I found a sensitive pet bereavement card, and morbidly calculated on whose Fido had outlived his lifespan, so I could dazzle with my condolences.

Today, I was too distracted to fondle the books or arm myself with the perfect Pearl Harbor Day card. I explored a Feeling hovering in my chest, poking it with my brain. It slid around evasively but I pursued it, determined. I was focused on this chase when I was grabbed and hugged from behind by a human who needed sudden sharp movements to release some of the energy rattling through her body.

"Mentally spending the gains from your food poisoning lawsuit?" she mocked my unshakeable food poisoning suspicions. Imogen is six feet tall and has beautiful curly hair that is pure white and makes me sigh with envy every time. One time I gave myself highlights at home and turned chunks of my hair white, but on me it just looked like a duck's butt. I slunk to the salon at dawn and paid the colorist an enormous amount of money to repair my hair to a nice ordinary color.

"No," I said darkly, "but you'll regret the diminishment of your cut when my eventual food poisoning lawsuit award is slashed for contributory negligence in returning to this unsanitary establishment. Stapled stomachs score big with juries."

"Mmwah." She kissed my check. "I'll check on the table while you molest the books." She bounced to the host stand, drawing eyes across the room in her wake. She dazzled the host. He looked stupefied. She waved me over. We were led to a choice table on the sidewalk.

"So, what'll it be?" enthused Imogen once we were seated with menus. "The Nouvelle Leo or the Brie, Basil, and Tomato Omelet?"

"Very funny," I replied. I ordered the Veggie Huevos Rancheros.

"Do you want that with sausage?" asked the server. I paused. Imogen snorted.

"Yes, I would like my Veggie Quesadilla with sausage," I deadpanned.

The server didn't notice. "Anything to drink?"

I ordered a Bloody Mary, an orange juice, a coffee, and a Coke. The server looked at me. "I like a little drinks party," I said.

Imogen rolled her eyes. "A toast," she pronounced. "To prising you away from a *Wedding Story* marathon and getting you out on a Saturday."

"Ha," I said, but clinked. "And very funny on sending me the Bridezillas Season One DVDs. How do they make that stuff up?"

"Sweetie, it's not made up, that's the point," Imogen laughed.

"I don't believe it," I dismissed. "Getting married isn't like that."

Imogen snorted. "You are such a romantic. I guess you're going to find out, aren't you?"

Like me, Imogen was from Charlotte, North Carolina, happily moving to D.C. after college without looking back. A lobbyist for the Children's Defense Fund, she was my constant counsel in all things and recently appointed as vicarious bridesmaid as I partook in the weddings of three friends from home. Jen, Amy, and Lila had gotten engaged in quick succession, going down like freshmen on twenty-five-cent beer night.

I was thrilled. After years of misting up at romantic movies, I was part of the real deal. It felt grown up. But at the same time . . .

"So what were you mulling when I walked in? You looked very pensive."

I returned my attention to the Feeling. I mentally cornered it and examined it.

"It's a Feeling, isn't it?" asked Imogen.

"Yeah. I can't quite put my finger on it. You know, I'm excited about the weddings . . ."

"That's the understatement of the year."

". . . *Me* talking. So, I'm the maid of honor?" I relished saying the words.

"But?" prodded Imogen.

I hesitated. Was I a bad friend? "I also have a weird sort of Dismay over the whole situation. It's terrific that the girls are getting married, but I might be Disappointed in their choice of grooms." I had assumed that my friends had been dating their perfectly-nice-but-sort-of-boring boyfriends to fill the time until blazing passion showed up. Tuned in only by sporadic phone calls and occasional trips home, I was surprised when in quick succession they got engaged—snagged the Golden Ring, hit the bull's-eye, won the Big Lotto Billions, were having a *wedding*. It was the pinnacle. So it pained me to feel tepid about them.

"Any unacceptable undersides to the Dismay?" asked Imogen.

"No. It's pretty much Dismay. Perhaps accompanied by Fear and Anxiety."

Imogen sipped her coffee. I waved the waiter down and ordered a club soda with a lime. "What do you think it's about?" she asked. "Aside from the obvious of being involved in any wedding where Amy picks the dress you have to wear. In public."

I made a face. "Be nice." I focused on my Bloody Mary. I added Tabasco as I reflected. "Since our first kisses, we've supported each other through crappy relationships and broken hearts. I guess I thought the finale would be more thrilling."

Imogen drummed her fingers on the table, listening. Some part of Imogen was always moving.

"I thought all the juvenile trauma would be rewarded," I continued. "Our solace for Unfaithful Bob or Johnny-Not-That-Into-You was that someday the Perfect One would come. Smart, handsome, successful, intelligent, kind to his mother but geographically removed from her, lover of animals, possessor of an adorable puppy, a sailboat, and a vacation home, charming to strangers, waiters, and old people, an account at Tiffany's, just gay enough to hew his own furniture then discuss with you how to arrange it in the room, witty, sexy, not too hairy, no fetishes, you know. Perfect."

"And?" Imogen looked at me, rapidly bouncing her knee under the table.

"Oh, I don't know," I sighed. "I can't shake the feeling that they aren't in love. At least not like you're supposed to be. The guys seem sort of boring. I mean, Bill lives one square mile from where he grew up, never owned a passport, and looks exactly the same as he did in eleventh grade, with the addition of ten pounds and that faraway look in his eyes recalling the glory days of high school." Amy was marrying Bill.

"What about Hart?" Imogen named Lila's fiancé.

"Hart makes me think of an i-bot. Plus, I think he might be sneaky."

Imogen grinned and wiggled in her chair to release a burst of energy. "You think Barney is sneaky."

"Well, it's true," I huffed. "It's really creepy when an adult puts on a costume and wants a bunch of little kids to sit on his lap." I took a sip of coffee with a club soda chaser. "The Dismay is that I expected passion."

"And the Anxiety?"

I looked at her. "I've been dreaming about my wedding day my whole life. It's supposed to be the best thing that ever happens to you. But it should follow a fairy-tale romance, and none of the girls had that. What if it all turns out to be just . . . ordinary?"

Imogen reached across the table and squeezed my hand. "Honey, we're not going to marry anyone who doesn't knock our socks off. I promise you that." She paused. "Is it possible you're idealizing marriage? Splitting the bills and keeping groceries in the fridge and oil in the car is a practical arrangement at some level. Picking a partner isn't always romantic."

"I don't believe it." I said.

"Ah. Caleb."

I shrugged. "I'm not sure what you mean." Though I did. I fell in love with Caleb Carter on New Year's Eve at age seventeen and never recovered. Imogen rode me about giving that relationship iconic status.

"I think you're a little disappointed in the girls."

"What do you mean?" Like me, Jen had been with one guy, Bo Davis, all through high school, most of college, and beyond. We both felt like we'd met our match, only, in a truly cruel trick of fate, we'd met them too young. I suspected my resistance to her choice was rooted in my own hopes about Caleb.

"Well, they let you down," Imogen said. "You want everyone to be this enlightened Super Woman holding out for true love. You can't accept that Amy just wants to get married and have kids. Bill has money and doesn't drool on himself, and Amy will rule her Laura Ashley smothered roost and watch her kids play club tennis just like her mother. Jen's finished looking and Louis is fine. Lila's more complicated, but made her decision based on family expectations. You're disappointed in them that they didn't act like you would. Like you *do*."

I frowned. "You make me sound horrible."

"No way, babe. You're great. Not everyone drives herself at the same level that you do. It's what I love about you. You make me improve my standards."

"Are you sure it's not a temporary loss of insanity? Like the Rapture?"

"As much as mass hysteria appeals to my flair for the dramatic, I suspect it's a Southern thing. At sixteen get your license. At seventeen drink cheap domestic beer at Twin Lakes while getting felt up by someone named Brian or Jimmy. At nineteen have your debutante season. At twenty-six get engaged."

I'd been the only one in my class to eschew the debutante season, opposed to the concept that a woman was deemed "marriageable" at a certain age. (Though I'd actually been sure I'd be engaged before graduation.) "I'm the oddball again, but this time I don't remember declining."

"Is this about you being left out?"

"No. I think that somewhere between 'debutante' and 'getting engaged,' I expected 'fall madly, deeply, passionately, and breathtakingly in love with the unique twin to your soul.' And I don't feel that from the girls. But I guess it's paternalistic to think I'm supposed to *do* something about my friends' choices," I conceded.

"Probably. And maybe blinding passion isn't what everyone's looking for. Or believes exists," said Imogen in a way that suggested she might be a member of that committee.

"Maybe." Imogen was jaded because her parents were divorced. I drank some orange juice and then some coffee, not believing it.

"Maybe it's the Anxiety back riding on my Dismay. I don't want to find out at the end of the day there's just someone named Bob who eats the same cereal and wants three kids and twelve place settings."

Imogen thought. Then she said, "For every person, the boundaries of what's possible are different. It doesn't have to be Bob. But at some point you have to stop treating the men in your life like tourists. You can be a little guarded."

"That's not true!" I defended.

"Vi, the only men you date for more than a week are somehow remote—either they're long distance or there's something else that prevents real commitment." It was a coincidence that most of the men I'd dated had been long distance.

"I dated Nathan for four months last year," I said smugly.

Imogen smacked my hand. "Nathan lives an hour away in *Annapolis*, and you stopped dating him when he wanted to see you more. And he was willing to drive here!"

"He was a bad kisser," I muttered.

"Whatever." She rolled her eyes. I was expert at eliciting eye rolls. "Are you done with your beverage buffet? If you want to hit the book signing, we'd better go."

I'm a wine buyer for a gourmet store called Darien & Dodd. I'd gotten the job through an accident of timing, and most of the time I was terrified everyone would figure out how little I knew about wine. In periodic fits of ambition, I determined to learn my trade. Politics and Prose was having a signing by a wine author, and after an embarassing gaffe with the Ggrich Hills distributor I'd coaxed Imogen into going. My self-improvement fervor had since cooled.

"We don't have to go." I hedged.

"Quit waffling and drink up. You might enjoy understanding your job for a change."

I threw a breakfast bread at her, and resigned myself to a boring afternoon.

CHAPTER THREE

Some Good Soldiers Go Down

We were holed up at Clyde's for Sunday half-price wine night. Given my job as a wine buyer, I fancy myself a wine snob despite only hazy "expertise." Like fashion, I recognize the hot labels but not the details. Clyde's has a wine list worthy of patronage and half-price night lets me pretend the discrimination my job (inaccurately) implies on the meager salary it provides. In truth, you'll find in my recycle bins Trader Joe's "Two Buck Chuck," also known as the eminently affordable $2.99 Charles Shaw cabernet.

There were already two dead soldiers on the table and the girls were snorting with laughter as I described the increasing demands of my maid of honor duties.

In the weeks following "Will you marry me," obligations had mushroomed like reality TV shows in the wake of *American Idol*. With Imogen and me were my D.C. girl posse, Mona, Ellis, and Babette, all bonded by our dedication to the half-price night ritual. Mona was my college roommate, and she, Imogen, and I had been coming to Clyde's since we first arrived in D.C. knowing no one but each other. We'd expanded our magic circle twice. Ellis joined us shortly after Mona and I discovered her occupying our usual Commentary Corner at a party. We'd stood apart dissecting the scene and watching Imogen work the room, and recognized a fellow in humor and temperament. Babette was a more recent addition after Imogen realized they were simultaneously dating the same man. They'd chucked the man but kept each other. For sarcastic but expectant single women navigating life, Sunday nights were sacred therapy sessions.

"So you have three weddings in three weeks?" Imogen demanded.

"That's a lot of weddings," Mona sympathized. "Imogen, you just kicked me. Stop jiggling your legs around—this table is too small."

Mona was a lawyer with straight brown hair, a wide smile, and a huge heart. Despite her hefty law firm salary, she was perpetually broke because she hemorrhaged donations to animal rescue charites. She was profoundly attached to an eleven-year-old cairn terrier named Moxie who had a thyroid problem and was going blind, and we all lived in terror of the day Moxie departed this earth and we'd have to put Mona back together again. Mona and I met in our college dining co-op. We'd been paired to bake bread on Sunday nights. From this alliance a great friendship, and the late night sport of Bread Ball, had been born. It involved balls of dough, rolling pins, and someone having to wash their hair eventually. After sophomore year we moved in together to split shampoo costs.

"What possessed them to stack up their weddings like planes coming into O'Hare? Don't they realize it's ridiculous?" asked Ellis.

Ellis was a National Public Radio program producer. She had straight red hair, was incredibly thin, and impeccably turned out at all times. Ellis was the classic preppy and never wore anything but cigarette pants and perfectly pressed button-down oxford shirts. I envied her this, as I loved her crisp look but couldn't pull it off with my "generous" cleavage. Whenever I wore a button-down shirt, it gapped between buttons two and three, looking completely tacky and sluttish. My penchant for three-inch heels was sluttish enough, so it was pullovers for me.

Ellis had once published a how-to book on navigating the chaos of T.J. Maxx. Stores like T.J. Maxx, with their endless racks and messy piles of oft-handled garments gave me a headache. I'd take one look at the forlorn fabric piles and head for Anthropologie to pay inflated prices for the pleasure of compartmentalized clothing displays. I hated to shop, and Ellis's true gift for any kind of shopping was indispensable on my biannual surgical strike missions to the outlet mall.

"Actually, they aren't really close—different schools, different neighborhoods," I told her. "The common denominator was yours truly, and since I moved away, nothing brings them together anymore. It's eerily coincidental that they're all getting married within three weeks."

Mona waved down our waiter, Charlie. Charlie was our favorite because he had a great ass and adorable dimples. The dimples were on his face. Mona and Babette had arrived early to stake out a choice table in his section. It was only 8:30 P.M. now, and nobody had to be home until *Grey's Anatomy* came on television at 10:00 P.M. With two bottles already down, it was looking grim for effectiveness at the office on Monday.

"Ladies?" Charlie flashed his dimples in a way he knew directly correlated to increasing his gratuity from female customers.

"There's something wrong with these bottles." Imogen waved at the empty bottles on the table. "Nothing comes out of them. You'd better bring us two that work."

"Will do," Charlie said. "Another Vanilla Stoli for you, Babette?" Babette was French and stunning. Contrary to all logic, she didn't drink wine. She dressed with great style in very, very short skirts and tight tops, but didn't really mind whether she received attention from men. (She always did.) She was a high-powered venture capital professional, and one of the ditziest human beings on earth. She lived and died by e-mail, but never sent a single one without a typo, often one that was meaning changing, such as encouraging me to "stay toned" when she had news to share or referring to a missive as "pact with information" (crammed with news and also consigning the reader to a secret agreement?). Babette's great goals in life were to finish the renovations on her kitchen and to find the perfect man for each of us. She was faring better with the kitchen. Sadly, she had a poor track record for selecting men who were "perfect for you." And half the time they were actually in love with Babette.

"Great minds have the same idea!" she beamed. Babette loved American idioms but never got them right.

"Vi, another root beer?" Charlie asked.

"No thanks. But I'll take a refill on the club soda," I replied.

"I'm on it." Charlie saluted and turned, letting us admire his second best feature.

"I've just had a lustful thought about a twenty-one-year-old," moaned Imogen. "God does that make me feel old."

"Don't get me started," I protested. "I just turned twenty-seven and I feel more like an old maid than a maid of honor."

"Don't blame me," said Imogen. "I'm not getting married."

"Who'd marry you?" I was rewarded with a kick under the table. It could've been intended, or just an excited burst of energy.

"Just you wait," Imogen predicted. "I'm going to meet a gorgeous Scandinavian prince with a gothic castle on a fjord and lots of hot, single royal cousins, and you will all be dying to crawl into my tulle."

Charlie returned at the tail end of Imogen's statement and gave her a startled look. She arched a brow. He sauntered off. We all looked at his ass. He paused without turning and dramatically wiggled his butt for us.

"Do you realize we might each be a bridesmaid at least ten times?" I relished the thought.

"You're off the hook with me," announced Mona. "I don't want any bridal party. I might elope." I goggled at her. How could anyone not want a wedding?

"Really? You don't want a wedding? But you're *Catholic*."

She laughed at me. She knew I thought Catholicism was mysterious and controlling. Like the people who set the line in Vegas.

"It's true. I don't want that sort of thing. So feel free to dis-include me from your bridal parties." I marveled anew. I thought I'd feel very left out if I wasn't chosen.

"Would you ever turn down being a bridesmaid if someone asked?" asked Ellis seriously. "I mean, if it wasn't family." Ellis came from a big family.

"Yes," chorused Babette and Imogen.

"No way," I said.

Mona paused. "Well," she said, "I'd have to balance how strongly I felt about it against the bride's feelings. If Imogen's Scandinavian prince turned out to have run a Nazi death camp, I'd definitely say no. But, in the more likely situation that I simply prefer not to call a lot of attention to myself or spend a lot of money on a horrible dress, but the bride's feelings would be really hurt if I said no," here Mona sneaked a glance at me, "I would just suck it up and say yes." I felt the guilt of being correctly identified in a less than flattering way.

"I know friends who've broken up over it," said Ellis.

"Well I think that is just silly!" exclaimed Babette. "If someone is close enough to you that you'd ask them to be in the wedding, how could you simply stop being friends if they say no? Americans have this crazy obsession with weddings that I do not understand. It is not such a big deal in France."

"In France, neither are fidelity, monogamy, and all the things that supposedly go along with marriage," countered Imogen.

"True," conceded Babette. "We just turn twenty-five and marry. Not much changes after."

"What about you, Vi?" asked Ellis. "I mean, you're in all these weddings but you think your girlfriends might be making a mistake. Does it bother you to go along with it?"

I thought about Ellis's question. "I'm excited to be in the weddings," I admitted. "It's thrilling. I also think a friendship could end over the bridesmaid thing if the bride felt judged," I ventured. "You can't be yourself around someone you feel judges you. You get defensive. I'm careful not to create that situation. I mean, just because I wouldn't marry these guys doesn't mean they're not good guys. What I struggle with is whether I'm being a good friend by shutting up and accepting their choices, or being a good friend by probing a bit to ensure they're making smart choices. So far, I'm playing it safe, and focusing on the weddings, which is fun."

I drank some wine as we all thought about it.

"Besides," I continued, "my opinion is just my opinion. I might be a tiny bit Disappointed that the girls didn't hold out for someone more challenging or romantic, but I'm trying to see it from their perspectives. They must be in love if they're getting married, right?"

Imogen reached over and gave me a big squeeze. "You're my favorite idealist!" she declared. "The way you believe gives me faith."

"Amen," agreed Mona, raising her glass.

"Ladies, a toast," ordered Babette.

"Vi?" Imogen looked at me.

I smiled. "To the reward for holding out—the Perfect One is out there," I said, raising my glass. "And that when we each marry, it's a delight and celebration for everyone we rope into it. Oh, and to Charlie's ass!"

"I heard that!" Charlie said as he walked by with a tray of drinks.

"Hear! Hear!" everyone agreed, and clinked glasses.

CHAPTER FOUR

In Which No Work Gets Done

When I woke up the next morning, I regretted it. On days when I didn't crawl home from Clyde's at midnight, I liked my job. I marveled that I had it. I graduated college with a fine arts major, equipped to do nothing. Add in no clue what I wanted to do. Within days my bank account was about to run dry, so I started a "temporary" gig at a Georgetown wine bar. I'd bartended a year and a half when the place went under. The day the manager broke the bad news, I was lamenting with a regular named Alfonso. Al was a short, dapper widower in his fifties, who came in most days, didn't ask me out, and was a good tipper.

"Well, Vi, what're you going to do?" Al asked. It was a good question. I had a week's lead-time on abject poverty.

"I'm not sure," I said. "Maybe see if Sean needs help liquidating the inventory."

"As in, swallowing it?" he joked.

"You got it." It turned out Al was the manager of Darien & Dodd's Georgetown store.

"Listen, Vi." He was earnest. "You know your wines."

I'm an excellent bluffer. I smiled modestly down at the bar.

"We've got an opening in the wine department. It's entry-level, but you can learn a lot. I think you'd be great at it."

And that was how my career found me. I didn't start out as a buyer, of course. I was an office assistant. Even an art major can handle that. By the time the buyer moved to Houston with her husband, I could mimic her job, and Al let me step in as interim buyer. Though not sizzling with originality, I managed not to bankrupt the business and organized a good event or two, so he gave me the job. It's not a ton of money, but I like my work. And I preen over the idea of being a wine expert—though my learning curve sort of stopped when the old buyer left. I'm quite deft at throwing out my job title then changing the subject before conversation progresses past generalities.

I don't however, love getting up for my job. I was dreaming a confused scenario where I tumbled through a huge crack in the ground with a bunch of Japanese schoolchildren and ended up in a jungle full of exotic birds when a persistent paw dragged me to consciousness. I opened an eye. Nigel was crouched on my chest, staring with enormous yellow eyes. NPR had moved from a story on the earthquake in Japan to deforestation. Nigel inched up to tuck his face under my chin. I embraced him like a papoose as I contemplated the depths of my headache.

"You're not fooling anyone," I said to Nigel. "I know what you're up to."

Nigel pressed his cold nose against my neck and snuggled further in. To anyone else it would seem like charming affection from a devoted pet.

"Seriously. You're so obvious," I repeated.

Nigel went for the kill, locking on my earlobe. He loved to sneak up on people and suck on their ears. He knew he had to move quickly because once people recovered from their shock, he was rapidly dispatched. He almost swallowed my stud once.

"Eeeuw, gross." I sat up, and then regretted it. Oh dear. Today would not be a good day. My tongue tasted nasty and my head pounded. Today The Movie Starring Me was called "Not So Bonny After Clyde's." Damn Charlie.

I staggered into work an hour later wearing wrinkled comfort clothes liberally embroidered with stray cat hair.

"Hangover, thy name is Clyde's," mocked our special events planner Giles, my compatriot and office mate.

"Ugh," I said.

Giles was an essential accessory to any D.C. girl, the stylish and very, very gay friend. He was tall, slim, and had glossy skin the color of dark chocolate. I thought he looked like a very skinny, very flamboyantly dressed version of Taye Diggs. Today he was wearing a tangerine shirt made of something flammable. Giles was one of my best friends, which is probably the only reason I hadn't been fired ages ago. He covered my back. And he had plenty of hangover mornings himself.

"What, J.R.'s closed early last night?" I named a trendy gay bar.

"I was saving myself for showtunes night tonight. Want to come?" he asked hopefully.

Damn. I *adored* showtunes, and Giles knew it. "Modern or old school?"

"Well hellloooo Dolly, oh helloooo Dolly, it's so nice to have you back where you belong," warbled Giles, criminally off tune.

Shoot. "What time?" I capitulated, even through my pain. After all, I could walk from my place, I rationalized. And sleep next year.

"Woo hoo," he crowed. "Let's go at eight."

"We'll see," I said, both of us knowing he had me.

Thankfully, my calendar showed a slow day. I had a tasting on Thursday but it was all planned. Today I could work on inventory and lick my wounds in my office.

"So." Giles returned to his computer. "Did you see the new baby pictures?" Giles and I share an avid love for the panda born at the National Zoo. I'm insanely jealous of the attending zoologists and suspect they examine the cub more than necessary because he's so cute. But, then again, so would I.

"Are they good?"

"Oh yeah." He was reverent. "He's adorable, more visible now and snuffling about."

"Really? Are they posted at the website yet?" Giles gave me a sly grin.

"They don't need to be. I'm on pandacam." His crow was unable to contain his glee. I gasped with envy. Live pandacam was always overloaded and impossible to get on.

"Really?" I breathed, jealous to my toes.

"Yep," he said smugly. "And I am going to stay on it *all day long*. Come have a look." Twenty minutes later we were oohing and aaahing over the cute little guy when a voice made us both jump and caused Giles to knock over his latte.

"And how is little Tai Shan today?" questioned my boss, Al. Giles frantically wiped up coffee while I turned, flushing.

"Oh, that's just a screen saver, sir," I blathered. "Giles was about to show me a wine pairings website he thought I might find helpful. Er, but that can wait." I put some distance between me and Giles's computer so Al didn't express an interest in the mythical pairings site. "What can I do for you?"

"Stop calling me sir, for starters," ordered Al. "Makes me feel like an old man."

"Gotcha . . . sir." I grinned. He rolled his eyes.

"I was checking on the arrangements for Thursday," he finished. "I want to figure out what kind of staff we'll need. Are the RSVPs coming in?"

"Yes sir." He glowered, and I rushed on. "I think we'll have a nice turnout." Thank God I was prepared—my capacity for ad lib was diminished. I plucked a cat hair off my shirt and pulled up the event spreadsheet, desperately hoping alcohol wasn't reeking from my pores.

"Well," said Al when we were done, satisfied. "You have everything under control, Vi." He laid a hand on my shoulder as he stood. "Remind me to thank Sean for mismanaging his business and cutting you loose." He smiled at me and walked out of the office. I preened, ignoring Giles's ludicrous faces mocking the teacher's pet.

"You're just jealous," I threw over my shoulder. I basked in my compliment. I knew I was inexperienced for my position. It meant a lot to know Al was happy with me. I resolved to be more responsible and reward him for his trust. I needed to be more grown-up. No more hangover Mondays, I vowed. No more wasting hours looking at shoes on Zappos.com or watching panda-cam. I was going to be a model wine buyer. I was going to conjure startling ideas to distinguish D&D as the vanguard of the wine connoisseur's ideal cellar. I was going to—

The phone rang, caller ID identifying Amy Bing from Charlotte. I'd make it quick.

"So can you make it for a bridal shower that weekend?" Amy asked.

I could picture her huge blue eyes beseeching. We'd been friends since meeting at a concert in high school during her flirtation with a punk rock persona. Black lace gloves and gobs of eyeliner was an image incompatible with her apple-cheeked face and Good Girl disposition, so Pat Benatar got her look back. We'd seen little of each other since college, but our friendship lived in that nostalgic space reserved for childhood friends. Though I'd been surprised to be appointed maid of honor. I loved Amy but wouldn't have called her *my* closest friend after these years. I decided for major milestones, you focus on old friends. It was a more attractive conclusion than being the "safe" alternative to rivalry among cousins.

"Sure," I agreed, with no idea what my schedule would be that far ahead.

"Great!" Amy's relief was obvious. "Mom was afraid it would

be difficult with you so far away." I felt a tremor at the thought of getting on Patsy Rose Bing's bad side.

"No," I assured her. "Wouldn't miss it."

"I want everyone to get to know one another," Amy went on, "so the wedding is cozy."

"Have you chosen the rest of the bridesmaids?" I felt maid-of-honor superior.

"Yes. I have to match Bill's numbers, but think I've figured it out."

"How many?" I asked absently, double-tasking on my spread-sheet.

"Fourteen," Amy answered.

"Fourteen?" My attention yanked back to the call. Cozy? "Seriously?"

"I know," Amy sighed. "But Bill has a lot of fraternity brothers. What can I do?" She laughed. "This thing is sort of getting away from me. I don't care really. Mom is *so* excited."

"You don't care really?" I was skeptical.

"Well, okay," she conceded. "I care a lot. It has to be perfect." There was a pause, then, "I've been planning this since my first kiss. Now it's for real. I keep pinching myself."

That sounded more like Amy. "I hope you don't let Patsy Rose run roughshod over you."

"That may be like trying to stop Hannibal and the elephants. We seem to agree on most things, though we're struggling with the theme."

"Theme?" I repeated.

"There's so much to choose from! You can do a period, like Western, Ante Bellum, or Renaissance, or a color theme, or a decorative thing, like 'Paris in the Springtime.' "

I pictured myself looking ridiculous in a large hoop skirt and prayed that they didn't go with Ante Bellum. "Those sound interesting," I said gamely.

"I'll probably do something connected to the South." Oh dear God, I thought. "Mostly, I just want to get married."

"Why?" I asked, genuinely curious. "Aside from the kick ass wedding and all."

"Well, Bill has all the qualities I think are important. He wants kids right away, and I won't have to work. He's got a great job, his family and my family get along. We both want to stay in Charlotte. He's good-looking and isn't losing his hair. Besides," she finished her prosaic summary, "he asked."

I frowned. "Is that enough?" It wasn't the I-knew-he-was-The-One-from-the-moment-our-eyes-met that I thought should dictate.

"Sure! I want to have kids while I'm young." Amy was the only child to older parents. She hadn't had a lot of the parent-child experiences I considered integral to growing up, like camping and playing in the ocean with your folks. She'd spent her vacations visiting the Ufizzi Gallery rather than Santa's Village. "You can't have an adult life until you're married, and I want to start mine.

I wondered at that. "But do you love Bill?" I persisted. "Is he The One?"

"Why not?" Amy replied. "There's nothing wrong with him. We agree on almost everything, and he's a nice person." She paused. "Don't *you* like Bill?"

Whoops. Not so subtle. I thought about my answer. It was always a relief to see Amy without Bill, but I didn't dislike him—he was just sort of *there*, like beige carpeting. He loved Amy, no question, but what she saw in him was a mystery. If I didn't follow sports, we'd have had nothing to talk about. I had to admit part of me felt resentful at losing Amy to someone I didn't enjoy. In my fantasy, I'd retain preeminence until my friends eventually married clever and fun men, and we would be a happy, jolly threesome. Instead I was trading girls' nights for stilted conversations. Though, if I were truthful, girls' nights had ended when I moved to D.C. Still, I felt Bereft.

"Of course I like Bill," I insisted. "I just want to make sure he deserves you."

"Oh, I think he does," said Amy.

"Well tell me more about the wedding plans." I pushed my selfish feelings into a small ball at the bottom of my gut. "Fourteen bridesmaids? Yikes."

As I half listened to Amy, I pictured myself advancing down the aisle, Jean Harlow, regally lovely in a gorgeous Parisian Nights dress. After we hung up, I surfed the Internet looking at bridesmaids' dresses. I would have to talk to Amy about Lazaro, I decided. I was still daydreaming when the phone rang again.

Caller ID told me it was Ethan, one of my best friends.

"Yo," he said. "Got your call over the weekend. What's up?" We'd bonded as Southerners equally disoriented by our Ohio cornfield college campus, and took that adaptability through Europe after graduation. If you can travel with someone well, you can do anything together—though I still scolded him over the time he fell asleep on the beach and got our backpacks stolen in Spain. We both looked sort of dirty in our passport pictures issued in Madrid.

"I finally got the dates from Amy and Jen about their weddings." I giggled. "You're not going to believe this." I told him the consecutive dates in May.

"Uh-oh," he said. "They're in May?"

"Yes. Why?"

"Well," he hesitated, "I can't go in May."

"Wha-at?" The blow was unexpected. Unless one of us was dating someone, which was almost never, Ethan and I were always each other's escort. "You can't come?"

"I'm sorry, darlin'. I have exams. You know I would if I could." Ethan was at Gerogetown Law School.

"Oh shit. I have six months to find a boyfriend." Giles raised an eyebrow at me, as if I'd announced I had six months to get a Ph.D. in metallurgy.

"May's a long way away. This town would be crazy if no one fell for you before then."

"Sure," I giggled nervously. Jeremy Piven will show up. Done and done." I had a sick feeling in my stomach even as I joked with Ethan.

"It's going to be a Danish prince." Ethan knew I had a thing for Danes. It's the height.

"Maybe." I tried to perk up, but got serious. "Do you think so?"

"You're so impatient. It'll all work out in the end. And if it hasn't worked out, it's not the end." His calming influence reached through the phone like a hug. "Hey." Ethan got my attention. "When it does work out it'll be so great you'll be astonished you ever doubted it."

"Promise?" I entreated.

"Promise."

As we hung up, my brain churned like Deep Thought. I *would* get a date, I vowed. Somehow.

I was creating a chart of the datable male population of my acquaintance and making notes when Imogen called.

"I just finished a meeting in Georgetown. Meet me at Barnes and Noble for a coffee." Barnes & Noble was up M Street from D&D.

"I should get some work done . . ." I protested feebly, knowing I'd go. The only "work" I'd been doing was notating in my date-matrix that Cassie and Christopher seemed to be arguing a lot, and he might be single by May.

Imogen did too. "See you in ten." She hung up. I ignored my Guilt. I'd stay late to make up for it, I promised myself. Besides, I could run my event ideas by Imogen.

"I'll be right back," I told Giles, sitting across the room. "I'm getting coffee." It was office courtesy to pretend we didn't already know everything from eavesdropping.

"Skinny latte," he said without looking up from his computer.

Ten minutes later Imogen and I were browsing audio books for my drive to Charlotte for Thanksgiving, me limited to one beverage because we were on the move. I was lamenting Ethan's unavailability.

"You'll find a date," she assured me. "What about the guy from the City Tavern party?"

"Too Republican," I dismissed. "He lobbied for the National Rifle Association gun lobby and thought if everyone wore bulletproof vests all the time, the 'gun hysteria' would go away."

"What about Jim's friend, Christopher. He was from North Carolina, right?"

"He wore an ascot and bright orange pants to Middleburg. I didn't know whether to fake a British accent or sing the Clemson Tigers fight song."

"He was attractive."

"Ascot. No one wears ascots outside of Merchant and Ivory films."

"How about the guy at the soccer game last week?"

"He wasn't very bright. When I used the word 'expedite,' he thought I was talking about a skin condition."

Imogen rolled her eyes. "Might our standards be a tad high?"

"I wasn't into those guys," I protested.

"And when was the last time you went on more than one date with a person?" she pressed.

I scrolled through my brain. "I went on a few dates with Brian."

"Doesn't count. You never kissed."

"Well, then Caleb." Imogen sighed. Caleb, at Wharton now, had been in Washington for an internship the summer before last and we'd spent all of our time together.

"That's your problem, Vi. You're living in the past."

"That's not true," I defended. "I'm open to meeting people. I date. But I won't date for the sake of dating."

"You need to move past Caleb," Imogen said. "Here's what you need." She yanked an audio book off the shelf. *"Miss Abigail's Guide to Dating, Mating and Marriage."*

I choked on my latte. "That cannot be a real book." I reached for it.

"Oh it is." Imogen fended me off, reading from the back. " 'In language quaint and curious, Miss Abigail offers relevant quotes, tidbits, and words of wisdom from her collection of one thousand classic advice books.' " She raised her eyebrows at me and continued to read aloud: " 'Nothing appeals more to a man than immaculate cleanliness. A stunny beauty, who looks even slightly soiled, will lose out every time to her plain-faced sister so pleasing to the senses.' "

I snorted. Imogen read on. " 'Above all, do everything you can to preserve your looks. While a kind heart and a beautiful spirit are wonderful assets, you can scarcely expect a husband to become thrilled at your inside beauty alone when the outside is neglected.' "

"Oh, puhleeeeze," I moaned.

"You're right. *The Rules* is better." Imogen held it out to me, grinning pertly.

"Saucebox." I stomped past her, I collected coffee for Giles, and hurried back to the office. I'd spent longer than I intended with Imogen. My eyes fell on the clock as I dropped into my chair. Egads—it was after four and I hadn't done anything but wedding stuff. I determinedly pulled out my notes from the morning's meeting with Al. I was going to make him proud. I just needed to focus.

"Ooooh, he's waking up!" called Giles excitedly.

"He is?" Let me see. . . ." I hustled over to check on Tai Shan.

"So where do you want to meet tonight for showtunes tonight?" asked Giles.

I prayed I wouldn't get fired before May.

CHAPTER FIVE

A Very Long Weekend

I dropped Nigel and Clementine off at Imogen's and started the six-hour drive to Charlotte the night before Thanksgiving. I passed the miles mentally planning my own wedding. I placed us all barefoot on a beach (Charleston? No, Bali . . .), and salted it with a gorgeous sunset and Jeremy Piven, my adoring groom. I struggled a little with the bridesmaids. I didn't want a crowd, but I didn't know how to choose between Amy, Lila, and Jen from home and Imogen, Mona, Babette, and Ellis, who were the mainstays of my current life. I liked the idea of Ethan there too, because I fancied myself as a wedding rebel with a male bridesmaid. Wrestling with these sticky questions preoccupied me all the way home.

I pulled up to my parents' house at 2:00 A.M, jacked on caffeine. I tossed in bed and reflected on the hours I'd passed planning my wedding right down to earrings and imagined conversations. No other prospect snared the imagination in the same way. I never fantasized in such detail about owning a wine bar, becoming a famous footwear designer, or my Academy Award acceptance speech after being discovered at a Pizza Hut. The only close parallel in terms of pleasant hours squandered was how I'd spend lottery winnings, but that was pure fantasy since I don't actually buy lottery tickets. Of course, at the rate my love life was going, odds on the lottery beat marriage potential.

I'd lied to Imogen. I hadn't tried to date since Caleb left. I'd been deliriously happy with him in D.C. and missed him terribly when he'd gone back to school. Distance had dwindled our communications, which felt sadly familiar. Our high school passion fizzled after just one year of college, and distance had unraveled each subsequent reconnection. Eventually, other than sporadic e-mail and some memorable holiday hookups in Charlotte, I'd cooled my efforts. I'd dated a guy named Steven, and instituted a no-Caleb policy to ensure I didn't stray. It turned out I needn't have worried. Steven was sleeping with his "friend" Tara the whole time, which I found out by walking in on them one day. A lesson in the downside of dating a trust fund baby—the sailboats and vacations are nice, but if he doesn't work, he has time to manage two girlfriends.

When Caleb arrived in D.C. for the summer, we'd met for a drink. The fireworks beat hello. I savored remembering the First New Kiss, knees touching on the couch at Russia House right before last call, and felt a trail of sparks shoot down my hoohah highway. We'd agreed our perfect summer wasn't serious. But no one else appealed to me after blissful days sailing on the Chesapeake, picnicking under the stars at Screen on the Green, curling together at night despite the humidity. I thought of Caleb counting all the freckles on my chest, nicknaming each one as he introduced himself and kissed it. I could pretend I wasn't, but in my secret heart I was hoping Caleb would return to D.C. when he finished school. But his radio silence stopped me from reaching out, too proud to see if he'd be in Charlotte for Thanksgiving. I dug the man's dimples but I wasn't totally lame.

I came awake groaning at the sound of my phone. It was my sister Maeve.

"Cruel wench," I answered.

"Get up," Maeve commanded. "You need to make sure Mom got a turkey." It sounded like she was chewing a bagel. Maeve was always eating into the phone.

"What?" I sat up. "Today is Thanksgiving! Dinner's in *six hours.*"

"And?" prompted Maeve.

Maeve had a point. My mother, an artist, was extremely flaky. I stumbled out of bed.

"Why didn't you take care of this?" I tried pulling on my jeans with one hand. "You live here! Hasn't Brick been home from college for a week?!" I got tangled up in my pant leg and fell over. "Ow!"

"And how would I pay for a turkey?" demanded my hopelessly broke sister. Maeve was also in college, in the loosest sense of the word. She was on the seven-to-nine-year plan for graduating. "You're the oldest. It's your job. What're you doing anyway?"

"Never mind." I winced, rubbing my ass. "Are you on your way?"

"I'll be there in twenty minutes." She hung up.

I finished getting dressed and went downstairs to investigate the extent of the Empty Cupboard Crisis. What I found was more alarming than no turkey. My father and brother Brick were out on the patio standing around a silver can and a scattering of metal parts, arguing over what looked like assembly instructions. They were also drinking. I stepped on the patio.

"Hey guys." They turned. My father beamed at me. He was wearing a sweater with a huge turkey on it.

"Sweetheart! Did you have a good drive?" He gave me a hug. My dad gave great hugs.

"Hey, Dad. It was fine." Brick got up from among the parts and gave me a hug too.

"Yo, cold!" I pulled away from the cold can of beer he'd pressed on my neck. "It's ten in the morning, kid." My brother was nine-teen and husky.

"What can I say." Brick's tone was laconic. "I don't like Bloody Marys."

"Want one, sweetie?" My father waved his Bloody Mary at me.

"Sure. Spicy, please. Um, what's that?" I gestured at the pile of parts.

Both Brick and my father gave me huge smiles. "We're going to fry the turkey this year," Brick told me. "See, you fill this fryer with boiling oil and cook the turkey in that." Boys and poten-tially explosive toys, mixed with alcohol. They were happier than pigs in shit. The Thanksgiving movie starring my family would be "Incendiary People." Or maybe "The Family Blown . . . Up." Hmm. Would I rather be played by Claire Danes or Sarah Jessica Parker? Who would more convincingly portray a charred lump of smoking flesh?

"Uh, okay. Do you know how to put it together?" I ventured.

"We'll figure it out!" my father assured me cheerfully from where he was fixing my drink at the patio bar. "I'm very handy." I held my tongue. My father was notoriously *not* handy, misled by male hubris.

"Hm. Okay. So do we have a turkey? Maeve wasn't sure."

"A big one. We'll be frying that sucker up by one P.M." My fa-ther handed me my Bloody.

"Well, no need to rush it," I suggested. "The important thing is assembling the cooker properly. You know, for, uh, safety. Say, did protection eye goggles come with that?"

They dismissed me, reabsorbed in bickering about which piece was the perforated poultry rack. Arguing was my brother's forte, and my father got sucked in every time. I was certain Brick would follow my dad into law—being paid to argue would be his Nir-vana. Dinners would be intolerable. Either way, the Connelly men were completely focused on fryer assembly and totally ignoring me. I gave up dropping helpful safety recommendations on deaf ears and wandered into the kitchen to take stock of other dinner essentials. Maybe the fireman would be cute.

Maeve bounced in as I was counting potatoes. Maeve looks like me, with long hair she vowed never to cut again after a shorn period. Today she wore it in two braids.

"Hi." I hugged her.

"What's the word on the turkey, lurkey?" I pointed at the massive defrosting bird.

"Wow. It's big."

"All the better to blow the house up with," I said, and explained.

"You know," Maeve said, "you really shouldn't eat something fried in oil. It has all kinds of partially hydrogenated fat in it."

"How about that." I was used to ignoring Maeve's food fetishes, which had cropped up after an eposide of illness. "Surprisingly, the food's all here. Potatoes, broccoli, green beans, cranberry sauce, stuffing. We'll need Mom to make the gravy. Otherwise we're in good shape." Maeve and I were used to managing dinners when my mother was working on a sculpture project, but some things absolutely required her expertise.

"I'll go drag her from the studio," Maeve volunteered.

"Grab a couple of pairs of protective eye shields while you're there," I instructed her. "I want to lay them suggestively around the patio."

"Pass the mashed potatoes," Dad asked Brick.

"Whoa, whoa, whoa," I said. "This way first." No mashed potato ever made it past my dad. I dumped a healthy scoop on my plate, passing the bowl to Maeve.

"Does anyone want more Cheetos?" Maeve handed me the bowl. I put a few on my plate next to the cranberry sauce. Maeve handed a Cheeto behind her to Oliver's cage on the sideboard.

Oliver was the talking cockatiel that Brick and I had bought for her birthday.

"Road trip! Don't forget the bird!" said Oliver, taking the Cheeto.

Brick started shoveling turkey into his mouth. "Hey!" I called a halt. "Shouldn't we say grace and what we're thankful for?" Everyone looked baffled. "It *is* Thanksgiving," I reminded them. Silence. We were neither a religious nor a traditional family.

"I'll start. Um, I'm thankful for my family, the food we are about to eat and, um, Nigel stopped leaving nasty slimy hairballs on the carpet where I step in them."

"That's nice," smiled my mother. "I am thankful to be surrounded by my lovely and healthy family," she squeezed Maeve's hand, "and that Congress finally passed a law to prevent telemarketers from calling and offering me insurance when I am trying to work, and that the neighbors finally put to sleep that dog that used to bark nonstop all the live long day at every leaf that fell from the trees." We passed a moment of silence for the dog, in surprise over our mother's legislative lucidity.

Brick said, "I'll be thankful when I can eat." I gave him the evil eye.

"I'm thankful I have such incredibly generous parents," said Maeve. Brick rolled his eyes. This sounded familiar. Maeve went on, studiedly casual. "So, Dad, I found the printer I want online cheaper than at Staples. If you give me your credit card number, I'll order it."

My dad snorted at her. "Not bloody likely." My sister was a fiscal nightmare on the scale of a developing nation.

"What?" she exclaimed. "It was just that one time!"

Brick resumed shoveling food into his mouth. The giving thanks portion of the evening was done.

"Last time I gave you my credit card number for your utility bill," Dad ranted, waving his fork in a way that threatened to send a bite of turkey flying across the room, "I found a charge from the

Mellow Mushroom three weeks later. Wanting a pizza and being out of cash does not constitute an 'emergency.'" My father would cancel cards once Maeve had only peeped at the number.

"Hey, some good turkey, right?" Brick changed the subject. I had to admit that fried turkey was delicious. I'd envisioned a giant tempura bird, but fried turkey was just like a regular turkey, only juicier.

"The taste reminds me of a large abstract piece I did in bronze for the Queen's College library," my mother responded. I remembered the piece and she was right. "So, Vi dear, how long are you in town?" she asked.

"Until Sunday night," I said. "I have a bunch of wedding stuff to do, looking at dresses with everyone. Oh, and Saturday night I'm having a drink with Edward." Edward was a boy I'd gone to high school with. A few years ago we'd run into each other at Providence Road Sundries and he confessed to having a crush on me in high school. We dated almost a year, traveling back and forth, but eventually drifted apart. When I was in town, we'd get together in a Not Just A Drink kind of way if we were both single. I'd targeted him as Potential Wedding Date Number One.

"Edward? Who's that?" My dad looked confused.

"Dad, for heaven's sake, I dated him for eight months!" I was irritated. My father never registered any of the men in my life. He would dismiss them with, "Well, they all run together to me," which nettled because they did *not* all run together for me.

"He was the diminutive one, dear," my mother replied, putting a green M&M on her deviled egg.

"No, no, *that* long distance boyfriend was Chris," Maeve interrupted. I'd dated Chris in college. Chris *had* been short, but he was cute and funny. And he graduated three months later and moved to Chicago. We stayed together until he met someone else, and I didn't mind.

"Is that the one that moved to Alaska?" asked my mother.

"Brick, please chew your food and don't swallow it whole. Blocked bowels stunt creative thinking."

"Edward was the one who wore ripped jeans to dinner with Grandma," Maeve finished. I glared. She portrayed innocence.

My father frowned. "Ripped jeans show a lack of respect."

"Dad, it was three years ago! He didn't know Grandma would be there.

"Well, Vi, you need to start thinking seriously about who you spend time with. You know, the advice I sent you off to college with was meant for college, not forever." I suppressed a snort. Bill Cosby my father wasn't. He'd sent me off to college with two pieces of advice. He'd said, "Vi, remember, there's no need to settle down anytime soon—try to play the field as long as possible." I think my high school addiction to Caleb had alarmed my parents. Caleb was one my father *did* remember. Then he said, "And hang out with the rugby players. They know how to have a good time, and sometimes you study too hard." This was the equipment I was given to start my adult life.

Brick looked interested. "What advice?"

"Never mind," I cut him off.

"Are you dating anyone now, dear?" my mother asked.

Maeve snorted. "Hellloooo . . . she's having a 'drink' with Edward." I looked at Brick. He winked, then licked his finger and stuck it in Maeve's ear.

"Oh gross," she howled. "That's disgusting. You're disgusting!"

"Thanks," I grinned.

"Pay up," he said.

I scooped the rest of my mashed potatoes, a Rice Krispie treat, and a dill pickle onto my bread plate and handed it to him.

"So, Mom, tell me what you're working on," I asked, deflecting the conversation as I grabbed another dill pickle from the sideboard and tucked into my delicious turkey. Thankfully, the conversation turned to her newest sculpture project and local gossip for the rest of the meal.

"Well, I feel slimed," Maeve quoted from *Ghostbusters* a while later, as she leaned back in her chair patting her stomach. Dad looked up from the Chips Ahoy he was munching.

"Am I the Keymaster?" he asked. "Where's the video?"

"I'll be the Gatekeeper," Brick said, pushing back his chair to make the popcorn.

"Oh, are we watching a movie?" asked my mother. Brick rolled his eyes. Our family had watched *Ghostbusters* after Thanksgiving dinner every year since I was fifteen, though no one really knew why. It simply made us laugh every time. And every year our mother watched in delight as if she'd never seen it before. "Can you believe that?" she would say. "That bad guy from the EPA got covered in marshmallow! Ha ha!" We all just shook our heads.

I pushed back my chair and began to clear the table.

"If we're watching a movie, let's just stack the dishes for now," my mother suggested, again as if it were a novel scenario. I snorted. I knew she'd be asleep on Dad's shoulder before Sigourney Weaver was rescued, and Brick and Maeve would disappear like morals in Vegas. Every year Dad and I ended up side by side up to our elbows in suds, embracing our martyrdom.

"We're ready," called Dad from the den, where he and Brick were in their traditional stations munching on Orville Redenbacher and Rolos.

"Road trip! Don't forget the bird!" chirped Oliver from the dining room.

I couldn't believe I was braving the day after Thanksgiving sales. I was barreling down Fairview toward Manzetti's while normal people were still home digesting and filling out insurance forms from turkey fryer incidents. Not me. While my sister was blissfully watching a *What Not to Wear* marathon on TLC, I was meeting

Lila for a necessary drink before going to a terrifying After Thanksgiving Day bridal sale. I suspected many non-normal people were lurking there.

Lila is five-one and bodacious, for lack of a better word. For someone as petite as she is, she has a *Baywatch* figure. She is perfectly manicured, styled, and coordinated at all times, with a seemingly endless supply of purses to match her shoes. Lila is also smart, which is what brought us together. In the South, the default assumption often is that pretty blond girls are not smart.

I walked into the bar and she waved at me from a stool. It was three in the afternoon and the place was virtually empty. Lila was sucking on a skinny menthol cigarette.

"Those things have ground up fiberglass in them," I inanely repeated some urban legend I vaguely recalled hearing but for which I had no shred of proof.

"Well thank God," Lila, said, laughing, "maybe it will take my mind off the pain of trying on dresses at David's Bridal." Lila laughed after almost everything she said.

I slid onto my bar stool. "David's Bridal?"

"Hart's sister is insisting. You know how cheap Hart is, right? Well, his family is ten times worse. I ordered you a Grgich Hills cab, by the way." Lila is a true wine snob.

"Is that possible?" I asked. Hart was pretty cheap. He was the kind of person who insisted on splitting the dinner check by each person paying for exactly what they'd ordered, and always saying things like, "Lila only had one glass of wine." Which was never true.

"One time I brought a bottle of Caymus to her parents house for dinner. The next time Hart and I ate at her place, I caught her pouring Two Buck Chuck in the empty bottle."

"Jesus." I laughed. "You drank Two Buck Chuck?"

"No way. I had gin and tonics."

The bartender sauntered over, leaning bulging forearms on the bar, and glistened at Lila with teeth so straight and white they could only have been the result of thousands of dollars worth of orthodonture. "Can I get you ladies anything else?"

Lila trilled at him. "We're okay right now." Lila was an irrepressible flirt. She flirted with anyone. When she was alone, she flirted with herself. Or inanimate objects. It was hard to picture her married. Pretty, lively Lila always had a boyfriend, but they changed names and faces so quickly that I couldn't keep track. What they had in common was good looks and money to spend on her. I'd been waiting for the day it would sound different when she talked about a man. I hadn't heard it yet. Fungible Hart had just seemed like more arm candy. Apparently he was the sticky kind.

"Thank God Albert's paying for this thing." Lila called her father Albert at his insistence. "Otherwise it would be a strip mall disaster."

"Does he know what he's in for?"

"Lord yes. My family's way, way involved in every detail. I feel like all of us are marrying Hart, not just me!" I always marveled at how much influence Lila's parents had over her. They were a very close, very Catholic, and very traditional family.

I laughed at the image of them squished at the altar. "Does everyone want to marry Hart?"

"They're over the moon. Since Guy's divorce, my mother has alternated between weeping fits and whispering in my ear that I'm not getting any younger." Lila's brother Guy married young and recently divorced without having children. He vowed never to marry again, and her parents had been reeling since. First, divorce. Second, *no grandchildren by the time they are fifty-five.* The horror. I counted myself lucky my parents were different. They wanted us to be happy for our own sakes, and you couldn't put a time line on that. Content in their marriage, they weren't trying to live through their children.

"You didn't get engaged for your parents, did you?"

"Oh no. *Please*. No, Vi, I feel like I finally found some stability. I don't know if life has been more chaotic with my whole family walking around as if Guy was dying instead of divorced, or if Hart's steadier than other guys, but he's become my rock."

"Really?"

"You know how emotional an Italian family can be. And we scream and yell and hug and cry and it's always emotions on the sleeve. And this divorce thing—God, it's worse than when my cousin transferred from Notre Dame to Berkeley and stopped shaving her legs. Hart's such a relief because he's even keel. It's a haven."

"Is he different than Richard?" I asked. Lila had dated Richard in college: he was dynamic and a lot of fun, but Richard hadn't pulled off the fidelity thing.

"Oh god yes. For one thing, Hart has career prospects. We're not supposed to care about that, but honestly, I do well for myself and want my husband to make at least as much as I do. With Richard, every idea was going to be the next big thing, but he never stuck with anything. I'm tired of little boys pretending to be men. Hart's a grown-up."

"Do you mind that he's not as outgoing as you are?"

"He doesn't mind. He lets me go out and do my thing. Being with Richard used to wear even me out, all that personality. After being 'on' all day selling, I like going home to a calm home and someone who doesn't expect me to perform."

"We're all looking for someone who lets us be ourself."

"Kind of. It's like he's my antidote, he diffuses my energy." I didn't like the sound of that, but Lila seemed sure.

"Tell me about the proposal. I never got the details."

"It was sort of an accident. He was going to take me to Hilton Head next month, but I found the box rooting in his briefcase for a pen, so we got engaged." It sounded like a dull thud when you wanted a reverberant gong. I dreamed of a sea of flower petals and poignant tearful declarations.

"Is the ring pretty?" I groped.

She held out a solitaire. Hunh. *Bo-ring.* I envisioned a unique design glinting in the sunlight as I waved to adoring guests from the back of an antique convertible, my veil streaming in the wind like a Chantilly Lace perfume advertisement. These engagements weren't meeting my expectations. Reality seemed much less romantic than *The Wedding Story,* featuring Rome by moonlight, hot air balloons, violinists.

One stereotype did hold true. "How are you getting on with your mother-in-law?"

"Oh fine. I ignore her when it comes to anything having to do with taste, and redirect to religion. They're as Catholic as we are. Usually I can make her forget about carnations by asking whether she wants a frosted glass or cross-embellished base for the unity candle."

"Carnations? That's painful."

Lila spied Hart's sister Angela coming through the door, and crushed out her cigarette. "Not as painful as this will be," she muttered, plastering a wide, false smile on her face.

David's Bridal is the JC Penney of bridal stores, strictly off the rack. The day after Thanksgiving the place was teeming with brides-to-be on a budget, sizing each other up over the racks. If someone grabbed the last size ten Gloria Vanderbilt with an organza ruffled inset, there could be a takedown. I wandered anxiously through the store eyeing gowns and keeping away from frenzied customers. There were some critically ugly garments.

Lila rounded a rack and grabbed me. "Come on. I've got some seriously good stuff." She winked. We shared an appreciation of the ridiculous.

Unlike most bridal salons, which offer large private rooms and tastefully covered chaises, David's Bridal was strictly mall changing rooms. I sat on the floor facing Lila's. Angela plopped next to me. To our left a woman with a bad perm swanned out of her closet looking like Little Bo Peep in a bell-shaped wedding gown with puffed sleeves and bonnet. I averted my eyes from the tragedy out of respect, like not staring at a wooden leg or a hairy mole.

It occurred to me that there might be a viable line of greeting cards offering wedding gown sympathy. I knew women who married in the high eighties and were now daily mocked by their wedding portrait. I pondered the market. Former bridesmaids to the bride? Enough time would have to pass so the bride would see the humor. The wife to the husband? Might stir up issues best left untouched. Daughters to their mothers, refusing to wear the legacy dresses? Hmmm . . . The last had potential. I was working on a rhyme for "Sorry about the excess tulle . . . at least Dad did not annul," when Angela spoke.

"So." she said, struggling a bit to make conversation. "Any idea what Lila has planned for us?" Angela was another bridesmaid.

"I'm not sure, but I think the color is maroon," I said.

"Oh," said Angela. She said "Oh" at least once per sentence. "Do you think we should look around?"

I mentally counted to three so my "No!" wouldn't come out too fast. I was allergic to synthetic fabrics. And ugly things.

"Well, I think she sort of has a plan already," I lied, practicing my Don't Mind Me I Am Being Merely Nice And Not Manipulative look.

"Oh," said Angela. "Okay."

"Ta da." Lila popped out of the dressing room. She was wearing the Little Bo Peep gown and bonnet. Next to me, Angela said "Oh." I wondered if she suddenly became aware that she was going to be punished for the David's Bridal trip by a parade of the Ridiculous and Revolting. I sighed. It was going to be a long afternoon.

*   *   *

Saturday morning found me again careening around Charlotte, along roads I no longer remembered trying to find a destination to which I'd never been. I was trying not to look at the clock, which radiated censure along with the time: 10:21. Brunch was at ten. Driving by my old high school, I reflexively slowed down and looked for where the "hidden" cop usually was stationed. I was regressing into my high school self. Before I knew it, Amy and I would be cruising Sean Montgomery's house to see if his car was home, and the highlight of our Friday night would be finding a 7-Eleven where the Slurpee machine worked.

After suffering the discomfiting recollections evoked by passing the neighborhood where Brian Dent said no when I asked him to the Homecoming Dance, the church where I was forced into junior high dance lessons from Bubba Gross and his son Bubba Jr., and the street where I got sick after too much vodka and vomited in the bushes of a guy known only as "Rader," I arrived with relief at Providence Café. A new restaurant, it was a Memory Free Zone. I thought I could get through brunch without vomiting.

I quickly slipped into an empty seat between Mary Francis and Mary Scott and smiled charmingly at the table. Patsy Rose Bing smiled back from underneath a stiff helmet of hair and continued her discourse on why white-candy-coated Jordan almonds tied up in silver net sachets were essential to any self-respecting wedding reception. In a pale blue St. John knit suit that inexplicably bore shiny epaulette-like accents at the shoulders, Patsy Rose looked ready to captain the helm of a perfectly accessorized, pressed, and White Linen scented army. Instead, she would be marshaling fourteen women of varying body shapes and degrees of recalcitrance into a single dress and one afternoon of perfect posture. She sounded the reveille by tapping her fork against a glass.

"Now that everyone has arrived," Patsy Rose began. I smiled charmingly at Amy's cousin Mary Louise and pretended the remark was not about me. I took a bite of chilly eggs made gourmet by the inclusion of some sort of herb, and poured myself a coffee, an orange juice, and a peach iced tea.

"We ah so delighted that ya'll ah here. Ah know Amy is just *thrilled*. Ya'll mean so much to her." I looked at the thirteen other bridesmaids and felt very, very unspecial.

"A young girl always dreams of her special day. When Amy was little she used to stand by the ocean for hours. I asked her, 'Amy, dahlin', what ah you up to out there just starin'?' She said, 'Mama, I'm wishin'. I'm wishin' for the love of my life to come up out of the ocean to me.'"

I was beginning to think I might have another vomiting incident.

"And so," Patsy Rose continued, "from Amy's girlhood dreams, we have planned something very excitin' for the weddin'. We're going to have an Under the Sea theme! And, girls, wait until you see the dresses!"

Amy was beaming. The youngest cousin, Beth Ann, was wiggling in excitement. I was very, very nervous. Patsy Rose beckoned a Distinctly Out of Place person wearing a pinafore and knee-length hose socks and introduced her as the seamstress. She reverently presented Patsy Rose with a garment bag. Patsy Rose opened the bag equally reverently, as if it contained a First Edition Junior League Cookbook, and withdrew the gown with a flourish. Mary Margaret and Martha Ann gasped in delight and clapped their hands. I gasped in horror. Patsy Rose looked my way and I smiled charmingly. With teeth.

The dress would look horrible no matter who wore it. Eyeing Patsy Rose's perfectly coiffed slim figure, I wondered if that was the point. The navy blue satin bodice mimicked heart-shaped scalloped seashells, from a tulip design that clung tightly to the hips and butt before flaring into a mermaid "tail." I mentally ti-tled The Movie Starring Me "The Belittled Mermaid."

"Now," Patsy Rose went on, "we were so delighted to find this gem that we ordered ya'll gowns raght that instant. So if ya'll can each get me a check for $345, that would be lovely. Ya'll can pay Maria directly for any alterations."

I gasped again. This time I wasn't alone. Patsy Rose turned a deaf ear.

"We thought it'd be fun to let ya'll gals pick your own shoes. Anything ya'll like. All we ask is that they be open-toe navy blue sandals, with approximately one and a half inch heels, and no shiny buckles." Anything we like. Just so long as it's what Patsy Rose likes.

The seamstress rolled a carpeted stool into a corner, and the fun began.

Patsy Rose smiled when it was my turn on the stump. I tried not to hunch as I waddled to the stool and awkwardly hefted my mermaid ass. Tails are so hampering.

"Vi! It will be a pleasure to fit you, dear. So slim."

"Well that is sweet of you to say. Thank you!" I practically sang, slipping into the language of the Southern Exchange. The seam-stress bustled about, touching me in inappropriate ways. After we were done, she might need to send me flowers.

"And how's D.C. treating you, dear? Such a big city."

"Oh, I like it. It's sunny," I declared, as if this meant anything in particular. But then again, what did "big city" mean? I jumped as the seamstress molested me. "How's the wedding planning coming?" I figured this topic could fully occupy our obligatory chitchat.

"Mah-velous dear. We decided on the most elegant invitation envelopes."

"Envelopes? Really? I've never thought about envelopes." Patsy Rose froze, as if I'd suggested I never considered closing the bathroom door. I rushed on. "What kind did you, um, and Amy, pick? I'll bet they're something special." God might strike me dead any moment.

"Oh, they ah lovely." She thawed at my repentant gesture. "We've chosen a 'pochette' style square with folding tabs on each side, which fold in to make the envelope. They ah made from pahchment, which is a *very* traditional version of wedding envelopes, with a subtle marbled finish, and a deckled edge, where the paper has a torn look, giving it a handmade appearance, dear."

She could have been Charlie Brown's teacher for all the sense it made to me. Did people really give a shit about this stuff? But I'm not proud. I can admit Patsy Rose scared me. I hid behind neutral. "Mmm-hmm. Wow."

Patsy Rose rattled on. "Of course etiquette demands that the invitation envelopes be hand-addressed. The ink naturally will be navy to match the Under the Sea theme."

Nervous *and* bored, I redirected to the weather.

"Well, we certainly were blessed with a beautiful day for our luncheon," I enthused. If I were a Harlequin novel, I would've said, "I enthused, gaily."

"Oh ahn't we? Was your drive down all rahght?"

"It was fine, I left late to avoid traffic."

"Now drivin' was smart during the holidays. Though ah do always meet such interestin' people on airplanes. Last time ah flew ah had a *lovely* chat with mah congresswoman."

"I have pretty firm views about not talking to people on airplanes," I said, truthfully. "Once I'm buckled into my seat, I want to read my book. If a person tries to broach a conversation, I'll shut them down. It really upset my dad once," I deadpanned. The seamstress finished her sexual assault of my torso and began pinning my hem so I could move a little. I reached for my drink.

Patsy Rose looked at me blankly, not sure if I was serious. "Ah.

Well, when shall we see your charming mother out on the golf course, dear?"

I tried not to snort my peach iced tea through my nose. My mother, with her fondness for Birkenstocks and natural fabrics, was definitely not joining any golf foursomes. It was all my dad could do to drag her to Prime Rib Night on Thursdays at the club.

"I know she'd love to play." I stretched "love" into three syllables to emphasize my sincerity. "But she is so busy with work these days." With relief I noted that the seamstress had stepped back to look critically at my dress and appeared satisfied.

"Well," murmured Patsy Rose, "perhaps when she's done." She was already looking past me to the next victim mincing unsteadily up to the hot seat.

"Mary Scott! Won't this dress be simply stunnin' on you with those blue eyes of yours!"

I managed an ungainly dismount and swished my way to the relief of normal clothes. I wondered if there was a sympathy card line for bridesmaid dresses.

Back home, I changed into jeans and walked across the street to Jen's house. I went through the garage and in the back door, calling out a loud hello.

"Vi? Is that you?" answered a male voice. Tom McIntyre walked into the kitchen. Jen's dad was tall and thin and tan and loved nothing in the world so much as golf, his azaleas, and his daughter. I ranked a pretty close fourth.

"Hey Mom," I said, and gave him a hug.

"Hi, son!" he beamed at me. Kevin, the son he never had. "You look great!"

"Thanks." I was already rustling in their pantry. Unlike our house, the McIntyre house always had snacks and that fine American champagne, Coca-Cola. Sodas weren't allowed in my house growing up, which probably explained my addiction today.

Forbidden fruit and all. When I went to the McIntyres' house—basically every day—I would beeline for a Coke. I could always tell if Marilou McIntyre was on a diet or not depending on whether there was regular or Diet Coke in the fridge. The Diet Coke times were dark days indeed.

Tom sat at the kitchen table. "How've you been?"

I retrieved bagel crisps, Allouete cheese spread, and a Diet Coke (oh dear) and joined him.

"A little worn-out," I answered. "Lots of dressing and undressing and whatnot."

"Don't I know it!" He grinned. "I stay out of their hair. They ask me things I'm completely unqualified to answer, like veils and the insides of envelopes, and then send me away, annoyed with my answer, telling me I don't understand anything. I just sign the checks."

"More crazy like a fox than unqualified to answer." I squinted at him. "You annoy them on purpose so they send you away to golf. Let me guess—you suggested recycled envelopes."

He winked at me. "Don't give me away, son."

"Secret's safe with me, Mom."

"Vi? Is that you?" Jen's voice floated down the stairs. "Come up quick! I need you!"

"The jig is up," I sighed, getting to my feet, armed only with artificial sweetener.

"Into the trenches," Tom said solemnly. "Good luck."

Jen had moved to Charlotte when we were eight, and we met under inauspicious beginnings that started with the Parental Dictate, "I think the new neighbors have a girl your age . . ." Once I gave the relationship a grudging chance, it stuck. Down-to-earth Jen understood the importance of having your own language, collecting golf balls from the pond, and eating powdered Jell-O straight from the box.

I headed along the familiar path to Jen's room. I found them flipping through a ten-inch-thick album of invitation samples in the guest room, now a Wedding War Room.

"Hey, Mrs. Mac." I leaned over to give Jen's mother a kiss on the cheek.

"Hello." Marilou smiled at me. She was a kind, plump woman who looked like what Nancy Drew would look like if she turned fifty and put on thirty pounds. At the moment she also looked fretful.

"Thank heavens you're here, Vi," she exclaimed. "We've just been in a to-do about the invitation envelopes. We simply cannot decide whether to have a plain matte or foil lining."

I looked at Jen. She rolled her eyes. I seriously doubted that "we" were much fussed about the envelopes. I recalled the Diet Coke.

"C'mon Mom," Jen said. "It doesn't matter to me. What do *you* like?" Jen shot me a what-do-you-think-the-odds-are-this-will-work look. None, it turned out.

Marilou snapped in exasperation. "Jen, the envelope is the first thing your guest will see. It's very, very important. I wish you would take this more seriously."

"How about an oversize parchment pochette, with a deckled edge?" I regurgitated, to forestall an argument. "It's a heavy paper with a subtle marbled finish. Traditional yet elegant."

I smiled charmingly at them. You don't spend a whole morning with Patsy Rose without picking up a thing or two.

Jen quickly recovered from her surprise. "I think that sounds great! Mom, what do you think?"

Marilou blinked at me. "Well, you certainly know your envelopes, dear. We won't have to worry about foil colors."

"If you want to work in colors," I continued helpfully, "you could use colored ink."

Jen stared at me again. Then her face cleared as she remembered where I'd been all morning. "Great idea!" She laughed.

"Well. My. Yes. That would work nicely. That lovely Jolene from the garden club offered to handwrite the invitations. And navy ink would look lovely on white."

"Navy?" I asked. "Seriously?

"Yep," Jen said. "Mom found a dress for you. And bought it. Without asking." I raised my eyebrows at Jen. She looked at me with sympathy . . . and a glint of humor. "Off the rack."

"Oh," I said, sounding like Angela when she saw Lila Bo Peep. "Super." There went my hopes of picking out a lovely dress since I was the only wedding attendant.

"Oh, yes," said Marilou, beaming again. "Let's slip it on. Size six, right?"

The size six fit like a glove. A giant navy Nun Suit of a glove with a great, large bow affixed underneath my breasts. I mentally renamed The Movie Starring Me "Too Cruel for Sister Sarah." Jen mouthed *I'm so sorry* over her mother's head. As I raised my hand to scratch my neck, itchy under the tight collar, I accidentally flipped the huge bow up to smack myself in the face. Jen doubled over with laugher. Marilou, who hadn't seen it, looked confused.

"What's so funny?" she asked. Jen toppled off the bed in convulsions. Marilou looked at me. I smiled gamely, my eye watering from where it had been smacked with the bow.

"I'm *so sorry*," Jen repeated later, as we sat in the backyard sipping iced tea. "I couldn't believe it when she showed me. But she was so tickled with herself, I couldn't hurt her feelings."

"It's fine," I lied. "I don't mind at all."

"Come on. It's awful. But I'm so tired of hassling about wedding stuff. It puts me in a foul mood to debate my mother and my future mother-in-law over every living thing. I end up picking fights with Louis, and he's blameless. How are Amy and Lila holding up?"

"They seem pretty normal. Amy's indulging in girlish fantasy, and Lila's running a precision haute couture operation." I paused. "It's kind of weird for me."

"You have reservations," Jen said matter-of-factly.

I remembered when Jen had first told me. I'd felt a pounding in my chest like the time I saw Jeremy Piven, my potential soul mate, in a New York coffee shop. Underappreciated by the film industry, I alone comprehended his brilliance. He simply had to become aware of how much he needed me. I figured a short conversation would do the trick, but I was paralyzed. As I sat there wrestling with myself, ten feet from *the* Jeremy Piven, I watched him walk away, wondering if I'd regret it forever. I had felt the same tension that day Jen told me she was marrying a man I wasn't convinced she loved. What was my role? As I'd struggled with my response, the second half of her pronouncement sunk in. Maid of honor. I visualized myself walking regally down the aisle, flowers perfectly clutched, smile graceful and a little mysterious. Eyes would be drawn from the bride to the arresting woman at her side. The ordinary people in the pews would be awed. I was seduced. Good-bye, Jeremy Piven. Hello, amazing dress! Now, my doubts whispered again.

"Yes," I agreed slowly. "I guess I do. I've always had one view of marriage. The fairy-tale one and getting swept off your feet by Prince Charming." I hesitated. "I don't really get that head over heels impression from you. Not like with Bo."

"I think you have reservations, because I gave them to you. I used to tell you I wasn't serious about Louis. Then, one day, I realized I missed it if I didn't talk to him every day. Then, I realized that talking to him was the best part of every day. It isn't the same crazy chemistry I had with Bo, but I found my best friend."

It didn't set my heart racing but made sense. I sighed. "Have I been a total bitch? For acting like you were settling?"

"God no," she laughed. "That's what friends are supposed to do. I respect you more for being honest. Do you feel better?"

"Yes," I said. And I did. "Do you think it happens that way for everyone? Lila and Amy seem to have done math to pick their fiancés."

"Everyone chooses their own solution. Remember how we used to say there were eight perfect Prince Charmings for you out there? There couldn't be just one because you could be getting a pedicure the day he wrecked his bike outside your house and you'd miss him. With eight, you'd be guaranteed to meet at least one. And you could marry the first one at eighteen and be as happy as if you let seven go by and married the eighth when you were forty. I also think there are different *kinds* of love, and you choose the one that suits you best. You're holding out for Charming One, which is dramatic. I went for Charming Two, which is comfortable, I guess."

"Do you believe in the Charlotte Lucas approach?" I cited *Pride and Prejudice.*

"Sure. She married a buffoon because her alternative was to be a burden and a spinster in her parents' house. The fact that her husband was annoying didn't matter. She was happy. If a woman wants something more than she wants love, then a spouse who can provide it to her will make her happy. The role of 'love' gets played by the kids, the mansion, or the oil well."

I could see the point, but it was flawed. "Yet, historically marriage is based on a theory of love. If you make a Faustian bargain for alternative gains, wouldn't you lose respect for your spouse, feeling that you beat the system? Without respect, no relationship can survive."

"Charlotte's did. She was sure what she wanted and content in attaining it. Anyway, I think marriage is actually based on a feudal theory of chattels," Jen teased me.

I ignored her. Medieval origins were so far from the romantic ideal, I couldn't consider them. I pondered her first point. "Then it's critical to know *exactly* what you want. How do we untangle what we *really* want from wanting to get married? We're raised to want to get married. People who don't really want to get married do it anyway because they're supposed to, or fool themselves into thinking they want to. Except George Clooney."

"Reality check," said Jen. "I don't think getting married is insidious wrong-minded brainwashing. Don't you want to get married?"

An image flashed of Caleb misting at the altar upon glimpsing me, a blond Audrey Hepburn in my slimming white sheath and elegant chignon. "Maybe. I mean, I do. But I'm in no hurry," I lied. "I'll know when it's right. When George is ready."

Jen elbowed me, laughing. "The way I see it, your vision of love is more Anne Elliott from *Persuasion* than Charlotte Lucas. The young lovers were driven apart, but patience, patience, patience led to a second chance at the love they never recovered from."

I shrugged.

"Just remember that Anne waited a long time," ventured Jen.

"Tell me!" Imogen demanded over the phone later that night. "Was I right?"

"Picture an upside down blue tulip with a scallop seashell bikini sitting on top. In navy." I grimaced thinking of the dress. "Now picture a gift-wrapped nun. In navy."

Imogen laughed so hard she dropped the phone. "Sorry," she gasped when she recovered. "I knew Amy would outdo herself, but Jen? It can't be that bad."

"It has puffed sleeves," I enunciated. "The last time I wore puffed sleeves I had an asymmetrical haircut and I agonized over whether Scotty Pitts would dance with me to something by REO Speedwagon in a semidarkened gym that smelled like feet. You should see the amount of fabric! This dress was designed by the guy who made M.C. Hammer's pants."

"Hey, those pants *made* M.C. Hammer."

"Where is he now? My adult wedding debut is turning into a

nightmare. I'd prefer my Holly Hobbie flower girl dress back. I paid Marilou $150 for the ugliest dress I've ever laid eyes on. And in navy!"

"Be glad they're not fuchsia."

"I'm not so sure. I think the consequence of an overdose of fuchsia is that you end up a gay male Broadway singer. I've always liked gay male Broadway singers. With an overdose of navy, you end up a Marine. I won't look good with a shaved head."

"You only know one gay male Broadway singer. And how do you know you wouldn't look good with your head shaved? It worked for Sinead. Not so much Demi Moore."

"I know," I stressed, "because of that thing I can do when I hit the top of my head in just that right place and it makes a timpani sound. That indicates a planar angle that if exposed would make my shaved head look like Gargamel from the Smurfs."

"I think you've been hitting your head a little too much."

"Pounding it against the wall," I agreed. "Standing still while someone designs an evil plot to make you unattractive is quite tiring."

"Speaking of the opposite sex, how was Edward?" she asked.

I huffed in annoyance. "Absent. His sister had her baby early."

"So inconsiderate. Don't worry. You'll get him next trip. When are you back?"

"Sunday night at seven," I replied.

"Come straight to Clyde's and draw the dresses on a napkin. Every horrifying detail."

I closed my eyes and pictured the dresses. "I shudder to think what tomorrow brings."

"Well," Imogen comforted, "the odds are that it's not navy blue."

"It's navy blue!" Lila laughed over the phone the next morning. "Isn't that a surprise?"

"Navy?" I sleepily repeated in definite surprise. "I thought it was maroon."

"Well, it was, but my mother-in-law found these dreadful maroon winceyette *garments*," Lila said in a tone indicating disbelief that such a thing rightfully could be termed clothing. "I had to take evasive fashion action. I found these navy Nicole Miller dresses, so I jumped on them before she could get herself to JC Penney to find some other monstrosity. *Winceyette!*" she huffed. "I mean, that's like *flannel*, for heaven's sake."

I approved Lila's fast action on the winceyette, but grimaced at the navy. And the Nicole Miller. Egads. That was going to put a dent in my wallet.

"Er, how much?" I braced myself.

"Not much," Lila said breezily. "Only $240."

I winced. At least I could recycle shoes.

"Oh," she went on, "and I found the most darling shoes for just a hundred bucks."

Sigh.

I'd crossed into Virginia when North Carolina reached out for me one last time.

"Vi, thank God," Jen sniffled into my cell phone.

"What is it?" I asked in concern.

"It's *Janet*." Her future mother-in-law. "We just had a huge fight about Maeve." Maeve? My sister Maeve? Granted Maeve was a bit of a disaster, but Janet didn't know that.

"She's hyper about numbers for the rehearsal dinner, and doesn't want Maeve there."

"Well . . ." I struggled for the right answer. "I'm sure that's okay."

"No it's not okay!" insisted Jen. "Maeve's like my sister too." Jen had no siblings. "Besides," she went on, "Maeve's my guest book attendant."

I was momentarily distracted. Maeve would be thrilled.

"So, we got in a huge fight. It's crazy, because they're inviting all these relatives I've never met, and my family is tiny in comparison. I mean, shit. Whose wedding is it anyway?"

"It'll be okay," I said, not sure. "Don't let Cowpie get to you." I used my nickname for Janet.

"She can be such a pain," wailed Jen. "It's not like *she's* getting married."

"Listen," I reassured, "Maeve won't mind." The hell she wouldn't, once she found out.

"No." Jen was resolute. "She's in. Period. I gotta go." She hung up.

I drove impatiently home, my earlier wedding fantasies replaced by the reality of ugly dresses, envelopes, and mothers-in-law. I humphed to myself. It wasn't at all the way I'd envisioned. Being maid of honor was getting less fun by the minute.

CHAPTER SIX

The Opposite of Luck

"You have to at least pretend to be interested," chided Mona over the phone.

I groaned. "It's going to be a disaster," I insisted. "You know Babette's bad judgment."

"Quit moaning. You have to put yourself out there or you'll never meet anyone. Where are you going?"

"We're meeting at Degrees Bar at the Ritz in Georgetown," I admitted.

"There," Mona pounced. "You love that place. What are you wearing?"

"The Christian." I had a series of dresses in my closet named after various ex-boyfriends. When I got dumped, I shopped. I had a whole section of Calebs. A brief fling was Christian, but a great dress, a clingy moss green wrap with a plunging neckline. It led to un-Christian thoughts.

"So you aren't completely without optimism."

"To admit Optimism would be to concede to its evil twin, Disappointment, if it doesn't pan out. I hold the line at neutral but well-dressed with shaved legs and enough cash for a cab home. In a word, prepared for any eventuality."

"You know," said Mona, "when you apply yourself, you can charm anyone. I've seen you in action. Men fall happily under your spell. Lately you've been keeping it under a bucket. Why don't you let yourself shine tonight?"

"An unfettered mojo can be dangerous. Ask Julia Roberts. I could wake up married to Lyle Lovett."

"You adore Lyle Lovett," Mona answered.

"Well, yes. But that's not the point." I paused. "What was my point?"

Mona laughed. "Vi—it's Saturday night. Go have fun and give this guy a chance."

After I hung up, I decided Mona was right. I embraced my date by settling on my three inch Via Spiga.

You can always identify the guy waiting for a date he has never seen by the way he glances up each time a woman enters the bar, a mixture of hope and horror on his face. The sadist in me savored his crushed expression when a stunning woman would enter, pause (raising hopes), and continue past to kiss some other guy.

Right away I spotted Dean waiting for me at the bar. I was gratified by his expression as I made solid eye contact.

"Hello." He stood with a relieved smile and held out his hand. I took it and smiled back engagingly. He had a nice handshake. He was attractive, with shaggy blond hair over his collar. I liked the look and approved the casual blazer and jeans. I ignored my inner whisper that the tug of instant sexual chemistry wasn't there, and determined to give the guy a chance. We sat at the bar, and Dean ordered me a glass of wine. Talking to him was easy, though I couldn't tell if he was nervous, deadpan in his humor, or completely lacking in irony. He was very literal. I decided that perhaps he was a scientist.

"So," I explored. "How do you know Babette?" Since everyone in D.C. asks what you do for a living with his or her first breath, I'm loath to ask (though keen to know), so I had to backdoor my way there.

"I'm an investor in one of her venture projects," Dean replied. Vague, but a good start as far as picking up the check was concerned. I'd have a second glass of wine.

"Are you also in venture capital?"

"No actually, I'm an inventor." Bingo. Scientist.

"How interesting. What sort of thing do you invent?" I smiled encouragingly.

"Well, I work with a company that's developing some nano-technology applications . . ." He registered my eyes glazing over and he rushed on. ". . . but it's some of my personal projects that are really interesting."

"I bet," I encouraged. "Can you give me an example, or is it top secret?"

"Oh no," he replied seriously. "I can tell you. Once you file your patent application, you secure the filing date for the invention while the application is evaluated by the examiner."

"Oh. I see." Uh-oh. It looked like Total Lack of Irony and No Sense of Humor were battling to overtake Dry Wit as we progressed down the stretch. I tried to remain Optimistic. "What are you currently working on?"

"Well, there are one or two that you might find interesting, as you're in the beverage field." He grinned at me. "For example, I've invented a portable bathroom device. Like if you're in a crowded bar or at a ball game or something, you don't have to leave to pee. You just go in the device and keep on drinking. I call it the Urine Luck."

Hey! That was actually funny. I laughed. Dry Wit raced into the lead. "That's hilarious," I applauded. "Urine Luck. Maybe someone should invent one."

He looked confused. "But I did. It really works," he insisted. I stopped laughing. Is it possible that he wasn't joking?

"Really?" I asked in carefully neutral tones.

"Oh yes. It works kind of like a condom, with a tight rubber part fitted to the penis. Then there's a tube attached to a bladder sack strapped to the thigh."

Oh my good God. Total Lack of Irony decimated the field and laid claim to the date. I was almost too stunned to speak. But, like staring at a train wreck or watching an episode of *The Bachelor*, I couldn't help myself.

"Er, so, are you marketing it?" At what, I wondered. Pantera concerts?

"Not quite yet. I'm working out a few kinks. But it definitely works. I tried it out. The first time I was home watching the baseball game from my favorite chair having a beer. Then, when I had to go, I didn't get up. I just went right there in the chair." He was completely serious. "After that I tried it out in public venues typical of my target consumer. Music clubs and sports arenas and stuff. It really works," he beamed. "And you don't miss a thing!"

And he'd looked so normal. I looked around desperately to see if the bar was on fire or a wild boar was rampaging on the loose—*anything* to permit a hasty escape. Sadly, I only saw yuppies sipping cocktails in distinctly nonthreatening ways. Dean kept talking.

"Actually," he looked at me as if about to share great news, "I'm working on a version for women." I felt a flutter of panic. If he asked me to product-test, I would die on the spot. I started babbling to forestall any horrifying solicitations.

"Oh. My. Well, that seems a bit more . . . uh, complicated. You know, just biologically, and all. And women like to, um, freshen up in the ladies room, too. And sort of chat." Like any self-respecting woman would walk around with a bag of warm pee strapped to her leg.

"Those are good points. That's why I am focusing on the NA-SCAR market. The bathrooms at raceways tend to be less clean and often don't have mirrors." Another potentially witty pronouncement battered to humorlessness by Mr. I Don't Have A Humorous Bone In My Body. Dean finished his drink and then smiled at me.

"Hey, are you hungry yet? Let's get some dinner."

I smiled weakly, anything but hungry. I could handle this, I assured myself. We'd steer clear of discussing his creative contributions to society or bodily excretions and I'd order the most expensive thing on the menu. It would be fine. But if he didn't excuse himself to go to the bathroom soon, I was going to get very, very suspicious.

"It was a *disaster*!" I cried as the girls cracked up. "In The Movie Starring Me, our date would be called 'Scary Nutter and the Chamber Pot of Pee Kept.' And you," I pointed at Babette, who was laughing as hard as everyone else, "this is your fault."

"How could I know?" She held up her hands in protest. "He seemed so normal. And I think you should call your movie 'U-Rain Man.'"

"No, no," interrupted Ellis, " 'Pee Harbor-er.' You know, like *Pearl Harbor*?" She looked at us expectantly.

"Ellis," Imogen laughed, "it doesn't work if you have to explain the movie."

"I got it, Ellis." Mona swatted at Imogen. "How about 'Catch Pee If You Plan'?"

"I know," offered Imogen, " 'Close Encounters of the Number One Kind'!"

"How about just 'A Time to Kill . . . Myself'?" I offered.

"I don't think it's time for that yet," said Imogen. "Clyde's hasn't run out of wine yet." We reflected on the greatness of that in a happy moment of silence, sipping our wine. Then Imogen knocked over Babette's Vanilla Stoli and we jumped to mop up the mess . . . almost as fast as Charlie hustled to replace Babette's drink. After order was restored, I spoke again.

"Seriously, though, guys," I said. "I'm letting it go. It's okay if I don't find a date. In fact, I'm off dating. I'm not dating anymore." Babette looked skeptical. Imogen gave a rude laugh, but couldn't make an accompanying discourteous gesture because Ellis had insisted she sit on her hands for three minutes so she wouldn't knock over anything else.

"What?? I mean it," I insisted.

"It doesn't have to be one extreme or another," suggested Imogen. "Stop worrying about getting a date. All you have to worry about is finishing your toast before you get smashed."

"Toast?" asked Babette. "You have to give a toast?"

"Oh wonderful. Topically less pleasant than Urine Man, if that's possible. Yes. *Three* toasts. It's all about equality these days. The maid of honor's toast follows the best man's."

Babette raised her eyebrows at Imogen. "I like how she's pretending she doesn't love the attention." I flushed. She had me there. I was preening at the thought of my perfectly executed salute to the loving couple, in language articulate, witty, and sensitive, under the admiring eyes of all the guests.

"Do you know what you're going to say?" asked Ellis.

"Not yet," I dismissed. "Something will come to me."

"Well, I don't envy you," Ellis replied with big eyes. "I had to do a reading at my cousin's wedding and I was terrified."

"Hmm." I murmured, feeling a twinge of Anxiety at her words. I shoved it down. It was forever away. I mean, it wasn't even Christmas yet.

CHAPTER SEVEN

Life's A Ski Boot

Before I knew it, it *was* Christmas. When I staggered into my parent's kitchen, groaning under the weight of Nigel and Clementine's crate, I found Maeve absorbed in scrutinizing the side of a loaf of bread.

"I'm allergic to wheat," she announced without looking up. I thumped the crate down with a huff, and together Maeve and I released a cranky Clementine and a skittish Nigel.

"Since when?"

"I saw it on *Oprah*," she said, "That's why my stomach's always upset."

"I thought your stomach was always upset because you eat mozzarella sticks, chocolate-covered Oreos, and fried egg and bacon sandwiches like they were a religion." I sidestepped Maeve's health sensitivity. Her diet fads were nothing new; she'd been a vegetarian for years. Nor were her Oprah Epiphanies, as I liked to call the revelations she had when an *Oprah* segment spoke to her very soul.

Maeve made a face. "Whatever. Want to go to the store with me to get some wheat-free bread and potato vodka?"

"Sure. Are you staying here over the holidays?" Maeve lived by the university.

"Uh . . . yeah. I sort of have no heat."

"No heat?" Even in North Carolina it got cold in December. "Are they fixing it soon?"

"Um. Well. It's nothing that $238 won't fix."

I groaned. "Oh, Maeve. Not again."

"It's not my fault!" she protested. "Those boots were *seventy percent off.* I'm always here during the holidays, anyway. I brought Oliver with me." I looked dubiously at Nigel and Clementine. Did Clementine perk up?

"Maybe you better keep Oliver in your room."

Maeve shrugged. "I'm keeping him there anyway. The battery was running low on my fire alarm last week, you know how it beeps over and over? Well, Oliver won't stop doing it. He's driving me crazy." Oliver would imitate anything he heard repetitively.

My mother walked into the room, smoking a pipe. That meant she had been working. She saw me and looked a little confused at first, then brightened.

"Vi! You're here. When did you get in?" Depending on how intently my mother had been focusing on her work, I could've been there for three days for all she knew.

"Just now." I received her hug. "You know you're not allowed to smoke in here."

"Oh, good." She puffed distractedly. "Just some problems with the curvy bits. Maeve, is there anything in there?" Maeve was peering in the fridge with a disgusted look on her face.

"Half a green pepper, a jar of pickles, Canadian maple syrup, cottage cheese, and some figs." I think the jar of pickles had been with my family as long as Brick had.

"Oh dear. I had a fig and cottage cheese sandwich yesterday

and I'm afraid it gave me bad dreams. I would prefer not to have another."

Maeve and I shot alarmed looks at each other. Maeve shut the fridge door decisively. "That's it. I'm going to Chic-Fil-A. Who wants a veggie wrap?"

"Let me dump my stuff," I said. "We can stop by the store afterward."

"Right. Potato vodka," said my mother. Sometimes she was spooky. She scooped up Clementine who, unnaturally, curled lovingly in her arms and purred.

"Well, off with you, then. Oh, and get some AA batteries. I think the fire alarm battery is running low because it keeps beeping." She wandered back to her studio.

As she left the room, I looked at Maeve. We both sighed.

We'd have to figure out all our family meals including Christmas, and get what we needed. Meaning I would have to get it and bill Dad later. Maeve was good for chewing gum, maybe, if she borrowed thirty-five cents. I mentally calculated my credit card balances, wondering if there was room to wedge groceries in among navy blue dresses.

"I've got the bows." Brick held aloft a shoe box he'd unearthed in the upstairs closet.

"I bought paper." I dumped six rolls of Christmas wrapping paper on the floor in front of the fireplace.

It was time for the annual Connelly Christmas Eve ritual. Each year we would gather and distribute the gifts we had purchased for ourselves for the rest of the family to wrap and give back to us the next morning. Not the conventional way to exchange Christmas gifts, but we were a practical family. Gift Wrap Night was very festive, with a roaring fire, Christmas carols on the radio, and wine. This year I had bought some chestnuts to roast. It was my favorite night of the year. I think we all enjoyed it even more than Christmas morning.

"Does everyone want red?" My father's voice floated from where his head was stuck in his wine storage cellar.

"Yes," we all chorused. "Beer," said Brick. My mother walked in from the kitchen with popcorn, and Maeve came behind her balancing a tray of cheese and crackers. The top half of my father emerged with two bottles of wine, which he opened and set on the coffee table, next to the glasses. We all settled into our usual places—me on one end of the sofa, Maeve on the other, my mother and father squished on the love seat sofa, and Brick on the floor in front of the fire.

"Okay," I said, peering into my bag. "Mom, here. This one is for me, from you."

"Oh, what is it dear?" she asked, taking the gift from me.

"It's a navigation system for my car," I told her. "It talks. Brick." I tossed him an Eagle day pack. Brick and I always tried to make each other wrap the most difficult or unwieldy objects. He just grinned at me as he caught it, so I knew his must be a doozy. Damn. "Dad." I handed him a box of Riedel crystal Bordeaux wineglasses. I was hoping it would inspire him to "plus up" the gift by throwing in a bottle of Riedel-worthy wine.

"Excellent choice," he commended me.

"Thanks. I got eight, I hope you don't mind."

"No, no, that's fine. Here." He handed me a four CD set of Beethoven piano sonatas. "I think I'll like these."

"Ooooh, easy to wrap. Awesome." I accepted it. Meanwhile Brick was handing Mom a copy of a ski magazine to wrap up.

"What's that about?" Maeve asked.

"I got skis," he said, looking a little sheepish.

"Skis! That's over budget!" Maeve screeched. Brick always went over budget. And always got away with it.

"Hey, it's what I wanted and it's from both of them. Here." He handed her a box. "You got me ski gloves and a hat." Then he looked at me with a devilish look and produced one ski boot. "You got me a ski boot," he said, grinning. "Wrap that."

"Give me back my day pack," I ordered. "You're giving me a garden hose."

"Too late." He thunked the boot into my lap.

My mother started handing around various bizarre things, including a rake, a beach chair, and, inexplicably, a set of plush dolls of common ailments. At Maeve's look, Mom explained, "They gave me some project ideas." Apparently I was giving her a vacuum food-sealer. Maeve and I didn't exchange self-selected gifts. We trusted one another to actually shop. It was nice to have some surprises. We also got socks every year from Mom, but we didn't know what they looked like. We also got an ugly sweater every year from our aunt Leigh, who worked at J. Jill.

"Did someone get the supplies?" my mother asked. I produced several rolls of tape, two pairs of scissors, gift tags, and some pens.

We all finished passing out the gifts and began wrapping. I saved the ski boot for last. Conversation and wine flowed, regularly punctuated with "Who has the tape?" and "Maeve, you're hogging the scissors again." Maeve and I competed to come up with the most ludicrous wrapping job, using as many and as intricate bows as possible. My father regaled us with ridiculous tales of unreasonable clients, and Brick related fraternity hijinks. Later Maeve and I would do the stockings. Several years ago we had hijacked this job from my father in a bloodless coup when the populace decided they no longer wanted oranges and nuts in their stockings but proper candy like everyone else. We just gave Dad the bill.

I looked at Maeve supplementing a bow with a miniature slinky and catnip mouse and was suffused with happiness. I loved Christmas Eve with my family. I turned my attention to my ski boot. I was going to make a bow that would kick Maeve's ass.

And I was going to figure out a way to attach something girly and pink to the boot that Brick couldn't get off.

As typically happens on Christmas Day, we ran out of knowing what to do with ourselves by three. I was flipping TV channels. Maeve was working on a crossword. Brick was half watching TV and half checking e-mail and sports scores on his laptop. Our mother was napping and our father was "watching the birds" on a lounge chair on the patio, which meant he was sneaking a cigar, napping, or both. Sometimes they "napped" together, which even for my smitten parents was too gross to contemplate so I didn't. I chose to believe he was watching the birds.

"Did you get anything good?" Maeve asked Imogen, who spent more of the holidays camped out on our sofa than at her own parent's house.

"Sweater. Perfume. Cash. You?"

"Perfume. I'm returning the sweater. I did get exactly the digital camera I wanted."

"You bought that camera and Mom wrapped it," Brick reminded her.

"Yeah, she did a good job," Maeve said. "What's a ten letter word for poverty?"

"Deficiency," Imogen said.

"Bridesmaid," I said.

"How about you, Brick?" Imogen asked.

"I got skis." Brick grinned at her. Imogen raised an eyebrow at Maeve and me.

"I know," I said. "It's scandalous. He goes ridiculously over budget every year and gets away with it. The male heir apparent."

"*Apparently* spending the inheritance right now, you mean," muttered Maeve. "What's a nine letter word for 'harridan'?"

"Patsyrose," I said.

"Termagant," Imogen said.

"Murphy's Law of Retroaction," Brick said, still grinning. "It's easier to win forgiveness than permission."

I found *Dirty Dancing* playing on the Oxygen channel.

"Absolutely not," said Brick. "I veto that. In fact I veto anything on the Oxygen channel."

"Nobody puts Baby in a corner," said Imogen.

"You aren't even watching," complained Maeve. "This is a good part, where the dad tells Baby she let him down and then she says no *you* let *me* down and—"

"Turn it," said Brick. "I mean it. Turn it, or it's dirty sock feet in the face for you. And I'm telling you, these are laundry day socks." I turned it. I have a thing about dirty socks.

"I'll switch back for the finale," I told Maeve.

"What's a four letter word for 'dismal'?" Maeve asked.

"Navy," I said. Imogen was stumped. Brick rolled his eyes like we were morons.

"You're living it. D-U-L-L," he pronounced.

"Its 'grim,' " Maeve crowed as she filled it in.

"That too." Brick went back to his laptop.

"Well." Imogen heaved herself up. "Should we motivate to Louis's for chili and football? The game starts soon." I felt too lazy to imagine being anywhere but the couch, but we had to make an appearance.

"Can I come?" pleaded Brick. "It can't be more boring dull grim than this. There'll be guys there. And football. That means nacho cheese dip. I love nacho cheese dip. If I watch any more Oxygen channel I'm gonna get my period."

"No. Go do laundry."

"I'll give you five bucks if I can come," Brick begged. "Each. I'm getting cramps."

"I'll bring you some cheese dip. And tampons."

"Don't let anybody put you in a corner," said Maeve, watching Patrick Swayze gyrate on the screen.

There were about twenty people at Louis's, mostly couples. The guys wore the Southern uniform of Tommy Hilfiger shirt, khaki Dockers, sneakers, and baseball cap, accessorized with Cheap Domestic Beer In A Can. I styled myself with one, as did Imogen. We found Jen and Louis talking to a couple introduced as Robin and Danny. They were all eating cheese dip.

"Vi! Imogen! Hey!" Jen gave us each a hug.

"Hey Jen. Hey Louis," I said. Louis and I went in for the awkward hug. Conversation floundered through the "thanks for inviting us's" and "glad you could comes." Then we all looked around. Danny saved us by being not the least bit interested in us and launching into a conversation about NASCAR.

I watched Jen indulgently gazing at Louis as he told her some race story he was jazzed about. I had to admit, they were cute together, with matching happy grins. And I couldn't fault her. In college I dated a guy who was really into competitive cycling. I was really into sex with him. I started reading Velo News and throwing around lingo like I knew what the hell I was talking about. He gave me my first multiple orgasm so I was willing to put in a little work to keep him around. My interest in cycling dropped off sharply after we broke up. My interest in multiple orgasms did not.

"How about Dick Trickle?" Danny threw out the famous driver's suggestive name, and both boys sniggered like eight-year-olds. I sighed. Jen saw something in Louis and that was good enough for me, but I'd never relate.

"Did'ya watch the Bobcats last night?" Danny thankfully moved on to another (tedious) sports topic. While the men spoke (at length) about the game (it was that bum Rush's fault they lost), Robin hung dotingly around Danny's waist.

"So, Robin," I tried brightly, "did you do anything exciting over the holidays?"

"My friend Jeanine came over and treated my split ends." She scrutinized the tips. We made sympathetic noises, and thus encouraged, Robin talked about split ends for another ten minutes. Imogen's foot tapping became audible. A Bruce-and-Cheryl joined us. Bruce immediately jumped into the boys' conversation ("that Rush is a bum"). As if by mitosis, we were dividing into two herds.

"Did ya'll see that article about infections from pedicures? I swear I've never been so grossed out in my life." Cheryl had a loud Southern twang. "They shouldn't put pictures like that in the paper. What if a child saw?" Presumably photos of corpses from war-torn nations were acceptable for children, but swollen feet were not.

"What're ya'll talking about?" asked a girl named Alecia.

"Infections from pedicures," said Robin, in a tone reserved for genocide in Rwanda.

"Ew, I saw that," Alecia said. "They shouldn't put pictures like that in the paper. Did ya'll see the one on public toilets? I was so freaked out." I felt Imogen vibrating next to me.

"Well, I never flush a public toilet with my hand," said Cheryl. "I kick it. People don't wash their hands." They all shook their heads over the baseness of the human race.

"So, Jen, what did you decide to do for New Year's Eve?" I turned to her, desperate to change the subject. Imogen came to attention.

"Well," Jen said, "we thought we'd try to save a little money this year, so we're going to have everyone here. We'll have just as much fun as if we went out." The girls all smiled and nodded, happy at the thought of safe, clean toilets.

"Oh," Imogen and I said.

"There'll be something," Imogen said confidently as we zoomed up I-95.

I grunted. "I hate New Year's. There's all this pressure to make it amazing and it never is."

"You had a good New Year's Eve with Caleb in Atlanta," she reminded me.

"Now that was cool," I admitted. "Caleb got us into this closed club by pretending I was an heiress and he was my bodyguard. He put my chapstick cap in his ear and kept muttering into his wristwatch. It was hilarious."

"We'll find something good," she assured me.

"Yes," I said. There was a pathetic meow from the backseat. We cracked up.

"You said it, Clementine." Imogen agreed.

We were silent for a bit. "Why don't you go home more often?" I asked Imogen.

She was quiet, then, "You have to ask? I don't fit anymore."

I had to admit that after a week in Charlotte, I was relieved to be heading home early. Home, I thought. I'd always called Charlotte home. Now it felt awkward.

"I don't think I fit either." I uttered the lurking admission I'd been avoiding.

"It's too weird," said Imogen. "And I'm not sucked back in like you. How do you do it?"

"I feel like I'm in this weird liminal space where I'm a Charlotte version of myself, one missing everything that happened after college. The Performer comes out and I fake it."

"And the Feelings?"

I reflected. "Simultaneously Claustrophobic and Alienated. I'm trying to act out who I might've been if I'd stayed here. But it's a bad idea. I like my life now."

"Stepping back in time makes you feel vulnerable?"

"In Charlotte I feel off schedule. Like I want things now and can't have them. I don't feel that way in D.C."

"We need to get back to reality," Imogen said.

"I'm afraid until after the weddings I'm stuck with one foot in my teens and one foot in my twenties. The Endless Parade of Joyful Events disrupts me from being very present in D.C. these days." A slow moving Taurus was making me twitch. "I bet Lance is having his New Year's party," I speculated as I pressed the gas to zip around the Taurus and get us to D.C. a little faster.

CHAPTER EIGHT

A Downhill

"Three, two one . . . Hurrah!" It was midnight on New Year's Eve. People blew little horns and everyone was kissing one another. I kissed Imogen and then Ethan. I looked over to kiss Mona but she was making out with a dead ringer for Dave Navarro, right down to the tattoos. I giggled and looked to point it out to Imogen, who was kissing Ethan, when my vision was blocked by Garrick, a cute boy I'd met earlier by the ice luge.

"I believe it's midnight." He grinned, I smiled back, and he leaned in for a kiss. A good kiss. We kissed again. For a while. And then we kissed some more. Coming back to D.C. for New Year's Eve had definitely been a good idea. I peeked guiltily over at Imogen, embarrassed to be making out in public, but she was still kissing Ethan.

Whoa. Wait a minute there! Imogen was still kissing Ethan??? I focused my stare, but Garrick snared my attention.

"Shall we celebrate the new day by returning to where we first met?" He smiled at me. Oh, he was cute. Dimples and blond hair, straight from a ChapStick ad. I could visualize him sentimentally tearing up on the podium as he held aloft his Olympic gold medal for alpine downhill and dedicated it to me, his inspiration. He led me to the ice luge for Jagermeister shots. That counted as a winter sport, right?

For once, New Year's Eve was turning into a fantastic night. Our friend Lance was having his annual New Year's Eve bash with a DJ and open bars at his enormous house on Foxhall. Everyone was having a blast and I'd met a cute potential Mr. Wedding Date. Yay me! Happy New Year!

At 2:00 A.M., Ethan tapped me.

"I'm heading home," he hollered over the music.

"What?" I shouted, cupping my ear at him. He dangled his car keys. "Nooooo . . ." I wailed. He grinned and nodded his head, yes. I knew the futility of arguing with level-headed Ethan over matters such as this. No amount of wheedling would change his mind. I looked at Imogen, who shrugged. Mona was still dancing with Dave Navarro's doppelganger.

"Want to stay and catch a cab later?" I shouted at Imogen. She nodded.

"I think she does too." She thumbed in Mona's direction. Cha, right.

I held up a finger at Garrick to indicate I'd be right back and walked Ethan to the door.

"Happy New Year." I gave him a hug.

"Happy New Year to you." He squeezed me back.

"You'll be careful driving?" I asked. Unusually, it was snowing beautiful fat flakes. Not life threatening but D.C. was notoriously ill equipped for snow, in both supplies and temperament.

"I'll be fine," Ethan assured me, tucking in his scarf.

"Hey," I remembered. "What was that with you and Imogen on the dance floor? You were making out! *J'accuse!*"

"We were not," Ethan denied. But he flushed.

"I think you were," I probed. Had I seen Ethan blush before?

"I kissed you too" he reminded, not looking at me as he extracted his gloves. I snorted.

"Not that long," I rejoined. "And not with tongue. Ew." Before I could press the matter further, Ethan kissed me on the cheek.

"You better get back to your gazelle before he wanders off. Be safe getting home. Don't take candy from strangers."

I returned to Imogen, Mona (still kissing), and Garrick. Imogen, Garrick, and I went to the bar for another round of drinks. I was feeling pleasantly floaty and happy. We'd enjoyed a couple of bottles of wine at dinner and I had sampled the chocolate martinis, the cosmos, the vodka tonics, and the ice luge at the party. I was now discovering that their cranberry vodka was excellent as well. As the bar ran out of mixers, I kept modifying my drink. Adaptable, you see.

We went back to the dance floor and were wiggling happily to Cher's "I Believe." Garrick's hand was on my hip and I tried to gyrate that curve sexily without tumbling over. It wasn't easy. He smiled at me. Then, focusing over my right shoulder, his smile froze and he snatched his hand from my hip speedier than a men's single's bobsled downhill.

"Meredith! Uh, hi. When did you get here? I thought you were going to call me?" Garrick stuttered, stepping back from me. An attractive brunette was advancing with a grim look on her face, none too pleased with the tableau.

"Garrick. I. Have. Been. *Trying*. To. Call." She ground out. "There was no answer. *Apparently*," she shot me a look of pure malice, "you were *busy*." I, wisely, decided to keep my mouth shut. I could sense the lovely Imogen edging into place behind me.

"Uh, gee, sorry baby," Garrick stammered. Baby? "Um, meet Vi. Vi is, uh, a friend of, um, Jay's." That Meredith couldn't care less who I was seemed perfectly obvious. "Vi, this is my girlfriend Meredith." He slung an arm over her stiff shoulders, looking desperate. My irritation boiled. Girlfriend? Jerk. My fantasy of

Mr. ChapStick at my side in May evaporated. Then I looked at Meredith's set face and pitied her.

"Yeah, Jay's a great guy," I said. Garrick's shoulders slumped in relief. "Well, it was good to see you, Garrick." I gave a half wave and dragged Imogen off. I could hear Meredith hauling Garrick to "The. Poor. Cab. It. Has. Been. *Waiting*. And. It's. *Snowing*." But I didn't look. I hustled straight to the bar.

"Are you okay?" Imogen trailed me.

"Actually, I'm fine," I told her. I really was. "If he did it to her, he'd do it to me. Besides," I giggled, "I got a nice New Year's smoochy-smooch."

"Too true." Imogen looked impressed with my nonchalance. The bar was now out of cranberry and vodka both, so I downgraded to beer. I'm a survivor. We returned to the dance floor in good spirits (though without spirits). Dumb Garrick wouldn't ruin my night. I started joyfully shaking my booty again.

"Hey, what about you and Ethan?" I shouted at Imogen. She pretended she couldn't hear me, but I suspect she did because she suddenly was very caught up dancing in a way that made her hair hide her face. Hunh.

CHAPTER NINE

Three Showers and a Funeral

"Please, please, please, please," I begged Giles.

"This is getting to be a habit," Giles tortured me, dusting imaginary lint off his paisley pants. We both knew he would give in.

"You know if I don't hit the road by three I'll be in traffic forever." I'd spun like a dervish to get my work done in time. I prayed I'd only ordered eleven bottles of the Pink Truck Rose rather than 1,100 as I'd done once before. It'd taken me some creative promotions to cover that mistake.

"What if I had plans that required an early slip-out on Friday?" Giles demanded.

"You'd have been crowing about them all week and I'd know," I said. "You don't. Just say yes, Giles. I'll come to a month of showtunes night at J.R's," I wheedled. It was almost three. We needed to hurry up the request-for-favor-meets-resistance-before-capitulation ritual.

Giles gave a gusty sigh. "Yes." Then he mimicked the evil principal in *Breakfast Club*, holding up four fingers. "But you're mine, Connelly. I got you for a month of Mondays."

I blew him a kiss and grabbed my coat. I would probably be at showtunes for the rest of the year by the time it was all over. I still had to skive off early for bachelorette parties and the weddings themselves. My friends would all gain husbands, and I'd lose my job.

I had a tight weekend schedule, with bridal showers Saturday at 2:00 P.M. (Jen), Saturday at 7:00 P.M. (Lila), and Sunday at 11:00 A.M. (Amy). Jen and Lila had been thoughtful enough to coordinate on the same weekend as Amy's. Amy simply told me the date her mother had selected.

My problem was a lack of gifts. While I deemed myself competent to come up with selections that communicated "style" and "elegance," I couldn't channel a gift that simply oozed "3:00 P.M.," as I had to for Amy's cutesy Round-the-Clock themed shower. *Nothing* happened at three except that my biorhythms hit the Mariana trench and I face-planted onto my desk for a few glorious minutes, until I slammed upright, blinking rapidly and feigning some busy action when Giles burst back into the office. Once, I was all the way home before I realized I had a paper clip embedded in my forehead. Giles had paid for that.

I also needed inspiration for "Foyer" (Round-the-House, Jen) and March (Round-the-Calendar, Lila). Tomorrow would be Round-the-Mall. I reached for my cell phone.

"Tampon," Imogen answered amid a chaotic din. At least that's what it sounded like. I suspected "hang on" is what she'd been going for. I heard noise diminishing.

"Sorry, I had to step outside to hear."

"Where are you?" I asked enviously.

"Rosa Mexicano. Come meet Ellis and me for pomegranate margaritas."

"Can't," I said. "I'm en route to Charlotte."

"Oh right, I forgot. Shower?"

"Downpour. Listen, what gift makes you think three P.M.? Or Foyer? Or March?"

"Three P.M. in the foyer . . . that sounds like kinky sex with the UPS guy. Get her a case of condoms and a French maid costume."

"How many margaritas have you had?" I asked.

"For March, get a bunch of Sousa CDs. I'll give you a dollar for everyone who gets it."

"Your money is safe."

"Just get them a vase." Imogen was ready to go. "I'm headed back inside. I'm freezing and someone might swipe the gazelle I've got my eye on. See you Sunday."

I sighed again. "I won't be back in time."

"Wha-at? You've missed two Sundays since Christmas. These weddings are starting to impact *my* happiness," Imogen huffed.

"Tell me about it," I said. "It makes me see white."

In the morning, I followed the smell of coffee to my mother reading the paper in the kitchen.

"Oh, hello." She looked up in surprise. "You're here?" She appeared conflicted.

"Wedding showers," I explained.

"Oh. Well, then. So, you're busy? All weekend? It's just that your dad and I have plans with Lisa and Andrew McCabe. We forgot you'd be here. Um, did we know?" I found it charming that my parents still dated and double-dated. Mom looked sheepish, but I didn't blame her. Lately I'd been living in their house more than Maeve.

"Surgical strike." I poured myself a cup of coffee. "Don't worry about it. So what do you think of when you think three P.M.? It's the hour that I got for the wedding shower. I'm also stuck with Foyer and March."

"They certainly make things complicated these days."

"Did you have a shower when you married Dad?"

"Oh no. We had a very simple ceremony. I never wanted another big white wedding."

I frowned. "Another?"

My mother looked back at her paper distractedly. "All that hoopla. Can you imagine, Jackie did it five times? I found it exhausting." Oh right.

"So," she continued. "Can't you just buy a vase?" Sigh.

I was heading out half an hour later when my mother intercepted me. "Vi . . . hold up." She strolled to the back door. My mother never hurried anywhere. I twitched impatiently. She smiled and handed me a note. "Have a good afternoon?"

"Sure, Mom." I gave her a kiss and dashed to my car, anxious to get three beautifully wrapped items in the backseat. At a stoplight, I unfolded the note, and read in her delicate handwriting:

> *March is planting season. I believe Lila and Hart have already bought a house? Yardley's Nursery is having a sale on flowering pear trees.*
>
> *Traditionally, 3:00 PM is the time of day when tea would be served. There is a Zen boutique at Park Place that offers tea sets. They do beautiful gift-wrapping there as well.*
>
> *A decorative wrought iron mirror would look lovely in the Foyer and has a practical aspect to give your appearance one last check on the way out the door. Judy Fletcher told me there are some lovely mirrors at Jacobsen's.*

Mostly absentminded, my mother had moments of visionary clarity. For someone who didn't have "hoopla" at her wedding, she knew what she was doing. Must have been all that practice with Jackie. I redirected to Jacobsen's, mentally singing my mother's praises. Two hours later I pulled up to Jen's shower, ribbons flapping from the tree hanging out of my car.

Three hours later tension was building across my shoulders. I was perched on an overstuffed floral sofa with a twee little tea-cup and saucer balanced on my knees, listening to Jen's aunt Harriet nattering away. Harriet was from a small town in eastern North Carolina and evoked a wombat with a nasal twang. Slow, not at all bright, but dogged.

"So." Harriet peered at me. "When will it be your turn, hmm? You two were always thick as thieves. I would think now that Jen's made the big step you'd be ready to race down the aisle yourself." Rub it in, I thought.

I gritted a wide, false smile. "Well, you know." I lowered my voice. "I'm having a hard time getting my initial elopement annulled. You'd think since he was already married and is in prison that the Church would be more sympathetic, but no amount of flirting with the priest changes his mind." I heaved a sigh. "It's sooo hard. Because there's this other guy I met when I was visiting the prison that I really fancy, and he'll be paroled soon." I gazed pensively into the bottom of my cup. "If you'll excuse me, I need some more tea." I extricated myself from the overstuffed couch and navigated a sea of Laura Ashley to the buffet table. I was abandoning my Future Accident of a sliver thin teacup in favor of a bottle of Perrier when Jen came up, merriment in her eyes.

"What did you say to Aunt Harriet?" she asked. "She looks scandalized."

"You don't want to know," I assured her. "But she deserved it. By the way, how far is the nearest prison, in case anyone asks about the commute?"

"You didn't! I'll hear about this later, you know." She laughed.

"Hey, *I* wasn't the one that had a pen pal from prison for a while."

Jen flushed. "Don't remind me." We met some guys at the beach one summer and one completely fell for Jen and wrote her long, tormented letters. Including after he was sent to prison for illegal transportation of stolen goods across state lines. Marilou had flipped out over the correctional institution return address and staged an intervention, convinced Jen was primed to elope (ignoring the logistical difficulties related to incarceration of one of the parties).

We heard the tinging of silverware on glass. Jen grabbed my arm.

"Don't you leave my side," she hissed, and dragged me into the living room for the opening of the gifts. I obediently sat by her and took notes. Jen performed the ritual perfectly.

"Oh look! A bread baker! We were hoping for one of these. It's for the kitchen. Isn't that perfect? It's from Mrs. Kramer. Where are you, Mrs. Kramer? Thank you so much." We all dutifully admired the bread baker. Aunt Harriet gathered the ribbons to stick on a paper plate.

"This is for the mock bouquet for Jen's rehearsal. Jen dear, be careful with those bows," she tittered. "Every ribbon you break will be one child in the marriage." Jen grimaced at her and reached for the next gift, sliding the ribbon off carefully.

"Oh look! A beautiful vase for the living room. Thank you, Carla. Carla's a friend from college, everyone. And look at this gorgeous vase. I'll pass it around . . .

"My goodness. Aunt Harriet, you shouldn't have. It's a night-dress . . . for the bedroom naturally. I'll pass it around. . . ."

"Oh look!" Lila exclaimed. "A bread baker! We were hoping we'd get one of these. Won't that be perfect for November? It's from Mrs. Smith. Where are you, Mrs. Smith? Oh there you are. Thank you so much." We dutifully admired the bread baker. Next to Lila on an overstuffed floral couch, I noted the gift on a pad of paper. Angela swooped on the discarded bows and stuck them to a paper plate.

"Lila, for every ribbon you break, you and Hart will have a baby," teased Hart's mother.

"Not if me and Ortho-Novum can help it." Lila muttered the

name of her birth control pills under her breath to me, while giving her mother-in-law a smile.

"Oh look, Christmas plates for December. How clever! Where are you, Whitney? This is Whitney, a friend from work. . . ." Lila bent down for the next gift and whispered to me, "Don't any of these people know what a goddamned registry is? If I wanted freaking ugly Christmas plates, I would've asked for them." I hid my expression by shoving it deep in my wineglass. One thing about Lila, she knew what she wanted. I was grateful that the beverage of choice at this shower was wine rather than tea. Lila came up smiling, holding a box aloft.

"Let's see. This one is 'For June, for the Honeymoon.' Oh my goodness, Susan. It's a nightgown, everyone. What a pretty color." (Aside to me . . . "Not.") "Susan, you shouldn't have. I'll pass it around to the right. . . ." (Aside to me . . . "She *really* shouldn't have. Like I'd wear something from Target made out of flammable material.")

"Well, it's a watermelon flag for the front porch, for July. How original. Thank you, Mrs. Leland. Mrs. Leland was my Sunday school teacher. Look everyone, a decorative flag for the house. (Aside to me . . . "Registry," barked like a cough into her hand.)

"It's a vase. And so pretty! For May—how clever, May flowers. I'll pass it around. . . ." (Aside to me . . . "Vain hope someone will drop it and break the hideous thing on the way around.")

When she got to my gift, Lila looked confused at the lonely little $4.99 trowel. Then she looked at the card. It read: "March. Over to the front door. And open it." She gave me a quizzical look and then said, "Vi's making me work for my gift, everyone. Marching for March." She opened the front door. There was my tree festooned with ribbons, roots anchored in a hunk of dirt wrapped in burlap. Lila clapped her hands and twirled.

"Vi, I love it! A tree for our new house! Thank you!" Around the room each of the ladies was speaking to the lady next to her.

"Is that a tree?"

"What month was she? Oh, March. That's good."

"What a clever idea!"

"So appropriate to starting a new home."

"My husband loves puttering in the yard."

I preened. I had pulled off the perfect gift. No asides for me. Then I heard the hostess.

"Is that thing getting dirt all over my stoop?"

Lila gave me a big grin and a thumbs-up. Then she addressed the room. "That's it, folks. Thanks so much. Everyone has been incredibly, incredibly thoughtful. Please continue to enjoy the food and drink and excellent company. Who needs more wine? Oh, wait. I do. . . ." With that, she beelined into the dining room. I popped right up after her.

That night, I pushed my way into an uptown bar, scanning the room for Edward. I was looking forward to seeing my cute former boyfriend. Edward had scruffy hair, and eyes that crinkled at the corners when he smiled. He was gentle and sweet but far too aimless to be a long-term partner. He'd do just right for a wedding date.

I was surprised at his choice of The Graduate pub. Prone to meatheads, it wasn't really our sort of bar. I did a double take when I saw someone wave at me. My eyes had skipped right over him, he was so altered. I approached the table trying to conceal my astonishment. The scruffy fellow from my past had his hair so slicked you could see comb lines, and was sporting tight white jeans and loafers, no socks. If we'd been in a gay rodeo bar, I'd have guessed a sexual epiphany.

"Edward," I sang, masking my surprise, "so great to see you! You look, um . . . great!"

He beamed. "Thanks! I know! Been working out." He flexed. I blinked. He was being serious. We sat.

"I'm so glad you were free," I said.

"Well, I'm pretty busy these days, but my plans for tonight canceled so it worked out." He smiled at me.

Ah.

"What d'you want to drink? I'm havin' a Corona Light." He winked. "You look like you've gained a little weight, so you probably want a light too!" he joked jovially. I gaped.

"That'll be fine," I managed, and watched the baffling new Edward swagger to the bar and order, winking at the bartender. When he returned with my beer, I said, "Well, wow. You look . . . transformed. Is that a muscle shirt?"

He smiled smugly. "Yep. Great, huh? I got a whole new look." Yes, and Hulk Hogan wants it back, I thought.

I said aloud, "It's so, *different*."

He raised his beer bottle and clinked it to mine. "Vi, I met a girl and she changed my life."

Oh.

"That's great," I enthused falsely, visions of a carefully re-dressed, gel-free "plus one" evaporating. "Tell me about it."

"Well, her name is Sheila and I met her at Park Lanes bowling one night. She's just the sweetest thing ever." He produced a photo of a woman who personified all the bad taste that North Carolina has to offer—long, bleached and permed hair, high bangs, white denim miniskirt with fringe, and jelly shoes. I recalled that I'd hadn't seen Edward in some time.

"She looks . . . nice," I managed, Edward too starry-eyed to notice my lackluster praise.

"She sure is," he praised. "She does nails at Wish You Were Hair, in the mall, and everyone loves her. She's the most popular girl. And she's real into body sculpting. She got me into this guy John Basedow and his fitness program. And look at me now!" He flexed again.

Indeed.

He looked at me intently. "You know, you could look sculpted too, with a little work. You should check him out at muscleweb .com. He's an inspiration." I was gaping again. I shut my mouth. And self-consciously sucked in my nonexistent gut.

"So, um, how are your folks?" I tried a topic other than my shape. I'd always liked Edward's parents.

"Great! They love Sheila!" He smiled. "She's such a joker, she calls 'em Uncle Bob and Aunt Lou."

"Great." I wondered what our tally on that superlative would be by night's end. Apparently the Vagina of Sheila could suck men's brains right out of their penises. Poor Edward was completely lobotomized. Unrecognizable.

"How's D.C.?" He asked.

"It's good. Work is going really well. I just—"

"Sheila went to D.C. with her mother last year to shop at Potomac Mills," he interrupted. "She's a little shopper, that one. Great taste." He paused, eyeing my tasteful outfit of black silk pants and red V-neck top. "You know, if you want a few tips, you could call her. She's so sweet she wouldn't mind helping someone out."

My mouth flopped open again.

"I'll get us some more beers." He jumped up, ignoring my full beer. "Corona Light is Sheila's favorite!"

When he returned, we made an effort at small talk, peppered with fascinating tidbits such as "Sheila loves the ocean" when talking about my trip to Charleston; "Sheila says Martha Stewart isn't a nice person," when discussing the wedding showers; and "Sheila went to Mexico once," when discussing Benicio del Toro's new movie.

"Well, you seem very happy," I managed, beginning to extricate myself from the inexhaustible torrent of Sheilaisms to head home.

"I tell you, I am," he agreed. He looked at me keenly. "But, Vi, I gotta say, you don't look so hot. Are you working too hard?

Have you been sick? Your skin tone is grey and your hair looks sort of lank. You might need some vitamins. John—that's John Basedow—he recommends them." He chuckled. "We're gettin' old, girl. We gotta take care of things or they slide. That's what Sheila always says."

I was too flabbergasted for words. The song "Crazy," by Gnarls Barkley came on the jukebox. Edward perked up. "Sheila loves this song!" He began rocking to the beat in his chair. Crazy, indeed. The song was our funeral dirge. It'd been crazy to think I could resuscitate an exhausted relationship just to have a wedding date. This avenue was as dead as my skin tone.

"Oh, Mother, look!" Amy squealed in excitement. "It's the bread baker! *Thank you*, Mrs. Morgan. It's from Mrs. Morgan," Amy instructed my note taking, beside her on an overstuffed floral couch. "Where are you, Mrs. Morgan? We *love* it!" We dutifully admired the bread baker. Mary Francis handed the discarded bows to Mary Scott, who fashioned them to a paper plate.

"Amy, you know you're supposed to have a baby for every ribbon you break," teased Mary Louise. Amy giggled, and tore the next ribbons with reckless abandon.

"Whoopsie," Amy sang. And everyone giggled with her. "Oh look! It's a cappuccino maker for eight A.M. Thank you, Peggy! Peggy's a friend from high school, everyone. . . ."

Peggy winked at me and I snorted. Like 8:00 A.M. was challenging. Cha. I dutifully recorded the gift along with 9:00 A.M. (waffle maker), 10:00 A.M. (waffle maker), 11:00 A.M. (lemonade pitcher), noon (picnic basket), 1:00 P.M. (serving platter), and 2:00 P.M. (vase), as Amy tore her way through wrapping with merry disregard for the bows.

When she got to my gift of a Japanese tea service, Amy hugged me tight.

"Vi, I *love* it. I used to love to play tea party when I was little.

Now I can really have a grown-up lady tea party!" She laughed in pure happiness.

Amy plowed through the gifts just delighted with everything. By the end she had two waffle irons, three vases, and four serving platters. I felt smug about my tea set. Then it was down to just one gift left.

"This is from me dear." Patsy Rose passed Amy a gorgeous silver-wrapped gift.

"This one's for midnight." Amy emceed, taking the gift. "It's from Mother. Oh my goodness, Mother. It's beautiful." Amy revealed a gorgeous ivory satin peignoir set.

"It's for your wedding night, dear." Patsy Rose smiled at her child. I felt a pang. It would be special one day to have such an exquisite thing to wear on your wedding night. I was envious of Amy's moment with her mother. While my mother had a certain eerie prescience, she was about as likely to shop at La Perla as Ivana Trump was to load her cart at Target. My *Wedding Story* wouldn't offer tearjerker moments like these. A little down, I kissed Amy good-bye, after extracting a promise of future tea, and gathered my things. I had a six-hour drive home and I was tired already.

CHAPTER TEN

Plus None

Late Saturday afternoon Imogen and I were browsing Crate & Barrel, looking at more kitchen implements than I knew existed as I clutched the registry printout without inspiration.

"Weddings seem to be about a lot of shopping," I grumbled.

"Don't be grouchy with me because you hate to shop." Imogen dismissed my invective and picked up a fondue set. "She got one." She pointed to a bread baker. "She got one." She picked up a waffle iron. "She got two." Imogen gave me a warning look. "How about a pasta maker?" She shoved one under my nose for consideration.

I shook my head, for the hundredth time.

Imogen frowned. "Right, quick, what's your favorite kitchen thing?" I mentally canvassed my kitchen.

"My corkscrew and my best frying pan."

"Perfect! Here's a ridiculously expensive frying pan." She held it out to me.

"You don't think it's too . . . boring?" I hesitated. I'm not sure what my hang-up was, but I was obsessed with giving a unique and perfect gift. Imogen took pity.

"Vi, I don't think it can be uncomplicated to watch all your childhood friends get married. Especially when you feel like you're just getting your feet under you here in D.C."

"It isn't. But I can't distance myself. I embrace the long phone conversations about minute details." A Feeling wiggled out. I identified it. It had a shadow, too. "It makes me feel Supercilious and Left Out at the same time." I sighed. "How dumb is that?"

"Not dumb at all." Imogen perched on a stack of bread boxes. "You're being swept along in the forceful wake of Patsy Rose et al, who are telling you what to do, what to wear, what to think, and so on. I think you've latched onto the gift as your only outlet for self-expression. But you'll wear yourself out if you try to find sneaky backdoor ways to present yourself in other people's weddings. Really, Vi, you don't have to want what the girls want right now."

"It's weird how irresistibly compelling the whole wedding thing is, even as it makes me melancholy. You don't think maybe we're missing out?" I pressed her.

"No." Imogen didn't even pause. Then she looked at my expression and sighed. "Okay, maybe once in a blue moon for a nanosecond really late at night. But, then, I figure it'll happen eventually, and right now I want to have fun before I settle down."

I twiddled with a Spoonula. "I used to think that," I said slowly. "Then I started to feel like I missed the boat."

"You didn't. You're catching a bigger, sleeker yacht later on. Now, how about the ridiculously expensive frying pan? It may not be the most original thing in the world, but what's original about getting married?" Imogen asked.

"I guess so." I wasn't bowled over with enthusiasm, but I could see that if I wasn't a Type Three "All About Me" Bridesmaid, I was quickly turning into a Type Three Gift Giver.

"Done." Imogen low-fived me. "Now let us hie to the Tabard Inn for a cheese plate, a Coke, a club soda, and two glasses of wine. All this kitchen stuff is making me hungry."

When we arrived at the Tabard Inn, Ellis and Mona were already there. It was surprisingly cold for April, and I love the Tabard Inn in cold weather. It has creaky wooden floors, low ceilings, and a merry fire in the ancient stone fireplace. You could imagine you were resting between stages of a carriage journey in the 1800s en route to visit the Darcys at Pemberley.

"So," said Imogen, once she was settled in. "How's the toast coming?"

"Urk." Despite her nagging, I'd managed to avoid thinking about it. Naturally, it played a critical part in my fantasies of being the clever, alluring maid of honor who arrested guests with her *je ne sais quois*. But the reality was a bunch of crumpled-up wads of paper on my floor. "I've got some ideas."

"Uh-huh." Imogen squinted at me.

"I do!" I insisted. I didn't. They knew it.

"How about this," Imogen suggested. "Over the altar, past the humdrums, look out Boredom, here they come."

I glared at her.

"You could change 'boredom' to 'bedroom' and it'd still work," she said helpfully.

"Poems are good." Mona looked at me sympathetically over her wine.

"Okay," chirped Imogen.

"There once was a Bride who said 'Fuck it,'
   All I want is blue on a pregnancy kit,
   Bill is a bore,
   But he has sperm and more,
   So it's no matter he's a half-wit."

"Gee, thanks," I said, "that is soooo helpful."

Giles swooped down onto the couch, looking sharp in a purple velvet blazer. "Ladies."

"Giles," squealed Imogen. Imogen a Giles adored each other, with the love shared by individuals who recognized a soul mate in their flair for extravagance.

"Darling," said Giles, giving Imogen a kiss. "What did I miss?"

"Yes, what's this emergency meeting about?" asked Babette, sliding onto the couch next to Mona. The waiter practically fell over himself coming to take her order.

"Well?" repeated Babette, when the waiter had gone to fetch her Vanilla Stoli, starry-eyed. Giles had to call him back to take everyone else's order.

I groaned.

"To date or not to date," Imogen announced, bouncing up and sitting back down. "Vi has to send in her reply card tomorrow."

"Oooh." They all gazed at me pityingly.

"What are you going to do?" asked Ellis.

"I don't know. If I take a date, he has to drive six hours, stay at my parents, and sit by himself holding my purse during a wedding where he doesn't know anyone. To agree, he'd have to be completely in love, enslaved by the best oral sex of his life, or a bigger loser than me. Options one and two are not applicable, option three not appealing."

"Lots of people meet people at weddings," said Ellis. She had started dating someone she'd met the old fashioned way. In a bar.

"First, I'll be starring in "Not-in-Good (Taste): An Abundance of Sleeves." It takes place in Not-in-Good (Taste) Forest. I won't be drawing them in."

"Maybe you can be Get Laid Marion?" Mona suggested.

"In those dresses? Besides, I suspect my fellow cast mates are a Band of Married Men."

"But there *is* something about weddings," Imogen said. "All that tantalizing future happiness dangling before you makes for frenzied mating."

"First of all, it's a myth. That you actually meet anyone, that is. The frenzied mating perhaps, but it always ends in disappointment the next day when the mania wears off. Second, I doubt I'll be interested in any fraternity brother of Bill's. Thus, see point one. And third, someone who lives in Charlotte falls into the category of Geographically Undesirable."

Imogen snorted and Mona hid a smile.

"What?" I demanded.

"Nothing." They both looked innocent.

"I do *too* prefer to date people who live near me," I protested.

"If you say so," Imogen placated, but with an amused quirk to her lips.

"What about Ethan?" Mona diverted me from more protestations.

I groaned. "He'll be in exams. To my father's eternal disappointment." My father adored Ethan.

"Wait!" protested Giles. "I thought I was your parents' eternal disappointment."

Imogen stroked him sympathetically as he theatrically laid his head on her shoulder.

"That's my mother," I corrected, "who couldn't spot a gay man wearing a rainbow spandex suit at a Pride Parade in San Francisco. She thinks we should date."

"Her mother loves me," crooned Giles.

"I know, dear." Imogen patted his head. He perked up when the waiter brought drinks.

"What about Giles, then?" asked Babette. "Since the gun is pointed at you."

We all frowned, until Mona whispered "under the gun," and everyone said "ah."

"Me?" Giles stopped clowning. "Oh no. Noooo can do. I'm allergic to calla lilies. Besides, the idea of this Patsy Rose woman terrifies me."

"This woman is really named Patsy Rose?" demanded Babette.

"Oh yes," Imogen and I murmured in unison. We knew an array of women named Patsy Rose, Pansy Ann, Pebbles, Buffy, Bunny, Binky, Mary Scott, Mary Francis, and Mary-Laura-Nate.

"Besides," Giles continued, "do you know what they do to girls like me down South?"

"Easy," I cautioned, drinking some club soda. I was easily riled by stereotypes of my birthright. It drove me through the roof when people said "North Cackilacky."

"Seriously, Giles, why don't you?" pressed Mona.

I cut off his answer. "For once I have to concede Giles's point. As I doubt he'd behave, it would be waving a red flag to bring him to this particular wedding." I visualized Patsy Rose's frozen smile as Giles, in a carnation-colored suit, pranced about the dance floor and flirted with the wedding singer. "Besides, we can't both be gone from work."

"Don't you have some dish stashed in Charlotte?" Giles deflected from himself.

"Edward. That's a no go." I'd reserved the horror of the Edward story for just Imogen.

"So you're going it alone?" asked Imogen, twirling her hair and jiggling her knee.

"I guess so." I couldn't think of any other options.

"It'll be fun," encouraged Ellis. "You won't have time for a date. In my sisters' weddings all I did was run around and get my picture taken. Having a date would stress you out."

"I'm all for reducing strain. Weddings are more trauma than I thought."

"It's decided," announced Imogen. "No 'plus one.' "

"By default." I wistfully imagined a Perfect Boyfriend who'd render the debate obsolete. I tried not to think of Caleb's hands. I loved his hands. They were capable and just slightly rough.

"Well then," said Giles. "Let's talk about that toast."

"Absolutely not," I insisted. "Babette, tell us about your date last night."

The next day I waited until Giles went to lunch, then stared at a blank e-mail. I was sweating, even though I wasn't moving. "This is ridiculous," I muttered, and began typing.

To: CCarter@wharton.upenn.edu
From: ViViVooom@gmail.com
Sent: April 6
Subject:

Caleb,

Hey stranger! We haven't talked in forever. I'm doing great—still the wine buyer for D&D. Though lately I feel like I'm on a revolving door to Charlotte. I've been traveling home a lot for a bunch of weddings—I'm Maid of Honor. Anyway, that naturally made me think of you (Charlotte, that is, not long puffy dresses). So, I thought I'd drop a line and see how you are and how school is treating you. Any chance I'll see you soon?
Hope all is well!

Love,
Vi

My pulse jumped when a reply popped right up.

To: ViViVooom@gmail.com
From: CCarter@wharton.upenn.edu
Sent: April 6
Subject: Re:

Vi,

Great to hear from you! I am delighted to hear you aren't imagining me in puffy ladies dresses. That's not how I hope to be recalled.

Things are good here but busy. I've got exams soon, and then I actually have to start real life. I'll miss Philadelphia but a summer vacation kite sailing in the BVIs should ease the pain. Not sure where or what I'll be up to after that, so can't say right now when we'll catch up.

I'm so glad to hear you are well. Make Charlotte treat you right—you're one of her best.

xo,
C.

I stared at the message for a long time, willing it to mean something. Did "right now" mean "but definitely sometime"? How *did* he want me to recall him? I reread the e-mail throughout the day. But when I shut down my computer to go home, even I couldn't convince myself there was anything momentous about it.

CHAPTER ELEVEN

Lost Weekend Number One

Amy Marries Bill

I pulled up to Mary Scott's apartment at 5:30 P.M. for Amy's bachelorette party, wondering what to expect. It was my first one. We were meeting for drinks, snacks, and gifts (naturally a purchase was required), and then a limo would take us to dinner.

Mary Francis opened the door. "Vi! You made it! We're getting Amy kitted up. Here." Mary Francis shoved a pink drink in my hands, with straw that had a miniature penis rubber tip. I followed her, tentatively sipping the penis. It tasted like latex. The drink also tasted like latex. Inside, a giggling Amy was wearing a KISS ME, I'M THE BRIDE! T-shirt with LifeSavers sewn all over it, and a giant penis tip rubber hat, topped with a tiara and veil.

"Hey Vi," she waved. "Check me out! Guys have to eat off the LifeSavers and sign the shirt!" She giggled again. More girls showed up, clutching latex-flavored drinks and sipping out of penis-shaped straws. Once everyone was assembled, we played games like Naughty Bingo, RoMANtic Trivia, and Pin the Hose on the Fireman, and opened titillating little gifts. Each gift got a little shriek and an "Oh my goodness" from Amy: furry handcuffs, penis-shaped lollipops, edible panties, Kama Sutra oil and book (this from me), naughty games, a tickle feather, and so forth. Drinks were poured at a rapid rate. I could tell Amy was getting drunk from her flushed cheeks and slightly glassy stare. I tried to pass her a glass of water but was foiled by other girls handing her all manner of pastel drinks with penis straws. The doorbell rang during the shrieking and giggling, and Mary Francis returned saying, "Ohmygodohmygodya'll, someone called the cops. . . ." Behind her was one of the cheesiest looking not-cops I'd ever seen. He was wearing a tight-ass "uniform" and carried a billy stick and . . . a CD player.

"Who's the young lady causing the disturbance here?" The so-not-a-cop flashed teeth that would make Donny Osmond jealous. He rolled the billy stick suggestively against his hand. "Where's the bride?" Girls squealed, "Here she is!" shoving a swaying Amy forward.

"Well," leered Officer Extra Friendly, "I hear you've been *very* bad." He pointed a remote at his CD player and dance music began thumping. Officer Pectoral began shaking his hips and dancing sluttishly around Amy, who shrieked in glee. With one motion he yanked off his shirt and pants (handy, that) and cavorted about ridiculously in a g-string and combat boots. He must shave all over, I mused, wondering how he kept the oil from staining his "uniform."

Things went pretty much as expected, with Amy getting pranced around and lap-danced. As maid of honor, I had to endure a lap dance, Officer Banana Sack's privates giggling in front of my face. Meanwhile everyone got drunker. I tried, but latex wasn't my flavor. So I found myself in the (unusual) role of concerned observer, my murmurings of "Shouldn't we be getting to dinner" ignored. And ignored. And ignored. The long, *ahem*, of the law packed up and left, and Mary Scott whipped out Jell-O shots frozen in—guess what?—penis molds.

An hour later I crouched beside Amy in the bathroom, holding her hair as she yakked her brains out in the toilet. I suspected that the other commode was in similar use, from the color of Mary Francis's face when I followed Amy's dash in here. Amy sat back from the Holy Bowl and moaned. I wiped her forehead with a damp washcloth.

"I want Bill," she whimpered. I patted her head and handed her some water. It was only 9:00 P.M., and we hadn't left the house.

"Shesh carnt shee Bell caush ish for girlsh only," Mary Scott slurred from the door. " 'Shides. Bellsh on bashelor night."

"Bill. Want Bill," Amy moaned. I patted her some more and tried to decide what to do. Nobody else was in any position to. I wasn't sure it was a good idea for Bill to see her in this condition. I was still wondering, when Mary Margaret lurched into view clutching her lime green drink and penis straw.

"Ish the boysh. They here!" She listed out of view. Problem solved.

"Bill!" Amy reeled to her feet, swaying toward the door. I easily intercepted her.

"Amy, wait." She blinked at me blearily. "You've been ralphing," I reminded her.

She furrowed her brow and pondered this fact. Then her face cleared. "Right." She staggered back to the sink and reached for Mary Scott's toothbrush. When she was done, I helped her to the living room.

"Bill!"

"Sweetie!" Bill was definitely more together than Amy. "We finished our steaks and cigars and realized we were bored without our ladies, so we came to find ya'll." He swept her into a hug. Even with barf-breath he held her like she was a delicate treasure. Amy closed her eyes and sighed with contentment. I felt a pang of longing, like I was outside in the snow looking through a window at a cozy den with a roaring fire. Bill met my worried eyes over Amy's shoulder and nodded. He'd take care of her. I closed my mind against a wistful thought of Caleb protecting me that way. I looked at the drunken bacchanal of wasted girls and had to laugh—it was only ten. At least I could still get dinner somewhere. I was starving and had a nasty taste of latex in my mouth.

I woke, well rested, to a deserted house the morning of the wedding. Under Patsy Rose's iron fist the rehearsal dinner had been a mannerly event, with everyone dispatched by 10:30 P.M. under orders to get a proper night's sleep. I was disappointed. I'd expected a bacchanalia and got a Tupperware party. What a waste of my best pink and black undies. I hoped tonight would be better.

The wedding was at six, but we had a bridesmaids' luncheon and had to be at Amy's for hair and makeup at three. I arrived ten minutes late to the luncheon and sat next to Peggy, who muttered, "Tardy slut."

"Smoking wench," I muttered back. Patsy Rose tapped her glass and we obediently fell silent. She smiled at us. Her lipstick was gleaming pink.

"We ah *so* happy to have ya'll here with us on Amy's special day. It means *soooo* much." Yeah it did, I thought grumpily. It meant at least $450, not including gifts and gas.

"Amy and I want to thank ya'll for participatin' with a special gift. We hope ya'll will use these today." Patsy Rose indicated bags in front of each of us, and we retrieved our goodies. I heard fourteen dutiful "oohs" and "ahs" around the table, some of which actually sounded genuine. Mine was not. I was looking at a scallop-shell clutch bag and scallop shell earrings. There were also two bizarre barrette-like things with shells on them.

"What are these?" I whispered to Peggy.

"You clip 'em on your shoes," she whispered back, rolling her eyes.

I sighed. Even my shoes were subject to Patsy Rose desecration. At least she wasn't billing me for them.

After a lunch of lobster bisque followed by a lobster salad, and the too short freedom of a coffee break, during which Peggy smoked no less than nine cigarettes—"stockpiling before the drought" she informed me—we presented ourselves at Amy's for the ritualistic painting of the faces.

"Ladies," announced Patsy Rose. "An important element of presentin' our theme is maintenance of a uniform appearance. Even the little details can be so critical. So, we have invited Graciela here to do ya'll's makeup, using a similar palette. And, Rosemary will style ya'll's hair. Ya'll can trust them to make you look your very best." I could smell disaster.

Patsy Rose continued. "Now, ah went ahead and paid for all ya'll." That was a relief. "So if ya'll can each get a check directly to me for sixty-two dollars, that will cover it." I blinked in disbelief. I mentally considered the state of my bank account and the number of days until payday and wondered if Patsy Rose would accept a postdated check.

I was the first guinea pig. I nervously eyed Graciela's heavily made-up face and bottle green eye shadow. My concern amplified when she spun the chair so my back was to the mirror. I normally don't wear much makeup. With my fair coloring, I'm convinced I look like a harlot with bright blues or greens. Graciela's "palette" was all blues and greens.

"Perhaps just something light," I suggested. Graciela didn't even pause in squirting a copious amount of foundation onto a sponge.

"Ms. Bing, she want same for everyone," Graciela dismissed me. And then she attacked.

"All finish," she announced twenty minutes later and spun my chair around. I started. I looked like an alien drag queen. The abundant foundation gave me a slightly orange look, to showcase my eyelids, lined and heavily covered in blue. My frosty pink lips were unnaturally outlined with a perfect line of rose. I snickered. Given how ugly the dress was, I decided the makeup was just right. I proceeded to be tortured in the hairstylist's chair.

I looked at the stiff and brassy curls Rosemary was sporting and embraced my fate. "Can you make it big?" I asked. I might as well go whole hog.

"I dunno." She smacked her gum doubtfully. "It's awful fine."

"Do what you can," I encouraged. "I want it to look like yours."

When she was finished I was delighted. It looked awful. A big pouf helmet, stiffly sprayed into place. After the wedding I'd swing by a casting call for *Mars Attacks!*

"Perfect," I nodded. Not a hair moved.

"Don't you look nice," Peggy grinned. I shot her a look that would have Ghengis reconsidering his invasion of China had they used it. Then I smiled when Graciela called Peggy's name.

At 5:00 P.M. the mermaid chorus line was lined up for inspection. Our frill sergeant Patsy Rose reviewed each of us, straightening here, tucking there, and readjusting sandal shell clips everywhere. At last we were approved and ordered directly to the church. If Patsy Rose had been in charge, the South never would have lost the Civil War.

St. Gabe's was a pointy modern building that didn't gel with my idea of what a church should look like. The Presbyterian church my family graced on Christmas and Easter looked like it came off a Vermont Christmas card. St. Gabe's looked like an artist's studio in Aspen. Father Ted, unlike his church, looked just like he ought to. He was a tall, thin grey-haired man who looked both kindly and intellectual. He would be very at home in Mitford.

At 5:59 on the dot we were marshaled to order, woe betide the tardy guest. At six Patsy Rose had to grudgingly relinquish control and be escorted to her seat to the swelling of Pachelbel Canon in D, gracefully acknowledging with a nod of her head all her supplicants in the pews. Amy didn't mind at all. She was a pink-cheeked porcelain doll of a bride, with a big fluffy white dress and four-foot train I'd have to bustle in a confounding manner later. She was absolutely glowing. No way Patsy Rose could steal the attention away from the vision of joy that was Amy today. I squeezed her hand.

"Excited?" I asked with a smile.

"Oh, Vi," she breathed, "its *thrilling.* It is my *wedding day!*" She couldn't stop beaming. "This is the best day of my life!" she insisted. "I can't wait until you have all this." I felt a pang before I squeezed her hand again and let go, preparing to take my turn down the aisle.

"Me too," I said, wondering when my BDOYL would come.

Then, for the first time since I was six, I was parading before the eyes of an entire church. It felt a little stiff . . . and not just because of my hair helmet. I plastered on a smile and held my flowers at exactly the position Patsy Rose had instructed us, simultaneously concentrating on posture and not popping out of my dress. The aisle seemed really long. At last I reached the altar, crowded now, and squished into place next to Mary Francis.

The music changed and I watched Amy, a bridal vision, floating down the aisle to the traditional wedding march. I got a little teary. Father Ted smiled benevolently at the bride and groom and began the blessed sacrament. His radiating warmth dimmed slightly only when Ann Elizabeth labored through reading First Corinthians, when his eyes took on a glazed look.

Twenty-two minutes later we were done.

Afterward, we all crowded in front of the church and waved good-bye to the new Mr. and Mrs. Bill as they got into the limo that would take them the approximately one and a half miles to the reception, where we would see them again. Father Ted gave me a high five.

"Flawless performance," he complimented me.

"Thanks," I said. "I'm glad it's over and I didn't fall down or anything."

"You did well. See you next week," the kindly fellow bid me farewell.

His lips were moving but I wasn't registering a word. I was at the reception. We'd finished a surf and turf dinner (I was getting really sick of lobster), and I was sitting next to the best man, puzzling. I'd just met him, but he looked oddly familiar. I couldn't put my finger on it. He noticed the depth of my concentration and flashed me a smile, showing off the tiny bit of *au poivre* stuck between his canines.

"So that's when I realized I have a gift for working with people . . ." he droned. I tried to recall the topic of his Seemingly Endless Story but couldn't. Something to do with Pittsburgh.

"I like Yuengling," I said inanely. He beamed at me. *Au poivre.* His eyes suggested it was natural that I should find him irresistible. Oh dear. I tried not to create the misimpression that I found him attractive, but I wanted to solve the mystery of his familiarity.

He was good-looking, but while not actually swathed in yellow crime scene tape, he might as well have been. The report from Amy was that he'd recently broken up with his live-in girlfriend and they were "seeing other people," but still shared the same apartment while they debated who had to move out. Rebound zone, potentially psycho ex-girlfriend in close proximity, and incipient homelessness all constituted a little something I liked to call "issues."

His name was Alan. He had thick brown hair, regular features, and slightly olive skin, a little shiny at his brow.

Wait. I stared intently at his eyebrows. They were thick and dark, and the surrounding skin had a raw pink tint. No way. He again preened under my intent stare. The vague familiarity dawned on me. I recognized that shiny pink look around the brows, having stared at it myself once every four to six weeks. The best man had just had his eyebrows waxed.

I was fascinated and repelled. I tried to concentrate on the conversation but my eyes kept sliding back to his brow. His neatly trimmed, no stray hairs, beautifully sculpted brow. I tried to be more understanding. I mean really, wouldn't I rather a man wax periodically than have a Cro-Magnon unibrow? I reached for my glass contemplating this. Then I contemplated why my glass was full of seltzer. Where the hell was the alcohol?

"So I said I don't buy that whole 'metrosexual' thing at all, that those boys were just plain gay. I mean what kind of real man wants his nails manicured?"

I choked and seltzer came out my nose. Wax Boy was ranting against metrosexualism?

"Well, there's a little more to it than that," I ventured. "I think it's about attention to grooming and a sense of style more than—"

"Whatever," he interrupted. "I sure don't need five gay strangers coming into my house to help me get women. I fight them off."

With hot wax? And whom was he fighting off anyway? The five gay strangers or the women? A grammatical mystery.

"Excuse me," I said. I scanned the crowd, looking for an out. It was as depressingly devoid of interesting singles as it had been when I last looked two minutes ago. I smiled across the table at Mary Francis and Mary Scott. They smiled back and resumed talking, declining to rescue me.

"Come with me—I have a girl emergency," ordered a voice at my shoulder. I turned to see Peggy. She grinned. I loved her.

"Sorry," I said to Wax, not at all sorrowfully. "Duty calls." We escaped the room.

"Bar?" I asked, but she was already bustling that way. We awkwardly hefted our mermaid butts onto the stools. Monty, the bartender for at least a hundred years, took our order.

"In a flash." Monty hadn't moved in a flash since the Crimean War.

"God, these dresses!" Peggy wrestled with her scalloped bodice.

"But you'll be able to wear it again." I laughed.

"Yeah," she muttered darkly. "When I moonlight as a Disney Princess."

Monty delivered our drinks and Peggy took a grateful swig.

"To the worst being over," she said.

I groaned. "Speak for yourself! I have to do a toast."

"Sucks for you." She lit a cigarette. "Do you know what you're going to say?"

"Is 'sort of' a bad answer?"

"Not for me," she laughed. "Nothing's more entertaining than someone making a public ass of themselves." She sounded deadly serious.

"Oh God." I was regretting my theory of spontaneity. I reassured myself I was good at speaking on my feet. It wouldn't matter that I hadn't practiced.

"Maybe I should practice on you," I said anxiously.

"Too late," Peggy said, spying Patsy Rose bearing down on us. And it was.

We returned to the ballroom, and Patsy Rose marshaled me toward the stage. Alan took the floor and proceeded to deliver the epitome of a bad best man's speech, from references to sex (Patsy Rose turned the color of a beet), jokes about marriage ("Marriage is more than a word, it's a prison *sentence*"), and corny marital advice ("Remember these three little words, 'You're right, dear' "). It was tired material. I could do better than that.

He wrapped up. "Seriously, though, if there's anybody here this evening who feels slightly apprehensive about what happened today, it is probably because you just married Bill, Amy, but you'll feel better after a few drinks." Patsy Rose was eyeing her mother's cane. "So please raise your glasses: to the bride and groom." Everyone clinked glasses, and then Alan held out the microphone. Oh shit. Panic ballooned in my chest.

I smiled numbly at the audience. I was gratified that Patsy Rose appeared calm.

"Hi," I began. "My name is Vi and I'm the maid of honor. I'm here today to speak for the bride. Well, both the bride and the groom, since it is a wedding and there are two of them, of course, but I guess the maid of honor sort of comes from the girl's side." Oh God. I was babbling. I needed to focus. Everyone looked at me politely.

"I want to say what a great guy Bill is. I was so happy when Amy started dating him. Bill has always been polite, kind, and well-mannered to everyone. Really, everyone. It's a little spooky. As a couple, they have the perfect balance. Bill grounds Amy with traditional values, and Amy keeps Bill from becoming boring." I was word-vomiting and I couldn't stop.

"In a good way," I hastened to add.

"So. Um, basically we're here today because of love. I thought I'd share some quotes about love. H.L. Mencken said, 'Love is the triumph of imagination over intelligence.'" Oh no. Did they think I was saying I thought Bill was dumb? Shit. "Even cynical people like Nietzsche believe in love. Well . . . believed. He's dead now. But when he was alive, he said, 'Perhaps the feelings that we experience when we are in love represents a normal state. Being in love shows a person who he should be.' Martin Luther King extolled the virtues of love. He said, 'Hatred paralyzes life; love releases it. Hatred confuses life; love harmonizes it. Hatred darkens life; love illumines it.'" Oh dear. Was that too political? Was it wrong to be political at weddings? I should make it more romantic. Poetry. Yes. Poetry was romantic.

"If the poet Rilke is correct, Amy and Bill will be rich. Rilke said, 'This is the miracle that happens every time to those who really love; the more they give, the more they possess.'"

Okay. I'd run out of quotes. I scrambled to think of a story I'd found in my limited preparation for this speech. I dredged it from my memory.

"I heard a story once that offered some good advice. The advice was, 'Be able to ride a tandem.' This couple went on a biking holiday, and they had solo bikes. It was fun, but the next year they decided to use a tandem bike. The husband's words were, 'We didn't want to go in two different directions.' And I think that he hit the nail on the head. On the tandem they learned about going in the same direction. There is a famous French quote that says, *'Aimer ce n'est pas se regarder l'un l'autre, c'est regarder dans la meme direction.'* That means, 'Love isn't about looking at each other. It's about looking in the same direction.'" Okay, that bit wasn't so terrible. Maybe analogies were the way to go.

"Really, love should be like a rubber band. It's a circle with no beginning or end. Like a ring. Um. A *wedding* ring. Only it's not hard and inflexible. A rubber band has the flexibility to change shape and adjust over time and under pressure—adapting but not breaking. Marriage should be like a rubber band, like that. Let the circle, rubber band, stay unbroken." Good Lord. Was I going to launch into a chorus of "Kumbaya" next? Patsy Rose caught my eye and actually tapped her watch. I swallowed.

"Well, so, uh, gee. The brain is a wonderful thing. It never stops working from the time you're born until the moment you have to make a speech, huh?" Here I did get laughter. I was desperately grateful. The last five minutes had been like walking on a broken leg.

"I'd like to close by asking you to please join me in wishing Amy and Bill a lifetime of happiness together." I scuttled off stage, drowning in humiliation. Amy, of course, was beaming at me. She didn't have a harsh or judgmental bone in her body. I, on the other hand, had enough for two, and the self-flagellation currently under way could easily last until December.

"Hey." I looked up. Peggy was waiting for me with a glass of wine. I took it gratefully and sent her a pained look. She laughed.

"Don't worry," she said. "You can do better next week." I groaned.

"Ack. I need to properly lick my wounds before I can even contemplate that hell."

"Perhaps a little advance planning next time," she teased me.

"Oh, I thought I'd just adopt the best man's speech word for word and use that." I drained my glass. "Let's hit the bar. This glass seems to have a hole in it."

"It's supposed to," she retorted. "It's where your mouth goes."

"Well, my mouth needs to go on about sixty-three more to ease the pain," I said grimly, and plowed through the crowd to the bar.

CHAPTER TWELVE

Preparing for Battle

"The *only* upside to the situation was that with so many bridesmaids, conceivably the guests couldn't tell who gave the World's Most Awful Toast." I buried my face in my hands.

"Can you handle a glass of wine?" asked Ellis gently.

It was the day after Amy's wedding, and I had a vicious hangover. Peggy and I had done our best to drain the reception of alcohol, and then again at the after party. I was pretty sure I'd kissed Alan. I woke with a shattering headache and a vague cigar taste in my mouth, but I hadn't smoked a cigar. Alan and Bill had. I cringed away from too much recollection. I'd made the briefest and most haggard of appearances at the wedding brunch, and then driven directly to Clyde's. I called the girls from the road to arrange an emergency summit earlier than our usual time. It was barely six-thirty, but Mona and Ellis were already there.

"Yeah," I said. "I think I'd better." Mona beckoned Charlie.

"Darlin'," he looked at me sympathetically, "you look like you've been hit by a truck."

I sighed. "Can I have a club soda, Coke, and coffee. Wait. Can you do iced coffee?"

"Sure can," he said. "Rest of the gang coming?"

"Yes, Babette will be here," said Ellis. Charlie flushed. "So keep an eye out. We'll need lots of drinks. There's been a tragedy." She thumbed at me.

"So I see." He grinned and patted me on the head, which hurt.

"Seriously, it was terrible," I moaned.

"Don't you dare start detailing your humiliation without me." Imogen bounced up with Giles, whose shirt was a shade of yellow that hurt my eyes. "I want every gory detail."

"Me too," said Giles.

"You're not allowed here," I told him. "It's ladies' night."

He shot Imogen a hurt look. "She said I wasn't a lady."

"There, there." Imogen patted his hand.

"How long do we have to do the campy gay routine?" I sniped.

Giles took pity and hugged me. "Sweetheart, was it that terrible?"

"Yes. It was. And if you're going to stay, sit here and be a barrier. I can't sit next to Imogen because she bounces too much and my head will explode." Imogen flipped her hair and flounced to the other side of the booth. They settled in just as Babette arrived and Charlie returned with drinks.

"So," persisted Imogen, as Mona poured the wine. "Spill. Not you, Mona."

"Imagine the most humiliating thing that has ever happened to you and then amplify that by ten." I cringed just thinking of it. "I don't know if I can bear to recall it." I winced.

"Were you drunk?" asked Ellis.

"Not then. I was terrible all by my own self. I got up with only the vaguest of plans. And the verbal diarrhea began." I closed my eyes in pain.

"Details!" insisted Imogen.

"Oh God. I just stared spewing. I actually said Bill was boring." Ellis laughed. "Then I quoted Nietzsche and then reminded everyone that he was both cynical and dead." I groaned at the memory, thunked my head on the table, and regretted it as my headache roared.

"Then what?" prodded Imogen.

"Do you pull over and take photos at car accidents?" I asked waspishly.

"No, I use watercolors," she retorted. "I like the creative license."

"I actually got the watch tap from Patsy Rose. I hid in humiliation the rest of the night."

"Except for the part where you may or may not have made out with the Best Man, who waxes his eyebrows," reminded Mona mercilessly.

"He waxes his eyebrows?" Imogen repeated in joyful disbelief.

I hid behind my Coke. Then I defended myself. "It's not clear that we actually kissed. There's limited circumstantial evidence that points in that direction, but I've chosen not to mentally explore the matter further, so it will remain a Great Un-Memory for the time being. I choose to interpret the ambiguity in my favor."

"Was Amy upset about the toast?" Asked Ellis.

"No, she's too sweet. *But*," I stressed, "I *cannot* go through that degradation again, and I have two more toasts to do. I need to be *prepared*."

"Ooooh. You sound like a Boy Scout," trilled Giles. "That's hot." I cuffed him. "She keeps hitting me," Giles tattled to Imogen.

"Don't make me separate you two," warned Imogen.

"I'm serious!" I insisted. "I need help. I have some of the finest brainpower in D.C. collected before me. I need two pithy, fun, and charming toasts. Stat!"

"Why don't you start by announcing that the bride is pregnant?" suggested Giles. "Then you can say, 'Just kidding,' and move on, but everyone will be so shocked they won't really take in the rest, so you can say anything." We ignored him.

"Well, I for one would be a wreck if I had to do a toast, like the cat with the canary," said Babette, pulling a pad of paper and a pen out of her briefcase. "I'd screw up and start laughing and it'd be all over. I'll help the best I can. If you don't mind spelling mistakes." She smiled.

"Thank you," I said gratefully.

"Okay." Imogen drummed her fingers on the table. "Basic ingredients: witty introduction of self. Three one-line jokes. A tale of the Bride. A comment on the Groom. Two heartfelt quotes about love. A Sweet (and short) Analogy about marriage. A humorous quip or two of Advice. A sincere and loving close. The whole thing should be no more than five minutes. Giles, you and Mona take pithy and funny. Vi, you work with Ellis on the personal stuff about Lila and Hart. Babette and I will draft sincere and loving statements. Each team should identify at least one meaningful quote. If we get a generic outline down, we can recycle for Jen and Louis."

"This is like the time Vi saved my ass organizing my parents' anniversary gig." Ellis said.

"I'm earning back the time she coordinated my twelve cousins' en masse visit," Mona agreed.

"Many times I would have been in a pond without a paddle without Vi," Babette agreed.

We did musical chairs to sit with our partner. Glasses were refilled and heads bent in pairs. Looking over the table, I was suffused with affection for my friends. If you could bottle this warm feeling and turn it into words, I thought, that would be the perfect toast.

CHAPTER THIRTEEN

Lost Weekend Number Two

Lila Marries Hart

I knew I'd get a nice dinner at Lila's bachelorette, and I was right. We were sipping wine and Lila was shaking her head in amazement as I told her about Amy's bachelorette party.

"A stripper, really? Gross."

"It was," I agreed. "And I had to pay Mary Scott forty dollars for my skeevy share."

Lila's evening was running with the precision of Alvin Ailey choreography. There were eight of us and we'd met at Lila's, where the stretch limo (thanks to Lila's father, Albert) took us to Pewter Rose for dinner. We'd opened the obligatory sex gifts: furry handcuffs, sexy panties, leopard print panties, garter, risqué negligee, edible panties, Kama Sutra oil and book (me), furry panties. Lila wasn't the chocolate penis type. We were now finishing a gorgeous meal. After that, we had mapped a Bachelorette Scavenger Hunt for Lila. She had to do a bunch of tasks or get things from random guys in bars. I had no doubt in Lila's abilities—she loved

a challenge. Before morning there would be several underpant-
less guys gingerly making their way home.

Lila finished her wine and glanced at her scavenger list. "Let's
hit it," she said. "I feel the need to collect phone numbers, a sock,
a serenade, some condoms, a lap dance, some boxers, and lots of
free drinks. And I can't *wait* to use the ruler and the Polaroid
camera!" She winked at me. She paused, tapping her lower lip.
"Let's start with Tutto Mondo. It's a more erudite crowd. I can get
a poem and serenade there. Then Ri Ra. I'm bound to have luck
with free drinks and goofy behavior. Later, we can hit Cosmos
Café. Men will be throwing off clothes by then and we can clean
up in the garment categories." She looked at me with a smile.
"Shall we? And get that fucking thing off my head," she commanded as her friend Elizabeth tried to put a little veil on her. She
rolled her eyes at me. "As if. Ready?"

I was. But I wasn't so sure about the unwitting male population of Charlotte tonight. Poor little gazelles.

By midnight I was collapsed onto a bar stool at Cosmos. Tire-
less Lila was flirting with a rapt circle of men. She'd demolished
most of her scavenger list, and I was toting around a bag full of
underwear, socks, condoms, and phone numbers. The tallest of
her champions was now getting on his knees as Lila climbed on
his shoulders. He did a lap around the bar with her and I took a
Polaroid. She could scratch off item number 16. I put the camera
back in the bag and considered whether I could handle another
martini. I ordered a club soda.

"Can you watch the stuff?" I asked Angela, who said "Oh." I
took that for a yes and plunged into the packed crowd toward the
restrooms. I had almost fought my way through when I saw it. It
was just a flash of a back as the crowd parted, but I froze.

There's something in a body you know so well that you'd recognize it anywhere, even at a glimpse. At a distance of a thousand yards I'd recognize the gait, the curls, the hand gesture. Caleb

Carter was at the bar. I pushed through the crowd until I was behind him. I took a deep breath.

"Caleb?"

He turned and my breath caught. God he was handsome. Caleb had beautiful hazel eyes and thick brown hair that flopped in a wave over one eye. He was tall enough that I had to crane up at him. His college fraternity brothers used to jokingly call him "the Lure" because that curl on his forehead was irresistible to women. They couldn't help brushing it out of his eyes. Right now he was talking to a pretty blonde perched on a bar stool that seemed eager for the job.

For a moment we were both caught, awkward. Then, "Vi," he swept me into a tight hug. "What the hell are you doing here? Are you part of the ruckus over there? I should've known."

"Lila's getting married. I'm in town for the wedding. I'm the maid of honor." I had no idea what to say to him. Catching him out chatting up girls in a bar wasn't a good tableau.

"Lila married? I never thought she'd settle down so soon. Lucky guy."

"What are you doing here?" He should have been in Philadelphia.

"My mother had to have some elective surgery. Nothing serious, but she asked if I could come home and shuttle her back and forth and be there for the procedure."

"Is she okay?" Caleb's mother and I had never gotten along. She thought my skirts were too short and that I was corrupting her boy. If she only knew.

"Oh yeah. It was really nothing. I tucked her in bed and came out to meet Chandler for a drink." He gestured to one of his fraternity brothers who lived in Charlotte. Chandler looked over, started at the sight of me, assessed our threesome, and beat a hasty retreat. Caleb and I caught each other's eyes and there was an awkward pause.

"How long are you around?" I asked, wild hope flaring that he could come to Lila's wedding.

"Just until Sunday, but I'm crazy busy. I promised my mother I'd repair the deck. It's taking every minute I've got." I wasn't sure what that meant. Was he putting me off?

We looked intently at each other for another long moment. Caleb and I called our current relationship just friends, but there was so much history, and chemistry, the boundaries were blurry. I wasn't sure what my role was. He reached up and brushed a thumb across my cheek.

"Hi, I'm Bonnie," the blonde said, shoving a hand under my nose.

"Vi," I said, tearing my eyes from Caleb. I eyed the two, gauging the vibe. It was sex.

"Bonnie and I just met," Caleb jumped in. "She went to U.Va too."

"Wow," I said. "A U.Va grad in Charlotte. Imagine the odds." Bonnie smiled daggers at me. She sensed her gazelle was in danger.

"Caleb—" I began, when I heard my name.

"Vi? Vi, where are you?" Lila hollered. "Where's my maid of honor?"

"Duty calls." Caleb gave a nod. It felt like a physical push. It hurt. Bonnie looked pleased. That hurt more.

"Would you like to join us?" I tried. "Lila would love to see you."

He looked at me seriously. "I'm really sorry, I can't. I promised Bonnie I'd give her a ride home when her friends left." He looked contrite. He did it well. "I really am sorry—I had no idea you were in town. This isn't a good weekend. It was great to see you, though."

Oh.

I nodded numbly and forced a carefree smile. "Too bad—there are still some interesting items left on the scavenger hunt!"

He smiled at me and gave me a long kiss on the cheek and a tight hug.

"Take care, Vi." I walked away, taking deep, deep breaths.

In the limo on the way home I pulled out my phone and looked at it for the hundredth time. No missed calls. I sighed. I flipped it closed. I tried to concentrate. I could leave a breezy message. Just to let him know where I'd be all weekend. I flipped the phone open again. Lila gently took it away from me.

"I think you've had too many drinks to operate that thing," she said kindly. She pulled me in for a squeeze. "It's going to be okay. It'll all work out. I have faith. We have ups and downs, but God has a plan. Sometimes I have doubts about Hart too, but he's a good man, and if you start with that, the rest will work out. I don't know if you can ask for more."

I recalled what I conveniently often forgot with Caleb—the highs were the best and most intense, but the lows were dramatically awful too. Maybe Lila and Jen's vision of a nice steady relationship that wasn't as passionate but more even-keel had appeal.

I took back the phone.

"I really need to make this call," I said. Lila looked mulish and ready to challenge me when I said, "Does anyone know the number for Dominos? I want that pizza waiting for me."

"Do you think it looks like rain? I think it looks like rain," Lila said for the hundredth time, peering out the window.

"It doesn't look like rain," I lied to her. "It's just cloudy. It'll blow over."

"You're lying to me," Lila accused.

"Yes, I am," I answered. "I'm afraid to unsettle a woman formidable enough to drink red wine while wearing a white wedding gown, *before* her wedding. Not to mention that it's not allowed in here." We were in the bride's dressing room at St. Gabe's. Lila had smuggled in a bottle of Silver Oak cabernet, and we were very, very carefully having wine while we got ready.

Lila waved her hand dismissively. "Catholics even drink *during* church," she scoffed.

"It's called communion." I continued sticking stephanotis flowers in her hair. "And it's allowed. Though they're stingy—the cups are very, very small."

"You know stephanotis means happiness in marriage," Lila said offhandedly. I stopped and looked at her. She seemed remote, staring out the window at the looming storm.

"Of course it does. You'll be very happy," I assured her.

"Oh yes. Everyone is happy," she said. "My parents are thrilled."

"And you're happy too?" I coaxed.

She turned to me with a wide smile. "Of course," she laughed. "I'm just ready to get this show on the road." I put the last flower in her hair and she stood up shaking out her dress. She looked absolutely beautiful. Her blond hair was swept up on her head, with flowers woven into her curls. Her dress was a cream-colored satin Vera Wang, with delicate beading.

"You look amazing," I said, hugging her carefully. She glowed.

"Thanks," she said, "you too." And actually, she was right. The bridesmaid dresses, despite being navy blue, were lovely. They had thin spaghetti straps and gentle A-line flowing skirts to the floor, with pretty pointy 1950s style high heels dyed to match. Expensive as hell, but very feminine. I stifled a wish that Caleb could see me in it. As if signifying God's disapproval of my thought, we heard the first raindrops hit the glass. Lila sighed resignedly and turned her back to the window.

"You know, Lila," Angela said, "they say it is good luck if it rains on your wedding day."

"Bullshit," Lila laughed. "Did you ever notice that the things 'they' say are good luck all suck, like rain on your wedding day or getting shit on by a bird? It's a load of crap to make you feel meaninglessly superior when something rotten happens."

Everyone was shocked into silence, unsure of Lila's mood. I had to laugh. Lila would always be Lila.

"I don't think you are supposed to say 'shit' in church," I whispered, an aside, "or 'crap.'"

"Crap on that," Lila said, and sashayed over to her wine. The wedding coordinator bustled in. She looked like Aunt Bea in a blueberry costume.

"Okay girls." She clapped her hands breathlessly. "It won't be long now. You should all find your bouquets." She turned to me. "You have the ring?"

Oh shit. I'd left it in the car. "Er, it's in the car," I stammered awkwardly. Aunt Bea looked appalled. For a short woman, she had a powerful presence.

"Its okay!" I assured the room, feeling like an idiot. "The car is here. With the ring in it. At the church." I stuttered to a halt with everyone staring but Lila, who was pouring more wine. "I'll just dash and get it," I declared, backing out of the room.

Lila waved at me. "Meet us in the vestibule," she instructed.

I nodded and hurried to the back door, which opened to the parking lot. I bumped into Father Ted.

"First mate!" he grinned. "Are you ready?"

"You betcha." We clunked fists, then he disappeared into his office.

When I opened the back door, I froze. It was bucketing rain. I looked around for an umbrella or a hat. Nothing. Oh hell. I *did not* want to walk down the aisle looking like a drenched rat, or the dead girl from *The Ring*. Hey, I distracted myself. That was kind of funny—*The Ring*, today's Movie Starring Me. Oh, wait, no. Bad. That was bad. I did not want to look like wet scary dead girl when walking down the aisle. I heard Pachelbel Canon begin in the church and panicked. Pachelbel was the music for the grandmothers to be escorted down the aisle. Desperate, I noticed a trash can lined in plastic. I peered in, and it seemed like most of the trash was of the paper variety. Fine. I denuded the can and pulled the plastic liner over my head, tearing a face hole. Glamorous I was not, but it would do.

Shielded, I dashed to the car, keeping my face down to protect my hair and makeup. I hastily snatched the ring and scurried back to the church in relief. Disaster averted. I pulled off the trash bag and returned it to its origins. Then I checked my makeup and smoothed my hair and dress, all of which seemed intact. I sighed in relief. I readjusted my shoes and then opened the velvet ring box to slip the ring on my thumb. My bright blue thumb.

I stopped in horror. My thumb was bright blue. As were my fingers. I closed my eyes in dread and then mustered the courage to look at my shoes. My formerly dyed-to-match shoes were now a splotchy bleeding blue and white drippy mess. Oh shit. The right shoe bore evidence of direct contact with a puddle, with a water line indicating the puddle's depth. the left shoe sported four perfect dye free circles on the top where raindrops had landed.

I heard the music change to "Jesu Joy of Man's Desiring." That meant Lila's mother was advancing down the aisle. I was out of time. I walked to join the others in the vestibule, dragging my feet. My gown was long, but not long enough to conceal the ruined shoes. I tried crouching over a little bit, but I looked like Quasimodo. I tried bending my knees and walking.

Hey, that might work. I bent my knees but held my torso straight. It lowered my hemline enough to allow me to walk without revealing too much of the shoes. I reduced my paces to tiny steps and the shoes remained completely concealed. Perfect! I would just hold this pose and no one would be the wiser. I minced to the vestibule. Lila gave me an odd look, but before she could comment, the wedding coordinator stepped between us.

"Thank God!" she cried. "Got the ring?" I nodded, concentrating on my knock-kneed stance. "Good, now, here's your bouquet." She thrust my flowers and I nearly toppled. Lila tried to steady me, no small feat after two glasses of wine, and I nearly took her with me.

"Whoa, you okay?" she asked curiously, after her father had steadied us all.

"Fine," I managed through a big fake smile. I had to concentrate. Given the look on Lila's face, I wasn't sure I was pulling off the "look natural" bit. The music changed. It was our turn. The wedding coordinator was practically frothing.

"You, now, go!" She fired each bridesmaid off with military precision. I was careful to leap out on command, convinced I'd fall over if she shoved me. I plastered on a big smile and took the aisle in my awkward unnatural duck waddle. I began to hope I'd pull it off.

"Oh dear," I heard someone whisper loudly. "I hope she can hold it until the ceremony's over. She really should've gone before." My humiliation was complete.

I attained the relative security of the altar and adjusted myself into an uncomfortable standing squat. Father Ted looked at me with kind eyes, but I avoided his gaze, smile cemented in place. The wedding march began and Lila advanced down the aisle on Albert's arm, beaming. Despite my discomfort, my smile became genuine. Lila did look lovely.

Lila joined Hart at the altar, handing me her bouquet. I wobbled when I reached for it. She looked at me strangely. Beaming brightly, I reset my balance. Father Ted raised his hands over Lila and Hart and we began. I was distracted by my discomfort, but it penetrated that Father Ted seemed to be saying more than he had when Amy was married. I recalled that this ceremony was a full Catholic mass, with communion. My thigh muscles sent shooting pains through my legs to let me know what they thought of that. I agreed with them. I gritted my teeth through the recital of First Corinthians and invoked all the yoga classes of my life. What had Nietzsche said again about suffering? And why was I always thinking of Nietzsche at weddings?

After an eternity passed in a haze of pain, Lila and Hart kissed and walked back down the aisle. Gratefully, I loosened my locked leg muscles and waddled out of the church. In the vestibule, guests were clogging up behind the wedding party; no one left the church because of the rain. The wedding coordinator had managed to locate a bunch of umbrellas during the ceremony and was passing them around. No feat, really, since the ceremony had allowed enough time for her to fly to Burberry headquarters and back. As I watched the chaos, I had an evil idea. I grabbed four umbrellas.

"Hey." I grabbed Kathy, one of the bridesmaids. I handed her an umbrella. "Quick, we need to help. See Hart's grandmother stuck in the corner? Quick, escort her to the comfort of her car. We don't want her to get wet or chilled." I blithely ignored that it was late May and not chilly. "Go, go." I shoved Kathy, channeling all the force of the wedding coordinator and looking so earnest that Kathy didn't question my wickedness. Next, I thrust an umbrella and sent Angela after her mother. Angela was used to taking orders and complied meekly. I sent bridesmaid number three, Ellen, on a similar mission to rescue Lila's elderly aunt. I saved the carefully constructed, highly visible heroism of ferrying Lila's grandmother to her car for myself.

"Here, Nana," I called loudly. "Let me get you to your car. We don't want you to get wet." I yanked Nana out into the rain under my umbrella before she had time to respond.

"Well, thank you, dear." She jogged to keep up with me.

"Watch the puddles," I hollered. "*I'll* handle the puddles. You stay dry." I peeked to see if people were watching. They were. Albert gave me a smile and I returned with a friendly wave. I deposited Nana into her car, accepting the thanks of Lila's uncle. I turned back to the church and saw Ellen step squarely into a puddle as she escorted her mother. I turned my evil smile inward, then winced when I overheard one matron say to another, "I'd have thought she'd have dashed straight to the ladies' room. She must have a remarkable bladder."

Father Ted smiled when I regained the vestibule. "Well done," he said with a twinkle.

"Thanks." I assumed he meant "rescuing" the old ladies. Then I paused. Father Ted's office overlooked the church parking lot. He gave me a wink.

"See you next week," he said cheerily, and disappeared into the back of the church.

As if on cue, I had to pee. I self-consciously slunk to the toilet under knowing gazes.

The wedding reception proceeded smoothly. After taking photographs, in which the photographer artfully seated the bridesmaids so as to conceal everyone's ruined shoes (Awww, who knew *that* would happen), we proceeded to the reception. I enjoyed the wine, and flirted with a coworker of Hart's named Chad who had nice blue eyes. I was enjoying myself until the band fell silent and the emcee tapped the microphone.

"Hey everyone! I'd like to get your attention please. If we could all gather by the stage, the best man and maid of honor have a few things they'd like to say to the bride and groom."

My heart plummeted to my blue-stained feet. The humiliation of Amy's wedding haunted me. I swallowed. At my side, Chad grinned at me, and I grimaced back through stiff lips. I didn't hear anything the best man said. Then, there was applause and clinking glasses. Crap! I should've crammed during the best man's speech. We'd worked up a good toast and I was prepared, but what if I forgot it all? It penetrated my panic that everyone was looking at me, and the emcee was holding out the microphone. I advanced to the stage.

"Do you think she has to go to the bathroom again?" I heard someone ask in a loud whisper. "Maybe she has one of those nervous bladders." I loosened up at the recollection that I'd already looked ridiculous tonight. What difference did one more snafu make?

I took the microphone with a shaky hand. Okay, I commanded myself, pull it together.

"Hey," I began, and the microphone squealed. I jumped a foot.

"Hold it away from your mouth," the emcee called. I cleared my throat and began again, awkwardly distancing the microphone several inches.

"Hey again," I tested. It seemed to work. I squashed my nerves and focused on my carefully memorized speech.

"Before I start I'd like to say that, Lila, you look absolutely stunning. Hart, well, you just look stunned." People laughed. Thank God.

"For those of you who don't know me, my name is Vi, and I've been friends with Lila for close to twenty years. For those of you who do know me, I'll have my usual, thanks." More laughter. I began to relax.

"When Lila asked me to be her maid of honor, I took my duties seriously. I thoroughly researched the origins of the custom of having bridesmaids. Historically, the bride was the most important person on the wedding day, and many customs were designed to protect her from misfortune. In the old days, sometimes marriage was by capture or force. Therefore, a maiden . . ."

Here, I winked at Lila, and said in a staged aside, "Don't worry, I won't blow your cover on *that* one." Lila and Hart lived together. She laughed delightedly.

"The, ahem, *maiden* was guarded by her family to prevent seizure. Cue the bridesmaids. They'd act as decoys by wearing a similar dress to the bride to confuse kidnappers and deflect evil spirits." I paused and looked around significantly.

"Yeah. *I* thought so too. 'Hey, I know. *You* be the one abducted and pillaged. Wear this dress. It's an *honor,* I swear.'" Everyone laughed, and I started to enjoy myself.

"So, you ask, why would a person subject themselves to possible kidnap, torture, or an ugly dress? I'll tell you why. Love." I paused to swallow a lump in my throat.

"Two kinds of love, to be specific. One, the love between close friends. And two, celebration of the special love that Lila and Hart have found in each other.

"Now, I'm not going to follow the traditional wedding speech route to give advice or tell revealing stories. I'm single so I don't really have much advice to give. Evidently." Here Chad blew a kiss at me. I felt a little thrill. "Though, Hart, as Lila's close friend for many years I can recommend the following. Go ahead and set the ground rules and then do everything Lila says. And never be afraid that Lila will leave you, as she's spent a lot of time training you and she won't give that up lightly." Was it my imagination, or did Hart look slightly stressed out by the volume of everyone's laughter, Lila's in particular?

"As for the embarrassing stories. Well, most of those escapades involve me, and in avoidance of self-incrimination, I'll stay silent. Plus, our parents still don't know the half." Albert belly laughed and Lila smiled hugely at me. I was going to give the perfect toast! I flooded with warmth for Lila and Hart and Albert and Father Ted and everyone.

"Lila, thank you for the love you've always shown me. As Christopher Robin said to Winnie the Pooh, 'Promise you won't forget about me, ever. Not even when I'm a hundred.'" I started to get choked up, and felt tears welling in my eyes. I struggled to speak clearly.

"I'm so happy that you found someone. . . ." I was getting really worked up now, my throat closing with emotional tears. I struggled to finish—I still had a personal bit about Hart, two sensitive love quotes, and the heartfelt closing—but my voice was barely a whisper.

"We all celebrate the joy you have brought each other . . .

sniff . . . and . . . sniff . . . those around you . . . in seeing your . . ."
I was full crying now, my graceful speech disintegrated. Everyone
was looking at me. I labored to end the humiliation, too choked up
to continue.

"To Lila and Hart," I burbled in a snotty and congested way,
and raised my glass blindly. I heard a chorus of "Hear hears"
from the guests as I bolted from the stage.

I was sitting on a floral cassock in the ladies' room blowing my
nose when Lila found me.

"Hey, you big goof," she said.

"Oh, I'm sorry," I sniffled. "I'm such an ass. Can I stay here for
the rest of the night? I can hear the band." I could. They were
playing the wedding staple, "I Will Survive." It seemed a little
early for that, and I suspected it was dedicated to me.

"You're not an ass. It was lovely." Lila sat on the cassock next to
mine and hugged me, her dress pooling around us both. "Very
sincere."

I pulled back and gave her a suspicious look. She looked back
innocently, but her lips twitched. "Yes," she repeated. "Very, truly,
obviously and evidently extremely heartfelt on your part. Fer-
vent, in fact." I swatted her, and she couldn't hold back her laughter anymore.

"Wench." I smiled and laughed as well. And hugged her back.

"That is Mrs. Wench to you now," she sassed.

"Cha, right."

"Oh, I brought you a glass of wine," Lila remembered. Of
course she did. Lila had her priorities right. She retrieved the two
glasses of red wine she'd brought and handed me one.

"Love you, babe."

"Love you back," I responded. We happily clinked when the
band began playing the first notes of a new song. Lila froze and
raised her head with the alert awareness I'd expect from a wild
animal that's smelled gunpowder in its midst. Her face contorted.

"Is. That. The. Tacky. Chicken. Dance?" She spat out, not seeing me anymore. Her wine glass clunked down, abandoned on the counter. "Oh no. Not at *my* wedding they won't." She leapt to her feet, her face a grim mask, and charged out of the room, an infuriated Valkyrie, her dress swirling about her. I took another sip of wine and pitied the emcee his immediate future.

CHAPTER FOURTEEN

Shorter

"Shorter," I insisted.

"Shorter?" asked Babette.

"Shorter," I repeated. "I probably have about two minutes before I get too choked up to finish. Complete disaster. The Movie Starring Me was *Titanic*. I went down under a ton of water while talking nonsense about love."

"Okay," Imogen said thoughtfully. "Delete the advice and commentary on the groom, focus on introductory humor, a brief story about the bride, one sensitive love quote, and a heartfelt closing toast with a hint of analogy. Absolutely *no* Winnie-the-Pooh."

"Sounds like a plan," Giles said, rolling up his sleeves.

"This time I brought my laptop," said Babette, pulling it out. "I researched some quotes today and downloaded them."

"I brought some reference books," offered Mona, holding up *Words for the Wedding*, *The Pocket Guide to Wedding Speeches*, and *Bartlett's Quotations*. Imogen took *Words for the Wedding* and *Bartlett's*.

Ellis turned to me, pulling out a notepad. "Tell me about Jen. Let's focus on stuff that gives you *fond* feelings but not anything *overly emotional*," she suggested politely.

"You guys are the best," I said. "I love you all."

"Oh no, she's going to cry," sassed Imogen.

"Shut up," I dismissed her.

"Let's get to work," said Imogen. "Babette, get Charlie's attention. Is he even here yet? I don't think I've ever been in Clyde's by four-thirty P.M. before."

CHAPTER FIFTEEN

Lost Weekend Number Three

Jen Marries Louis

"This is the best bachelorette party I've ever attended," I declared to Jen.

She grinned. "Me too," she agreed.

It was 2:00 A.M. and we were sitting on a hill overlooking the sixth hole of our neighborhood golf course. The moon shone over a balmy southern night. Earlier we'd had dinner at Sir Edmund Halley's, then cruised by the Gin Mill (Maeve bartended part-time) and Providence Road Sundries, a bar we dubbed the "High School Reunion." After last call at Selwyn Pub we weren't ready to go home just yet, so I'd grabbed beer and bagels (still nothing in the fridge) from my house and we'd walked to our old spot.

I handed her a beer and popped one open for myself. "I can't believe you're getting married in forty-eight hours," I said, taking a sip of beer. It was frosty cold and tasted excellent.

"I know," she said. "I don't feel any different."

"Happy?" I passed her a bagel.

"Hmmmm." She chewed. "Content. Glad the planning is over,

that's for sure. Hopefully after this weekend I won't have to talk to Janet except for Christmas and Thanksgiving."

"Yes," I agreed. "And Ralph Nader will vote Republican, Britney Spears will become a classy dresser, and I'll marry Johnny Depp."

She jabbed an elbow at me, playfully. "One can always hope."

I jabbed back in retaliation. Then I fell quiet. "I kind of feel funny about you getting married," I finally said in a low voice. She looked at me in the moonlight.

"I know," she said. "But you're not really losing me."

"I know." I was pensive. "It's selfish."

"No, it's not," she reassured me. "You were there first. It's a natural feeling."

"It sort of feels like an ending," I thought out loud. "When you marry, it's drawing a delineating close to childhood. To *my* childhood. Only *I* didn't do anything. I feel like I don't belong to an era in my life anymore. Like I'm in this straddling place."

"Well, perhaps you don't. At least not down here. Remember what you told me when you went back to college the year after you graduated? There were little changes, but it was otherwise the same. Only you were out of place because it belonged to other students then. And it made you feel funny."

"Yes," I remembered. "It made me feel like putting on an old coat that looks the same on the outside but is too small and feels uncomfortable."

"I think that's what you're feeling now. Your friends have moved into the next phase of their lives and you aren't there yet. But you can't freeze things the way they were."

I sighed. "I know." She was right. But I didn't feel this way in D.C., in my own life. We both took a sip of beer.

"Nothing will change between us," she said to me. It wasn't true, but it was a nice idea.

I put my head on her shoulder. "I love you," I said.

"I love you too," she said back. We sat there side by side for a long time looking at the moonlit golf course.

"Wake up. I can't sleep. I'm hyperventilating." A tense voice penetrated my sleep. I groggily opened my eyes. I was in Jen's guest room. I could feel her staring at me in the dark.

"What time is it?" I was completely disoriented.

"It's five A.M. I've been up for hours. I've had four fingers of schnapps. The wedding is off." That snapped me awake.

"What!" I cried. "What do you mean?"

"The wedding's off. Louis lied to me."

"What! When we went to bed everything was fine!" I switched on the lamp. Jen's eyes were red and puffy and she looked like she was in the middle of an anxiety attack. "Tell me."

"He called me after the bachelor party. I can't marry him."

After the bachelor party? Holy shit. What had Louis done? I put a calming hand on her shoulders. "What did he say?"

"Remember how I told him no strippers? I made him *promise* me no strippers. Well, they had a stripper. It's that jerk Jesse's fault."

Oh God. Louis had slept with a stripper. "And?" I prompted, bracing for the worst.

"And what? There was a stripper. He broke his promise. It makes me sick."

"Um. Did he *do* anything with the stripper?" I gently probed, to figure out the problem without upsetting her more.

"*Do* anything? Louis? With a *stripper*? Oh, that's gross. No, he didn't *do* anything. But I asked him to make me a promise, it was important, and he broke it. If he can't keep his word when we're about to get *married*, what does that *say*?" Jen put her face in her hands.

"Honey, shush." I sat up and put my arms around her. "It'll be okay." Tonight's movie was "The Night of the Wedding Dread." There was more going on here than strippers.

"How?" she pleaded. "How can it be okay?" I was stumped. I wasn't Louis's hugest fan, to be sure, but I found it hard to get worked up over a stripper at a bachelor party. If I could recover from seeing my father get his face slapped between two enormous stripper breasts on his fiftieth birthday, she could recover from this.

Then I felt Guilty for judging. At least she wasn't afraid to try. I'd been going through the bridesmaid motions from a distance, so her choices couldn't undermine my own convictions. It was time to become a participant.

"Okay." I used my confident tone. "The first thing is to calm down."

"How can I calm down?" she asked plaintively.

"Well," I tread my way, "it's not as if Louis cheated."

"No," she admitted. "But he *lied* to me. He *promised* me—no strippers." Oh boy. This wasn't going to be easy.

"Do you want to marry Louis?" I asked.

Jen sniffled. "Yes."

"Okay." I channeled Rogers & Ury, *Getting to Yes.* "Let's focus on what you really want. You want to marry Louis, but you asked him to promise no strippers, and he broke it."

"Yes!" She nodded vigorously.

"But maybe you knew that would be a pretty hard promise to keep. And maybe you also know Louis wouldn't really want that, um, fun." Jen looked at me, waiting. Pause. "So," I coaxed her, "maybe, there's more going on here. . . ." I hinted.

"Like I'm afraid to get married?" responded Jen haltingly.

"Maybe. Are you?" I used my measured tone.

"I don't know," she whispered.

"Jen, it's okay," I reassured her. "You can want to get married and be nervous at the same time. Just don't pull a Lady Macbethian thing, you know, so far steeped in the gift registry it's better to go fore than aft. If it's wrong, you call it off. Period."

Silence from Jen.

"But," I continued, trying to read her, "if it's right . . ."

"I think it's right," she ventured at last. "I'm just a little scared. Of giving myself up. Of trusting someone that much. When they can slay you with one stupid act."

"Oh honey, I know. Vulnerability blows. But without it there's just a lot of Blockbuster and Häagen-Dazs." I couldn't believe I was dumping on my own life like this, but there was a truth to what I was saying. And my situation was different. Clearly.

Jen thought it over. "I do want to marry Louis. But you need to totally trust the person that you marry. And the stripper thing was a big thing for me."

"Okay," I said, thinking. "But you said it was really Jesse's fault." Jesse was Louis's best friend.

"Jesse is a pig. I hate him."

"Right. But you love Louis. Focus on what you want rather than your position."

"What do you mean?" I had her attention.

"Well, too often we focus on our positions—like 'I'm mad at you' or 'I said this and don't want to yield'—and we get committed to the position and not to what we actually want. You may be upset, but you don't really want to call off the wedding." I was astonished to find myself talking Jen into this marriage. But it felt like the right thing to do. "So. It wasn't his fault that Jesse got a stripper. And, he called you right away. That's a form of honesty."

"I don't know. . . ." she said.

"Tomorrow we'll talk to Louis. You can see how you feel after you talk to him."

"Do you think I should?" Jen's tired eyes begged me.

"I do," I said. "But what you need now is sleep. Can you?"

"I don't know, maybe." Now her eyes were drooping.

"Your mom's going to wake us up at nine. We won't tell her.

We'll meet up with Louis so you can talk." I had another thought. "Does he know?"

"Yes. He kept calling, so I turned off my phone." She was vague now.

"Good," I said, relieved. "He'll want to see you." I smoothed her hair. "It's going to be okay," I pronounced.

"Really?" Jen pleaded.

"Yes," I said. "Now wait here." I slipped into her room and found the schnapps. I poured her a shot and brought it to the guest room.

"Oh I couldn't," she protested, but I insisted. She needed to sleep.

"Do you want to stay in here with me?" Jen nodded and slipped under the covers. When she was settled, I put an arm around her. She curled closer and we both exhaled. Soon, her breathing was deep and regular and I let myself fall asleep.

"Jen? Where are you?" Jen's mother, Marilou, popped into the guest room. "Oh, look. Just like when you were little. Wakey-wakey. We have a big day," Marilou trilled. My eyelids felt gritty.

"Oh God. Make the mean light go away," Jen groaned.

I fought the urge to throw a shoe at Marilou. A pointy high-heeled shoe. I tried to jump-start my brain. We had to see Louis. My life as a mediator was about to begin.

"Wow." I raised my eyebrows at Jen. "It's nine. We need to scoot to get our nails done."

"Oh. Today?" Marilou looked befuddled. "I thought—"

"No, Mom, today." Jen slid her perfectly manicured hands under her pillow. We'd spent two hours at the spa yesterday.

"Oh, well, okay," fumbled Marilou. I felt bad taking advantage of her ditziness. But Marilou had often been our sucker. "When are you done?"

"It should only take an hour or so," I suggested. "But we should hurry, Jen."

Marilou capitulated with, "Well, have fun, girls. But be back by noon—we have work to do." She smiled and left the room. Jen collapsed face first.

"C'mon." I poked her. "Call Louis." She grabbed her cell phone and turned it on.

"Twenty-two missed calls," she groaned.

"Good," I said. "Let's go."

A half hour later, after a "baseball cap shower," we pulled into Starbucks. I so rarely wore a ball cap that when I did people looked right past me, even my sister. It was convenient for invisibility. Jen hesitated as I parked.

"Come on," I bulldozed her. "It'll be fine." We walked into Starbucks. Louis was there with Jesse. Jen stiffened. Uh-oh.

"Coffee first." I waved at Louis and steered Jen to the counter. We ordered our lattes.

"Remember what we talked about on the way over?" I coaxed. I'd given Jen a crash course in Rogers & Ury's *Getting to Yes*. "Remember the four principles?"

Jen ticked them off on her fingers, "Separate the people from the problem, focus on interests rather than positions, consider a variety of solutions, and base your agreement on objective criteria."

"And," I nudged her. She sighed.

"I'm not angry at Louis. Louis is not a bad person. I'm having strong feelings of vulnerability because of his failure to keep a promise. My interests are to communicate this so that he understands and can adapt his behavior to minimize situations that give me these feelings. Oh, and I'm going to kill Jesse."

"You are ready, oh, grasshoppah. Let me talk to Louis."

Louis radiated misery; Jesse, scorn. We were all wearing baseball caps. I rapped Louis on his.

"Let's chat. Jesse, take a hike."

"Whatever, dude. She's out of control." Jesse sauntered off.

"How'ya doing?" I sat down.

Louis looked at me mournfully. "I didn't want to upset her. I didn't *do* anything."

"I know," I consoled him. "But here's the snapshot. She's upset. Last night alarmed her and she needs to come to terms with her feelings and your response to them before she's comfortable entering a life partnership with you."

His expression was dazed.

I sighed. How to explain? "She's scared that because you broke your promise, you might not keep other promises."

"I didn't even *want* the stripper."

"It's not about the stripper. Let me put it this way. If I told you that I'd drive you to work, but then I didn't show up, would you trust me the next week if I offered you a ride again?"

"Probably not." He said. "But I'm *never* having a stripper again," he assured me.

"That's great," I reinforced. "But more important is that you show Jen you understand what she's feeling—*without* judging her." He nodded. "And that she can count on you."

"That's true," he said eagerly.

"Super. So, Louis, have you heard of some guys called Rogers & Ury? They're really smart about ways to talk to people after a fight."

"No," he said.

I smiled at him. "Want a crash course?"

He looked at where Jen was sitting, shoulders hunched, clutching her latte, and swore, "Definitely!"

When Maeve and I arrived at the club, cocktail hour was in full swing. "*Somebody* needs a *spanking*," Maeve said under her breath as she accepted wine from a tuxedoed waiter. Maeve dug guys in uniform. I didn't share her tastes. If there'd been anyone worth flirting with, I'd have made a bigger show of parading my cute cocktail dress (Caleb II), to ensure they saw me in a normal, flattering outfit. But there wasn't, so I didn't.

"So," I asked, "still allergic to wheat?"

"Hell no," she declared. "Have you ever tasted wheat-free bread? I couldn't stand it anymore and one night I made sweet, sweet love to a Wolfman pizza."

"Hey." Jen joined us. "God, get me a drink. I'm going to kill my mother-in-law."

I laughed. "What now?"

"You don't want to know," she said crossly.

"Well, don't worry. If Cowpie gets on your case, I'll throw my body in front of yours and take the bullet."

"Um. About that . . ." Jen said hesitantly.

"What?" I asked.

"Well, you aren't exactly sitting at my table."

"Oh, okay. Are you doing just family?"

"Um. Not exactly. See, Janet did the seating arrangements." She avoided my eyes.

"Okay," I persisted, curious now. "And?"

"Shit, Vi, I'm sorry," Jen groaned, facing me. "You're sitting in Siberia with Uncle Sal."

"Uncle Sal?" I parroted in disbelief. "You've never *met* your uncle Sal."

"I know," she wailed. "This is punishment over the Maeve thing. I'm so sorry! I just found out or I would've changed it."

"What Maeve thing?" demanded Maeve.

Jen and I stopped and looked at her. "Never mind," we said in unison.

"Listen," I comforted Jen. "Don't worry about it. Don't let her upset you. This is your night." Humph, I was thinking. This didn't accord with my idea of maid of honor glories.

"Are you sure?" sniffled Jen.

I gave her a squeeze. "Of course I'm sure. Now go mingle. No sad faces."

"Thanks," she said gratefully, and followed my command.

As soon as she was out of sight, I dumped my full glass of wine into a plant. I handed my empty glass to Maeve and did the same thing with hers. Then I headed to the bar.

"What the hell?" demanded Maeve. "What are you doing??"

"C'mon," I commanded with a wicked smile. "I feel the need to run up Janet's bar tab."

Maeve returned a nefarious grin and trotted after me. "What Maeve thing?" she asked again.

When a (tuxedoed) gentleman rang a bell for us to take our seats, Maeve and I looked for our name tags. Maeve finally found them, at Table 16. If we were at the theater, the seats would be called "obstructed view" and we'd get a discount. Maybe Janet knew I called her Cowpie.

I chose a seat that would give me a glimpse of the bride if I leaned waaaay back in my chair. Maeve sat next to me. Also at our table was the aforementioned but never encountered Uncle Sal, along with his wife and son, and a mousy looking couple that turned out to be Janet's dog groomer and his wife. His name was Rufus, which I thought was a testament to career preordination. Making conversation, I asked Rufus what breed he preferred, in terms of coiffure style. He looked at me blankly, as did his wife Cecily.

"We don't discriminate among breeds," he responded stiffly. I assured him I was suggesting no such thing.

"For example," I said, "I'm a wine buyer. I equally sample all variety of red and white grapes, but I personally like cabernet the best."

Rufus stiffened. "I don't drink on the job," he huffed. His wife looked scandalized. Maeve bit her lip to keep from laughing.

"Of course not," I sighed. "Not with all those sharp objects around." I glanced enviously at (what I could see of) the center table. Just when I was wishing for a pair of sharp dog clippers to slit my wrists, Uncle Sal arrived. Uncle Sal looked like an Uncle Sal should. He had a great round belly and a bulbous red nose. As soon as he sat down, he waved over a waiter and demanded wine, as well as a side of scotch rocks for himself. When the waiter hesitated, Sal barked, "Hop to it boy!" and the waiter hustled off. Sal clearly had enjoyed the cocktail hour. I thought of Janet's ballooning bar tab and decided I liked uncle Sal.

The waiter returned with a bottle of red and poured everyone a glass but Sal. He gave Sal the scotch and began to retreat.

"Wait a minute boy!" boomed Sal. "Where's my wine?"

The waiter faltered to a stop. "You want wine, sir?" he stammered.

"Why wouldn't I?" demanded Sal.

"Well, your—your scotch, sir . . ."

"Doesn't it look like I have two hands? Now pour me some wine and skedaddle. But not too far. We don't want any empty glasses at this table tonight." The waiter eyed Janet across the room, then Sal, clearly trying to assess the lesser of two evils. Sal raised a bushy eyebrow and won neatly. The waiter hastily poured him a whopper of a glass of wine. I looked at the label and sighed. It was going to take a lot of drinking to run up the tab. Frankly, I didn't think my palate was up for it.

"Well." Sal turned to me. "Who'll make an ass of himself first tonight? My money's on the chap with the SMU tie. A pug nose indicates a man that can't hold his liquor."

We listened to Sal hold court through the salad course, receiving smothering attention from our personal wine steward. For the second course they put steaks in front of everyone.

"Um, excuse me." Maeve quietly got the attention of a server. "I don't eat meat. May I have the vegetarian option?" Maeve had been a vegetarian since *Oprah*, May 1999.

He looked at her blankly. "There's no vegetarian option," he said. "Only the filet."

"I don't eat red meat. They must have a vegetarian option," Maeve insisted.

"We're serving everyone filets. It has herb butter on it." It did indeed have a lovely pat of herb butter melting unhealthily over it. It made my mouth water. I didn't wait—waiting for Maeve to work out food issues meant starvation. I cut into my perfect medium rare steak and took a bite. Heavenly. For all her faults, Janet had just served me a divine filet.

"It's really good," I moaned in bliss to Maeve, who shot me an annoyed look.

"What's going on?" Jen appeared at our side.

"Nothing," I said, giving Maeve a warning look that said shut-up-now-and-I'll-drive-you-to-Pancho-and-Lefty's-later."

"Are you okay here? Is it awful?" Jen lowered her voice and crouched beside me.

"No," I assured her. "It is fine. Sal's hilarious." Jen caught sight of Maeve's plate.

"Maeve! Are you eating meat again?" she asked in surprise.

Maeve looked panicked. I knew she was thrilled to death about her first wedding appearance. She didn't want to do anything wrong.

"Yeeess," she said haltingly. As if she suspected she wasn't wholly convincing, she cut a small corner of steak and put it in her mouth. "This is delicious," she mumbled, her face stretched as she tried to avoid touching her tongue to the flesh inside her mouth. She smiled gamely at Jen and swallowed.

"Oh, okay," Jen said. "When I realized there was no veggie option, I was trying to get you a salad. Well," she looked over her shoulder, "got to get back. Enjoy."

As soon as she left, I resumed eating my perfect steak. "Don't worry, babe. I'll take you out for something as soon as this is over. Whatever you want."

"That's okay." Maeve had a strange look on her face. I wasn't paying attention. I inhaled the steak, along with the delicious mashed potatoes and asparagus. Negotiating the Treaty of (tra) Verse-the-Aisle had taken a lot out of me, and we hadn't really had time to eat. My steak was gone too soon. I sat back, wanting more. My eyes fell on Maeve.

"Oh great!" I perked up. "I'll eat your steak."

I reached for her plate and she whacked her fork on the back of my hand.

"Ow!" I yelped in shock.

"Back off," she commanded, shoveling steak into her mouth. I gaped at her.

"Maeve! You don't eat meat!" She'd consumed three-quarters of her steak.

"Only because no one told me it was this good. Damn. What a waste of six years." She looked at me. "Tell me more?"

"Ribs," I said firmly, "with Maurice's sauce. And pulled pork BBQ sandwiches from Allen and Sons. Bacon. Mmmm . . . bacon. Five Guys' cheeseburgers. Chili dogs from Ben's Chili Bowl . . ." I was silenced by the tapping of a microphone. Sal perked up and waggled a hand at the waiter to top us all off as he settled in gleeful anticipation of someone making an ass of himself. I relaxed. This time it wouldn't be me. And when tomorrow came, I was prepared.

The first phone call came at 7:30 A.M. Seriously.

"Vi?" came a panicked voice. "It's Darla. The wedding manager at the club?"

Her voice went up in a question mark. Was she asking or telling me? I made a noise into the phone.

"I was calling because the pedestal isn't here. You know, the column for the central floral arrangement?" Again with the question that wasn't a question. I blinked my gritty eyes and tasted my tongue. And regretted it. Uncle Sal was no longer my friend. He was an evil, wine-pouring punisher.

"What do you need me to do?" I managed. Besides keep it from Jen.

"We need a pedestal." Darla sounded anxious. "It's central to the entire vision of the room. The florist was supposed to deliver one but the flowers are here, and no pedestal?"

"A pedestal. Where do I get a pedestal?" I asked. "That's a question, by the way."

"What?"

"Never mind. Where?"

"Um, try Jen's florist, KaBloom. If they don't have one, maybe they can recommend someone else. But we need it here sort of early. By noon?"

"Noon. Got it." I staggered into the bathroom and felt immense relief after I brushed my teeth. I popped a few aspirin and surveyed the damage in the mirror. Puffy, but not irreparable. I could sleep another hour before the florist opened. I was pulling back the covers when the phone rang again.

"Vi? It's Mrs. Mac," whispered Jen's mother.

"Hey Mrs. Mac. Why are you whispering?"

"Well dear, there's a teeny, little problem. But I don't want to alarm Jen. The printers only gave us half the programs. They have the rest at the shop. Someone's on the way over now to open up for us, so we need a person there to . . . ?"

No doubt when Marilou was asking a question. "I'd be glad to." I resignedly released the bedcovers. I put on jeans and my invisibility White Sox cap, then thought of one thing that *would* make me feel better.

I noisily banged open Maeve's door with an evil smile and flopped on her sleeping form.

"Wakey, wakey," I sang in a loud and annoying voice. "We have mission critical errands to run. Come on. Plaaaaaayy with me!"

"Please die," ordered a weak voice from under the covers. Uncle Sal had gotten to her too.

1. *Drive across town to printer at insanely early hour to get extra programs—check*

2. *Take programs to Mrs. Mac for inspection, despite fact they were printed the same time as other, already scrutinized, programs, then deliver to church practically adjacent to printers—check*

3. *Pick up coffee to stop Maeve's bitching—check*

4. *Pick up sausage McMuffin because actually up in time for McDonald's breakfast (miracle) and encourage Maeve to try one—check*

5. *Get yelled at by Imogen for calling too early to practice toast—check*

6. *Return home for thirty-minute bathroom break as Maeve's body reacts to her newly carnivorous diet—check*

7. *Practice toast to disinterested father—check*

8. *Drive unsuccessfully all over town to four florists looking for three-foot white pedestal for centerpiece—check.*

9. *Pick up Chic-Fil-A to stop Maeve's bitching—check*

10. *Drive back to first florist, where they found pedestal in way, way back room—check*

11. *Deliver pedestal to Club at 11:59 to anxious Darla, who weeps in relief?—check*

12. *Practice toast to Maeve—check*

13. Pick up extra tea lights and tea light candle holders from mall for reception—*check*

14. Deliver candles and candle holders to frenzied Darla at Club—*check*

15. Practice toast over phone to Ethan—*check*

16. Pick up accidentally overlooked box of monogrammed napkins from McIntyre house—*check*

17. Deliver monogrammed napkins to near frantic Darla at club—*check*

18. Return to McIntyre house to collect rings—*check*

19. Deliver bride's ring to Best Man Jesse and endure "maybe I'll just lose the ring and stop the wedding" jokes—*check*

20. Practice toast over phone to Mona—*check*

21. Nervously check that groom's ring is still in purse—*check*

22. Return to McIntyre house for engraved champagne flutes and silver cake knife—*check*

23. Nervously check that groom's ring is still in purse—*check*

24. Deliver engraved champagne flutes and silver cake knife to now hysterical Darla at club (consider giving Darla Valium)—*check*

25. Nervously check that groom's ring is still in purse—*check*

26. Return home to gather wedding outfits and necessities—*check*

27. Emergency removal of spot from Maeve's navy blue skirt—*check*

28. Get hand smacked by Maeve while nervously trying to check that groom's ring is still in purse—*check*

29. *Emergency removal of cat hair from maid of honor dress—check*

30. *Get cell phone taken away by Maeve when trying to call Ellis to practice toast—check*

"Egads. Are we done yet?" Maeve flopped onto the sofa. I collapsed next to her.

"Except for the wedding part," I groaned. "What time is it?"

"Time to go." Imogen bounced in, fresh from a morning of leisure. "Chop chop. We were supposed to be at Jen's five minutes ago. You don't want to make her anxious on her big day."

I gave her a pointed look. "I have spent all day ensuring that Jen has no anxiety." Imogen muscled me off the couch.

"See you at the ceremony girls." My mother drifted through the room.

"It's at *six*," Maeve and I shouted in unison. She waved over her shoulder.

"Make sure Dad knows when and where," I told Maeve, and she and Imogen nodded.

"Here." Imogen handed me a Starbucks cup as we crossed the street to Jen's. "Skim latte. I picked it up on the way so it's totally tepid, just how you like it." I accepted gratefully.

We were barely across the threshold when Jen pounced.

"Tina's ready for you. She's set up in my room. Hey Imogen." Jen gave her a hug.

Imogen hugged her back. "What can I do to help?"

"Nothing really," mused Jen. "Everything's going smooth as pie. We're totally organized."

I muffled my snort.

We arrived at the church at five-forty with nothing to prevent being relentlessly hounded by the photographer in pursuit of "candids." Jen was tranquil, snacking on dry Froot Loops.

She gave me a huge smile. "I'm so ready. I feel great. I'm getting *married*." Her smile became goofy. "Louis left roses on the doorstep this morning with a note about how excited he was to begin our lives together. I think he's nervous I'm still mad." She squeezed my hand. "Thank you, Vi, for everything yesterday. This is the best day of my life. I'm so happy." She focused on me. "Because of you."

"Me too," I said, wondering why I felt bittersweet. I knew I didn't deserve any credit. I'd only done what I thought was best for her. I had no idea what *I* wanted. What I knew is that I loved her. I was going to miss her.

Ten minutes later we were walking down the aisle. Twenty-four minutes and one "love is patient, love is kind" later, Jen and Louis were married. Afterward Father Ted and I did our hand jive and looked after the departing bride and groom like proud parents.

"We did it," Father Ted mused.

"All our babies are married now," I joshed. "I'm so darn proud of those kids!"

"I'll miss my first mate," said Father Ted, and I knew he meant it. My eyes watered.

"I'll miss you too." I hugged him.

"Good luck with your toast," said the sympathetic minister.

"I'm ready," I assured him. We clunked fists one last time and I went to be photographed to death.

My second wind kicked in at the reception. This time I was sitting with the bride and groom, having a ball joking around with Jen's father. The food was delicious. I had the salmon. Maeve, nearby, had the steak. Then finished our mother's.

After dinner Jesse rose for the Best Man's toast. I felt Jen steel herself. I filled her champagne glass to the brim.

"My name's Jesse and I'm the best man.

"In preparation for my Best Man duties, I bought a book. I read to page five, which said that 'to maintain a clear head during the wedding it is vital for the Best Man to remain sober at all times.' I threw the book away." Here Jesse theatrically took a big slurp of his gin and tonic, while his fraternity brothers hooted. I squeezed Jen's hand under the table. She clamped on it like a death vise.

"But in those first five pages, I learned three key elements of the wedding. First, the Aisle—the longest walk you will ever take. Second, the Altar—where two become one. Third, the Hymn—a musical celebration of marriage. I think Jen may have read the same book, because as she walked toward Louis today, I'm sure I heard her whispering Aisle Altar Hymn, Aisle Altar Hymn, Aisle Altar Hymn." The fraternity boys cracked up again. Jen sucked in her breath. My hand was going numb.

"Louis, it's been an honor being your Best Man. Even if I couldn't talk you out of it. Heh. Just kidding, Jen. I'm thrilled Louis has found someone he believes will make him happy. He deserves a good wife."

My hand was verging on permanently dead. I whispered to Jen, "Nothing can spoil this day." Her grip eased a fraction. The amputation surgeons could rest easier.

"On behalf of the Bride and Groom and their families, I invite you to toast Louis and Jen. We wish them well." At last he sat down and Jen released my hand to clap tepidly.

Then it was my turn. I took the microphone with the confidence of a trained athlete. There was no way I was screwing this one up. My *parents* were here.

I smiled at the room.

"Hey there," I said brightly. "My name's Vi, and I'm Jen's maid of honor. Jen and I've known each other since we were little kids. Like all friends, we've had our downs as well as ups. I can remember times when a petty argument would arise from nowhere. Jen would call me smelly, and I'd call her a cow, and we'd each end up in tears. But sure enough, the next day, Jen would drop me an e-mail from work and we'd make up." Everyone laughed.

"When we were seventeen Jen inherited a red Karmann Ghia from her cousin. You can guess who was overcome with delight, right? Yep . . . my father." More laughter. "See, I'd been nattering to my dad about wanting a Karmen Ghia for ages. When Jen got her car, my father was thrilled. He told me I could live vicariously through Jen. He didn't realize at the time how prophetic his words would be. More than a cool car, we all want one thing out of life. That's a soul mate, and true love. Jen and Louis have found this rare thing, and I've learned a lot about love and trust by watching their example. From them I've learned that the truest manifestation of love is when both individuals strive to grow and change in an effort to become the best version of themselves, despite the fears that go with vulnerability. And they succeed because they're inspired and supported by each other. I know I wouldn't be the person I am today if it hadn't been for my friendship with Jen all these years. And I know Louis is the man for her because I've watched how they make each other grow. What I mean to say is best captured in a quote: 'And now my friend, who are we? We are who we never would have been without each other.' What's lovely about a wedding is that it allows everyone here to see the ones we love with fresh eyes, and remember what's most important. I'm blessed that I see that every day through my parents' example of a perfect marriage." People in the audience looked at each other, a little misty-eyed. A few couples held hands. My parents beamed at me. Awesome.

"Traditionally a toast offers advice to the groom, but Louis—I don't have much advice to give. Jen seems to have you well in hand. And take heart—there are only two times when a man can't understand a woman. That's before marriage and after marriage." Everyone laughed.

"Folks, I started planning this speech nine months ago, and you must feel like I've been delivering it equally as long. So, I'll wrap up. I wish Jen and Louis the very best in their future journey. I hope, when they look back years from now on their wedding day, they realize it was the day they loved each other the least. Please join me in a toast to Jen and Louis."

I raised my glass to Jen and Louis, who were beaming at me, and had my first sip of alcohol for the evening. Imogen caught my eye and inclined her head. "The Perfect Toast," she mouthed. I nodded too. "Get Me a Goddamn Glass of Wine," I mouthed back, smiling.

CHAPTER SIXTEEN

The Cost of Living

I was wading through the pile of mail accumulated while I'd completely neglected my life for three weeks. I stared at my bank statement in horror and did some quick math. Nine trips to Charlotte (three by plane)+three shower gifts+three wedding gifts+three pairs of shoes+three blue dresses+extras=over $4,200. Yep, I could've bought a one-way plane ticket around the world, or a small, only slightly dinged used car, for what the weddings had cost me. Hopefully I still had a job on Monday.

"Look at it this way," Imogen had said. "You bought a heaping helping of experience. You can't put a price on that." I remembered a line from a movie where the mother said to her daughter, "You may be in a hurry to lose your innocence, but if you won't fight to keep it, I'll fight for you," and I felt traction. I longed to recapture the awe and aspiration I'd felt at Jackie's wedding. Three blue dresses had forever diluted it. The weddings themselves were lovely, of course, but I had a hard time comprehending the rationality with which my friends chose grooms. I secretly, unshakably believed I'd be different, I'd have elevating love, and passion. Despite Jen's apparent satisfaction, I spurned the idea of choosing anything less than magic. Perhaps I was wrong. But, despite recent romantic blows, my heart of hearts whispered that if I held out I'd be the lucky one.

Imogen was right too. If I wanted real love, it was time to give dating an honest chance. I had to stop assuming Caleb would rescue me from it all. Our last encounter made that clear. As much as I loved him, I liked myself more.

I felt Melancholy. Caleb wasn't the only past I was letting go. My drive back from Charlotte after Jen's wedding brunch was an ending. I wouldn't be returning any time soon. It seemed a poignant irony that at the moment I should've been closest with my friends—maid of honor on the best day of their life—I had little in common with them anymore. I sensed this chasm would grow as they embarked on the alien terrain of married life. Our friendships wouldn't end, of course, but I knew without feeling defeat that they would downgrade. I wasn't sure I'd have it differently. Often we remain friends with a person merely based on longevity. Who else remembers when we had Adam Ant posters on our wall? I was Melancholy because I'd dissected the last Feeling. It was Relief. I'd spent the last year stepping into a past, playing an outgrown role and unsure of the script. It was time to move forward. There is a comfort in old friends, but it can become a discomfort when we try to wear the friendship with the same intensity as when we were young. A graceful loosening is necessary to allow us all to breathe. I was Relieved to return to D.C., where I could be myself.

My attention was drawn to something colorful sticking out of my mail stack. It was a postcard from Los Angeles. I turned it over curiously and read on the back:

My darling, when will you return to me? Life is empty without you. I miss you and I long for you. Love and kisses, Jeremy Piven.

I laughed, recognizing Mona's writing. I thought about Sunday nights with the girls, and Ethan and Giles. They were my family now. Maybe growing up wasn't that scary if you had the right team. It was obvious to me now that I'd moved on from my first team to a new team in D.C.

"At any rate," I assured the silently reproving bank statement still in my hand, "we'll have a nice long recovery. New Team is wedding free. In fact, this is a wedding free year." I smiled in happiness at the thought.

A year later I would remember that moment and laugh so hard I would pee my pants.

Part Three

FOURTEEN WEDDINGS IN TWELVE MONTHS

CHAPTER SEVENTEEN

Mission Impossible

"I'd like to propose a toast." Ethan tinged his fork against his glass to quiet the chatter. "To Vi Connelly on her twenty-eight birthday."

"Here, here," came a chorus of voices, clinking glasses. The gang had taken me to Sushi Taro to celebrate my birthday. Twenty-eight. Ack.

"Vi, what are your goals for this year?" asked Jack, Ellis's now serious boyfriend. He'd produced a diamond ring, so we'd admitted him to the inner circle.

"To survive it." My answer was prompt.

"The mean streets of Washington getting a little tough for you?" mocked Imogen.

"Huh, no. It's the queen sheets of Crate & Barrel I'm worried about. I have twelve weddings in the next twelve months." After Jen's wedding I'd hallucinated I'd have a nice long interlude before my next one. Cha. Last spring had only been the beginning. In the intervening six months a barrage of Save the Dates and thick parchment envelopes had assaulted my mailbox. My bulletin board hadn't seen so many like-patterned postings since I'd tacked up all the job rejection letters I received after college as motivation.

"Twelve weddings!" Giles radiated disbelief, suppressing a shudder.

"That's my version of hell," said Braxton Barnett, Ethan's room-mate, who often tagged along for group activities. Braxton was a good old boy from North Carolina, who always wore cowboy boots and loved to hunt and drink beer. Mona swore he looked just like Christian Bale (in a camouflage jacket). Then she got a little breathless, but I never pressed her on it.

"Or Ethan's," said Imogen. "Who's going to schlep her to them all?" Her voice had an odd tinge.

"No comment," commented Ethan.

"I don't think I know twelve people I like well enough to put on a suit," quipped Jack. "Now funerals . . . that's a different mat-ter. I'd gleefully attend a number of funerals." Jack liked to pro-voke people with outrageous statements. His warm brown eyes and dimples diminished the intended effect.

"Well, I apologize for my part in it," said Ellis. She and Jack were getting married in May. "But don't think that means I'm let-ting you off the hook." Mona and Imogen groaned.

"Maybe we should add to Vi's goals for the year," Ethan sug-gested. "Let's get her a boyfriend to go to all these events."

"Oooooh," said Imogen. "Mission impossible."

"Mean." I sulked, though I was practically a neuter, my only date prospects a gay man or a pal. All my men thought of me as a dear friend. Not that I wanted them putting the moves on me. Ick. But still. At least they could've tried.

The waiter interrupted us with an enormous tray of sushi. There was a chaos of sorting out what was what. I studiously avoided the eel. We ordered more sake and settled into wolfing down our dinner.

"So." Imogen wouldn't let go of a topic guaranteed to torture me. "What qualities does Vi need in a man?"

"Laid back," said Ethan, as he sniffed a California roll suspiciously. He wouldn't touch raw fish, my urging to sample a fish-free California roll futile.

"Are you calling me high maintenance?" I huffed.

"Yes." Ethan didn't blink. He set the sushi at the every edge of his plate, as if it might infect his steak.

"I like lots of drinks, that's all," I defended myself. "Different drinks go with different things." I drank some club soda, followed by some sake. Then I chased a spicy tuna roll with Ichiban beer, to prove my point. When Ethan looked at me, I showed him my mouth full of chewed-up sushi like an eight year-old. He just rolled his eyes.

"Not a morning person," offered Giles.

"Hardee-har har," I said.

"Smart," said Babette. I flushed with pleasure. Then paused. Did they think I needed a smart man because I couldn't handle things myself? Hmm.

"Southern," Braxton pronounced.

"You think everyone should be Southern" scoffed Imogen. "And shoot things that move."

"Liberal," said Ethan. "An unreasonable pinko commie just like her so they can go to rallies together with people who smell and don't shave, and when they get all gooey they'll call each other 'granola muffin.' He should have at least three tie-dye shirts. Two of which he made himself."

"Natch," agreed Imogen.

Ethan winked at me. "You know you're my favorite liberal."

I patted him reassuringly. "I sleep better at night knowing my vote cancels out yours," I replied sweetly. While we agreed to disagree on critical political areas such as welfare reform and the integrity of Republican politicians, we had a pact that one day Ethan would run for President, I'd vote Republican for the only time in my life, and he'd appoint me Chief of Staff.

"He'll have to be outgoing so he can handle us, and all these weddings," said Mona.

"You got that right," said Jack, who'd survived the trial by fire.

"Vi, any special requests for Mr. Connelly?" Giles asked.

"Mr. Connelly is my dad, thanks very much. Right now I'd like to enjoy my meal without indigestion." I smiled at the table, all innocence. "Who needs a boyfriend when I've got you?" I declined to share the secret Seize The Day Plan I'd devised after Jen's wedding. It was time to take action for the love life I wanted. I'd put the plan into motion soon enough.

"Here here," everyone replied.

"Does she really think we're buying that?" Imogen asked Giles.

"Shut up," I commanded. "I want my presents. Now. Pony up."

CHAPTER EIGHTEEN

Tempest in a Teacup

My dad must have oiled the door hinges, because my gentle hip bump caused a Richter 7.2 slam. I flinched, and was muttering about dangerous home repairs when I nearly jumped out of my skin. My mother was sitting like a stone at the kitchen table staring at a teacup. She hadn't twitched.

"Hey Mom. I'm here," I stated the obvious. It was gloomy, but no lights were on. She didn't move. It was weird.

"Mom? It's Vi. Home for my birthday dinner." More obvious.

Her eyes focused on me. She managed a wan smile. "Vi. Welcome home."

"What's going on?" My mother wasn't prone to melancholy. Emotional extremes were my department. She looked as if she didn't know how to answer my question. "Do you want some tea," I offered. She was fixed on the empty cup. Maybe it was an experiment to concentrate tea into existence. I reached for it, but she grabbed my wrist.

"No . . . don't . . ." I sat down and waited. She sighed. "It's a gift." She frowned. "No, that's not right. It's a bequest."

"A bequest? Who died?"

"Maggie. Maggie remembered me." She rubbed her face.

"Who's Maggie?" I'd never heard her mention a Maggie.

She looked at me with tired eyes. "She's my first husband's mother."

I blinked.

"She died last week. I hadn't seen her in thirty years." She traced the teacup's handle.

I had heard wrong. "You mean your first boyfriend? She was the mother of your first boyfriend?" My mother wasn't divorced.

She touched her throat. "I wore her pearls at my wedding."

"Grandma Kate's pearls, you mean," I corrected. "You wore Grandma Kate's pearls at your wedding."

"Vi, are you having auditory comprehension problems?" My mother's voice was suddenly less dreamy. "Maggie was Daniel's mother, and Daniel was the boy I married before I met your father." She looked at my face and sighed. "I'm sorry. I shouldn't snap. I'm feeling a little emotional. I haven't thought about that part of my life for a long time. This must be a surprise."

"Surprise!" I squeaked. I couldn't breathe. My mother had a secret life. Something shiny in my mind tarnished. "How could you do this to me?"

"To you?" She looked confused. "How does this affect you? It was a long time ago. Before you were born."

"But . . ." I shook my head. All this time I'd thought my parents' marriage was a faultless gleaming model for me. I'd counted on their example, and they'd deceived me. "I'm . . ." I stopped again. I didn't know what to say. I felt like crying. It wasn't right. I needed their experience to have been perfect so I could believe. I didn't have to settle for Ordinary or Disappointing, because if you did it right, you wouldn't make a mistake. But . . .

My mother laid a hand on mine. "Vi, when I was very young, too young, I married my high school sweetheart. . . ."

I sucked in my breath. "You had a sweetheart other than Dad?" I was aghast. My ideal was crumbling.

"Vi, be reasonable. Your father and I both dated other people before we met. It would be silly to think otherwise. It doesn't mean—"

I pulled my hand away and jumped up.

"Vi," my mother frowned, "you're being—" But I couldn't listen. I was shaken. I practically trotted from the room. As I reached the door, my father came in.

"Welcome home!" He beamed, sweeping his arms wide for a hug, but I brushed by him and ran to my old room. At least there I knew nothing had changed.

CHAPTER NINETEEN

Deck the Holiday Inn

Holly Marries Eli, Washington, D.C., December

"I can't believe," Holly fumed on the phone, "that they sold the hotel to Holiday Inn two weeks before my wedding. It's so unfair."

I made a comforting noise into the phone.

"I refuse to get married at a Holiday Inn. So, now I personally have to call every single guest because the invitations went out *weeks* ago, and Eli can't be trusted. Anyway, we're getting married at the Calvary Baptist Church."

I laughed. "You're an atheist and Eli's Jewish!" She had Perfect Wedding Syndrome *bad*.

"Whatever," Holly dismissed. "They were available and walking distance."

"The reception is still at the Holiday Inn?" I asked carefully.

"Yeah. Everything we planned will be the same. Only the sign's changed. There's no chance of finding another reception location on short notice during the holiday season."

"Well, I'm looking forward to it." It was my first wedding since

Jen's, and I *was* looking forward to being a regular guest. Everyone said weddings were a great way to meet other singles. Now that I wasn't distracted with bridal duties, I could check it out. Being a guest must be where all the fun happens. I declined to probe the psychological connotations that I preferred the role of observer to participant.

A call rang on my second line. It was my parents' number. I felt my chest tighten. I'd been dodging my mother. I didn't want to punish her, exactly, but seeing her made me anxious for reasons I hadn't dissected. I avoided it.

"I've seated you next to a friend of Eli's from school," Holly said. "He's supposed to be good-looking."

Alarm bells pinged. "You've met him?"

"Not yet," Holly dismissed my apprehension. "But he'll be great. He's single."

"There will be lots of single people, right?" I pressed.

"Sure, sure." She was less than convincing. "There'll be some."

Hunh. "Some" didn't match my wedding reception fantasy rollicking with loads of good looking, snazzily-attired people discreetly winking across the dance floor.

"What's his name?"

"Irving," Holly said. "You'll love him."

I knew I could not love a man named Irving, ever. But I was amused. With the wedding only two weeks away, Holly had morphed into full Bridezilla and would brook no obstacle less insurmountable than change in ownership of a major international hotel chain's holding properties. I'd bet that if she could've gotten the CEO on the horn, she would have argued him into postponing. I stood no chance of persuading her to skew her seating charts by allowing me to bring Ethan. I wisely held my tongue.

"Listen, I've got to run. I have a *ton* of phone calls to make. 'Bye!" She hung up.

As I considered our conversation, I admitted that my overwhelming Feeling was Optimism. I was looking forward to the wedding as a chance to meet someone.

With that Optimism, I refreshed the website I'd been perusing when Holly called. Sid Dickens was a Canadian artist who designed hand-crafted decorative plaster tiles. They were pure art, some finished to a porcelain-like quality, others cracked to create a faux look of weathered stone. I'd finally found the perfect wedding gift. And just in time for the marathon. Feeling cheerful, I dialed the number.

"Sid Dickens, this is Ben speaking. How may I help you?"

"Hey Ben, this is Vi Connelly calling," I announced.

"Uh, hello Vi. What can I do for you, eh?"

"Wow," I pounced. "Canadians really say 'eh'? I mean really? Or, wait. You just said that because you know Americans would be impressed by the colloquial Canadian charm. Do you have caller ID, Ben? Is the 'eh' a marketing tool?"

"I do have caller ID," he replied civilly. I thought I could hear a smile but he offered no more.

"Okay, okay. Keep your marketing secrets," I yielded. "Ben, I've been looking at your website and I'd like to order a wedding gift. These tiles are beautiful."

"That is a lovely idea." Ben accepted the praise calmly.

"My friend Ellis saw your tiles in a decorator's magazine. Frankly, I don't like to shop," I chattered. I'd long ago determined that endearing rather than alienating telephone sales representatives behooved the caller. Something about the isolation of phone communication liberated people to rapidly degenerate into name-calling, aspersions on job qualifications, or huffy disconnections among even the best of people. Starting off with cheerful camaraderie can cement goodwill and elicit an equally positive—if cautious—response.

"We sell a number of tiles as wedding gifts." Ben didn't comment on my rambling.

This was good news. It was risky going off-registry but I still had issues with vases and soup tureens. "What do they choose?"

"It depends on the couple. As you know, Sid offers a range of designs."

"You sound like a catalogue, Ben. Help a first-timer, would you?"

Ben coughed. "Perhaps one of our classic tiles. Have you seen T-18, which is Script?"

I scrolled the website.

"That's not very romantic is it?" A voice said in my ear. I jumped a foot.

"Jesus, Giles!" I clutched my heart. "Don't sneak up on a person like that!" I scrabbled below my desk to recover the phone, taking deep breaths.

"Since this is *my* office too, and I reasonably returned from lunch approximately one hour from the time I left, I don't consider my return to be the least stealthy." Giles sniffed.

"Ben?" I panted into the phone. "Sorry. My office mate sneaked up on me. But he might have a point. Do you think that tile is romantic enough?"

"Reasonable point." *Reasonable point,* I mouthed to Giles, who preened. "You might consider tiles T-02 or T-66."

"Yech. No hearts." I rejected the tiles outright. Giles nodded vigorously.

"Then perhaps tile T-125, the Tree of Life, or T-57 of Leaves. The growing plants could symbolize new life, the putting down of roots."

"Now that's poetry, Ben," I praised. I looked at Giles.

"I like the Leaves," he suggested. "It's seasonal."

I nodded. "Okay Ben, I'll take T-57."

"Excellent choice," Ben replied. I gave him credit card and shipping information, wincing at the pair of Charles David shoes it cost me.

"What would you like the card to read?" Ben asked.

"Card?"

"It is traditional with a gift, so the receiver will know from whom it came." I squinted at the phone. I deeply suspected that Ben was making fun of me.

"How about, 'Congratulations, Holly and Eli. Thank you for including me in your special day. May your new life together be decorated with beauty beyond this gift. Love, Vi.' "

"Very thoughtful," Ben said. "That order will be shipped in approximately eight weeks."

"February!" I cried. "But that's way after the wedding!"

"Unfortunately, Christmas is very busy for us. Under traditional wedding etiquette, you have one year to provide a gift. It will arrive close to Valentine's Day, eh?" Definitely. He definitely was mocking me.

"There you go with the 'eh' again, Ben. Now I *know* you're teasing me. For that I expect it to arrive *on* Valentine's Day."

"I'll see what we can do," Ben said, in a tone that managed to convey kindly that he had no such intentions whatsoever.

"One down," I said to Mona over the phone the morning after Holly's wedding.

"How was it?" she asked sleepily.

"Efficient. I was betting on twenty-six minutes, but the cousins were speed-readers so love was patient, kind, unenvious, and non-bragging for only thirteen seconds, and in under twenty-three minutes we were trailing the bride and groom out of the church."

"How can people feel like anything important happened in twenty-three minutes? An informercial takes longer." I agreed with her. "How was the guy?"

I snorted. "Pleased with himself."

"Oh."

"I could've overlooked the lazy eye, but I couldn't get past the name."

"What, was he named *Irving*?" She used a heavy nasal accent.

"Did I tell you?"

"Seriously?" she laughed. "I was just guessing."

"Yeah. But it didn't matter anyway. Under OFW, no hook-ups unless I've met the guy at least once before, or the bride does a thorough background check."

"OFW?"

"Nowadays 'wedding' is an umbrella term, potentially incorporating up to seven different events. Operation Frock and Withdraw is the perfect wedding surgical strike. Limit pre-wedding activities, show up in a stunning dress, and withdraw with the minimum possible entanglement and maybe a groomsman."

"You know you don't have to go to every one," Mona suggested.

"What? Don't be silly. I love weddings." I was surprised. Why wouldn't you go?

"Never mind. So how does OFW work?"

"Limit your attendance and your purchases. Unless you're related within one bloodline, you attend either an engagement party, a shower, or a bachelorette party, never all. And efficient gift giving. Find a good thing and stick with it." I was particularly pleased with this one.

"And have you?"

"Did I tell you about this guy named Ben?"

CHAPTER TWENTY

Caleb Redux

Katrina Marries James, Pittsford, New York, January

"Sid Dickens, this is Ben speaking. How may I help you?"

Hey Ben, this is Vi Connelly calling. Remember me? The Leaves tile, eh?" I prompted.

"Oh yes, of course. Ms. Connelly. Was there a problem with your order?"

"Vi, please. No, no problem at all," I assured him. "I need another one."

"Well I am delighted to assist you." Ben said, sounding sort of sincere.

"Okay, see, my ex—his name is Caleb—and I used to spend a lot of time with Katrina and James. We haven't been that close since Caleb and I broke up. Again. But we used to hang out all the time. A couple of different times. It's complicated."

"I see," said Ben.

"Well," I flustered, "so, um, my gift has got to be extremely perfect. Just right . . . I chattered. Ben seemed to be waiting. "Okay, it has to be way better than what Caleb gives them," I got out in a rush.

"I suspected that was where we were going," responded Ben. "Don't worry. I'll help you find just the tile." I let out my breath. Ben was so nice. He understood me. Maybe I should go to Vancouver, if everyone there was as nice as Ben.

I told him what I knew.

"So they were long distance for a while?" he probed. "I have just the thing. Check out T-112, the Postmark. It's about being connected across time and distance." It was perfect.

"Ben, you deserve a million dollars. Throw it on my card, will you?"

"I'll need to get that information from you again," he said.

"Ben," I teased, "I'm hurt. You didn't save my number?" I gave him my information. "For the card, how about: 'It's a delight to celebrate the marriage of a couple so perfect for one another. I'm honored to be included in your special day. Love, Vi.'"

"How very original," Ben said.

"Get off my back, eh?"

"So, are you coming home for Dad's birthday?" Maeve crunched ice in my ear.

"I can't." I was only partly fibbing. When I'd handed Al a list of days I needed off for wedding travel, his usual smile had been missing. He'd given me the time off, but his "Just make sure you get your work taken care of" was more abrupt than normal. The panic fluttering in my chest was real. With the sense it was at risk, I realized that I wanted to keep my job. I didn't really have time for Maeve's call.

"I don't know what your problem is with Mom," Maeve said. To be honest, I didn't understand either, but my stomach twisted when I thought that my mother had worn another man's name before Connelly, and I'd felt strained around my parents since then. I still loved them, but it was easier to avoid them from the safety of D.C. than try to untangle my inexplicable sense of betrayal. Plus another day off was out of the question.

"Don't you want to see Edward?" Maeve teased.

"I'm too busy body sculpting," I retorted.

"Poor Ethan." Maeve knew my wedding roster. "Suffering the consequences of your dating dysfunctionality."

"Bite your tongue," I replied. "I have a plan." I instantly knew I'd said too much.

The crunching stopped. "That has Caleb written all over it," Maeve reproved.

"I gotta go." I hastily hung up.

I thrashed hangers, creating total disarray in my closet and causing Nigel and Clementine to frolic in delight chasing tantalizing bits of twirling fabric.

"I have nothing to wear!" I howled.

Mona sat on my bed reading *Us* magazine. By describing *Us* magazine as "reading," I'm being generous. The only words in *Us* magazine are photo captions. I loved it.

"Wear something from the Caleb Couture Collection," she suggested without looking up.

"No," I shot out, too quickly. *That* would be weird. Mona stopped leafing and looked up. "Um, I mean. It's just not right. For tonight. *Nothing* is right." I hid my face in the closet.

She regarded me for a minute. "I don't know why you're getting so worked up," she said. "It's just an engagement party. Pick a basic black dress and be done with it."

"I want to look nice," I frowned. "And I don't want to wear boring black."

"I see." Mona's stare was level. I started to squirm. Then she looked back at the magazine. "All I'm sayin' is anyone who doesn't think *she* has an eating disorder is crazy." She held up the magazine. "Get that girl a sandwich!"

"Mmm-hmm." I returned to my morose examination of my closet. Maybe I was going about it all wrong. Maybe I should start from the shoes and build up. Behind me, Mona slid casually off the bed. Then she darted past and grabbed my cell phone. Too late, I lunged. It was no good. She went right to the call log.

"I knew it," she groaned. "Vi, honestly, again?"

"What?" I avoided her gaze. "We're going to the same party, that's all. I met Katrina and James through Caleb." I grabbed the phone, not that it made a difference now, but I didn't need her to see that there might have been more than the one call.

"Do you really think this is a good plan?" she crossed her arms and gave me a Look.

"What? Yes. No. I don't know." I sat on my bed. "I really don't know. There's no plan. He just called to see if I was going to the engagement party."

"Right," Mona said, unconvinced.

"Okay, so I'm a little wound up. I haven't seen him in a long time." Our paths hadn't crossed since Caleb moved back to D.C. after business school. Except in multiple fantasies played out in my mind. "I just want to look nice tonight, okay?"

"Babe," Mona said, "do you *really* want that mess back? Sometimes what seems like a victory isn't. And pride can skew our perspective quite badly."

"What do you mean, pride?" I asked.

"Well, you guys always get back together. But then it ship-wrecks the same way every time, where Caleb can't commit. Maybe your goals in seducing him back are pride-related. You want him to *want* to have a relationship with you."

"I didn't say I wanted him back," I huffed. "I just want to look nice when I see him." The Feeling that skirted my mind was definitely Dishonesty, chased by Guilt, though it wasn't clear who I was deceiving. I didn't have a very clear head when it came to Caleb, so untangling my Feelings was a complicated business.

Mona looked at me in a way that let me know she knew exactly what I was thinking. "It's like you keep reliving this scenario with Caleb, thinking that eventually you'll 'get it right' and he'll pick you. He clearly has c-c-c-c-commitment issues." Mona drew out her stutter, making me laugh. "And at the end of the day if you 'win,' you end up with Caleb. Do you really want that? Or do you just want him to finally choose you?"

It sounded pretty bad when laid out that way. I thought it over. "I don't know. Sometimes I really think we're meant for each other and maybe we just met too young. Maybe we've grown up."

"Maybe," Mona said. "Just be careful. You are," she chose her words carefully, "romantically impetuous. Your faith in people's redeeming qualities is something I admire about you. But be mindful of it as well. Sometimes you blind yourself to who a person is because you focus on who they might be in their idealized form. Besides," she pointed out, "it's got to screw up your perspective to see everyone around you getting married. It's a hyper idealized event."

"Tell me about it." I flopped onto the bed. "I'm almost thirty and single, and every other weekend I'm celebrating another couple's happy joy. What's wrong with *me*?"

"There's nothing wrong with you." Mona flopped next to me. She headed off Nigel, who was slinking in for some ear, and rolled to face me. "The cost of holding out for something amazing might be that you have to be a little more patient."

"Well I'm tired of waiting," I grumped.

She paused. "Are you talking to your mother yet?"

"No."

"Don't you think—"

"No," I shut her down firmly. I was still sorting out my feelings on that one. If my mother had felt anything about her first love the way I felt about Caleb, was her whole marriage, my *family,* a lie? I couldn't think about it. Seeing Caleb could help me figure it out.

Mona relented. "All right. Let's find you a drop-dead outfit. No matter what you decide, Caleb most definitely will have one thing on his mind when he sees you."

"Regret?" I scrambled off the bed.

"Okay, *two* thoughts." Mona grinned and winked.

We agreed on a shimmery bronze cocktail dress that I'd bought just because I liked it and not because I'd been dumped, which we agreed was good karma. The dress came to mid thigh and, with three-inch bronze pumps, showed a dazzling amount of leg.

"Perfect," Mona said. "I can drop you off on my way."

"On your way where?" I asked.

Mona flushed and looked away. I zeroed in on the fact that she was wearing her favorite skirt and boots. "I sort of have a date."

"Hey, that's great! With who?" I beamed.

"The guy I met at that Democratic fund-raiser," she hedged. "We'll see. I'm not sure how he feels about dogs yet."

I gave her a mock stern look and wiggled a finger. "If I'm— what was it?—'emotionally impetuous'—then you err too far on the side of caution. Instead of trying to evaluate the totality of his moral character immediately, why don't you just enjoy the date?"

She regarded me. "How about this—for every modicum of restraint you exercise with Caleb, I'll loosen up an equal amount."

"Woo-hoo!" I cheered. "You'll be dancing on the table tonight!" She laughed.

"Let's go," Mona turned me toward the door. "We have dates with destiny."

"Oh," I scoffed. "Didn't I tell you? I had to dump Destiny. It approached everything with a tedious sense of inevitability, was constantly making portentous statements, and *always* insisted on the last word."

Mona dropped me off and I smoothed my dress unnecessarily. I felt sweaty despite the February cold, so I flapped my arms about to dry my armpits, then pinned on my attitude of Casual Nonchalance and entered the house. Katrina and James greeted me in the foyer. I darted my eyes around, trying for casual.

"Caleb's not here yet." Katrina sweetly shattered my illusion of subtlety. I smiled weakly.

"Oh yes. He did mention he was coming, I recall now." I convinced no one. "So are you excited for the wedding?"

"We couldn't be more ready," James said in an ambiguous way, laying an easy arm over Katrina's shoulders while she beamed at him. A twinge of envy pinched me.

"We're so glad you're coming," said Katrina.

"I'm glad to be included," I replied dutifully. The front door opened. I jumped a foot, ascertained it wasn't Caleb, and realized I had to blot my sweaty armpits. Damn the man. Even his nonpresence worked me up.

"We'll catch up more later." Katrina gave me a squeeze as they turned to greet their new guests.

I found a bathroom and blotted my armpits on overly fancy Renoir print napkins. I checked makeup (good) and attire (great), and went back to the party. A wandering waiter offered me wine from his tray. Practically in my ear a deep voice said, "Make that two," in a way that eradicated all my efforts to have sweat-free armpits. I turned to face Caleb.

"As I live and breathe," I said, "it lives and breathes." Caleb smiled, and suddenly there was no air in my lungs.

"Vi. You look amazing." He clinked my glass, and the Lure flopped over his eye. My hands twitched and I clenched them around my wineglass to prevent reaching out. I focused somewhere near his Adam's apple, where I could glimpse chest hair peeking out from the crisp white shirt he wore open at the neck. He smelled manly.

"It's good to see you, Vi." He looked at me intently. Oh, it was good to see him too.

"Is that so," I answered evasively. "I wouldn't have been able to tell." He tipped my chin up and forced me to look at him.

"I know it's been too long between friends"—that word weighed six hundred pounds the way he said it—"like us. But I've been traveling constantly since I started work at McKinsey, and I'm usually out of town. And, Vi, I'm really sorry about when we ran into each other in Charlotte. It was so unexpected and I felt so awkward. I would have much rather been with you, you know that. How could I not?" He looked right into my eyes when he said this. Suddenly I relaxed. Caleb was not some mythical being or human Mount Everest. He was my Caleb, who'd been in (and out of) my life since I was seventeen. I smiled at him.

"Do you like work?" I relented. He smiled back and placed a hand possessively in the small of my back, guiding me to a side parlor. A waiter passed, and he scooped two brimming wine-glasses to supplement our already full glasses.

"Come with me, said the spider to the fly, and I shall tell you all about it . . ." he whispered in my ear. I shivered in delight and felt the old charge rocket straight from my brain to my hoo-hah and back.

"Don't you think we should join the party?" I allowed him to urge me along.

"I had my two minutes with Katrina and James, and other than that I came to see you. And that's what I intend to do." A part of my brain whispered that I should probe him on why suddenly the full court press. But I didn't. Mona would have been less than impressed.

The parlor he guided me into was cozy. We sat on a love seat in front of a small fire. I was conscious of the length of Caleb's leg touching mine. He put himself out to charm me, and I was an easy mark, relaxed and happy. At one point he retrieved more wine.

"I'm going to be tipsy." I dubiously eyeballed the drinks. "Usu-ally when I have four glasses in front of me, they all contain different beverages, at least one of them water." Caleb winked and whipped from his pocket a mini-bottle of club soda. He knew me so well.

He "walked" his wineglass across the coffee table to lean toward mine, and said in a falsetto voice, "Hey, who invited the nonalcoholic to the party?" I laughed.

"Do you remember the time . . ." I started, and he raised his eyebrows at me. I blushed.

"How could I forget?" He leered. If it was possible to blush more, I did.

His voice gentled. "You were amazing. You *are* amazing." I caught my breath and stared. He clinked my glass without taking his eyes off mine.

"Are you trying to get me drunk on purpose?" I demanded.

"Most definitely." He smiled and put a hand on my knee. "Do you mind?"

Most definitely not. "Jury's out," I said.

Caleb laughed and then launched into a story about his recent jury duty appearance in a dog bite case. "So." He handed me one of the remaining full glasses of wine. Oh my. Was I really on my fourth glass? "You're going to Pittsford. I'm going to Pittsford—where in God's name is Pittsford, by the way?—shall we go ensemble? It makes sense."

Sense wasn't what I was feeling. I was suffused with a warm glow. It wasn't just the wine. It was the feeling I got when Caleb singled me out for his undivided attention—the feeling of being the most important girl in the world. And I was, wasn't I? I reassured myself. After all, it was me he kept coming back to. He was looking at me expectantly. I thought of all the things that *might* happen if we shared a room together. Delicious things.

"Sure," I agreed, wondering if I felt Slightly Compromised. I pushed the Feeling away.

"Excellent. I was thinking surgical strike. We fly in Saturday for the wedding and leave Sunday. We can be back in time to put our feet up and watch football."

I tried not to feel Disappointed that he didn't want to spend the whole weekend. "Sounds good to me." Then I wondered if he meant we'd watch the football together.

"That's my girl." He held up his hand for a high five. When I gave it, he caught my hand and brought it to his lips to place a kiss on the inside of my wrist where my pulse beat wildly. We froze like that. Caleb shifted my hand to cup his cheek. Then he slowly leaned toward me.

"There you are!" a bright voice interrupted. Then giggled. "You two. Not again," protested Katrina. "Come along and join the party. Caleb, James has been mourning for you. He's had about all of the formal 'Thank you for coming' and 'Yes we're so excited' that he can handle for one night. I think you and he and a tequila bottle are about to make three." She surveyed the row of empty glasses on the coffee table. "Not that you need it . . ." She giggled again. "Come along now. Up! Up!"

We were shepherded off by Katrina's efficient effervescence. Caleb shot me a look of regret and I swear he mouthed *Later* at me. I couldn't be sure, though, because as I stood I staggered as the alcohol made itself felt. I needed food. I walked carefully to the buffet and piled a huge plate of food. I was stuffing chicken fingers and mini egg rolls into my mouth when I intercepted Caleb's look of desperation from where he stood by the bar with James and the predicted tequila bottle. I took pity and brought a plate over. James turned when I approached.

"Vi, remember when we went to the Outer Banks and that baby possum was in the downstairs bedroom? It couldn't have been more than six inches long and Katrina was running around screaming that there was a bear in the room. And you walked in cool as a cucumber and bundled the little guy up in a towel and took him outside." James laughed.

"That was nothing compared to when the Jacuzzi caught the deck on fire because *someone* turned it on without checking to see if there was any water in it," I scoffed.

"How was I to know the realtor was a slacker?" Caleb defended himself. He slipped his arm around my waist, stealing food off my plate. I leaned into him and it felt right. We were different people, but still the same. This time it would be different.

CHAPTER TWENTY-ONE

$Vi + Caleb = Plural$

"I think I might still be drunk," I said as I accepted a glass of wine from Ellis.

"Fun party?" she asked, pouring herself some. Babette was sipping something milky, on ice. I decided not to ask.

"Mmm-hmm," I answered noncommittally.

"Any talent?" asked Babette. I considered how to answer. It was inevitable that the truth would out, but I wanted to forestall the harangue as long as possible.

"Nothing new," I said truthfully. "What did you guys do?"

"Well, Jack and I had absolutely no fun this weekend at all. We looked at invitations, listened to dreadful wedding band audition tapes, and fought four times—the band, his mother, tuxedo styles, and his mother again."

"Scale?" I asked.

"Moderate. The worst one, about his mother, was only a 4.5. But he absolutely *insists* on inviting her." Ellis cracked a smile. "I suppose I'll give in, but only after he expends valuable political capital, enabling me to triumph in the tuxedo debate." She sighed. "All we accomplished was getting on each other's nerves. So we get to waste more weekends. And the dumbest part," she meditated, "is that I never thought I gave a rat's ass about tuxedos, yet now it's consuming me. Wedding planning isn't fun. The only upside is that you get to taste a lot of cake."

Mona and Imogen bustled noisily up to the table. Actually, Mona just walked up to the table. Imogen bustled noisily.

"Well." Mona lanced me with a look as she reached for the wine. I sighed and braced myself. It was Game Over. "Did you sleep with Caleb last night?"

Direct shot across the bow. Oh man. It was going to be worse than I thought. A hush fell over the table. I looked down at my hands and peeped up guiltily through my lashes at faces frozen in mixed expressions of shock and horror. Imogen recovered first.

"Whaa-aat?!" she screeched. I winced. We all winced.

"Hey, man, don't break the glasses," Charlie called as he passed by the table.

I shot Mona a dirty look. She smirked back, pleased with herself. "Well?"

"No," I emphasized. "I did not." Only because James had insisted on dragging Caleb out for a boys' night after the party and I was too drunk to think of a clever way to foil the plan. Then I went home and passed out, sleeping through several late-late-night missed calls on my cell phone. But they didn't need to know that.

"You Went Out With Caleb?!" Imogen stared.

"Well, for heaven's sake," I flapped. "It's not like he's a serial killer or Karl Rove. We're old friends and we were at the same engagement party. That's all." I crossed my arms, ready for the next assault. It came from Land Mine Mona.

"Well, I think it's good you guys caught up," she said. I relaxed, vindicated. Imogen boggled at Mona and drew in a breath to blast her when Mona continued. "Because that'll make it less awkward when you share a hotel room in New York for the wedding." She gave me a fiendish grin while Imogen erupted.

"Are you absolutely insane? Do I need to march you home and parade half the contents of your closet before you?" I started sliding down in my seat. "Caleb is Bad News. Bad News, I tell you. Have you seriously lost your mind? What on earth prompted this?" Imogen was flailing now. I went lower. Everyone held their drinks safely away from her waving arms. Mona and Ellis each grabbed one of mine with their free hands, as I kept sliding and couldn't reach. My butt hit the edge of the seat. I looked longingly under the draping table cloth. It looked safe.

"Imogen." Babette braved the dervish and put a calming hand on her shoulder. "Stop the mountain from a mouse house." Imogen windmilled to a stop and huffed in exasperation. She slumped back in her seat to glare at me, muttering.

"Whoa," I said from below the table. "Tell me how you really feel. Geez—it's not like anything is happening." Everyone looked skeptical.

"Vi, sit up and face the music," Mona commanded. I reluctantly pushed myself into a grown-up sitting position. "So, how was it?"

"It was, it was . . ." I let out a breath. "It was *wonderful*. But nothing happened!" I hastily assured Imogen.

"Yet," she grumbled darkly.

"But he was charming and attentive. And thoughtful." I smiled, recalling last night.

"And still hot, we may presume," Ellis's tone was dry.

"What?" I snapped back to them. "Oh, yes. Definitely. Mmm-hmm," I nodded. I looked around the table seeking understanding. "Guys, what if he's my one true love? I mean, he's the one I think about whenever I think about the future. I compare all my relationships to him. And my scalp hasn't tingled since we broke up."

"Scalp tingling?" asked Ellis.

"My scalp only tingles when I kiss someone amazing. Look, on the one hand you can see it like Caleb broke my heart. But the reality is that we were nineteen and living on opposite sides of the country when we broke up. *Nineteen.* No one stays serious from nineteen. Think of what I would've missed if I had." I rushed past this bit because, brilliant in theory, in practice I hadn't done anything earth-shattering with the time. "Since then it's like we're hooked on each other. We try other things and then come back. But we haven't been in the same place since high school. Maybe this is our time."

"The time line doesn't change the fact that when he left after these 'casual summers,' you were devastated. Even if he didn't do anything wrong, *you* got hurt," Imogen pointed out.

"Imogen . . ." I pleaded. She softened, and reached for my hand across the table.

"Honey, I'm trying to understand, I really am. I've seen you two together, so I get it more than you think. But it was also hard to see you inconsolable. I don't want you to set yourself up for more avoidable anguish."

"I think it'll be different this time," I argued. "I really do. You should've seen him last night. He was devoted and lovely and . . . well . . . *mature.*" I wasn't sure what I meant by "mature," since tequila shots and late night booty calls didn't epitomize maturity, but it was a persuasive sounding argument and I was sticking with it.

"It's not that I don't like Caleb," Imogen responded. "I really do. But I worry that he's not the settling down type. And I have doubts that relationships can be successfully reinvented."

"I guess I need you to trust me to figure it out," I said slowly. "Let's see how New York goes. Nothing may happen." I looked around the table. Nobody was buying that one.

"You're a smart young lady and I know you can take care of yourself." Babette reached out and squeezed me affectionately. "We just hope you know what you're doing."

"I do, I do," I assured them all.

* * *

"You're doing what?!" Ethan's voice reflected disbelief. I gripped the phone tighter.

"Um, just going with Caleb to this wedding we're both attending."

"As in the Caleb? The love-of-your-life-to-date Caleb?" Somehow, despite the words, Ethan didn't sound thrilled for me. "The broke-your-heart-three-times Caleb? The I-left-you-for-a-girl-named-Edna Caleb?" Ah. Now that was much worse.

"Her name was Agda. And, um, yes. That one. But the whole Agda thing was complicated." After college freshman year, Caleb had asked me to spend the summer in San Francisco. Worried about money, I stayed home. He met a girl named Agda and dumped me. "If you recall, she broke up with him because she said he was hung up on me and we'd end up married." I defended. It was not a memory I savored.

"That's not how I recall it," Ethan said sternly. "As I recall, it was pretty simple boy meets girl. Boy meets other girl. Boy forgets about girlfriend. Unoriginal Plot Number Seven."

"Are you going to lecture me?" I pouted. "I thought you might be a teeny bit happy for me."

Ethan was quiet for a moment. "I do want you to be happy. I'm just worried this will make you sad. And difficult to console. Then I'll have to grocery shop alone because you'll be home doing waterworks or something and Imogen will have a very bad time of it."

"Honestly, I think people are more concerned about the impact this relationship will have on Imogen than on me."

"Especially Imogen," Ethan agreed.

"Not that it's a *relationship*," I rushed to correct. "We're just pooling resources."

"Right. Until you're pooling bodily fluids."

"Oh, Ethan, yuk." I got warm thinking about pooling with Caleb.

"Listen, kid, you know I want you to be happy. I'm just not sure about this guy."

"I'm being careful, Ethan, I swear," I promised him.

"Well then, I hope you know what you are doing," he said.

"I do, I do," I assured him.

"Wow," said Jen over the phone.

"Yeah," I opted to laugh, choosing my own interpretation.

She was quiet a minute. "You guys always had quite a thing," she mused. "If it works out, it would be quite the fairy tale, wouldn't it?" she mused.

"Or fate."

"Just be careful."

"I know what I'm doing," I promised.

"Are you serious?" Maeve asked.

"Yes." I tried not to sound defensive.

"I hope you know what you're doing." She sounded like she was eating an apple.

"I do, I do," I assured her.

What the hell am I doing? I thought as I strapped on my seat belt. I felt woolly and disoriented from sleeping on the plane. I'm not a good napper. I go too deep under.

"Feeling woolly?" Caleb massaged my neck. I blinked blearily at him.

"Hmm? No. Fine." I opened my eyes really wide to seem alert.

"I got you a treat." He grinned, dangling an icy cold Coke between two fingers. I snatched it gratefully and took a deep swig, sighing with pleasure.

He chuckled and settled his arm across my shoulders. "I'm glad you're here."

"Me too," I said. We were quiet a while.

"So," he tugged my hair, "what do you think Pittsford will be like?"

"Small." I laughed. I'd looked it up on the Internet. "I got all excited at first because Pitts*town* is in the Hudson Valley, with acres of beautiful parks and over five hundred lakes and ponds."

Caleb looked at me with a smile. "And?"

"And?" I repeated. "And what?"

He tugged on my hair. "If I know that remarkable brain of yours, you've ferreted away a few fun facts about Pittstown. Or Pittsford. Whatever."

"Well," I launched in, "Pitts*town* is in Rensselaer County, which is named after the guy who founded the oldest degree-granting engineering school in the English-speaking world. It was an iron producing area, and forged the old ironclad battleship the *Monitor*. Remember the battle between the *Monitor* and the *Merrimack*? Local iron makers also made the replacement for the cracked Liberty Bell. And the moniker 'Uncle Sam' was coined from a meat packer named Sam who shipped provisions to U.S. troops. Oh, and Herman Melville wrote his first two novels there."

"But . . . ?" Caleb raised a brow, smiling.

I puckered my brow. "But that's *not* where we're going. We're going to Pitts*ford*. No acres of trails. No five hundred lakes. Just one canal," I said in a disappointed voice.

Caleb laughed out loud. He brought my hand to his mouth and planted a kiss on it. "You are one of a kind. And I do enjoy you." He settled back into the driver's seat, still holding my hand. "Now tell me about Pitts*ford*."

"Well," I flushed with pleasure, "Pittsford is a historic Erie Canal village . . ."

It seemed we arrived at the Renaissance Del Monte Lodge Resort and Spa within minutes of leaving the airport. As we parked the car, I felt my nervousness return. We hadn't discussed our status. Despite the flirting and handholding, fairly normal for us,

Caleb might think we were just bunking together as buddies. Which was perfectly fine, I assured myself. I'd just like to know. To avoid completely humiliating myself in the manner of flirting and smiling at a man until you realize he's actually flirting and smiling with someone over your shoulder. Right. Expect nothing. Be composed and calm. Aloof.

Caleb grabbed our bags and headed for the reception. I followed after him, composed and calm. On the outside. Inside I was doing a boogie. He was carrying my bag. That meant something, right? A brunette stick with boobs was working the reception.

"Ah, Mr. Carter. One nonsmoking king room, for one night?" asked the perky hostess. I held my breath, waiting for Caleb to demand two beds.

Instead he gave the hostess his most charming smile and said, "That's right."

She fluttered a bit as she checked us in. I was momentarily too giddy to fume over the flirting. King bed! Yay! I'm about to have a romantic, sexy weekend with the former love of my life. Suddenly I love weddings.

"And you're with the Milhorn wedding?" According to her tag, the hostess's name was Dani, and it seemed that she was taking an inordinately long time to check us in.

"Yes, ma'am," Caleb twinkled. Dani beamed at him. I hated her. I wished I was comfortable enough to drape myself on Caleb, but it was too early for that. Not that I was the draping type, mind you. Come on, Vi, I chided myself, get a grip. Caleb held my eyes a minute, as if he could read my thoughts. I forced my game smile on.

"I have a little treat for you." Dani handed Caleb a gift bag, brushing her fingers over his as he accepted it. Tart.

"I believe we should have *two* gift bags," I cut in on her assault. "My name's Vi Connelly." She gave me an assessing look. I smoothed my hair. When Dani turned to check the bags, Caleb gave me a wink. I got the feeling he was enjoying this.

"I'm sorry," she meowed, not at all sorrowfully. "I only have a Kevin Connelly."

"That's me," I declared. She looked doubtful. I raised an eyebrow. "Want to see some ID?" I challenged. Caleb interceded.

"The lovely lady is indeed Kevin Connelly," he assured Dani. I was a little mollified, but still bristling in the presence of a competitor she-cat. She wasn't getting her claws into *my* gazelle.

"Well, then." Dani refocused on Caleb, who was unabashedly amused now. "Here you go," she purred, handing over the room keys. "I gave you one of our best rooms." I'm not sure how she managed to ensure that "you" conveyed singular and not plural, but she pulled it off.

"Well thanks." Caleb flashed his lethal smile again, tugging the key envelope from her.

"You" (singular) "have a good night, and don't hesitate to call if you" (singular) "need anything," Dani persisted. Yeah, Dani. Sure thing. I'd ricocheted from giddy to murderous in approximately fifteen seconds. How did being around Caleb do this to me?

He slipped an arm around my waist and said to Dani, "I've got everything I need right here." He looked in my eyes and gave me a squeeze. Dani looked crestfallen, I noticed smugly through my euphoria as we (plural) walked away. Ricochet.

We were silent in the elevator. Caleb led the way to the room, dominated by an enormous bed. He hung his garment bag, and put my duffel on the luggage rack. Then he approached, staring intently at me. My heart began to pound. He took my fidgeting hand and inspected it carefully. Then he met my eye.

"Just checking," he said, quirking a brow.

"What?" I was confused.

"Making sure you've retracted your claws," he teased. "I wouldn't want to get scratched in the cross fire." I flushed. God, this was embarrassing. Men couldn't stand a possessive bitch. Especially Caleb. I'd made him completely uncomfortable and now he wanted me to disappear.

"So, I thought we'd clear one thing up, little kitten with claws," he continued seriously. Oh God. He was going to sit me down and explain that he wasn't looking for a relationship. That I'd completely misunderstood. That we were friends sharing a room for convenience. That he was going to meet Dani for a drink when she got off work and please don't come in if there's a sock on the door.

"Um, no need," I blustered, unable to meet his eyes, and tugging on my hand. Perhaps I could salvage my pride at the bar. Right now. It was acceptable to drink at, oh, noon, under extreme circumstances of humiliation and discomfort. Like this.

"Vi." Caleb caught my chin. "Look at me."

I looked up miserably.

"There's no one I want to be with but you." He lowered his head to mine, and before I recovered from my shock, he was kissing me. I felt all the air whoosh out of my lungs, and my pulse exploded and scalp tingled. I loved to kiss Caleb. And kiss him. And kiss him. And I did.

I sighed as he lifted his head. He smiled and tapped me on the nose with his finger. "I'm glad we cleared that up. One room, one bed, one couple. Simple math." One night, I thought, but pushed it aside. "So," he bent to nibble on my neck, sliding his hands around my waist. "We have four hours to kill before the wedding. What *shall* we do with ourselves?"

"Wedding," I murmured. "What wedding?" He chuckled against my skin and I shivered.

Several hours later we were driving to the wedding and I couldn't wipe the goofy grin from my face. I was decked out in a 1950s strapless tulle dress, with delicate ribbon sandals. Caleb was dashing in his black suit. He caught me looking at him, and reached out for my hand, lifting it to his lips. "Delightful," he said quietly. My insides somersaulted.

The wedding was very tasteful, the service longer than twenty-two minutes because Katrina had a cousin who could sing. The reception passed in a blur. We sat with Caleb's college buddies. It was an odd feeling, both old and new at the same time. As comfortable as it seemed, it also felt fresh. We kept unnecessarily touching one another in the manner of unsullied infatuations. After dessert, a swing band began to play and Caleb held out his hand, which I took with alacrity. The best thing about Caleb was how we danced. Well, the *second* best. I was pretty light on my feet thanks to Southern training, and with Caleb I walked on air. He twirled me, and I spun into a temporal plane of undiluted happiness, only surpassed later when we made our excuses to duck out early and, clutching hands, hastened back to our room. This was definitely right, I thought. Definitely.

"Helllooooo." Babette snapped her fingers in front of my eyes.

"What?" Startled, I jerked my attention back to the present. It was Sunday night. Oh, right. I was at Clyde's with the girls. Caleb and I had returned that afternoon from New York. I smiled to myself. Caleb . . .

"There she goes again," said Ellis in fascination.

"It's fantastic," Babette marveled. "I've never seen anything like it! She's on the moon."

"I have," said Imogen in disgust. "Four or seven times."

"It *is* like she's in outer space," said Ellis. "Let's get her to sign a bunch of legally binding documents. Mona, write something up."

"I still can't get over the fact that she hasn't ordered any extra drinks. She's just having wine." Babette sounded awestruck.

"Hmmm?" I refocused on the table.

"So." Mona was laughing in her drink. "Tell us about the wedding."

"Oh, it was nice. Really nice." I stretched really into extra syllables. Then I nodded. "Mmm-hmm. Nice."

"We can see that," Mona grinned. "And how was Caleb? Did he go?"

"I don't know if he went but he definitely came. Several times from the looks of it," muttered Imogen, drumming her fingers on the table.

"What?" I concentrated on them. They were uniformly smirking. Except Imogen, who had a unibrow. "Man do I feel good."

"So sayeth a woman who's had sex for the first time in over a year," commented Mona.

"Not just sex. *Good* sex. No, *amazing* sex. Curl your damn toes four days later just thinking about it sex," I corrected Mona. Babette laughed delightedly.

"Well, I am elated," She beamed at me. The French always favored more sex.

"Well, I hope it lasts," Imogen said sourly.

"Imogen," Mona chided. "Now's not the time."

"Imogen, it's going to be fine," I reassured her. "Caleb was amazingly sweet. Did I tell you what he said about how there was no one he wanted to be with but me?"

"Yes," said Ellis.

"Yes," said Babette.

"Yes," said Mona.

"You mentioned it. One or a hundred times," said Imogen.

"Well it was sweet. Oh, and then he—"

"Said all he needed to be happy was right here," chorused Mona and Babette, laughing.

Ellis looked at Mona. " 'The Sixth Sense'?"

"I think 'The Chronicles of Pornia,' " Mona countered.

"Okay, okay." I waved my white napkin. "I concede. I'm being a total git. But, you guys, it was an *amazing* weekend. He's perfect."

"Did she just say 'amazing' for the eighth time?" Ellis asked Mona.

"She did, but blessedly we're only clocking in at four for 'perfect,'" Mona reported.

"You undersexed harlots can all just bite me," I grumbled. "Jealous wenches."

"This has verged on the ridiculous," pronounced Imogen. "Vi, did you actually attend the wedding? Or just the hotel?"

"Oh the wedding was nice," I replied.

"That is nine for 'nice,' the dark horse, hurtling past 'amazing,'" Mona muttered to Ellis. I ignored her.

"The bride was gorgeous, the food was delicious, and the band was awesome. We danced all night long. Caleb is *such* a good dancer." Imogen's eyes fought to roll completely back into her skull.

"So when's your next wedding?" asked Ellis.

That brought me down with a bump. I grimaced. "God, it's on Valentine's Day. Can you believe it? What kind of saccharine freaks get married on Valentine's Day? Even good sex afterglow doesn't make me imbecilic enough to think that is charming—it's cheesy."

"But you're going?" asked Mona.

I looked at her surprised. "Of course."

Mona laughed at my answer. "You know, Vi, you don't *have* to go to all these weddings."

"Well, sure I do." I was bemused. Who doesn't want to go to a wedding? If I hadn't been invited, my feelings would've been a little hurt.

"Is Caleb going with you?" Imogen spoke up, examining her nails.

"Are you being mean?" I asked suspiciously. She met my eyes, and I thought I detected a gleam of Guilt.

"No." She shook her head. "Sorry. Just curious." She waited for my answer. I fidgeted.

"I don't know. We just got back. I haven't asked."

"So," Imogen failed at sounding casual, "when do you see him again?"

"Actually, I don't know yet." I failed at sounding nonchalant. "He's in Houston for work until Friday." Truthfully, I did wonder when I'd hear from Caleb. He said he'd call me. After our amazing weekend, I was sure it'd be soon.

"Oh," said Imogen.

CHAPTER TWENTY-TWO

Crossed

Chris Marries Chris, Sugarbush, Vermont, February 14

I stared in disbelief at the heavyweight, oversized cream-colored envelope I'd pulled from the mailbox. I mentally ran through the lengthy list of friends getting married and came up blank. The return address in Harrisburg, PA, was not helpful. I opened the thick paper bomb and extracted the inner envelope. *To Mrs. Kevin Connelly.* I sighed. No *and Guest.* It was from Dee, a social friend. I'd vaguely heard she got engaged, but never expected to be invited. Normally I felt graced by receiving a wedding invitation, but my usual delight was tempered. I know it's a rite of passage in your late twenties to attend lots of weddings, but thirteen? When Mona and I got the invites for our friend Adele's four-hundred-guest wedding, Mona had speculated what exactly one would have to do to be left *off* the list. The gleam in her eye when we'd agreed that sleeping with the groom's father might do it had alarmed me. But she'd had a point that it was hard to convincingly feel special among four hundred similarly "special" others. I wouldn't invite Dee to *my* wedding. Nonetheless, I was free that weekend. Sadly, it was in Harrisburg. I looked regretfully at my treasured, but costly, copy of the Sunday *New York Times*.

"Oh, Book Review, I hardly knew you," I muttered, and picked up the phone to cancel it.

"Sid Dickens, this is Ben speaking. How may I help you?"

"Hey Ben. It's Vi." I announced.

"Ms. Connelly. How delightful. How can I assist you today?" Ben responded brightly.

"By calling me Vi, for starters," I instructed. "And I need to order three tiles."

"This must be a special couple."

"Oh, no. It's for three separate couples. Didn't I tell you I had thirteen weddings?" I was amazed there was someone left I hadn't bitched to.

"You're a popular young lady."

"Word got out about my great gifts. Invitations are bucketing in. I've narrowed the last one down to either my hairdresser's niece or my boss's mechanic." Ben laughed. I was elated. I got Genteel Ben to laugh! We were tight now.

So," he resumed his serious air. "What shall it be this time?"

"Okay, for couple number one, that's Chris and Chris—" Ben started to cough. I squinted at the phone. "You really should get that cough looked at."

"I'll see to it the instant we are off the phone," Ben lied.

"Right. Okay, Chris and Chris . . ." I paused for another cough, but Ben remained composed. He was good. I ran him through the tiles.

"I particularly like that tile myself," Ben said as I gave my last order. I felt ridiculously pleased with his approbation. "Shall I charge these to the credit card on file?" Ben shattered my pleasure bubble. I winced in embarrassment.

"Actually, I'm going to divide it up." I felt like a college freshman, splitting a Dave Matthews Band ticket across multiple credit cards.

"It's understandable, Vi. Weddings in bulk can be expensive," Ben sympathized.

"Tell me about it," I sighed. I gave Ben all my credit card numbers (and I mean *all*) and decided that I'd better cancel Showtime channel. Farewell dear *Weeds* Monday nights at 9:00 P.M. Henceforth my only *L Word* (a wedding-free program) would be Liability, for my debts. Or maybe Loanshark. Hopefully not Leg reconstruction.

Chris and Chris were actually Christopher and Christina, but they'd each always gone by Chris and saw no reason to change now. Astonishingly, Chris was taking Chris's last name, indicating a misplaced reliance on people's diligence in using a middle initial when addressing mail. The Chrises were athletic, jocular types who sealed their love through a series of extreme sport adventures and tender application of plaster to one another's wounds. I liked spending time with them, though frequently I felt like a battered hockey teammate after all the sport, shoulder slapping, and enthusiastic clunking of beer steins. I tried to avoid rafting, hiking, or skiing trips and stuck to competitions I could win, like meeting for drinks. The wedding, however, was a group ski trip to the slopes of Sugarbush, Vermont, on Valentine's Day. It loomed the Saturday after next.

I'd been invited with a guest, but hadn't replied with one. I was counting on there being at least one sexy ski bum. Chris (Y-chromosome) definitely had attractive, athletic friends. But now I was fretting over Caleb. Even at this late date Chris (X-chromosome) would happily include him if I asked. The kicker was, I couldn't ask her because I hadn't asked him. Hadn't been *able* to ask him, I corrected. Crap.

It was Thursday night and I was on my couch alternately

stewing and eating ice cream. The Movie Starring Me was "Cone Alone." I stared at the phone with Hate. It'd been four days, and I hadn't heard from No Call Caleb. Supposedly he was returning from Houston tomorrow. Pathetically, I hadn't made weekend plans. Which I'd been sure I'd spend with him. Over the week, my confidence had eroded. I knew they had phones in Houston. My cousin Jared lived there. To Jared's astonishment, I'd called him this week for the first time in eons for no reason whatsoever. Just checking in. On his phone line. It worked fine.

Part of the problem was the looming double deadline. First, Valentine's Day, the vilest holiday of all, was the nine-hundred-pound Gorilla in the room—pretending it wasn't there was equivalent to wondering how the New Testament was going to end. If you had any romantic connection with a sentient being, you had to address it, either scoffing or serious.

Second, the whole fake holiday thing made it doubly awkward to invite Caleb to the February fourteenth wedding. And I felt time pressure. I hated when I wanted to plan something but couldn't get other people in gear. So, I was getting exorcised, when Caleb had no idea he'd done anything upsetting. I punched at the sofa cushion. Nigel woke up.

"You'd go to Vermont with me, wouldn't you Nigel?" I cooed. He blinked his lantern eyes and did a lazy meow, which came out sounding like "ick." Then he did mashed potatoes on my chest with his piston paws. Then he zoomed in on my ear.

"Bleah." I wiped off the drool and shoved him to the end of the couch, where he happily curled up, sure in the knowledge that the gig was up for the night. Clementine disdainfully observed from her perch on the back of the couch, tail flicking restlessly.

I went back to my own flicking, channels. Nothing was on. I called Mona.

"Isn't Valentine's the vilest holiday of all time?" I demanded.

"Yes," she agreed without hesitation. "So, he still hasn't called?"

"No. Should I be freaked?"

"No. You're getting yourself knotted up because you're a Type A control freak and you're desperate to nail down the details for the Vermont ski weekend. It doesn't mean anything outside your own head."

"Thanks. I think."

"You're welcome. I gotta go." She said something muffled that sounded like Charlie Brown's teacher, whispering close to the handset through cupped hands.

"Oh, right." I remembered. "That guy's there. Seeya later, 'bye." I hung up.

The next day at four-thirty I miserably checked my Gmail account for the nine thousandth time. Nothing. Friday night and I had nothing to do. Not Saturday either. I didn't want to go out anyway, I thought. I wanted to stay home and wallow. Forever. They would find me years from now with long scary curling fingernails and hair like Cousin Itt from the Addams family, mumbling unintelligibly to myself and compulsively tapping my head.

The phone rang.

"Can I use olive oil for the chocolate wonder cake recipe if I'm out of vegetable oil?" Maeve asked.

I grimaced. "Ugh. No. Use margarine."

"Genius. What's going on? How's the baby panda?"

"I haven't checked today," I said listlessly.

"Why so glum, chum?" It sounded like she was eating chips.

"No reason," I sighed.

"Oh boy. That's a Caleb sigh, isn't it?"

I sighed again. "He hasn't called."

"Tell me." I did. She was quiet. "He'll call," she finally said. "Be patient. After Pittstown—"

"Pitts*ford*."

"Whatever. Pittsville. He'll call. But Vi, you know I love him, but be careful." Her reassurance left me feeling no better.

I refreshed Gmail. Nothing. I considered asking Giles to send me a test e-mail, weighing the net negative of his mocking jibes against the benefit of knowing Gmail was functioning properly. Doing actual work didn't even cross my mind. The phone rang again.

"Vi Connelly," I said listlessly.

"Hello, darling," Caleb's voice sounded richly in my ear. I jerked upright so quickly I had to clutch my desk to keep from toppling. Giles raised an eyebrow.

"Caleb." I struggled to calm my breath. "How'd you get this number?"

"It wasn't easy. Vi, you have no idea—it's been like Chinese water torture not being able to call you and wondering what you must be thinking."

I perked up. This sounded good. "What do you mean?" I went for casual.

"First of all," he said, "I miss you." He paused a beat. "I really missed you. I wore the tie from James's wedding to a work dinner this week and it had your perfume on it. My client caught me sniffing it. I was an utter disgrace." I smiled in delight.

"Anyway, I got sent to Dubai for four days and, jackass that I am, left my cell phone at home in a jacket. So I'm in the Middle East with no computer access and no way to get in touch because your number's only in that phone, and you know I can't remember a number for shit once it's in my phone. I know it sounds outrageous, but I swear it's true. I really wanted to call. I googled your work number the minute I got to a computer today. I hope this isn't a bad time?" he apologized.

He was so forgiven.

"Not at all." Forgiven or not, no way are you hanging up without asking to see me, big fella.

"Listen, I've just got a minute. I'm heading to the airport for my flight to D.C., but I'd like to see you tomorrow night if you're free? I've only got the weekend before I have to come back. This project is brutal."

"Saturday? I think so." Giles rolled his eyes at my line of total crap. "Let me see . . . yes, yes. Saturday should be fine." Yes, yes, yes!!! Caleb was coming home and wanted to see me. Hurrah! I did a hippy shimmy in my chair. Then had to grab the desk again.

"That's good news," Caleb said evenly, but I could hear the smile in his voice. "I can't wait to see you. What do you say to something low key? Nice dinner and then maybe a movie on the couch at my place? Or even order in?" He sounded hopeful. And tired.

"That sounds perfect." I was elated. "I just want to see you."

"Great. Listen, I've got to go. I'll call you tomorrow." I blew a kiss at him and hung up, transformed. Ricochet.

"Giles, what're you doing tonight?" I descended on him. "I'm in the mood to party."

He pretended to cower. "Oh my. You used a noun in a verb format, defying one of your own cardinal rules of grammar. I'm frightened." I laughed and levered him out of his chair.

"Let's go. Ethan's at City Tavern. Let's meet him for drinks on his tab. For starters."

I passed Saturday morning spending quality time with Nigel and Clementine and tidying the apartment. I was in such a good mood, I even called my parents for a brief chat, though it was limited to nonpersonal things. I was trying. At noon I motivated to lunch with Imogen and Ethan at Peacock Café in Georgetown. I wore my baseball cap for invisibility, saving my shower and hair wash for later. More than one wash a day could make my hair more limp (if that was possible), and I wasn't taking any chances. After lunch I hurried home to get ready for my date. My preparations were more tactically planned than the invasion of Normandy, and would take approximately two hours. Most would cause me to suffer discomfort of some kind—plucking, waxing, scrubbing, exfoliating, and unnecessarily itchy face mask. Then there was the tedious drying of the hair and laborious selection of the outfit (time schedule allowing for several changes). Caleb's preparations no doubt would take twenty minutes and involve (1) taking a shower (maybe) and (2) combing his hair (maybe).

At six-thirty I was ready astonishingly early, because I'd chosen my outfit (7 For All Mankind Jeans, Juicy Couture sweater, and red cowboy boots) without second-guessing. So I had to sit on my hands for half an hour and fend off Nigel's snuggle assaults so I didn't get covered in cat fur. Like that worked. At seven on the dot I defurred with the lint roller and hailed a cab.

Caleb opened the door and gave me his heart-stopping smile. My heart actually did stop. He drew me in for a kiss. "Good to see you," he murmured against my lips.

"Good to see you back," I agreed breathlessly, pressing against him.

After a minute he pulled back. "Come in. Hey, I got you something."

"You did? What is it?" I bubbled with delight as I followed him in. He grinned and tossed me a plastic bag. I looked inside and pulled out an I ♥ HOUSTON T-shirt.

"Awww. It's so sweet. I especially like how they spell out 'love' inside the heart, in case you weren't sure what it meant."

"I thought you'd like it," Caleb said. "It was either that, a Gay Asian Pride Houston T-shirt with a rainbow yin yang on it, or a T-shirt that said, 'Everything's bigger in Texas except my boyfriend's small penis,' which would not do." I felt a jolt. Boyfriend? Bliss.

"It's perfect. I love it."

"There's more." He handed me a plain white envelope with

a picture of a bow drawn on it in red pen. I opened it curiously. Inside was an airplane ticket stub from Houston to Dubai. "I wanted you to know I wasn't jerking you around," he said, and pulled me over for a long slow kiss. I thought I might melt or weep, I was so gooey.

"Come into the den." He tugged my hand. "I built a fire. Would you like some wine?"

"Yes, please." I contentedly settled myself onto his squishy leather sofa. *Especially* contented when he sat too and pulled me back against him.

"Tell me about your week," he said against my hair, so I did.

"How was Houston?" He groaned and reclined more, pulling me along.

"Don't make me talk about it," he begged, wrapping his arms around me and squeezing. "Houston is the armpit of the world, and I have to go back next week."

"All week?" I asked carefully. Vile Valentine's Day was Saturday. He hadn't mentioned it. But boys didn't really notice these things unless nudged, right?

"Yeah. But I don't want to think about it now. I just want to enjoy being with you." He gave me another squeeze. "Do you want to order takeout? I was thinking Thai." I battled my internal dialogue. Should I ask him about Vermont? Should I wait until he'd relaxed more? We were sort of on the subject now. But he needed to unwind. I would wait.

"So, Thai? What do you think?" Caleb asked. I would definitely wait.

"Um, Caleb, there's this wedding next weekend," I burst out in a rush. "In Vermont, at Sugarbush. I was thinking maybe you could come with me. It's a quick trip, but we could ski. I already paid for a room." His body tensed a little. I babbled on. "I know you'll be beat, but maybe it's just the thing, you know, get away from it all, the anti-Houston. Relax." Oh God, this was horrible.

I'd only been in the house for ten minutes and I was making demands.

Caleb sat us both up, and turned me to face him. "Babe, I'm not
insensible to the fact that next Saturday also happens to be Valentine's Day." I flushed and looked away. He pressed his lips to my
temple and said sexily into my ear, "Which I would be delighted
to spend with you . . ." My pulse skyrocketed and I swear I had an
honest-to-goodness hot flash. Ricochet. ". . . if I could." He pulled
back to look at me. "But I can't. I have to be in Houston all week.
Then, I promised some of the guys that we'd spend the weekend
in Austin. You know, they're all single and have nothing else to
do." He gave me a smile. "I promised them *before* Pittstown."

"Pitts*ford*," I corrected glumly.

He laughed and gave me another kiss. "How about this? The
weekend after next I'll be here. Why don't we pretend it's Valentine's Day then? We'll celebrate without the hassle of fighting
other couples to get a dinner reservation. What do you say?"

"You're sure you can't come to Vermont and ditch those dumb
boys?" I wheedled.

He laughed again and tapped my nose. "I'm sure."

I sighed. "Well, then, I guess that will have to do. But I want a
present."

"I have just the gay Asian pride T-shirt in mind," he said,
wrapping his arms around me and settling me back against him.
"Now, about that Thai food?"

"So, you're okay with it?" Mona asked sleepily. It was pretty early
for Saturday, ruling out a call to Imogen. All my morning phone
calls went to Mona.

"Fine," I said firmly. "He had preexisting plans."

"How's the snow?" Mona loved to ski too. I looked out the cab
window. "It looks good." I could hear Mona yawn. "Hey, I'll let
you go."

"Okay," she agreed.

"So," I asked, "what're you doing tonight?" There was a pause. "Mona?" I nudged.

"Um. Well. I'm sort of having dinner with Brad." I perked up.

"Really? That's the guy from the fund-raiser?"

"Uh-huh. But it's no big deal. I mean, it's just dinner—"

"It's *Valentine's* dinner." I started to hum "Going to the Chapel." She hung up on me.

The lodge checked me in early, dispensed my wedding swag bag, and directed me to a room with a gorgeous view of the slopes. It was only ten-thirty and I was itching to get out there. Before I went, I dialed Caleb's cell phone.

"Hello? Caleb's phone," a woman answered. Shock radiated through my body, and my lips went numb. "Hello?" the voice repeated.

"Um, hello . . ." I stammered. "May I speak to Caleb?"

"No, he's not here yet. He left his phone at the office, so I'm getting it back to him later. I thought this might be him calling. Can I take a message?" If Dani was perky, this woman was honeyed. Smooth and sure of herself. Suddenly, I was not.

"Um, okay. Can you tell him Vi called?"

"Oh, Vi. He said to tell you that he left his phone and would call you later somehow. He got your number from me," the rich voice suggested helpfully. I did not feel helped.

"Um, okay. Thanks, 'bye." I hung up quickly. I slumped on the bed, suddenly plagued with doubt. Was that as innocent as Honey had suggested or was something going on? I thought unbidden of Agda. I'd talked to her on the phone too, and there was always an innocent explanation. As it turned out, there'd been a not so innocent explanation too. But Caleb *was* prone to leaving his phone everywhere. Please, I prayed fervently to God, looking at the hotel ceiling as if eye contact could occur. If you're watching, please let Caleb be on the up and up. Don't I deserve it finally? I didn't believe in making rash promises to God ("I'll never drink again" or "I'll give more to charity") because, I mean, He's God. He can tell when you aren't telling the truth. But I wasn't above begging. My phone rang. I didn't recognize the number.

"Vi, it's Caleb." Did he sound anxious?

"Hey," I said neutrally.

"Babe, I'm so sorry—I wanted to call you right away to warn you that Audrey might answer my phone, but I wasn't sure when your plane landed. I'm sorry if that freaked you out. God, what a git I am about cell phones, huh?" I softened. Then I stiffened. Had Audrey told him that I had freaked out? I was distinctly certain I had *not* freaked out. "Baby?"

"I'm here. Hey, it's no big deal, I forget my phone all the time too." Not. "Where are you calling from?"

"Sanjeev's phone. We're in Austin. Man, Austin is great. I wish you were here."

"Hm. Me too. Vermont is gorgeous, though. I'm getting ready to ski."

Caleb laughed. "I'm torn! I wish I could be with you there too. I'd love to be in two places at once." Then he dropped to his sexy voice. "I couldn't sleep last night thinking about your skin." A glow suffused my body. Caleb was being more demonstrative than he'd ever been. People didn't say things like that unless they meant it. Or were feeling guilty, a nagging little voice in my head whispered. I ignored it.

"I miss you too," I said. "I feel like I haven't seen you in weeks. Oh, wait, I haven't." My tone was only half joking. I was getting annoyed with his travel schedule.

"I know, baby. But I'll see you next week. Will you be my Valentine?" he flirted.

"You betcha," I consented, "but it'll cost you."

"I can't wait until next weekend," he murmured into the phone.

"Me too."

"Listen, I have to run—the guys are waiting. Will you call me later?"

"Sure. What number should I use?"

"Oh you can call my cell. Audrey's bringing it 'round, so I'll have it this afternoon."

"Oh?" I feigned interest, feeling anxiety in my gut.

"She's coming to hang tonight in Austin. Cool girl. But nothing like you. I keep telling her how wonderful you are. See you soon." He hung up.

Oh.

At four-thirty that afternoon I crunched my way out to the slope behind the lodge hoping my stock winter wedding outfit of chocolate brown velvet long skirt and matching top would keep me warm, but I suspected the faux fur cuffs had limited warming capabilities. At the mountain base, where the green and blue slopes merged, a runner eased guests across the snow to folding chairs arranged before a wide trellis wreathed in evergreen boughs. I could see Chris's brother escorting his grandmother carefully to a front row seat. Grandma slipped and slid and didn't look happy. Other guests stepped gingerly, looking trepidatious and pulling coats on more tightly. By 4:45 P.M. we were all seated waiting for the ceremony to begin. I passed the time trying to read the program, but my gloveless hands were freezing so I gave up and shoved them in my pockets. After another few minutes I felt like an ice cube and was fantasizing about hot tubs.

A man to my left cursed. "Ridiculous nonsense. People should get married in nice warm places, with alcohol and padded seats." I think I nodded, but it may have been compulsive shivering. I tried to think sexy thoughts about Caleb to warm me.

The priest took his position at the trellis and the talk fell silent. I worried that everyone could hear my teeth chattering. Despite being glacial, I had to admit the view was stunning, a beautiful snow-covered slope dotted in evergreens spread before us. The chairlift lights twinkled on as the sun descended. I wished Caleb was with me. The tasteful piano music playing in the background got louder and changed to the "Chariots of Fire" theme. I stifled a giggle.

"Think they'll play 'Ironman' next? I left my Black Sabbath T-shirt at home," the man to my left said in a theatrical whisper. Then, at the top of the green run to the left, I could make out a figure skiing toward us. A billowing figure. I sucked in my breath in astonishment, then coughed as the frigid air hit my lungs. It was Chris(tina), in a wedding gown. I don't know why I was shocked. It was her wedding, after all. But I'd thought because it was a sporty outdoor wedding, she would wear . . . what? Ski clothes? No, naturally she would wear a wedding dress. It was just so . . . unexpected. Especially the flowing veil.

"Jesus, she must be freezing," I heard a woman behind me mutter.

No, *I'm* freezing, I thought, sitting in the cold like an idiot, turning blue. At least Chris was getting a workout.

"I hope she doesn't crash," her date sounded like he did.

"It's a bird, it's a marshmallow, it's the ghost of Christmas past, it's Polar Bride," sang the comedian on my left, as a second figure caught my eye. A tuxedo was skiing down the blue run.

Chris(topher) was skiing fast, cutting edges, and generally showing off. Chris(tina) was skiing precisely. It couldn't be easy maneuvering in that gown, but her run was perfectly controlled. They seemed on target to arrive at the trellis simultaneously. The bride slowed as she approached and executed a perfect stop directly in front of the priest, angled to face the guests. Chris continued to barrel down the slope, evidently planning to roar to a stop with an impressive spray of snow and fanfare. Just as he reached the altar and started to cut his skis, he caught sight of his bride. She looked beautiful in her wedding gown, with pink flushed cheeks, snowflakes in her windblown hair and veil, and sparkling eyes. His jaw dropped and he forgot what he was doing. The audience gasped as Chris, riveted by Chris, plowed on a direct collision course into Grandma.

Six people went down with Grandma and the groom. The bride screamed but was stuck in her skis. Guests not yet in deep freeze leapt up to right people and chairs and dust snow off Grandma. The groom was pushed upright and backward to his correct place at the altar. His mother fixed his hair and straightened his tuxedo. Everyone was uninjured, just startled.

"Let's get this goddamn wedding going so I can get inside where it's warm and get a drink, for Christ's sake," I heard Grandma bellow once she'd been reseated. "I'm freezing my goddamned ass off." I hoped I was sitting at Grandma's table.

CHAPTER TWENTY-THREE

The Have Nots

Traci Marries Tim, Washington, D.C., March

"I can't believe she's wearing a tiara," Caleb muttered out of the side of his mouth.

"Shhh." I poked him, giggling and looking over my shoulder.

We were at the Manor Country Club in Rockville with about 150 other guests, watching six girls march down the aisle in skimpy red dresses to the tune of "Friends" by Michael W. Smith. They joined six men with red vests, who I expected to burst into barbershop capella at any moment. Now, the bride, a cashier from D&D, hustled down the short aisle in a heavily beaded confection with a V-neck, long satin sleeves, and a Snow White skirt. Michael W. Smith barely had time for two stanzas of "I Am Sure" before she was in front of the minister tapping her foot impatiently, shooting looks at a young man off to the side. He leapt to stop the CD in mid-verse so a twelve-year-old could lisp through First Corinthians. After the briefest of secular ceremonies (seventeen minutes, a new record), we were ushered into the adjacent ballroom.

At the front table was the expected lineup of cards. I picked up mine, expecting to see a table number, but there was nothing. It merely read:

Miss Vi Connelly
and
Mr. Caleb Carter

Caleb didn't know Traci and Tim, but after two glorious months we were a settled couple, and he confessed to being a willing hostage for free booze and food. We'd snickered our way through the tacky ceremony in good spirits. Now, I turned our card over, wondering about its purpose. I noticed the man next to me

Mr. Niall Devlin

had something attached to his card. I looked at the man himself to ask what it was and sucked in my breath. I couldn't help it. Was he *ever* my type. He was maybe six-foot-three, with a body Maeve would spank even out of uniform. *Preferably* out of uniform, thought my naughty self. He had a delicately boned face with cheekbones like razors and rich dark brown eyes behind eyelashes wasted on a man, all framed by a wild mop of reddish, brownish curls. He smiled at me, revealing absolutely perfect white teeth.

"Glad to have one of these," he said in a lilting Irish accent. I didn't absorb his meaning, reeling from the effect of the sexy accent on top of the sexy human. I was trying not to swoon. I was also trying to inhale his smell. It was woodsy and masculine.

"Vi?" Caleb snapped his fingers in front of my eyes. "Where'd you go?"

"Huh?" I blinked at him. "Oh. Sorry. Spaced out." Long Legs

and Lashes had disappeared. I focused on Caleb. Did he look shorter? "Come on, let's find the bar."

We walked toward a bar set up behind a velvet rope. A man looking like Stone Cold Steve Austin in a tuxedo stood by a gap in the cord. I figured our card was an admission ticket and handed it to the guy. He looked at my arm.

"No wristband?"

"What?"

He sighed as if I was exceptionally thick, and repeated with exaggerated slowness. "Do . . . you . . . have . . . a . . . wristband?"

I recalled the cards with things attached. Ours didn't.

"This bar is reserved for the wedding party and special guests." My mouth gaped in disbelief. "You need to go over there." He pointed to another bar across the dance floor.

"Humph." Caleb gave a disgruntled snort. "Looks like they're hoarding the top shelf liquor." As we approached the steerage class bar, I saw a guest hand the bartender a bill. Uh-oh.

"Um," I started to say anxiously, when Caleb exploded.

"What the hell? Beers are five dollars and wine is six-fifty! You've got to be kidding! Who brings money to a wedding? It's a country club, for Christ's sake. Even members don't use *money.*" He spat the word with revulsion, as if he too had been raised with such privilege that to handle filthy lucre was beneath him. He turned to me. "Do you have money on you?" I desperately scrambled in my purse but knew I only had a twenty. Who *did* bring money to a wedding? I handed the bill to Caleb.

"Great," he said in disgust. "I have a ten. That's five drinks with tips. Hopefully they won't charge for food." He pointed a finger at me. "You're drinking beer tonight, princess. And no club soda. We have to ration." I felt irrationally guilty, even though the invitation hadn't said anything about a cash bar. I accepted my beer meekly. A waiter passed with a tray of mini hot dogs and chicken fingers. I helped myself. Caleb turned up his nose. I grabbed a few more in case he changed his mind. I suspected it might be all the food the lower castes got.

"Maybe they'll have a champagne toast," I channeled optimism.

"Nope," said a fellow walking by. "There's no free punch for the unwashed masses. Christ, I only brought twenty bucks. This sucks." Caleb perked up at the discovery of a soul mate and followed him out to the patio, where there was a rumor of cigars. I drifted toward the dance floor to watch, settling discreetly out of the way by the French doors facing the patio. To my right the glitterati in the velvet rope section were getting roaring drunk, guzzling champagne and happily snacking on stuffed mushrooms, crab cakes, steak satay, and salmon.

"And now, ladies and gentlemen, the bride and her father!" The bride approached the dance floor and, to everyone's surprise, unhooked a clasp and whipped off her Snow White overskirt to reveal that her wedding "gown" was actually a minidress. The DJ started pumping out "Baby Got Back," and the admittedly ample-bottomed bride and her father started "doin' the butt" for their father-daughter dance. It was a side of Traci I didn't see at work.

"I must say," lilted an enchanting voice. "You don't strike me as a beer-in-a-paper-cup drinker." I looked up. On the right side of the velvet tracks was Mr. Niall Devlin. I steadied myself.

"I hear hops are good for the skin. I thought I'd give it a try," I joked.

He appraised me. "Love, nothing could improve upon that fair complexion." He gave me a roguish smile. "Stay right there." As if a human being turned completely to liquid could move. He disappeared into the crowd.

The atmosphere seemed to diminish when he was out of sight. After a few minutes of ridiculing myself for waiting upon a Category One hottie who was *not* going to return, but nonetheless rooted to the spot, he reappeared. He sidled in a mock secret agent way up to the rope, without looking at me. He looked at the ceiling and bobbed his hips to and fro, whistling, as if idly passing the time. He cast a comic look over his shoulder, then stage whispered out of the side of his mouth, "I've got the goods. Don't let *them* find out or your man's wristband is a goner." He advanced a few steps and I could see that he had two glasses of red wine in his hands, which were clasped behind his back. He turned his back to the rope, so the wine was held toward me. I giggled. I sidled up to the rope with exaggerated nonchalance, casually looking in the other direction as I swiped the wine from his grasp. We sprang apart. I glanced back at him as he winked and tapped two fingers to his nose in a secret salute. Just then a willowy brunette came out of the crowd. Niall turned to her, shielding me with his back.

"Niall," complained a pouty voice. "You left me. Where's my wine?"

"Sorry love." He put an arm around her shoulders, effectively blocking her view, and herded her into the crowd. "That miserable beast Gregory snatched it from me. Let's fetch you another." As he walked away, he threw a last look and grin over her shoulder at me. I inclined my head back at him.

"Vi! Don't tell me you wasted our money on wine! I told you we'd get more bang for the buck with beer!" The peeved voice of Caleb pulled me back to the wrong side of the rope.

We took a minipoll and agreed that we'd never heard of a segregated wedding.

"That's *so* tacky." Ellis was horrified. "Did they really serve hot dogs?"

"Only to the proletariat. The noblesse got filet sandwiches and crab cakes. What really cheesed me was the cash bar. I'm so broke from all these weddings I keep retrenching at home. My one comfort is free food and booze."

"Retrenching how?" asked Ellis.

"So far, I've downgraded to Scott tissue"—everyone winced, and rightly so—"canceled my Sunday *Times* and premium cable, switched from lattes to regular coffees, taken to home waxing, generic shampoo, and sacrificed all nonwedding travel."

"When I was saving for spring break in Jamaica, I ate spaghetti with butter every day for a month. I didn't eat Italian for years after that," said Imogen.

"I sold plasma in college," Ellis offered. "Hurt like a bitch."

"Ugh, I worked at Rax," Mona said. "Seriously—there's a fast food chain in Ohio called Rax. Who thought it was a good idea to name a restaurant after the sound of barfing? I had to wear this hideous polyester uniform and visor, ring people up, and make milk shakes. In my third week my huge crush, Robert, came in with his girlfriend and ordered six shakes. It was abject humiliation. I never went back."

Imogen patted Mona. "Still stings?"

"Oh yeah."

"I had a roommate once who paid the rent by being a test subject for medical experiments," Babette said.

"They pay you for that?" Imogen asked.

"Yep. She would do all kinds of crazy stuff, like not sleep for forty-eight hours and take a test or eat weird things and run on a treadmill. One time she had to lie in bed for four days and not move a muscle. She couldn't even stand up to pee."

"And they paid her?" Ellis marveled. "Hell, Jack does that for free."

"It sounds like a job for Urine Luck," I joked.

"They pay pretty well," Babette said, "once you get on the NIH list." That caught my attention. NIH was just up the road.

"What kind of list?" I asked. Imogen squinted at me.

"I'm not sure but they never seem to get enough people because she dragged me along once when we wanted extra cash for a party. I had to take a thousand mgs of vitamin C every day for a week and report my feelings and undergo tests. I swear I was dizzy the entire time and my pee was neon. It was terrible." I thought it sounded like easy money. I noticed both Mona and Imogen looking at me now. I changed the subject.

"Well, hopefully there won't be any more cash bars. I'm running out of budget to trim."

"It sounds like Caleb was a cow's ass about the cash bar," Babette said.

I sighed. "Can you blame him? We only see each other on weekends, and I drag him to a tacky wedding where he doesn't know anyone, there's no food and a cash bar, and the music was of the Vanilla Ice variety. I'm surprised we stayed until ten."

"What a total waste," Imogen said. I thought of Irish Dream, but decided to keep that to myself. A nice interlude, but I'd never see him again. Willowy pouty brunettes got those guys.

"So how *are* things going with Caleb?" asked Mona.

Yesterday I'd have been singing, but last night hadn't been great. After the wedding he'd called a bunch of friends to go out, but no one answered. Sulking, we went back to his place, where he channel-surfed and drank beer. At 1:00 A.M., exhausted, I'd gone to bed alone. This morning he'd raced off to the gym first thing. I was a little hurt. It wasn't *my* fault about the wedding. I'd driven him to the airport on my way to Clyde's. I sighed.

"Things have been really good," I said. "But he *was* a butt about the wedding. And I Feel all Guilty, like it was all my fault."

"It wasn't," said Imogen. "And he shouldn't make you feel that way." I shot her a look. She held up her hands in surrender. "Hey, I'll admit, I've been impressed. He spends every weekend with you, and has committed to weddings through summer. Even I wouldn't do that." I made a face at her.

"I know. He's been great. But I'm tired of the work-travel thing. He's gone all week, and on the weekends he wants to see his other friends too, so we go out a lot. We don't get a lot of time alone."

"He won't be in Houston forever," Ellis soothed.

"What did you guys do this weekend?" I was tired of talking about Caleb.

"Nothing," said Mona.

"Nothing," said Babette.

Ellis made a disgusted sound. "Wedding planning."

Imogen spoke up. "Ethan and I saw *An American Daughter* at Arena Stage. It was really good." I was surprised. Imogen and Ethan were friends, but usually all three of us did stuff together.

"Really? He didn't mention it," I said, curious.

"Maybe he forgot. He was at school all day. You know how he is when he's studying." Imogen avoided my eyes. Hunh.

"Yes," I mused. "I do. So, how did you—"

My phone rang. Caleb. He always called when he landed. "Excuse me." I slipped out of our booth. Did Imogen look relieved?

"Hello?"

"Hey, babe."

"Hey back. Have you landed? That was fast."

"Long enough for me to kick myself aplenty." He paused. "Listen . . ." My gut clenched. Oh God. Not over the phone. "I was an ass this weekend. I'm sorry. You didn't deserve it."

I was so completely surprised I couldn't say anything. Ricochet. I clutched the phone, weak with relief but unsure where he was going. After it became clear I wasn't going to talk, he continued.

"What would you say to coming down to Houston this weekend? I'll get you a ticket." Did he sound anxious? "I miss you."

I relented. "I miss you too. And I'm sorry about the stupid wedding, Caleb." I wasn't sure what I was apologizing for, but I wanted everything to be right between us.

"That's okay," he said. "Listen, I have to run. Audrey's picking me up and I don't want to keep her waiting." I wrinkled my nose in distaste at Audrey's name, though I knew I was being irrational. "Email me the flights you want and I'll book it." It sounded like he was walking outside. "Can't wait to see you, babe."

I walked back to the booth, thoughtful.

Imogen stopped talking suddenly and grabbed her wine, jiggling her leg under the table. Babette wiped a grin off her face.

"I just love pinot noir." Ellis burbled. I looked at her oddly but was preoccupied.

"Who was that?" Mona shot a look at Ellis.

"Caleb," I answered, thoughtful.

"Good news?" she asked. I felt a smile creep over my face.

"Yes, I think so.

CHAPTER TWENTY-FOUR

What's In a Name?

Barbara Marries Norman, The Poconos, Pennsylvania, April

"Norman wants me to take his name." Barbara stirred her tea. We were sitting in the Pocono Cinema and Coffee Shop the day before my college friend got married at Skytop Lodge.

"You don't want to?" I was surprised. I wouldn't have pegged Barbara for a strong feminist stance in the name department. Her last name was Slutsker.

Barbara Slutsker laughed. "Are you kidding? The first time I fell in love it was because his last name was Smith."

I laughed. "So what's the problem?"

"It's *his* last name." I tried to recall it.

"I'm embarrassed," I confessed. "I don't remember it."

"My lovely fiancé's name is Norman J. Cartland."

I fell apart in giggles at the image of Barbara's head on the stout taffeta-clad body of the maven of bodice-ripping romance novels.

"Stop," the future Mrs. Barbara Cartland begged me, laughing. "It's not really funny. I finally get to dump Slutsker, and for what? It'll be 'Barbara Cartland calling,' and people will head for the hills thinking I'm hawking romance subscriptions." She shook her head. "You're so lucky. Carter is a lovely nice name."

I sucked in hot tea and scalded my throat. Barbara had to pound me on the back to stop my coughing.

"This is my kind of wedding." Caleb dropped a salt-flecked kiss on my lips. I wiggled my empty glass at him and he samba'd over to the Margarita Momma machine. I wondered where he'd found the sombrero. My gaze softened, then I caught myself sharply. I'd been having irrational wedding fantasies since Barbara's comment earlier. Vi Carter.

"You guys seem happy," Barbara commented, catching my stare.

I smiled. "We are." I felt the wispiest beginnings of a security that had previously eluded my grasp with Caleb. I also felt righteously vindicated. My parents might have screwed up the first love thing, but I wouldn't. Patience was the right decision.

Caleb returned and tugged me toward the handkerchief-sized dance area filled with couples. "It's time to salsa."

"Arriba!" He smiled at me. Damn, he was beautiful.

"Arriba." I repeated, letting him pull my body against his long frame. I felt the familiar zing.

He leaned close and whispered in my ear, "Come on, baby, and salsa with me." So I did.

My head had barely hit the pillow when Caleb was tickling me under the covers. I gasped and writhed to get away.

"Please stop, stop," I begged. My head was killing me. Too many margaritas.

"Come on, wake up," he said. "We can't waste this bed." Instead of Skytop Lodge, Caleb had insisted we stay at an over-the-top Poconos hotel with a heart-shaped bed and champagne-glass whirlpool tub. We'd tested it all last night.

"Tacky," I muttered.

"Sinsational," he corrected, kissing my neck and shoulders, and . . .

Bliss.

Several hours later we were seated under a tent, studying the wedding program.

"Oh look," Caleb gave his refrain. "First Corinthians."

"Look at their names." I told him. I waited for it to dawn. It did.

"You've got to be kidding," he laughed. "She won't take it, right?"

"Norman wants her to." I paused. "Would you?" I went for offhand.

"Wife?" Caleb laughed. "Who knows? I never thought about it. Marriage is an alien concept right now." He slung his arm over my shoulders and twisted in his chair to look up the aisle. "Wonder when this gig will get going? I'm starving."

His casual dismissal exposed the mental scab my insecurities couldn't stop picking. Shit. I'd been envisioning us frolicking in the park with a passel of tow-headed children and Caleb laughing down into my eyes in the sunlight. Did I want to get married, or did I just want to live a ReMax® commercial? Either way, he was only thinking about food.

The music changed and the wedding began. Out of habit I checked my watch. Thirty-one minutes later the minister held his hands over the beaming couple and announced, "I now present to you for the first time, Mr. and Mrs. Norman and Barbara Cartland."

Was it my imagination or did Barbara wince?

The reception was on the lawn of Skytop under a tent. Dinner was over and I was alone at the table drumming my fingers. Other couples were dancing, but my date was smoking cigars by the bar.

I was Ignored and Resentful. I picked up my wine and joined a group of girls, but didn't listen to their conversation as I glowered at Caleb. I passed an unpleasant half hour fuming and getting increasingly irritated as he (1) didn't notice the fuming and (2) didn't come for me. The thing I loved most about Caleb—his ability to become best friends with anyone he met—also drove me completely crazy, as I often felt excluded or cheated out of private time. I was determined that for our honeymoon we would go to some extremely remote island where he didn't speak the language so I could get him alone. Oh shit. Did I just imagine our honeymoon? Now I wanted a Carnival Cruise commercial.

Right. I could brood or I could do something about it. I marched over to where Caleb was entertaining his Merry Men. I waited until he finished his story before tugging his sleeve. He turned and grinned.

"Hey babe," he said. "Where've you been?" I waved about vaguely.

"Caleb, I'd like to dance." The band was swing, my favorite.

"Oh. Hey, listen. I'm not really in the mood for dancing tonight. Do you mind? I'd rather chill out and enjoy a cigar." Obviously I minded, if I came over to ask. Several of the guys feigned that they couldn't overhear this humiliating conversation.

"Can I talk with you a minute?" He looked like he'd rather not, but agreed.

He followed me out of the tent and down a path to a gazebo. "What's up?" he asked.

"You tell me," I countered. "You haven't spoken to me all night."

"Vi, that's not true. I've been with you all day. Remember the part where I sat by you at dinner and passed the butter? Don't I get a minute off the leash?"

"Leash?" I was incredulous. He looked repentant.

"Look, I don't want to fight. Let's go back inside and have

a good time. There's nothing sinister going on. Please don't over-think everything. You make yourself miserable."

"Pardon me for not trusting you," I snapped. He froze.

"We're not starting that again, are we?" he asked in a hard voice. I felt shamed. I was being unfair.

I hung my head. "No. I'm sorry. I just . . . I just . . . I don't know. I guess I was thrown this afternoon when you said you'd never considered getting married." I couldn't believe I was bringing it up.

He sighed. "I thought that might be it. Vi, I'm being honest when I say I'm not thinking marriage now. I want to be with you. But I can't promise anything beyond that. I'm focused on my ca-reer. I thought we were having a good time together? That you were happy."

"I am happy," I said miserably.

"Then come on, give me that smile." He tipped up my chin and wiped a tear off my cheek. I looked at his endearing face. I did love him. So, why did I feel like I was looking at a photo that's slipped in its frame, revealing a little of the cardboard behind?

"Is my girl in there?" he coaxed. I nodded.

"I love you," I said. He kissed me tenderly for a long minute, then took my hand and led me back to the party, where he contin-ued to hold it while laughing with the other guys. When the band played "It Had to Be You," he led me to the dance floor. It was only later as I lay awake listening to him sleep that I explored how I felt about him not saying anything back.

CHAPTER TWENTY-FIVE

Forever Hold Your Peace

Alfonso Marries Carmen, Alexandria, Virginia, May

From: ViViVooom@gmail.com
To: Ben@siddickens.com
Sent: April 12
Subject: You Get More of My Money

Ben,

Hi there! I need (another) Memory Block. Can you please send one T-110 tile to Alfonso Muñoz at 121 Prince Street, Alexandria, Virginia, 22314? I work for Al's wine shop, so I think he'll like the grapes on that one. Did I tell you I'm a wine buyer? You should tell me your favorite wine and I'll ship you a bottle. Have the card say something like, "Al, best wishes on your marriage to Carmen. I hope, like a fine wine, your relationship only improves over time. Love, Vi." Or is that too cheesy? Tell me if you think it's too cheesy.

Oh, and guess what? Barbara caved in. She took Norman's name. She's now officially Barbara Cartland. (Snicker.) Can you imagine? And remind me to tell you about Traci and Tim's wedding. Cheap bastards had a cash bar. Is there any way to get my tile back???

Tell Sid to name his Maserati after me.

Best,
Vi

From: Ben@siddickens.com
To: ViViVooom@gmail.com
Sent: April 13
Subject: Re: You Get More of My Money

Vi,

I continually marvel at the number of weddings you attend. You have quite the stamina for nuptials. I do hope you will continue to think of Sid Dickens for your wedding gift needs. I'm sorry to hear your access to alcohol at Traci's wedding required exchange of legal tender. Sadly, we already shipped the tile. Perhaps next time you should order your gift *after* the reception?

I will promptly see to processing the tile for Mr. Muñoz. I am sure he'll appreciate the thought you put into the gift. Your card is very sincere.

I feel for the new Mrs. Cartland. Perhaps name confusion will open some doors for her. Tell her to visit the Elizabeth Arden spa in New York, and instruct them to "put it on her bill." And let us hope you do not begin to date someone named Mr. Agra.

Sincerely,
Ben Applegate
Sid Dickens Sales Representative

P.S. I believe Sid drives a Mercedes Benz.

From: ViViVooom@gmail.com
To: Ben@siddickens.com
Sent: April 16
Subject: Re: Re: You Get More of My Money

Ben,

You're a funny guy. Don't worry about a Vi Agra. I've been seeing my old boyfriend Caleb again. Remember Caleb, from Katrina and James's wedding? It's been going great. Well, mostly great. Oh, I don't know. Sometimes it's great. I don't know what to think. I could use some advice.

—V.
P.S. So what are my tiles buying? Braces for Sid's kids? It eases the pain to know.

From: Ben@siddickens.com
To: ViViVooom@gmail.com
Sent: April 16
Subject: Re: Re: Re: Re: Re: You Get More of My Money

Vi,

I am at my desk. Call anytime.

Yours,
Ben

P.S. Take heart. I believe Sid sponsors a number of World Vision children from impoverished countries.

"So, thanks for coming," I said awkwardly.

"No problem." Caleb never took his eyes off the road. We were driving to Old Town, Virginia, for Al's wedding.

"We don't have to stay long," I reassured him. "I know the last thing you want to do is go to another wedding. Maybe we can meet up with James and Katrina later."

"Vi, it's fine. Stop apologizing," he ordered.

I fidgeted in my seat, tense. "So, how's Houston?"

"Same old, same old. Sorry I couldn't come back last weekend. I do nothing but work. I'm not very interesting these days." I wracked my brain for ways to coax him into good spirits. I was dying to know, but refused to stoop to "What are you thinking?" We rode in silence. I reached over and took his hand. He finally looked at me with a gentle smile and lifted it to his lips briefly.

It was a second wedding for Al and Carmen, both widows. They seemed perfectly suited. The gathering was small—family and a few friends. I'd been surprised—and flattered—to be invited. Al saw us enter the church and came over. I gave him a hug.

"You look great!" I smiled. He fussed with his collar.

"Do you think so? It's been a long time since I wore one of these."

"Definitely," I assured him, smoothing out the creases he'd

created. He seemed nervous, glancing around repreatedly. "Looking for the bride?" I teased.

His eyes jumped to mine. "What? Er, no. My son." Something caught his eye and he tensed. "Excuse me—there's Carmen's family. I should go. Take your seats—we'll start soon."

I squeezed his hand. "Al, I'm so happy for you." He gave me a grateful smile.

"What was that about?" Caleb asked under his breath as we entered the church. "He looked like he expected to be shot."

"No idea," I murmured back. "Maybe he's afraid Carmen is having doubts." A woman who looked like she'd sucked on a lemon handed us a program. Possibly her face was taut because her hair was scraped into an incredibly tight, hard little bun. My scalp ached looking at her.

"Bride or groom?" she pinched out. An odd question when there were only thirty guests.

"Groom," I answered. She pursed her lips more, if that was possible, and dismissed us to the right side of the church. We slid into a pew.

"Oh look." Caleb read his program. "First Corinthians."

A second later Giles slid in beside me in a lime green suit. "Did I miss anything?" he whispered.

"No. It hasn't started yet."

"No," he hissed. "Did I *miss* anything? You know, the *drama*."

"Drama? What do you mean?"

"You don't know?" Giles looked at me, not believing someone could live oblivious to the human spectacle. He rolled his eyes. "The extended families are *tragic* about this marriage. Apparently the children are devastated. Not ready to let go of mater and pater departed, think the old folk are rushing in."

Caleb perked up. Suddenly the wedding became interesting. We looked around. Few people were smiling. I recognized Al's son Carlos in the front pew with a grim set to his mouth. He was matched by a dour-faced woman across the aisle, presumably Carmen's daughter. There were other assorted displeased-looking people sitting by the daughter, including the hatchet-faced program attendant, a stern man who favored quantity over quality in hair product, and a teary young girl who looked like she'd just heard her Hilary Duff concert was canceled. It was a crowd more suited to a genocide trial than a wedding.

There was a swell of organ music and Al stepped to the front of the church in a before-the-firing-squad stance. Without fanfare, Carmen walked stately down the aisle wearing an elegant cream suit and determined set to her shoulders. She smiled directly at Al, who relaxed a little. Giles actually rubbed his hands together.

"You're morbid," I whispered.

"Shut up. You want something to happen too," he dismissed me.

"I definitely do," murmured Caleb.

Carmen and Al joined hands in front of the minister and the service began. The wedding program portrayed a graceful recognition that both celebrants had been previously married and mourned their lost spouses but were moving on. It progressed smoothly until Al's son rose to read a poem. He walked heavily to the podium and read as if announcing layoffs in Flint, Michigan. Halfway through he choked up and garbled the rest. The young girl began to cry.

Al looked like he'd been tasered. The minister was startled, but recovered and called the next reader. Hair Product man bit out something unintelligible that ended "gate breast peas ugh," but which I suspect was our old friend "the greatest of these is love." The girl's cries became more anguished. I winced. Caleb appeared to be trembling until I realized he was shaking with laughter. A harpist sat at her instrument and began to play. Guests stared hard at the harpist, trying to pretend nothing was awry. The harpist was sweating with so many eyes boring through her.

The girl was now keening with grief. Caleb covered his mouth with his hand as if in contemplation. I couldn't look at him or I was going to giggle with nervousness. Giles gazed fixedly at the harpist with a pious expression, only the quirk of his lips giving him away. The harpist finished her piece and fled the stage with obvious relief. The minister soldiered on, launching into his homily as Al and Carmen stared fixedly at each other. Carmen's knuckles were white as she clenched Al's hands. The girl wept on. In fact, most of the front pew seemed to be in tears. Finally, the minister began the vows.

"If anyone knows a reason this couple should not be joined in marriage, let them speak now or forever hold their peace."

We all tensed. The minister was rushing but there was still a pregnant moment. Giles looked around avidly. The girl bawled, the front row sniffling sympathetically. The minister raced on. After thirty-nine painful minutes it was done. The minister motioned the happy couple to face the audience. He beamed at the crowd and intoned, "I am pleased to introduce to you for the first time, Alfonso and Carmen Muñoz."

Al and Carmen clasped hands and faced their guests, smiles pasted on, while the sound of sobbing filled the church. Sitting next to Caleb, our bodies not touching, I knew how they felt.

Instead of a reception, Al and Carmen had invited their guests to join them for dinner at La Bergerie. We left as soon as it was over. By 9:00 P.M. we were driving back to D.C. and I was looking forward to a quiet night with Caleb. I was lost in my musings when he spoke, causing me to jump. I giggled at his look.

"Sorry." He smiled and tousled my hair. "Baby, do you mind if I just drop you off and head home? I'm beat, and what I want more than anything is a good night's sleep in my own bed." He looked at me with an expression that practically had an ® next to Earnest Look.

"Um, sure," I lied. We hadn't spent the night together in three weeks. "I understand." I didn't.

"Thanks." He steered the car toward my place. I felt like I'd been here before. Caleb and I were getting serious and he was pulling away. Or worse.

He put the car in Park as he pulled up to my apartment. He did look exhausted—there were creases around his eyes. He smiled at me. "Come here, kid." I leaned over and he kissed me. "Thanks for being a sport.

"Thanks for coming to the wedding," I said.

"I'll call you tomorrow. Maybe we can grab brunch before my flight?"

"I'd like that," I said, and slid out of the car. I shut the door and turned to say something through the open window, but he was already driving away. I watched his taillights in frustration. If only I hadn't had a wedding this weekend. If only I didn't have a wedding practically every weekend. Did he think I was trying to channel messages to him? If only I'd been more laid back as opposed to being stressed about how he was feeling. If only . . .

"How come you're home on Saturday night?" I asked Maeve a few minutes later when she answered the phone. I wanted to talk to my mother. I suspected she'd understand, but I didn't want to admit I needed that kind of advice. I'd called my sister instead.

She crunched chips in my ear. "It's damp out and I'm out of echinacea. I can't risk getting sick." I decided not to ride her about her hypochondria. "So what's up, buttercup?"

"I honestly don't know." I rubbed a contorting Nigel. At least one creature was happy Caleb had dumped me at home for the night. "Technically everything is fine, but I have a bad Vibe, you know?"

"Yeah, I know. The Vibe is never wrong. I got the Vibe with Andy."

"Andy made out with another girl right in front of you."

"Yeah. That was a bad Vibe." Maeve at least could always make me laugh. "So, are you coming home for Mother's Day?" Crunch, crunch.

"I'm not planning on it."

"This isn't still about Mom and—"

"No, no," I cut her off. "I've got too many weddings. When I have a free weekend, I want to relax." Nigel purred in accord.

"I think you're totally overreacting. So Mom was married for a nanosecond when she was younger than me. Big deal. Get over it."

"Tell me if this sounds like me hanging up," I said, and hung up. I was no longer sure what made me so squeamish. My conviction that my mother's secret previous marriage corroded her later, seemingly happy one, was slipping. Also, I missed her. What I did know was that I had a bad Vibe about my own high school sweetheart, and it made me a little panicky. If Caleb and I didn't work out, did that mean spinsterhood? Or could you love someone that much again? It seemed hard to believe. I shook myself and heeded the lure of the Häagen-Dasz bar in my freezer. I had to stop being negative. You are the thoughts you put out there, and it was premature to be pessimistic. Caleb and I were fine. I was sure of it. And my Jack Johnson CD was just the thing to drown out the whispering Vibe.

CHAPTER TWENTY-SIX

My New Career in Medicine

"Well, you look like a perfect candidate for a broad number of categories," beamed the perky woman at the NIH. She tapped at her computer. "In fact, we have something right now if you have time." I was startled. I'd been excited about volunteering at NIH for extra cash, but I hadn't expected to start immediately.

"Um, what did you have in mind?"

"It's a study of the effects of caffeine on cognitive responses. It only takes about an hour." My, she *was* perky. "That one pays forty-two dollars." Whoa. For drinking coffee? Cha.

I was all smiles. "Where do I go?"

Two hours and the equivalent of a zillion cups of coffee later, I'd trembled my way through an SAT-like test and was white-knuckling my steering wheel and sweating profusely. I thought my heart would burst from my chest.

"Drink lots of water," the researcher had advised as I left. She'd patted my shoulder, and I'd jumped a mile.

At home, I raced to the kitchen and guzzled an entire liter of water standing in front of the open fridge. This could not be good

for you. I didn't want to do any more volunteering at the NIH. I
might actually be having a heart attack. I dialed Maeve. A benefit
of hypochondria, she knew the symptoms to everything.

"I'm dying," I told her.

"What from?" she asked. It sounded like she was munching
carrot sticks.

"Caffeine. I did this thing at NIH. I think I'm having a heart
attack."

"Are you feeling a squeezing in your chest lasting several minutes, with pain spreading to the shoulders? Light-headedness,
fainting, cold sweats, nausea, or shortness of breath?"

"No."

"You're not having a heart attack."

"Are you sure? How can you be sure? I feel like I'm having a
heart attack."

"I'm sure."

"Myocardial infarction? A little one?"

"Nope. Drink some water. Did they make you take an SAT?"

"What? Yes. How did you know?"

"I volunteer at Carolinas Medical all the time. It's good money
and like a free checkup. I just don't like the ones where I get the
trots." Now it sounded like she was eating a sandwich.

"I don't want to know."

"For future reference," she said, "don't take any of the caffeine
ones after lunch."

Oh great. I was going to be up all night. Definitely no more
NIH for me.

"How's Caleb?"

I was quiet. Then, "I think the Vibe was right. He's doing the
thing, you know."

She was quiet. Then, "It's never wrong. I'm sorry. He doesn't
deserve you."

"Thanks."

"I love you, babaloo," she said.

"I love you too."

After I hung up, I heaved myself off the couch and got the mail, which included a creamy parchment envelope. I sighed. I wondered how frequently the NIH ran experiments.

"Sid Dickens, this is Ben speaking. How may I help you?"

"Hey Ben, it's Vi."

"Vi! How delightful! I was going to lunch but this is better. Do you mind if I snack while we chat?" As if I wasn't used to that. I heard the rustling of paper.

"What's for lunch?" I was curious. Ben's personal details remained a mystery. With his courtly manners and indeterminate voice, I had no idea if he was twenty-two or sixty-two. Unless it was a turkey sandwich, his lunch might give me a clue.

"A turkey sandwich," he told me.

"You're good to make your lunch. I always end up buying," I fished.

"Actually, I'm not usually this good. I frequently visit the deli around the corner. But my mother made my lunch today." That got my attention.

"Really? Did she put a note in your Transformers lunch box, next to the fruit roll-ups?"

"Your humor is scintillating. My mother's been staying with me because she had an accident. She's been forcing lunches on me to compensate for her dependency. *I* am happy to accept my mother's kind ministrations."

I ignored his dig. I didn't want to talk about my mother today. Especially as I was starting to feel foolish about it. "Nothing serious I hope."

"She just took a little tumble." Ah ha! Another possible clue.

"Yes," I ventured. "She should be careful, at her age. . . ." I let the solicitation dangle.

"Indeed." Ben revealed nothing, suppressed laughter in his voice. My disembodied friend enjoyed thwarting my nosiness. It was like having a relationship with God, or a big white rabbit named Harvey. "So," he prompted. "Another wedding?" I brought back my focus.

"Ellis and Jack. I was thinking two tiles."

"Since you've been such a devoted customer, perhaps we can find a discount to allow you to purchase three tiles as sort of a referral fee. Have you put some thought into the tiles you'd like?"

We spent half an hour trying different combinations and bickering back and forth, until finally we were both satisfied.

"Well," I eyed the arrangement, "that works. Can you have them for the wedding?"

"I'll see what we can do," Ben promised, this time not lying. "And I'm glad you let go of your attachment to T-05. It simply didn't work. I believe Ellis will be quite pleased."

"You didn't have to call me a nitwit," I sulked.

"My apologies." Ben was smiling, I could tell. I relented.

"Forgiven . . . if your mother sends me some fruit roll-ups too."

"I'll speak to her immediately." He fell quiet. Then he said gently, "How's the other thing?"

"I don't really know," I sighed. "Lately it . . . isn't. He's been gone. I mean *really* gone. It's like he's disappeared even when we're together." It was scary to say something out loud you didn't want to be true, as if voicing the words would make it stronger than it already was. I liked talking to Ben about it because he was remote. It was like having a free shrink. Sometimes when I talked to Mona or Imogen about Caleb, I felt foolish and repetitive. Ben was a fresh ear and I craved his unfettered objectivity. He never judged. I plunged in.

"Caleb and I have this intense bond. I call it the Light Switch theory. When I'm around Caleb, I'm *on*—funnier, smarter, sexier, more confident, more everything. Because that's how *he* sees me. But I guess the weaker parts get amplified too. I'm not a jealous person, but he pulls that out of me too. And insecurity and all that."

"It sounds tiring." Boy did he hit the nail on the head. He continued, "There can be things that are good in some ways but not so good when you calculate the whole picture."

I thought a second. "Like recycling," I suggested. "It's great because you can rescue a tangible soda can from becoming landfill and get moral satisfaction. But if you actually look at the cost-benefit economics of recycling, there are strong arguments that it can be detrimental to long-term green economy goals."

Ben laughed. "Your approach is unique as ever, Vi."

"But, Ben, everyone still recycles. Somehow, the value of keeping that one can out of the landfill overcomes more rational calculations. Even if the bottom line is 'in the red,' maybe having that one nugget of true passion is more valuable than the bottom line. If I could be sure of Caleb, like we were engaged, the anxiety would go away and I'd have nothing to worry about."

"For what it's worth, they say the relationships meant to work aren't really work at all."

"Who are 'they,' anyway," I demanded, frustrated. Ben knew I wasn't snapping at him.

"I think they're the ones that set the line in Vegas." Ben poked fun at my Vegas cabal theories and I snorted, but my mood lightened.

"Ben, you always put me in a good mood, eh," I told him, smiling. "Thanks, pal."

"Vi, it's a pleasure," he replied evenly, but I thought I detected gratification in his voice.

"Vi, it's your father calling." My father always announced his phone calls.

"Hi, Dad," I wondered if I was in trouble. My father rarely called.

"I have a question for you. They are about to release the 2005 Domaine Lamarche Echezeaux Grand Cru from Burgundy, and I'm debating whether to buy a case. I heard they had some trouble with this vintage. I was hoping you could share your insider knowledge."

I panicked. I had no idea what he was talking about. "Um . . ."

"Are you expecting significant sales?"

Deep breaths. Think. Buy time. "Sorry, Dad, Al just walked in. Can I call you back?"

"Sure, sure. I don't need to decide until next week."

I hung up, humiliated. It was ridiculous that I couldn't answer my father's question. I thought of a look I'd recently caught in Al's eyes and my chest tightened. It said he knew I wasn't applying myself. Had I ever?

Oh God. I was pretty sure I'd lost Caleb. I didn't want to lose my job. I turned to the Internet.

Four hours later I was proudly emailing my father his answer, when the phone rang. I was surprised to hear Jen's voice. Since the wedding, our communications had become rare, each of us preoccupied with the life in front of us.

"Whatcher doin'?" Her greeting was the same. I smiled to hear it.

"Watching it about to rain and gauging the absolute earliest I can skive off work. You?"

"Skived off already and going to Chic-Fil-A. How's Caleb?"

How to answer? "Not good," I admitted. "I haven't heard from him in a couple of weeks.

Jen was silent a minute. "I'm sorry," she finally said. "I was hoping it'd be different this time."

"But you didn't think it would, did you?" I was curious.

She sighed. "Who ever knows, Vi? All I know is that after a few rounds of that on-again, off-again roller coaster with Bo, I just wanted off. I wanted stability. And I found it."

"And you're happy?"

"Yeah," she laughed. "That's why I'm calling. I'm pregnant!"

I was astounded. "Pregnant?"

"Yep," she said. "Eight weeks. It's still early to tell people, but I wanted you to know."

"That was fast," I said. They'd been married less than a year.

"I know," she laughed, "but we're ready. And my goodness, that's nothing compared to Amy. I ran into her at the grocery store last week and she's huge!"

I was shocked again. "Amy's pregnant?" I'd had no idea.

"Seven months along. She didn't tell you?"

"No. Since the wedding, she disappeared into Bill Land, ne'er to be seen again," I joked.

"Oh. Well," Jen said. We were both conscious of our own lapsed communications.

"I'm so happy for you," I rushed into the space, and she talked about her pregnancy, and I talked about my work, and we pretended we could relate. After we hung up, I sat for a long time and listened to the sound of a gap widening.

I threw down the *Wine Spectator* I wasn't absorbing and glowered out the window. It was raining, which suited my foul mood.

"Are you sure?" Imogen asked gently.

"We've hardly spoken at all in the three weeks, since Al's wedding. We used to speak every day. I've left multiple messages—not psychotic, mind you, but perfectly reasonable given that he's my *boyfriend* and I have *no idea what's going on*. He only returned one call, and it was after I told him I was going to a movie, so he knew I wouldn't answer."

"Maybe he's in Dubai." She tried to be optimistic.

"If a guy doesn't call, he's not trapped under a refrigerator or affected with a debilitating brain disease. He just doesn't feel like it," I said darkly, slumped on her sofa. I buried my face. "He's doing it again," my small voice said into my hands.

"I can't believe he'd be so callous," Imogen said.

"I just wish I *knew*. I mean, who am I kidding? It's so clearly over. He hasn't called in weeks. But until I hear it from him, it's like there's this ridiculous hope it might not be true. That maybe he *has* been under a refrigerator crying out my name until he lost his voice or consciousness or both." I sighed. "If I don't get closure, I can't let go."

"Well, you know what to do, don't you?" Imogen prodded. I looked at her. "Call him and tell him you're going to the movies, and then wait for him to call back."

I laughed. "You're devious." Then my laugh caught. I took a deep breath. "It hurts," I said.

"I know," Imogen said. "I know."

CHAPTER TWENTY-SEVEN

A New Dress Redux

We were gathered at Rizik's to have our bridesmaid fitting. The Lazaro dresses were beautiful tea-length lime green. Mine fit perfectly. Imogen was being pinned when my phone rang. I saw Caleb's name and a jolt of electricity shot through me. I felt slightly sick. I stepped away from the group and answered.

"Hello," I said neutrally.

"Hi. It's Caleb." He seemed to be trying to gauge my reaction. I gave him nothing.

"Hello. Where are you?"

"I'm in Dupont Circle. I was hoping we could get together." Ah. At last. We were going to have the Talk. A small part of me desperately hoped it wasn't the case, that he'd just been busy, that he still loved me. But when it came to a Bad Vibe, I was never wrong.

"Sure." I tried not to quaver. "What did you have in mind?"

"How about Teaism?"

"Sure." My vocabulary had evaporated. "Now?"

"Are you free?"

"Give me twenty minutes."

"I'll see you there." I remained where I was for a long moment after he hung up, girding myself for what was to come.

"Vi?" Ellis called my name. "Where are you?" I walked slowly back to the gaggle.

"Hey," I said. "I think I have to cut out, you guys." They all looked at me.

"What's up?" Ellis asked, concerned, after seeing my face.

"That was Caleb. He wants to meet me at Teaism. It's going to be the Talk," I said heavily.

"Are you sure?" asked Mona sympathetically.

"I have a Bad Vibe," I told her. They all nodded. "I'm sorry I'll miss lunch, Ellis. I need to get this over with."

"Don't sweat it." She paused. "Um, good luck?"

I walked out of the bridal area and paused at a mirror to check my appearance. Despondent. Imogen appeared behind me. She met my eyes in the mirror. She gave the slightest small nod, then wrapped her arms around me and squeezed.

"Why don't you come over later," she suggested. "I'll keep lunch short and be home in an hour. Ellis will understand."

I nodded. "That should do it," I said. She squeezed me again and let me go.

I was a bundle of nerves when I walked into Teaism. Caleb was already there, and had ordered tea for both of us. He knew I liked the passion fruit. He was still beautiful. I leaned down to give him a kiss. He turned his head slightly and kissed my cheek, so I kissed his in return as I felt something dying inside. I slid across from him and cupped my hands around my mug for warmth and to conceal any trembling. I forced a bright smile on my face.

"Hi, stranger," I said lightly. Breezy.

"Vi," he said, looking into my eyes. "It's good to see you."

"It's not as if I haven't been around to be seen, Caleb," I

responded. I saw no point in small talk. I'd been his girlfriend, he disappeared. The weather was of no interest to me.

"Yeah." He looked away. "I guess I owe you an explanation for that."

"Yes," I agreed. I said nothing else. Sometimes I find it satisfying to unnerve others, saying just enough to be courteous but not making it easy on them to deliver unpleasant news.

"Um, yeah. Well, look, my situation now is just not one where I can have a girlfriend."

"You've made that quite evident," I said evenly. "Though why this conversation couldn't have happened three weeks ago is not apparent. Nor is it apparent why, knowing you didn't want a girlfriend, you pursued a relationship with me anyway."

"Vi, for God's sake. This isn't easy. I know I haven't been great to you, and I've felt all this pressure. It makes me feel terrible." Funny how we were talking about his Feelings.

"So what's the problem?" I asked.

"I'm focused on work right now, and can't be worrying all the time about letting you down. And, you and I, it isn't just dating. There's too much there."

"And?" I prompted. "Why did you start? You knew all this going in."

He looked at me earnestly, then reached out and traced a finger down my cheek. "With you, I can't resist. You were my first love and I'll always be partly in love with you. You've been the most important woman in my life until now. The selfish part of me always wants to be with you when I can. But my rational brain knows that's unfair because I don't want to fully commit. And you deserve more."

You bet I do. "Partly in love" wasn't good enough. I considered him carefully and thought about "until now." There was more.

"And," I prompted. He looked away and twiddled a packet of sugar. He cleared his throat.

"Well, there's this thing. Not a big deal, not a *real* thing. At least . . . I don't know. Maybe. But, um, sort of a thing. In Houston." Ah-hah. A Thing. This *was* familiar territory.

"Is it Audrey?" I steeled myself.

He twiddled some more. "It just sort of happened," he said.

"Is it Audrey?"

"Does it matter who it is?" He shrugged his shoulders impatiently, not looking at me.

"Is it Audrey?"

He sighed. "Yes. I didn't mean for it to happen. I'm sorry, Vi. But I feel something with her. Right now I want to be with her and I don't want to lie to you."

He looked like a little boy, puffed with bravado, but sort of quaking inside over how I'd react. I looked away. His face was still so dear to me. A black hole yawned at the thought of no Caleb. But I felt something else too. I closed my eyes and explored.

"Are you okay?" he asked.

"I must be okay, because my heart is still beating." I spoke more to myself than to him, stealing the words of another to frame this experience. I opened my eyes and looked at his face again, expecting to feel Anguish or Humiliation, at a minimum, Pain. I released myself to let the Feelings flood in. But nothing happened. I probed. I stared at Caleb, and he looked so . . . normal. Shorter, actually, his face marred by the spoiled look on it. Suddenly, I did feel something. And I swear I could almost hear the rushing of wings as I released what I had been clutching in my chest and felt it fly away. I'd always heard the expression about rose-colored glasses, but truly, in that moment when they came off, it was cinematic. I laughed in pure surprise, which took Caleb unawares. He eyed me nervously, like I might get hysterical.

I felt Relief. And Freedom. No more Anxiety over whether it

would "stick this time" or Nervousness about being good enough for him. Actually, he wasn't good enough for me. He was immature, noncommittal, and sort of lacking in substance. I looked at his handsome face and smiled. I actually felt Maternal. He was a mess.

"I'm fine," I assured him. I reached out and covered his hand in mine. He tensed a bit, as if the contact was undesirable. But, for the first time, the little physical rejection didn't bother me. I was done collecting and reviewing his million little rejections a day. I squeezed his hand.

"I hope you're happy," I said. "I hope it works out. Oh, and tea is on you." I stood and picked up my bag. I paused to tuck the Lure behind his ear one last time in a farewell gesture. "Be well, babe. I love you."

"Vi . . ." He stared after me, bewildered, as I walked out the door with a smile on my face. He'd be back, I suspected. But I wasn't buying anymore.

The lack of Pain didn't stop me from sobbing on Imogen's sofa a few hours later. I wasn't sure what I was crying for exactly, but they were sincere sobs and it felt like the right thing to do.

"There, there," soothed Imogen, patting my heaving back. "Let it out, sweetie." I cried until I was spent and then I energetically whimpered and sniffled for another ten minutes. Imogen just sat silently rubbing my back. She understood that sometimes you don't want advice, you just need to let it out in the presence of another. After I calmed down, she spoke.

"Want some tea? Häagen-Dazs?" Imogen asked gently.

"Dea," came my snotty and garbled response. Imogen disappeared and I sat tentatively upright, relinquishing the comfort of my fetal position for one more suitable to an adult. I padded to the bathroom and looked in the mirror in disgust. Red, watery eyes stared back from a puffy face streaked with tears and mascara. I splashed cool water on my face and blew my nose, then returned to Imogen's living room and gratefully accepted a cup of tea from her.

"Okay?" She smiled at me. I nodded.

"Incurably stupid," I said. " 'The Dummy Returns.' "

"Hearts are funny things." Imogen contradicted me. "They do a lot without our permission." I sniffled and sipped my tea.

"Is it funny that I feel kind of good?" I asked hesitantly. She smiled hugely at me and gave a little happy bounce.

"I was hoping I detected a wee rite of passage in all those tears," she enthused.

"I think so," I said cautiously. "I saw Caleb today in a way I never had before. Even though he broke up with me," here my eyes welled up again, but I fought it off, "I feel like I'm the one that gained freedom."

"Sweetie, that's so good to hear."

I sighed. "It's sad too, though. Like I said good-bye to an era of myself. Not only my relationship with Caleb, but the naive romantic optimism that went with it. Suddenly I feel . . . old. Cynical."

"It doesn't have to be that way," Imogen responded.

"How else can it be? You only truly fall in love the first time. Then your heart breaks for the first time. You realize love doesn't last forever, and you never give all of yourself again. You reserve a little bit out of self-protection, so when it doesn't work out the next time you're not totally destroyed. And the more times it doesn't work out, the bigger the reserve gets. I'm starting to wonder if we get so guarded we *can't* truly fall in love."

Imogen regarded me thoughtfully. "It's true about holding back your heart, but I also believe that as we get wiser, we're less likely to be distracted by fool's gold. By holding something back you're actually giving more of yourself—being real, not chasing a fantasy." She paused, then said carefully, "Look at your parents."

I exhaled. "Caleb was definitely a fantasy. I worked so hard to redeem our first, pure love, like it had superpowers, when what I was working for didn't really exist. There was so much about him right in front of me, but I only saw this other version of what he *could* be. I blamed the problems on myself."

"You wouldn't be the first person in the world to do it," Imogen said.

"And all these people racing to marriage. How can everyone be so sure?"

"Maybe they are and maybe they aren't," speculated Imogen. "We live in a marriage-oriented society. Your community, your religion, pop culture, all teach you to get married."

"But how do they find each other?" My eyes welled up a bit. "Why doesn't anyone pick me?" I wailed plaintively.

Imogen smacked me on the forehead. "Don't be a melodramatic ninny. Someone will pick you. You haven't been open to it, frankly. You were always snared by Caleb fantasies." She was right. "And it's not clear that all marriages are a good idea. Sometimes, people get it wrong. It's a seductive daydream to have someone cherish and care for you all the days of your life in perfect security. But when the wedding's over, you simply have the same two people and marriage doesn't change them. People see it as a panacea—like exchanging vows wraps the relationship in armor and protects it. But it doesn't work that way."

I thought about it. Marriage did promise a firewall that could stop infidelity, or anything. I'd been convinced that if Caleb proposed, I'd feel secure and everything would be perfect. But he would've still been the same man with the same tendencies and I would have still been insecure from all the ricochet. How can you firewall that? I felt foolish.

"Marriage gives you a false sense of security," I mused.

"Perhaps," Imogen said. I became a little lighter. I'd felt like a failure that Caleb had dumped me when all my friends were getting married. But marrying him to avoid being alone would have been the real failure.

"How's this for a greeting card," I offered slyly.

"We had ten good years of fun, sex, and drinking,
 Except when you jumped like a rat from a ship sinking,
 I can't help but wonder . . . as I lay here tears blinking,
 To stay with you that long, what the hell was I thinking?"

Imogen applauded. "How about: 'When we were together, you said you'd die for me. Now that we're apart, make that promise be.'"

I closed with, "It's only fair, you see, I'll throw in the cyanide for free," and Imogen and I both collapsed in laughter.

"I'm fresh out of cyanide," Imogen wiped tears from her eyes. "Wanna go to Bistrot du Coin for a bite?"

"Yes. But first I want to make a quick call to my mother."

"It's good to hear your voice." My mother sounded surprised, and a little guarded, a few moments later. Who could blame her?

I jumped right in. "Mom, I'm sorry I've been a jerk." She was quiet. I went on. "I'm not sure I know how to explain it, but I think it comes down to me being a lazy person," I admitted. "I was punishing you because you forced me to realize that relationships are about difficult choices, and sometimes mistakes, and I couldn't deal."

"That's something you're going to have to accept, I'm afraid," my mother's laugh was rueful.

"I know," I sighed. "I was clinging to the idea that certain things are pre-ordained, because it's easier. If your soul mate is already decided, it's simply a matter of meeting him and the rest is easy. You don't have to do anything or risk anything. Just wait."

"If only it were that easy."

"Watching my friends get married, it spooks me that you can never know for sure if you're making the right choice. And if you choose wrong, it's your own fault and you're stuck with the consequences."

"Fault is a strong word, Vi."

"Okay, but you're responsible for your own life. You have to *choose*. It's so much easier to believe in fate. So I convinced myself that you and Dad were destined. And I convinced myself that Caleb was the one for me. Finding out you'd been divorced blew that out of the water. Especially, that you'd divorced your high school boyfriend."

"It's perfectly understandable, Vi." Her voice was warm.

"No, Mom. I wasn't allowing you to be a real person. You were braver than I've ever been. You didn't fail because you got divorced—you gambled on something better. At least you took charge. I'd probably have stayed with Caleb forever if he let me. I didn't want to have to think for myself, so I clung to a fantasy."

"The idea of destiny is very comforting. It absolves us of responsibility."

"But it doesn't work that way."

"No." Mom was quiet a minute. "Vi, I can't tell you what to do to ensure you never get divorced." A pang told me that in the back of my mind I'd irrationally hoped that maybe she could. "But you are an intelligent young lady with a good head and a great heart. I have every faith you'll figure it all out just fine."

"Thanks, Mom." I blinked back tears.

"You're welcome. Now, I have to run. They're having a sale on old anatomy textbooks at Joseph Beth and I want to get over there before all the good ones are gone."

From: Ben@siddickens.com
To: ViViVooom@gmail.com
Sent: May 23
Subject: From Your Friend Ben

Vi,

You are a remarkable young lady. Caleb doesn't deserve you. Someday, when you've met the man of your dreams, you'll look back in astonishment that you ever wasted your tears. I promise.

Your friend,
Ben

CHAPTER TWENTY-EIGHT

Oh, I Do

Ellis Marries Jack, Eastern Shore, Maryland, May

"Well, ladies, this is it," beamed Ellis from inside her wedding gown. We all stood a respectful two feet from the dress, which created a stiff radius around its pearl. The gown's perfect choreography around Ellis's body matched the perfect choreography of the entire wedding—I'd never been part of such flawlessly executed nuptials.

Now, we were all arrayed around Ellis in our lime green tulle like a bridal Mountain Dew commercial. I could see it now: "Do the I Dew—soda for the hipster wedding generation." It would involve the groom parachuting onto a cliff top for the vows.

Instead, we were civilly situated at The Oaks on Maryland's Eastern Shore. I was still a little raw about Caleb—I hadn't expected to attend this wedding alone. But I was determinedly refusing to mourn him. It was over and that was that. I forced my Intellectual Understanding into prominence, focusing on the fact that he made me Unhappy and Anxious. It didn't make me miss him less. Pretending there wasn't this yawning chasm in my mind,

I corralled my brain far from the precipice. Whatever was there, I didn't even want to peek. I suspected it would wash over me and be too much.

"So, the first of the Clyde's Brides," Ellis said. "I'm one down. Who's next?" The chasm yawned. Until recently the logical answer would've been me.

The wedding coordinator popped in. She too looked like a variation of Aunt Bea. I wondered if it was a job prerequisite. She gave a wide smile and asked, "Ready, ladies?" in a breathy little voice. The girlish inflection called for pink rose adornments, and her dress didn't disappoint.

"Yes!" Ellis popped up, unnecessarily smoothing a dress that wouldn't wrinkle after a flight to Fiji. "It's time."

"Circle up!" Imogen ordered, and we pulled into a huddle. Ellis stuck her hand in the middle, and Babette, Mona, Imogen, and I put ours on top. "Goooooo team! Hoo-ah!" Ellis's eyes were bright with tears as she looked at us.

"Oh no. Don't do that," Mona ordered, blinking rapidly. I began to well up myself

"Clyde's Brides, take one," Babette announced. I had a scary vision of myself wrinkled and alone at an empty table being served by a grey-haired Charlie. I prayed hard that Ellis wouldn't slip away from my life as Amy, Lila, and Jen had.

"You guys are the best A-Team ever," Ellis gushed. We fell into a group hug. Then she commanded, "Now line 'em up and march!"

"I love it when a plan comes together," said Imogen as she led the charge.

Ellis and Jack were married on a lawn sloping down to the water while the sun bathed everything in a rich golden glow. As they gazed at each other over clasped hands, I fastened on my Bridesmaid Smile and subtly scanned the audience for Ethan. I spotted him on the bride's side about four rows back. He winked.

I tried to wink back but ended up shutting both eyes in a wince. I'm a terrible winker—I can't do just one eye. Ethan's grin conveyed that I was hopeless. I started to sweep my glance back to Ellis and Jack when my gaze caught. My mouth dropped and hung open for several moments before I recalled where I was standing and snapped it shut. Sitting in the same row as Ethan, was Mr. Niall Devlin, Irish Hottie Extraordinaire.

I stared. There was no mistaking it. The World's Hottest Man was sitting in front of me. He was wearing a sharp suit and his hair was sexily tousled. He was casually slung in his chair as only long and lean men can manage without looking like Ichabod Crane, idly tapping a finger on the wedding program. And looking right at me. I started as our eyes met dead on. There was a zing right down the hoohah highway. Then I realized I'd been gaping at him for several minutes and he was probably wondering whether I was (a) deranged, (b) convinced he was on America's Most Wanted, or (c) retarded. I collected myself, about to look away, when he winked. I gaped. Again. I had to restrain myself from looking over my shoulder in the manner of a bad sitcom to see if he was winking at anyone else. I was pretty certain that only the minister was behind me, and odds were good that the cleric was not the object of Irish Dream's merriment. No, it was undeniable. He had winked at me.

I elected not to try to return the wink, as I'd inevitably close both eyes and he'd think I had Tourette's. I ventured a small smile. He curved up one side of his mouth in a grin. I was entranced. I beamed goofily at him. Then I realized that the person next to him was also looking at me. And the person next to her. Everyone, in fact, was looking at me. I snapped my eyes to the altar. Ellis's eyes were boring into me.

"Um, ahem. And the rings?" the minister prompted, for what I was pretty sure was not the first time.

"Oh yes! The rings! I have them!" I blushed the color of a

Persian carpet and hastily pulled the rings off my thumb. Out of the corner of my eye I could see Imogen struggling not to laugh. I wanted to sink through the earth. Had the entire wedding noticed I was gawking like a lovestruck teenager at Mr. Devilishly Good Looking? I peeped a glance at him. Now, both corners of his lips were definitely curled in a grin in my direction. He knew. Oh dear Lord, I wanted to die. But what a sweet, sweet death it would be.

The minister blessed the rings and started nattering on about commitment. I was desperately impatient to get Ellis off the altar and ask her about Niall Devlin. I know it was her wedding and all, but this was important. I tried not to jiggle. I drew in a deep breath. I had to calm down or I'd burst out with, "Yes, yes, yes, we've all heard it before now get to the good bit where they're man and wife so we can go." It was hard enough not to chime along with the permanently-burned-into-my-cortex First Corinthians.

After what seemed an eternity of physical struggle not to look at Niall, but was in fact approximately thirty-eight minutes, the ceremony was over. Mr. and Mrs. Ellis and Jack Brent laughed out loud in happiness as they faced the guests and gaily trod back up the lawn. I followed behind them with Jack's brother Jed. I couldn't resist a Casual Glance at the Object of My Lust as I passed. I found myself looking straight into amused rich brown eyes. I snapped my glance away. Breezy . . . I'm breezy, I intoned like a mantra.

"Are your palms sweating?" Jed asked me curiously. Crap.

As soon as we were out of the church, I rocketed toward where Ellis was standing on the lawn. I was almost there when my momentum was abruptly halted and I nearly toppled backward. Imogen had a handful of my skirt.

"Whoa there, Lust Cowgirl," she called with a grin. I flushed.

"What? What do you mean?" I stammered. She gave me a pitying look.

"My darling unsubtle friend. You are sprinting to the bride, mere seconds after her marriage, arguably the happiest moment in her life, to sniff out some piece of tail that you spied in the audience. I, selfless being that I am and constant foil to your pratfalls, have taken it upon myself to intercept you in order to suggest that a moment a little further in the future, say, oh, at least half an hour, might be more appropriate for your Him-quisition. Hm?"

I sighed. She was right. I was once again starring in the movie about myself ("Crush Hour," perhaps? Yes, I liked it) and failing to think of others. Ellis was aglow and bubbling with giggles as people congratulated her. Jack looked like he'd won the lottery, grinning and perpetually twisting the alien-feeling ring now shining on his left hand. Ellis beamed over at us.

"Come on." Imogen tugged at the folds of skirt still in her grip. "Restraint."

"Breezy!" I promised. We went to Ellis and hugged her and touched her rings and giggled. The other girls joined us, and then the photographer hustled us off to tramp around the grounds: Magnolia Tree Shot, Dappled Sunlight Shot, Wide Terrace Shot, Sloping Lawn Shot, etc. He was all business. I got schooled for whispering. Finally we were released for good behavior, but warned that we could be recalled at any time.

"Thank God," moaned Mona. "My face hurts."

"It's killing me," Imogen quipped.

I decided that slogging all over the grounds was an appropriate cooling off period for just-married euphoria, so I sidled up to Ellis as we awkwardly minced back to the inn, trying not to aerate the grass with our heels fence-posting into the dirt.

"Oh, Vi, wasn't it perfect?" she breathed, clutching my elbow for support with one hand and raising her gown with the other like a one-winged swan.

"Flawless," I agreed, plotting my contact with the soft earth carefully. "Except the part where I almost kept the rings." Ellis giggled. She was doing a lot of that today. "So, I thought I saw someone I met at Traci's wedding," I ventured casually, once we attained the relative safety of the flagstone path. "Niall Devlin. Do you know him?"

"Niall Devlin? Hmm, no, doesn't ring a bell. But I have to confess that I don't know everyone. Maybe he's someone's plus one."

Curses. I hadn't thought of him being someone's date. Then I sighed. What did it matter anyway? I wasn't the type of girl that amazing men wanted to be with. I didn't have the zing of an Audrey. Caleb had made that perfectly clear. I suddenly felt old in my heart. Forget Niall Devlin or Caleb Carter, I vowed—I was going to have a good time tonight. Ellis's radiant-because-I'm-in-love smile staked me a little bit, but I managed an equally bright smile for her.

"Shall we?" I forced.

"Martini bar here we come," she trilled as Babette caught up with us. Mona appeared to be spiked into the lawn and Imogen was extracting her.

After reprising my recurrent starring role in "The Bustler," I excused myself, slipping away from the concern in Babette's eyes, and breathed a sigh of relief when I locked myself into the bathroom stall. I needed a moment alone. I leaned my head against the cool wall. I didn't know what was wrong with me. I was completely Happy for Ellis but Aching at the same time.

No, I resolved. I was not Aching. I was Fine. I squared my shoulders, took a deep breath, turning up the corners of my mouth to cue my emotions to fall in line, and walked determinedly out of the bathroom. Babette was sort of floating about the hallway when I emerged. She looked at me and gave a quick nod.

"Check this out," she said as we walked to the terrace. "It's a customized martini bar." The bar menu offered the MetropEllis (a cosmopolitan), the Jack Attack (dirty martini), the Brent Would (a chocolate martini), and the Shore Thing (apple martini).

I cocked an eyebrow at Babette. "Two Shore Things?"

"Would you ever turn down a Shore Thing?" she quipped.

"Not if your room is five hundred yards away." I laughed.

"How enticing a thought," said a delicious voice in my ear. I looked up into gorgeous brown eyes and had a wave of adrenaline so strong I thought I might swoon. Those lashes really were wasted on a man.

"Oh, Uh," I said, brilliantly.

He smiled, shooting wattage down my spine. I forcibly pulled myself together before I drooled. Babette looked on with interest.

I struggled for a clever remark. "You need a wristband for *that*," I glanced pointedly at his hand. "Tsk tsk . . . I see you don't have one." Cha, right, I thought. An image flashed in my mind of me wrestling him into my room. More like a Whore Thing.

"To be so lucky," he murmured. Jeeesh. There went my armpits. Sweat glands definitely working. I tried to subtly hold my elbows away from my body to air out without looking like I was prepping for the chicken dance. He seemed to be waiting for a reply, but my stupefied brain was not responding. I smiled inanely.

"So, we meet again," he finally said.

"Technically, we didn't actually meet before," I reminded him.

"A secret agent never reveals his identity," he pointed out. "But my alter ego, Niall Devlin, is absolutely delighted to make your acquaintance." He held a hand in my direction. I prayed my palm wasn't sweaty.

"Vi Connelly." I smiled back and touched his hand. Zing. He didn't recoil. In fact, he held my hand for an extra two beats before dropping it. Rather, he held it for what would normally be two beats, but at my current heart rate I managed close to twenty-nine beats. I wondered if it was possible to pass out from a toxic crush.

"Yes, I know," he said silkily, reluctantly letting go of my hand. I felt another jolt and preened. He'd been asking about me! He dangled the wedding program and I deflated. Naturally. My name was right there in the program for all to see. "A headlining role," he commented.

"Not much to it really," I was determined to act casual. "Don't fall, don't let the bride mix alcohol and antidepressants, trip the groom if he bolts up the aisle before it's legal, don't lose the rings. . . ."

His smile widened and, and I winced. Damn.

"I considered pawning the rings for a luxury trip to Aruba," I bluffed, "but I wouldn't get far in an electric golf cart. Plus, I didn't want to miss having a MetropEllis."

"Yes, about that . . ." Babette put in. Niall and I looked at Babette as if just realizing there were other people on the earth. I sighed. Here we go . . . another swain falls prey to the lovely and lovable Babette.

"This is Babette," I made the introduction. "Babette, this is Niall Devlin." I braced myself not to be disappointed at his reaction.

"Delighted to meet another lime fairy." Niall smiled enchantingly at her. Then, to my surprise, he directly turned his gaze back to me. "So, Miss Vi Connelly, here we are as alcohol equals, and yet I'm impeding your way to the bar. I prefer my former role as enabler. I believe I heard two Shore Things were in order? May I?" If only he would.

"You may," Babette said, smiling.

Niall kept his eyes on me. "Excellent," he said, and maneuvered to the bar. Babette turned an enormous grin on me.

"Well, well, well. Someone's been keeping a bush under a barrel," she teased, brows raised. "Who was that tender morsel?" I flushed, recalling I was out of Niall's league.

"It's no one. Just someone I met at a wedding."

Babette smirked in total disbelief. "No one. Right. Shall I ask Imogen?"

"No!" I burst out, too quickly. The last thing I needed was Imogen deciding what was best for me and humiliating me by throwing me at Niall. "Imogen doesn't know Niall. Honestly. I only met him for a second at Traci's wedding."

"Traci's wedding?" Babette's brow furrowed. "That's the cash bar one? With Caleb."

"Right," I said relieved. Now she would drop it.

She looked pensive, then smirked again. "The plot thickens." I must have looked alarmed because she patted my arm. "Don't worry, sweetie, I'll let you work it out for yourself. But I'll say this—he had eyes for only one of us. And it wasn't me. And those eyes. Whooooo."

At that moment Niall returned balancing three drinks. He handed us each a frosted martini glass, and then clinked them with his own. "Cheers."

"Dexterously done," Babette complimented. "I could never manage three glasses."

"Comparatively easy drink-getting here, really," Niall said lightly. "Did Vi tell you about the last wedding we went to?" It sounded so casual and couplelike that I took in a breath. I had a flash vision of the two of us surrounded by friends as Niall said "that was like the time Vi and I were in Africa teaching small children to read in the sunlight . . ." arm casually slung over my shoulder while everyone looked on admiringly. I was physically gravitating toward his side when I snapped back to reality. I hastily righted myself.

". . . And the quest for a free drink nearly resulted in fisticuffs," he finished. Babette laughed. "This wedding is loads better on all fronts," his eyes rested on me. "The bridesmaids," he paused, "*dresses* are particularly lovely."

"You're just saying that because an Irishman has to favor green," I countered. I eyed his tan suit. "Where's yours?"

"If I have green shamrocks on my undergarments, does that count?" he joked.

"I'm afraid not," I chided, trying not to imagine him in his underpants, "unless an actual leprechaun sprouts out." Babette choked on her martini and started coughing. I realized what I'd said and a bright red blush burned across my face. I wanted to die on the spot. Niall looked like he was struggling mightily not to guffaw but took pity on me, glossing over my innuendo.

"You see, this is what happens when my charade as an American fails." As if he could pull that off with his giveaway lilt. "I'm left completely exposed to ludicrous expectations that I have a pot of gold, or might whip out a wee flute or dance a jig or other such cinematic nonsense."

I laughed, so grateful to move past the leprechaun-in-the-pants gaff that I passed on the obvious "wee flute" opportunity. "I feel your pain. I initially rejected my Irish-American heritage out of iconographic disgust for Ireland's unassailable position in Hollywood as the last remaining source of the rustic life. The overly-romantic depiction would put anyone off—thatch-covered, candlelit pubs as the only freestanding structures, and a population consisting entirely of old men fiddling or fluting, feisty flame-haired beauties, and stalwart farmhands who drink Guinness and dispense homespun wisdom with a mystical bent? No way."

"And?" Niall arched a brow at me.

"I was somewhat embarrassed on my first visit to find that thatch-covered, candlelit pubs were the only freestanding structures, and the visible population consisted of old men and feisty flame-haired beauties who drank Guinness in pubs, where farmhands would spontaneously produce fiddles and homespun wisdom."

Niall threw his head back and laughed heartily. When he recovered, he defended himself. "In Galway, we actually have a university with some rather nice structures made out of stone and lit with electricity and everything."

"Naturally," I agreed. "Where else would one go to learn how to brew stout and play the fiddle?"

"Right," he countered. "Where I first lived in America there was either a McDonalds"—charmingly pronounced MAC-donald's—"or a church on every block, and to get from one to the other everyone drove an SUV."

"And when I was in Ireland, the snowy-haired man wore an Aran knit wool sweater and told me stories about the auld folk who all eventually turned into seals."

"I give up, I give up," he yielded, laughing. "It's true. I was, in fact, once . . . a seal."

"I know how you feel, though," I conceded. "I grew up in North Carolina, and the first time I went to Ireland, people asked me if the roads were paved where I lived, whether my father was a member of the KKK, and if we had indoor plumbing."

Niall looked at me with a completely serious expression. "And?"

"Oh puhleeze," I said in my best twang. "Who needs tar on them thar roads?" I was laughing up at his chuckle when our eyes met. My breath caught and something flashed between us. I forgot we were at a crowded reception, forgot to breathe, until someone jostled Niall and he looked away. I turned to Babette to cover my awkwardness, but she'd faded into the crowd without my noticing. I had no idea how long she'd been gone.

"So, Miss Vi Connelly," Niall recaptured my attention. He seemed a little flustered. He cleared his throat. "We appear to be in the reprimandable position of partially obstructing access to the bar. Shall we edge our way out of the crush?" I followed him to the edge of the patio overlooking the water. I smiled over my martini, and felt a bubble of happiness as his eyes met mine. I couldn't believe I was having a conversation with Niall Devlin.

And I was being funny and normal! Well, aside from the lepre-chaun thing.

"So what brings you to—" I started to ask, when an attractive redhead walked toward us.

"Niall?" she called. I froze. Oh Lord, I was an idiot. I'd forgot-ten the plus-one thing. He was someone else's date. He was prob-ably talking to the only person he knew while his girlfriend was in the toilet. I prayed it hadn't been obvious I was flirting, while cursing the unfairness of it all. Dating people should wear physi-cal cues as well as married people. An ear tag or something so you don't make a fool of yourself.

An expression that looked like chagrin crossed Niall's face. He replaced it with a warm smile as he turned to greet his date. She was pretty, with long curly hair and a bright smile.

"Hello," she said pleasantly in an Irish brogue as she held out her perfectly manicured hand. "I'm Fiona. Your dress is absolutely lovely, and you carry it so well. I was telling Niall that you were the best attendant I'd ever seen. Textbook flower position." She was a perfect statuesque match to Niall's height. She also seemed genu-inely happy to meet me and nice to boot. I couldn't dislike her.

"Vi Connelly." I smiled back, feeling stumpy. "I've had lots of practice."

"How lovely. I'm sorry to interrupt." She looked genuinely apologetic. "But Niall, this is the best time for me to introduce you to those people we were speaking of. Would you like to?"

"Yes, yes, of course," he agreed. He smiled at me. "Vi, it was a pleasure, but I must excuse myself. I'll look for you later and we can finish our conversation and perhaps enjoy an Irish reel on the dance floor?"

Fiona laughed. "Watch out for that one," she warned brightly. "Himself will lure you out there and spin you until you feel quite sick. I've learned my lesson!"

I forced a weak smile. They were a charming couple, and obviously completely secure in one another.

"Of course," I said. "Lovely to meet you." As they walked away, Disappointment washed over me and I felt tired again. In just fifteen minutes with Niall I had relieved the exhausting cycle of my (most recent) relationship with Caleb: Titillation, Anticipation, Hope, Happiness, Disappointment, Defeat. I felt oddly teary. My emotional coffers were like Argentine currency—one poor investment would bankrupt the reserves and cause the entire system to collapse. Lately I was pretty shaky on self-image.

I caught sight of Imogen crossing the lawn. I knew everyone was babysitting me today and figured it was her shift. I recalled my resolve from the bathroom and gathered it about me like armor. Niall was a slip-up. Forgivable, because he was a preexisting condition, but allowable no more. I was staying away from men for a while. I needed to strengthen the reserves before I ventured back into the shark-infested sea of love.

"Hey," Imogen joined me. She had two pink drinks. "Metrop-Ellis."

"Gesundheit," I accepted the new drink. We clinked glasses. A band was playing bossa nova in the corner of the lawn. Imogen wiggled her hips at me.

"Shall we?"

We samba'd our way to the knot of lime green girls, jiggling our hips and wiggling our shoulders in a spontaneous salsa-meets-limbo choreography designed to groove without spilling our drinks but mostly probably just looking silly.

Braxton joined the group and handed Mona a pink drink. "Have a meto, . . . cosopol . . . what the hell ever . . . have a pink drink. I don't know how you drink that pastel stuff. Give me a Miller Light anytime."

"Philistine." Giles walked up with Ethan. And I thought I'd been joking when I accused him of a carnation-colored suit.

"Where'd you find a beer?" asked Ethan. "And how'd you convince them not to put it in a fancy glass?"

"Southern charm," Braxton chuckled.

"Braxton is a human dowsing stick for beer," Imogen said.

"Braxton, is that a clip-on bowtie?" Giles asked. "For the love of God man."

Braxton grinned. "They're lucky I'm wearing a damn monkey suit at all. It's a lot to ask of a man on a Saturday. I should be in my cowboy boots."

"I am shocked and awed to note that you *are* in your cowboy boots," pointed out Giles. We all looked at the dusty tips of Braxton's cowboy boots sticking out below his tuxedo pants.

"Oh." Braxton grinned. "That's right. So I am." He took a satisfied swig of beer.

A bell rang and we walked to our table, Mona's Brad completing our number.

"Hey," said Brad to Braxton. "How'd you get them to give you the beer without a glass?"

Dinner was delicious. I determinedly did not scan the room for Niall-Not-Available, and it was definitely by accident that I knew he and Fiona were seated at a corner table with Jack's work colleagues. He was facing me and his tie had come loose, but it was unavoidable. I knew this because if I looked up accidentally-on-purpose in just the right way with my chair tilted, he was directly in my line of sight when the fellow opposite him went to the bar. It was merely a matter of physics. Once, physics resulted in our eyes catching across the room. He smiled and I looked hastily away, poorly pretending that I hadn't seen his look. My hormones weren't getting the Memo From My Brain that he was off limits.

After dinner, Ellis and Jack danced sweetly to Israel

Kamakawiwo'ole's version of "Somewhere Over the Rainbow." Then the bridal party joined them. As I twirled with Jed, I fancied that Niall was gazing intently at me. I was hallucinating, though, because he had Friendly Fiona from the Homeland. Still, on one twirl I calculated a casual glance over Jed's shoulder. My breath caught when Niall's eyes squarely met mine. He looked thoughtful. I wrenched my glance away, and was relieved when the dance ended. I scurried back to my table.

"So," queried Babette as I sat down. "How is the charming Mr. Devlin?"

"He's an extremely charming plus one," I answered.

"Who's Mr. Devlin?" Imogen reclaimed her seat.

"What does that mean?" Babette furrowed her brow.

"It means he's the date of an equally charming woman," I stressed. "He's not available."

"Who's Mr. Devlin?" Imogen repeated.

"I do not believe this." Babette shook her head. "He was definitely into you. He was . . . *quelle est le mot* . . . *glowing* at you."

"No, he was just being nice," I said.

"Who's Mr. Devlin?" Imogen's voice rose a few octaves.

"I do not believe it. I saw what I saw, and what I saw was spading."

"Spading?" asked Mona, sitting down.

"Spading . . . it's like flirting, tilling the soil to create fertile ground. Spading is overlong or overheated glances, unnecessary casual contact, leaning into someone when you speak to them, a hand on the knee for emphasis."

"And this guy was spading Vi?" Mona asked.

"Definitely," Babette insisted. "No handshake takes that long."

"Are they talking gardening?" asked Ethan.

"I'm blind, deaf, and dumb," said Giles. "I just let them go."

"He's not interested," I maintained. "He was just being nice."

"Who's Mr. Devlin?" Imogen was practically strident.

"Imogen, hush." I looked anxiously over my shoulder. Niall was leaning his head toward Fiona to catch something she was saying. I felt a stab of Disappointment. Then I felt Disgust. Even though I knew he had a date, I'd still coaxed myself into a fantasy that he *had* been shooting me heated glances across the dance floor. I sighed. Hubris is not your friend.

"Niall Devlin is a very nice guy I met at Traci's wedding for a nanosecond, and who is here with a very nice and very pretty date. Babette, contrary to all reason, has decided that he likes me. Which he does not," I explained.

"The guy in the crowd." Imogen eyed me closely. "You're crushing," she pronounced.

I opened my mouth to deny it, then gave up. Imogen (a) knew me too well and (b) wouldn't let it go. Easier to yank the Band-Aid—the inquisition would pass faster. "Yes, I fancied him," I admitted. "He's *gorgeous*. And *so* nice. And funny—*really* clever. And he has this *amazing* Irish accent," I mooned.

"She is speaking in italics," Mona observed. "She italic *really* italic likes him."

"And he's really italic *taken* italic," I responded. "So can we please let it go and for one minute not obsess over Vi meeting a man, because I just broke up with one and frankly I'd like to think that maybe, possibly, there's a universe where it's okay for me to be just Vi, no plus one. I don't have the energy to like someone right now." I felt tears welling suddenly. I quickly swallowed them back and set my face, hoping no one noticed. Mona looked stricken and Imogen abashed. Imogen came and squatted by my chair.

"I'm sorry." She met my eyes seriously. She gave me a hug. "It's just that we don't want you to feel sad even for a second, and a new man is an easy patch. It was lame. It's always better to be happy on your own. Boys are dumb."

"Hey," protested Ethan and Giles.

"Definitely," Mona agreed.

"Well, I don't care what you say," Babette persisted mulishly. "He digs her. And she gets all breathless around him."

"I'm going to the bar," I announced. I headed to the bar with a purposeful mission and ordered a glass of wine identical to the full one I'd left behind.

"Hey Vi," Brad was standing by the bar talking to an extremely short man.

"Hey guys." I flicked my eyes around the tent, letting their conversation flow over me, knowing that if I ever needed such thorough knowledge of chili recipes, I'd just call Brad. Most people were dancing. Others were standing in clutches talking. One was striding toward me. It was Niall. I gave a squeak of alarm. Brad and his companion stopped talking.

"Did you just squeak?" Brad asked.

"What? Oh. Maybe. I've gotta go." I scurried away from Niall's certain destination, the bar, and fled to the table, collapsing into the seat between Giles and Braxton.

"What's up, darlin'?" Braxton shot me a quizzical look.

"Nothing. Just being a goof." I slouched into the chair.

"As usual," he said, and went back to his conversation with Mona.

"Pardon me," said the sexiest voice imaginable. "I've come to rectify my abrupt departure from our conversation earlier." I looked up into Niall's handsome smile. His eyes gleamed at me. "Could I coax you into a dance with me?"

All conversation at the table died as everyone stared at Niall. I panicked. If I danced with him, my schoolgirl crush would be embarrassingly evident, my mooning eyes the female equivalent of a hard-on. Dammit. I was not *ready* to like someone—especially not someone with a girlfriend. I looked desperately for Ethan, my make-believe boyfriend. I spotted him on the dance floor with

Imogen. It penetrated that it was a slow dance. I definitely could *not* dance a slow song with Niall. No way. He was looking at me expectantly. Recklessly, I firmly planted my hand high up on Braxton's thigh. He jumped in surprise.

"Um, I don't think I can this time," I said with forced casualness, trying not to turn tomato red at the fact that my palm was perilously close to Braxton's privates. "I promised this one to you, didn't I, honey?" My eyes shot Braxton a look that promised decapitation if he didn't play along.

"Um, yeah," he agreed, confused.

"Oh, I see," Niall said in a flat voice. "Well, perhaps another time."

"Yes, perhaps," I chirped brightly. Niall flashed a lackluster smile and walked away, shoulders set. I breathed a sigh of relief and slumped back in my chair.

Babette gave me a look of disgust. "You're an idiot," she pronounced.

I realized my hand was still on Braxton's thigh and snatched it back. He wiggled his eyebrows at me. "You want to see me naked, don't you?"

"Oh shut up," I muttered. "And c'mon. Now we have to dance." I stomped to the dance floor.

After an hour of dancing and working up a sweat, I escaped to the bar with Ellis.

"Whew, I'm hot," she exclaimed.

"Well, yeah. You're like a great white dervish out there," I teased her.

"Post-wedding-planning stress discharge," she grinned. We clinked glasses and leaned tiredly against a table.

"Good day?" I asked.

She gave me a radiant smile. "The best ever. Thanks so much, Vi, for everything."

"Thanks for not making me give a toast." She laughed.

"By the way," she said absently, looking around for Jack. "I met your Niall Devlin. His sister works with Jack. I can see why you were interested." She nudged me, with a grin.

I froze. "Sister?" I demanded.

Ellis looked at me in surprise. "Mmm-hmm, sister." Comprehension dawned on her face. "Ohhh . . . did you think . . . ?" She giggled. "Vi, you're really too much. Watching your comedic errors is like a bad John Hughes movie. The old mistake-the-sister-for-a-date thing. Too clichéd for words." I stared at her, my mouth an O.

"He's available," she enunciated, as if speaking to someone mentally disabled. She laughed and gave me a shove. "Go find him."

"Oh no," I said. "I'm not—"

"Suit yourself," Ellis cut me off, shaking her head good-humoredly. "I'm going to find my hubby. Mwah." She dropped a kiss on my head and wandered off.

I stayed where I was. Niall Devlin was single. Wait, I corrected myself. Not necessarily *single*, just not dating Fiona. Maybe Babette was right. Was he interested? I recalled my hand on Braxton's thigh and blanched. Crap. Why had I been so extreme? Not that I was interested, mind you. I definitely wanted to be on my own for a while. But still. He was a nice person and there was no harm in being friendly. I should say good-night.

I scanned the room. I would also casually mention that Braxton was Imogen's boyfriend. Not that I wanted anything to happen with Niall, but it seemed only fair to clarify.

"What're you looking for?" Mona intercepted me. With his height, Niall should've been easy to spot, but I couldn't see him. I began to be apprehensive. What if I'd blown my chance?

"Have you seen that Niall guy," I asked, casting my eyes around the room. Mona raised her eyebrows at me.

"Not since you did a prostate exam on Braxton," she said wryly. I flushed. "What's up?"

"Nothing," I said evasively. She looked at me. I sighed. "Fiona was his sister," I muttered. Mona cracked up.

"I love it. That's what they call karma. Or dharma. Something. Your life is like a bad John Hughes movie. The old 'it was really his sister gag.' Too much . . ." She wandered off chuckling. I made a face after her. I was beginning to get the idea I'd been "discussed."

"What was that about?" Ethan walked up.

"Mona being right. Hey, have you seen that Niall Devlin guy?"

"The Irish guy? I think he left. I saw him and his date getting their coats."

"They're not a couple," I moaned. "Sister and brother. And not a word about John Hughes movies."

Ethan looked at me sympathetically. "Oh, Vi."

"I blew it," I said miserably.

"Well," he mused thoughtfully, "maybe not. You know what you said about being emotionally bankrupt? Maybe you need to spend some time recharging. You're still reacting to Caleb. Something new would be really hard right now. If you go for something when you're not ready, *that's* blowing it."

I thought about his words. "Maybe you're right," I said slowly. "Of course, I'll never see that guy again." I sighed.

"There'll be another one," he assured me. "When you're ready."

The band started to play "I Will Survive," and Ellis waved from the edge of the dance floor. "C'mon!" We hurried to join Mona, Imogen, and Babette, and threw ourselves into dancing. Ellis laughed in pure delight and I joined her. Maybe I had everything I needed right here.

CHAPTER TWENTY-NINE

My Boyfriend Pedro

Paula Marries Mark, Warrenton, Virginia, June

From: ViViVooom@gmail.com
To: Ben@siddickens.com
Sent: June 12
Subject: Me Again

Ben,

Ellis and Jack loved the tiles! I'm attaching a wedding photo. Ellis is in the white dress—ha ha. I'm next to her. The dresses aren't bad, huh? Imogen is the ten-foot-tall blonde next to me. Mona is next to her (remember, she's the one with the dog?). It's too bad her eyes are closed.

So, next are Paula and Mark. I was thinking T-169, Porcelain Royale. Paula's a pretty no-nonsense girl. Can you put this one on the Visa ending in 2716? I think I cleared enough room. But honestly, if I look at another peanut butter and jelly sandwich I might boot.

How's your mother feeling? Has the swelling gone down? It's a blessing it was only her ankle. Hopefully your brother is helping her out around the house more.

Cheers,
Vi

From: Ben@siddickens.com
To: ViViVooom@gmail.com
Sent: June 13
Subject: Re: Me Again

Vi,

Thanks for the picture. Ellis looks lovely. I'm pleased she liked the Memory Blocks. It was a pleasure to provide tiles for the young lady who referred you. By the way, who is the woman standing next to Mona?

My mother is much better, thank you for asking. She has been able to hobble around and take care of herself again, which has been a relief for me, as you can imagine. Hopefully she'll avoid future spills off the porch. She also loved the flowers. That was very kind of you.

I've processed the tile for Paula and Mark. It should arrive in six weeks.

Speak with you soon,
Ben

From: ViViVooom@gmail.com
To: Ben@siddickens.com
Sent: June 14
Subject: Re: Re: Me Again

    Aw Ben, you old dog. Even you're not immune. The lovely lady next to Mona in the picture is Babette. Of Babette fame. Perhaps if you sent me a picture of yourself I could share it with her???

Vi

From: Ben@siddickens.com
To: ViViVooom@gmail.com
Sent: June 15
Subject: Re: Re: Re: Me Again

Vi,

    Sadly, I do not have any digital photos of myself. Hopefully you shall not perish from the suspense.

Ben

P. S. Thank you so much for the pinot noir. It was quite lovely.

Imogen lounged on my bed, Nigel purring on her lap, while I folded laundry. Clementine was curled up on a pillow, her tail snapping back and forth, flick, flick, flick.

"So whose wedding's this weekend?"

"Paula and Mark."

Imogen laughed. "That'll be a precision affair." It was true. Paula was a dynamo. We were relatively close in the way of two fairly competitive women. She was a real estate agent specializing in downtown lofts, which I suspected she did to throw herself in the path of eligible men. She'd loudly lamented being single over pedicures until she sold a loft to Mark Boyd, a handsome unassuming lawyer. She'd clotheslined him and that was that.

"Ethan going with you?" Imogen asked in a decidedly offhanded way.

I looked up at her odd tone. "Do you know something I don't?" I asked, and was surprised at how startled she looked. "Does Babette have another blind date in mind?"

"No, uh . . ." She looked like she wanted to say something, then shrugged. "Just curious."

I didn't know if I was Relieved or Disappointed. "I let Ethan off the hook. You know Paula surely has an agenda for me." Dealing with Paula could be like negotiating with a wave.

"Will it be a good crowd?" Imogen asked.

"Hard to tell," I mused. "Mark's so sweet. If his friends have personalities and salaries like him, sharp-eyed cheetahs would have brought down those gazelles long ago."

"You must be optimistic, if you're not taking Ethan," Imogen pressed. Was I? I was emerging from mourning and appreciating the life I had. Choosing life without Caleb also had me thinking seriously about my job. I dedicated myself to not disappointing Al. But it wasn't enough to satisfy me. I'd let my job choose me the way I'd let Caleb choose me, without my active involvement. It was time to decide if it was a long-term relationship or if it was time for something new.

"I don't think I really care," I said. "I'm on a Break, remember?

I'm going for Paula. She's a good friend, especially when she's five pounds thinner than me."

Imogen rolled her eyes. "You're compelled to attend weddings. It's okay to say no."

A whisper of how nice it would be to have a weekend to myself wiggled out. I squished it. "What's wrong with going to weddings?" I defended.

"Nothing's wrong with it," Imogen said reasonably. "If you actually enjoy it. But it's like you feel validated by wedding invitations. If Ann Coulter invited you to her wedding to Satan, you'd go. You throw around wedding references like other people name-drop celebrities."

"Let me get this straight. By accepting a wedding invitation from friends, I'm social climbing?" My pitch rose to a hostile tone.

"No, no," Imogen placated me. "You're a lovely and giving friend to a lot of people who like to have you around, but you shouldn't need a wedding invitation as proof. If Mona got married and didn't ask you, you'd still be her best friend."

"No," I said mulishly. "I don't understand." If Mona got married and didn't ask me, I'd be devastated. Was Mona mad at me? "What are you trying to tell me?"

Imogen sighed. "Nothing very well," she said. "Just perhaps you put too much importance on being included. Perhaps wedding invitations shouldn't mean as much as they do."

"A wedding is the best day of a person's life," I protested. "Being invited is an honor."

"Maybe," Imogen said. "Or maybe you invite people you barely know and will never see again because they're friends of your parents. Remember Uncle Sal? Frankly, I'd rather skip the wedding and be the friend that has dinner with them before and after."

"Are you upset that Paula didn't invite you to the wedding?"

"Aaargh." Imogen stood, tumbling Nigel off her lap. He blinked sleepily, then bonelessly resettled himself into a ball. "Come on," she said. "We're supposed to meet Mona."

I hauled myself up and trailed dutifully after her. I was thoughtful.

"Is Mona mad at me?" I started, but Imogen gave me the Heisman hand and kept walking. I sighed. Maybe I *had* been a bit more jumpy since Caleb and I broke up. But who could blame me with all these weddings?

"So," I said brightly to Paula. "Are you ready?" We were having lunch outside at Sequoia in the Washington Harbor. It was one of those blessed days where the humidity wasn't out of control. Flags snapped in the breeze and the air smelled loamy. Paula, as usual, was impeccably turned out in Dolce & Gabana. She'd remade herself when she arrived in D.C. in her early twenties. If you asked Paula where she was from, she would generally offer "outside of Philadelphia," which was technically true in the way that Seattle and Dubai are "outside of Philadelphia." But Trenton wasn't exactly the Main Line inference Paula was angling for.

In addition to looking smart, she seemed quite composed. She nodded briskly. "It's just the last-minute details now." I pitied the detail under Paula's beady eye. It didn't stand a chance. "I asked you to lunch because I wanted to hand off something. One of my 'last-minute details.'" She laughed. She reached beneath the table and pulled up a good-sized document box. "It's my imaginary boyfriend," she said seriously.

I blinked at her. Had she just said what I thought?

"It's what?" My question was hesitant.

"My imaginary boyfriend, Pedro." She was deadpan. "I don't need him anymore." She pushed the box across the table to me. It practically took up the whole surface.

"Um. You have an imaginary boyfriend?" I kept my voice neutral.

"Had. Yes. It was an expedient solution to a problem. I have four married siblings. And everyone was constantly on my case about when I was going to settle down. I got sick of it, so I created Pedro. He's Spanish and works for IBM in international sales—good solid American company, but requires him to travel a lot. That's why they've never met him. He has a green card, so it's legal. It's all in there." She tapped the box.

"All?" I repeated in disbelief. She talked about him like he was real.

"You know, photos, letters, mementos, souvenirs from trips we took together, you name it. There are even some of his things in there, like boxers, old sneakers, a second toothbrush and Speed Stick that I leave around my place when family comes to visit. You have to Photoshop if you want pictures together. I never could be bothered."

"And people bought this?" I was incredulous. Paula raised an eyebrow at me.

"Honey, they bought him *Christmas presents*. All I had to do was order a few Spanish souvenirs off the Internet and fake a few phone calls. They ate it up. People will believe what they want to. They were devastated when Pedro and I broke up."

I envisioned trying to pass an imaginary Spaniard off on my family and suppressed a giggle. "Then what?" I was as fascinated as if it was a real relationship. "How did you end it?"

"That part was easy. I had him transferred permanently back to Spain. Of course, he remained madly in love with me and wanted me to come, but I wasn't prepared to move to Europe. And voilà, suddenly there was Mark."

"And Mark?"

"As far as Mark's concerned, Pedro was my boyfriend when we met. I think it made me less threatening. Conveniently, Pedro and

I broke up right when I was sure of Mark's interest. *Adios y gracias,* Pedro."

I boggled at her. She was bordering on delusional. She acted as if Pedro was real. And she was bequeathing him to me.

"Why me?" I asked, alarmed. Paula just raised an eyebrow.

Washington was beautiful all week until the day of Paula's wedding. I took one look at the sky and knew without a doubt it was going to rain. I also knew without a doubt that this would not settle with Paula's vision. I joined her for brunch at the Mayflower with her mother, sister Helen, and her bridesmaids Claire and Mary. Paula was vibrating with tension. Everyone else looked wary.

"Hey guys." I helped myself to a croissant and coffee, then flagged down a waiter for orange juice and a club soda.

"Hi." The usually unflappable Paula was terse. "What do you think? Will it rain? I have to decide. Do I move it inside? It was on the lawn but they can move it into a ballroom."

"Yes," I said firmly. The others looked a little shocked that I suggested altering Paula's perfect wedding plan. "Paula, if you don't move it inside, you'll be tense until the second of the wedding or scrambling at the last minute. If you move it, you can relax."

"But it's so nice outside. The lawn is gorgeous." Paula clung to her vision.

"It's kind of nippy even if it doesn't rain. I'm sure no one planned for it to be this cool." This was self-serving, to be sure. I was wearing a strapless number, the Steven.

Paula was nodding. "Yes, yes, you're probably right." Paula could be mercenary in pursuit of her vision but she had common sense. "I'll move it."

Paula's mother sighed in relief. The waiter delivered plates of food.

"Are those scallions?" Paula's sharp eyes skewered her omelet. "I said no scallions. No onions. None. I can't eat this." She pushed the plate away and twitched. The waiter shot her a hateful look and took the plate.

"It's wedding nerves," Paula's mother whispered to him, and I thought Paula was going to stab her with a butter knife.

"It'll be nice inside," I said. "I bet the room is beautiful."

"Oh yes," everyone chorused. Paula's look beseeched me.

"Do you think so?" I'd never seen her this unnerved.

"Definitely," I said with conviction. It was all about confident delivery.

"Okay." She nodded slowly, drawing resolution from my un-wavering expression. Hey, ladies! No tragedy! We'll just move inside! We'll just fix that runner with some nail polish!

Paula's father walked up. "I have some bad news, sweetheart." After gradually relaxing, Paula instantly again looked like she might crack into pieces.

"What? What now?"

"The weather's bad all the way to Jersey and flights are getting canceled. Folks that were coming this morning aren't going to make it."

"Oh God." Paula looked like a deer in the headlights. She was practically rattling now. "But the seating. I spent hours on the ta-bles."

"Oh well, Paula, remember that by moving inside we are switching from twenty-five tables of eight to twenty tables of ten." Her mother patted her hand. Paula got wild-eyed.

"I . . . can't . . . I . . . don't . . ." I feared she might hyperventilate. Everyone stared at her. I got impatient.

"Oh, I'll do it. It's just a matter of moving chairs. Paula, what you need is a massage. I'm calling the Black Horse Inn to book you one. While you're doing that, I'll do the tables."

Her eyes clung to me. "Really? Will you? But the oranges and the programs—"

"I'll get it taken care of." This unraveled version of Paula threw me. And it certainly didn't make getting married look pleasant. "Mary will check on the flowers." Mary nodded. "Claire can see to the programs and I'll deal with the tables." I finished my coffee and stood up. "Be right back." They smiled gratefully, relieved to have a director. Fifteen minutes later I returned.

"Right, Paula. Massage in an hour. Let's go." When we got to the Black Horse Inn where Paula was getting married, Paula handed me a bunch of Ziploc bags and an envelope.

"I have the names on slips of paper. Each bag is a table. The tables were eights but now they're tens. And a bunch of people won't make it." She started to look frantic again.

"Easy, peasy," I said cheerfully. "I'll rearrange."

"Okay," Paula said distractedly. "But the Torrances and the McFarlands hate each other and can't be anywhere near each other. And the Maryland Franklins can't be sitting with the Pennsylvania Franklins. They don't speak. Oh, and Maggie George and Tom George are divorced and should be seated apart. The Hathaways must be with the Simons—they're the only ones who can tolerate Mrs. Simon. Try to keep as many of the Boyds together as you can. They can be a little abrasive, and we try to only put them with other Boyds. Oh, and put John Gorman out of my mother's sight line—she can't stand him. Did I tell you about the Torrances and the McFarlands . . . ???"

I dashed off shorthand hieroglyphics of who hated whom and who was stuck on the tarmac somewhere bitterly eating airplane snack mix. Paula got twitchy again, but I bundled her off to her massage. In the ballroom, the staff was shaking crisp white linens over tables. The linens floated down gracefully with a gentleness that seemed to whisper it would be all right.

"Like it's going to make a difference," I muttered under my breath. "No one cares whether it's indoors or outdoors so long as the booze is free."

I sat down to the task of rearranging tables and soon my head was spinning. I felt a stab of panic. Who hated the McFarlands? Was it the Franklins? Someone hated the Franklins. The Simons? I tried to decipher my scribbles, cursing my reliance on arrows and plus/minus signs rather than the more easily understood "hates" and "likes." Why had I thought a mini skull and cross-bones next to the letters J.G. would be helpful? In the end, I just made sure every name I'd scribbled down wasn't sitting with any other jotted name, except for one I couldn't decipher at all. Well, they were on their own, whoever they were.

"Everyone's just going to have to wear their Big Boy pants today," I muttered to myself.

Once I had people clustered into groups of ten, I opened the envelope with the formal calligraphy place cards and read the instructions from Paula:

An orange with a place card will mark each guest's place.
Each card should be attached to the orange with a straight pin,
alternating pins with green balls and pins with yellow balls.

I spied a crate full of oranges against one wall. I blinked in disbelief. There had to be two hundred names in the envelope. Was she kidding me? The Movie Starring Me was "A Poke-Work Orange." I contemplated hiding the oranges and just laying out name cards. "Oranges? What oranges? I didn't see any citrus!" Then I thought of Paula. This detail could devastate her in the manner that brides react with disproportionate sorrow to minor deviations from the Dream. I hauled the crate of oranges to my chair and began the arduous task.

Two hundred oranges later my thoughts were not very charitable. No fruit at *my* wedding, unless it's served on a silver tray with lots of clotted cream. Two hundred is a ridiculous number of people to invite, I cursed, sucking my sticky finger where I'd poked myself. I looked at my watch and cursed again. I only had thirty minutes to get ready. I pushed back my chair and jostled an orange so it rolled the card reading Michael McFarland facedown. I righted it and adjusted the orange for Ellen Torrance next to it. Then I glanced at my watch again and panicked. As I ran from the room, a Thought niggled my brain. Something about Ellen Torrance. I frowned, trying to remember, but came up blank. Oh well. I didn't have time now to fret about it. I only had thirty minutes to stop smelling like a breakfast drink and get to the chapel.

Paula made an amazing bride. Back to her usual self, she was perfectly composed and coiffed. Her blond hair in a sleek updo, she looked like a runway model in her heavy satin dress. I'd been glad to be part of the bridal gnat swarm, despite the oranges. It made me feel better about being on my own. I didn't need a date. I'd met Niall at a wedding, right? I ignored a twinge over that blown opportunity and focused on the possibilities.

The program was minimalist, without names or details, just the order of service. It was difficult to guess how long it would take. There was one reading, and I was willing to put my money on First Corinthians. I was betting on twenty-two minutes. We were ten in.

"And now the couple has chosen the first book of Corinthians as their ceremonial reading," intoned the minister. Heh. "I invite our reader to come up at this time." I tried not to smirk as I glanced at the program to see who was doing it, but it only said "Reading." There was no movement in the church.

"Oh shit!" Paula burst out. "I forgot." Everyone froze. The minister looked aghast—Paula had shouted "shit" at the altar. I gaped—Paula had *forgotten* something. She looked at me.

"Vi," she said urgently, "*you're* the reader. I forgot to tell you." Her eyes begged me to comply. I gaped some more, then leapt up.

"Excuse me." I trampled feet on the way out of the pew. I hurried to the altar hoping my bra straps weren't showing. The minister seemed a little wild-eyed as he handed me his careworn Bible. "Just read from here." He pointed at some minuscule Bible print.

"The whole thing?" I whispered back, anxious.

"Yes, yes. All the way to here." He pointed at some more minuscule Bible print.

I hurried to the podium and faced the church. Everyone faced me back, alert now. I took a deep breath, then relaxed. This was fun. And it wasn't as if I didn't know First Corinthians. Cha.

" 'Though I speak with the tongues of men and angels . . .' " I began.

After the wedding, we danced between raindrops from the chapel to the (indoor) reception, Paula trailing a procession of guests like the tail of a comet. As I've noticed happens, once the wedding was over, Paula stopped caring entirely about the ins and outs of the reception and simply beamed at everyone, particularly Mark. It was all very jolly and the reception was lively. There was some sort of commotion when we arrived, back where I'd staked the oranges all afternoon, but I couldn't see what it was. After a while the shouting stopped and things settled down.

I was buoyant. Paula was delighted with me. I'd risen to the occasion. Given her profanity, I'd done a better job than she had. Later, I heard her explaining to the minister about mild, high-functioning Tourette's syndrome that could flare under stress. I learned something today, I thought to myself like a *South Park* episode. It didn't matter that I hadn't been a bridesmaid. It didn't matter that I'd saved the day. Even Paula wouldn't remember in several hours. What I learned was, despite the hype, minutiae of a wedding are just that, forgettable.

I enjoyed my stardom until the dancing started. Then, music leached couples from the tables like roots sucking nutrients from soil, leaving fewer seated guests than attendees of an Adult Children of Normal Parents convention. My euphoria faded. What was I doing here, alone on the barren mud of an empty table for ten? As I tried not to think about my conversation with Imogen and whether there was a hole in my life I was filling with false gods, an ominous shadow fell across the table.

"Excuse me," interrupted a nasally voice. I looked up. Before me was a heavyset man with a red-flushed baby face who looked like a consummate sitcom character called something like Richie who would sport a beanie cap with a propeller. I'd swear he had highlights and a perm, like a (very) poor man's Drew Carey.

"My name's Richie." He stuck a hand practically in my nose, revealing inches of pudgy wrist his too-short plaid jacket didn't cover. "You're a wonderful reader. I was wondering. Would you like to go out sometime? I like movies. Do you like movies?" He looked hopeful.

"Oh, thank you, Richie. That's very kind," I hedged. "But, um, I have a boyfriend. Yes. His name is Pedro. He's in Spain right now, actually. Do you want to see a picture?"

CHAPTER THIRTY

Rash Behavior

"I'm so broke," I moaned.

"Are you talking to anyone in particular?" asked Giles.

"American Airlines." I studied my computer screen. It was a lot of money.

"Vacation or wedding?"

I didn't even dignify him with an answer. The cost was making me feel tight in the chest. A thought skittered across my brain. I *could* decline.

"Where to?" he persisted.

No, I'd told Aurora I'd come.

"Amherst," I said absently. There was no way around it. My thrifty nature rebelled, then ached as I typed my credit card information. After I hit Submit, I skipped over to my online bank account and grimaced. Then I panicked. I was flat broke, with my credit card steadily inching upward. Insult to injury, it felt totally wasteful to stay in a hotel alone.

"Who's going with you?" Giles asked, as if my lament was audible. I winced.

"No one. It's too expensive to ask Ethan." Giles looked at me sympathetically but refrained from saying anything. He'd met someone a few months ago and had been intolerably giddy about it since. He was acquiring that grating air of couples that pity singles.

"Giles, can you cover for me this afternoon?" I asked suddenly.

"Sure. What's up?" He looked at me curiously. I'd been a model worker lately, and it was only 10:30 A.M.

"Nothing," I hedged. "Errands and . . . stuff. Call my cell if anything comes up. There's pretty good reception in the waiting room." As I'd deviously calculated, Giles got the alarmed look on his face men get when they suspect they're perilously bordering on a discussion of Personal Women's Issues. He became engrossed in an order sheet. Should Al inquire about my absence, Giles would scare him off with hushed references to "lady doctors." And frankly, both Al and Giles had been avoiding me since I began pestering them in my newfound fervor for my job. A little knowledge is truly a scary thing. I'd become obsessed, and pelted Al with proposals. My current bailiwick was Virginia wines. Al's current priority was sidestepping me.

I typed a quick e-mail asking Ben to hold off on the tile I'd selected for Paula and Mark until I could fit it on my credit card, then escaped. Half an hour later I parked at NIH with grim determination. Evelyn, the perky administrator, looked eerily like a character from a *Far Side* cartoon. Today she was wearing a white plastic barrette identical to ones I'd worn when I was nine.

"Vi! How nice to see you!" she chirped.

"I'm just happy to help," I responded in the tone of an earnest funeral home host.

"Let's see now. Oh yes! We've got you for some ointment testing and, ooh looksee, you're doing non-movement this weekend! Friday afternoon through Monday morning, right?" She looked at me through her pointy glasses and giggled. "Won't that be a kick?"

Not, in fact. No kicking, no walking, no muscle reliance whatsoever, just laying in bed and staring at the TV for sixty hours.

While people dream of such sloth, I suspected it would be maddening in reality. But it paid $400. That almost compensated for using a bedpan. I planned to go easy on the liquids.

"Well, let's get you started! You'll be in Salon 6." It remained a mystery to me that people as smart as NIH doctors fell for the fallacy that if you call something a "salon" it's somehow more appealing than a "room." Either way, it was a clinical drafty cubicle with fluorescent lights, vinyl furniture, and industrial pea green paint. Evelyn burbled on. "Do you have magazines? Usually we don't provide magazines, but since you are becoming a real regular, I can let you in on my secret stash!"

I thanked Evelyn, but no, I had my book, thanks all the same. Internally, I wondered about the state of my life that I was entitled to secret magazines for regulars. In Salon 6 a nice young researcher asked me to take off my pants and graciously informed me I was permitted to keep my top under the hospital gown. I gritted my teeth and did as I was told, feeling awkward in the way people universally do in hospital gowns. I suspect hospital gowns are a great physician conspiracy to distract patients from whatever ailment brought them to the hospital in the first place. Surely the wealth of modern technology and design could yield a more comfortable and covering garment. But this would leave patients free to pay more attention to and vocalize their discomfort, or offer self-diagnoses that are so helpful to physicians. Instead, preoccupied with keeping their bum covered, distracted patients leave doctors to treat them in relative peace. I half listened to my instructions as I wiggled on the table, trying to get comfortable without inspiring a chorus of Moon River from the researcher.

"Don't rub the lotion off or rub my legs together, stay here. Got it," I said, not listening. I lay back on the table and pretended to be engrossed in my book while the technician applied a smelly cream on my legs from mid-thigh to mid-shin. When she was done, she set a timer and left.

I tried to focus on the newest Jasper Fforde novel. That Jasper, he keeps getting better and better, I told myself in anticipation. This was true, however, my brain wasn't buying it. My brain was focused on the itchiness expanding through my body. Even abatement of the lotion's noxious odor as it dried didn't make up for the increasing irritation. I refocused on the sentence I'd just non-read eight times. If I could do bikram yoga hung over, I could do this.

"I can't do this." I tossed my book aside after what seemed like enough time to evolve down to four toes, but was only seven minutes. I squinted at the timer. The arrow seemed ominously far from zero. The itching was getting worse.

"This isn't worth fifty dollars," I muttered. I struggled to sit upright without rubbing my legs together. This resulted in a gown malfunction that would've been terribly embarrassing had anyone been in the room. I adjusted. I was no longer cold, but sweating. The fire on my legs increased. I squinted at them under the cream. Was that a rash? I peered so intently that I accidentally bumped my nose to my leg. I jerked back in horror, rubbing my nose. God forbid I got hives on my face.

I was convinced I was having a reaction. And not a good one. Normally I'm not a crazy hypochondriac, but my legs definitely felt inflamed and I was sure that beneath the completely opaque yellow cream they looked redder than they should. Okay, maybe I *was* a hypochondriac. But not as bad as Maeve, who once spent an entire summer convinced she had malaria. On second thought, had that been me? Regardless. Childish foolishness did not change the fact that I was now in the throes of a flesh eating virus.

I looked around anxiously for a call button. There wasn't one. There was a phone, but who would I call? I eased off the bed and hobbled to the door, trying both to preserve my modesty and prevent my legs from rubbing against each other, which were incompatible goals. I stuck my head out into the (deserted) hallway. I could hear a lonely wind whistling. I counted to ten. Nothing. I counted to ten again. Crickets chirping. Damn.

I considered my options, none of which seemed great. Stay where I was and allow my legs to be chemically eroded for another—I looked at the timer—twenty minutes. Or shamble down the hall seeking a rescuer, hoping no one noticed I had little elephants on my underpants. I looked at the timer again. Right. Shamble it was.

I began my awkward toddle down the deserted corridor. As I was approaching a corner, I heard voices. I sped up in happy relief. Ignoring my ignominy, I rounded the corner ready to embrace the unsuspecting stranger . . . and looked up to see Niall Devlin walking down the hall deep in conversation with a white-coated, official-looking man.

I slammed myself back around the corner so fast that my head ricocheted off the wall. The pain brought temporary relief from the relentless itching and, now, panic. What was Niall Devlin doing there? More important, how could I avoid him? There was no way I wanted to be caught covered in Pungent Unguent and flashing pink pachyderm panties. I didn't think I'd been spotted, but they were approaching fast. I looked around desperately. There weren't many options. The voices were getting closer. I sized up a door across from me. I had no clue where it went, but on short notice it was the lesser of two evils. I leapt across the hall, yanked the door open, then slammed it shut behind me and my billowing gown.

I pressed my ear against the door, panting and listening, and wondering what I was going to say to the four shocked faces turned in my direction. The idiot voice in my brain suggested that maybe if I didn't say anything, they'd go away. From the way I could see half-chewed tuna fish in the hanging open mouth of one of them, I doubted it. But my attention was first focused on using all of my mind powers to hurry Niall and his companion along to another destination. Preferably Asia. I was reminded of my total lack of mind powers when they stopped to finish their conversation right outside the door.

"So, they're hydrating him now. That should take about half an hour, and then you'll be able to take him home," said an older American voice.

"And do I need to do anything for him once I get him home?" came the divine Irish lilt.

"Excuse me," a high-pitched nasal voice sawed in from the table behind me. I waved a hand to shush him as I continued to focus on the other side of the door.

"Lots of fluids," the other man said, "but, obviously, no caffeine. Alcohol's not recommended. He needs to hydrate, eat nourishing food, and get some sleep."

"Excuse me!" The voice was more strident, with the petulant twang of someone used to being ignored. "You're not allowed in here." I ignored him.

"Grand," I heard Niall reply in relief. "Thanks so much. May I go to his room now?"

"Certainly. You'll find him in Salon 14. At the end of this corridor, turn left." I slumped in relief as two sets of footfalls departed.

"Hey, you need to leave," the voice insisted peevishly. "Patients are not allowed in staff break rooms." I knew he'd be skinny with a big Adam's apple before I turned around, and he was and he did. He was puffed up like a bantam as he tried for bravado, but couldn't carry it off. Everyone else sat wide-eyed, looking from him to me—more interested in diversion than concerned about the prohibited presence of a pachyderm panty-clad patient. I gave him the same amused look I would give a Chihuahua straining its leash to get at a German shepherd. I wasn't focused on him, though. My brain was calculating. If I hurried, I could cross paths with Niall as he left. I was dressed distinctly *not*-hip retro in an oversized and shapeless carnation-colored sweater left over from 1988 (complete with spot and cat hair), and definite Drowned Rat hair, but it couldn't be helped. According to his conversation, I had thirty minutes.

"Listen," yapped the Chihuahua. "You must leave."

"You're right," I confirmed. "I have to be at the studio in thirty minutes to film the segment on my last undercover health care exposé. Can you please send someone to Salon 6 promptly to effect my discharge? If you're quick, I might forget to mention in my piece how easy it is for patients to access off-limit areas." I strode out the door. Once it shut behind me, I flew down the corridor to Salon 6. The timer read eleven minutes left. I quickly turned it to two minutes and hopped onto the table just as the researcher hurried in.

"What's going on?" she asked, looking confused. "I got the weirdest message."

"Sorry about that," I said. "I was trying to find you. I think I may be having a reaction."

"Why didn't you just pick up the phone like I told you? It connects directly to the monitor's desk when you lift the receiver." Ah. That must have been the bit I didn't listen to.

"I guess the lotion affected my brain," I said, wiggling on the table in impatience. I peeked at my watch. Twenty-five minutes. On cue, the timer pinged. "But, hey, so can we clean me up really fast? I just remembered that I have to go. Now."

The researcher led me to a shower stall and bench and used the shower nozzle to clean my legs. I tilted my head up so spray didn't land on my hair and exacerbate the wet rat look.

"Oh my God," the researcher said.

"What?" I looked down in alarm. My legs looked like the cheeks of a fifteen-year-old *Star Trek* devotee. There were angry red bumps from my thighs to my calves.

"You must have a sensitivity to the ointment," she said in concern. "It looks like an allergic rash reaction." She gently touched my leg with her gloved hand and I jumped.

"Yow! It looks like a swarm of bees attacked my legs. And feels like it too."

She was sympathetic. "I'm so sorry. I'll give you something to help with the swelling. You can rest as long as you like."

"What? No. I don't have time." I looked desperately at my watch. Fifteen minutes. "I have to go!"

"But it'll be much better if you—" I was already shaking my head. The researcher shrugged, took some photos of my reaction, and made copious notes on her clipboard while I jiggled with impatience. At last she was done.

"At least let me put some ointment on your rash and give you a shot of steroids to help with the swelling," she begged. I looked at my watch. I had eight minutes.

"Okay. Make it quick," I consented grudgingly, as if she was the Avon lady hawking Paradise of Plums eye shadow, rather than a medical professional trying to treat my disease.

She disappeared and I brushed my hair and reapplied lipstick. I looked at my watch impatiently. She returned and quickly applied a much better smelling lotion that felt like a cooling hand on my legs. I actually sighed as she applied it, it felt so good.

"Are you sure you won't stay—" she started to ask.

"Nope, nope. Thanks but can't." I looked at my watch. Three minutes. "Gotta go."

"All right." She shook her head over my foolishness as she left. "You're released."

I dumped the gown in the trash and grabbed my jeans, then paused. How was I going to put on my jeans? Two minutes. What the hell, I thought. I gingerly pulled up the jeans. It felt like Clementine was clawing her way up my legs. I took a few deep breaths. Then I ventured a step. Then I took a few more breaths. I looked at my watch. Shit.

You can handle this, I steeled myself. I slipped on my shoes and headed out the door. Walking chafed but I could bear it. I straightened my back and practiced a casual looking saunter, then dropped the act and raced toward the lobby. Evelyn looked surprised as I flew past.

"Vi," she called after me, but I didn't stop. Near the lobby, I dropped into a casual saunter. I strolled across but didn't see Niall. I got a drink at the water fountain. Then I lingered while the information desk clerk looked at me. I got another drink of water. I read a CPR poster as if I'd never seen the information before. So *that's* how you help a choking victim! I loitered some more (nonchalant). So *that's* where the fire exits are located! I looked at my watch. It'd been forty-five minutes since the overheard conversation. I fretted. Had I missed him? I fought the urge to manically rub my legs against the furniture in the manner of a wild animal.

After five more minutes I decided he was gone, and my legs were driving me crazy. I had this paranoid idea that the pestilence was slowly infecting the insides of my jeans. If I didn't wash them soon I'd be afraid to wear them again. I turned to go, mentally cursing the NIH, as if Niall's nonappearance was somehow its fault, when I heard a familiar lilting accent.

"Easy there, mate." I saw Niall emerge from a hallway, steadying a ruddy-faced man. The fellow said, "I'm okay man. What do I gotta do to get out of here? I just wanna go home." Niall pointed to the checkout desk and his friend ambled over carefully. Niall looked after him, smiling in amusement. I admired his long lean body. He turned and caught sight of me watching from across the lobby. Recognition came over his face and he smiled and started toward me.

"Well, hello." He grinned engagingly. Delicious. "So we meet again." I beamed goofily. "What brings you to this exalted institution?"

I blinked. "Oh." I racked my brains for an idea. I had a stroke of brilliance. "My girlfriend works here—I think you met her boyfriend at Ellis's wedding, the one I'd promised to dance with when you asked? Anyway, he has a potbellied pig and he's going out of town so she's looking after the pig. He was running behind today and didn't have time to get her his keys, so I said I'd drop them off." A professor once told me, if you're going to lie, lie big. I smiled engagingly at him.

"And you?" I asked. "I didn't know they treated patients here." I gestured to his friend. Then I mental head-slapped myself. How would I know his friend had been treated? Niall didn't notice my clairvoyance.

"If you can believe it, a mate from my rugby team was the subject for experimental testing. It's the daftest thing you've ever heard." He laughed and shook his head. "He needed some extra dosh and heard that NIH pays plonkers like himself to be test subjects. So your man comes out here and ingests an unholy amount of caffeine. Only it turns out he has a sensitivity to caffeine. He booted all over the researchers, had convulsions, and generally distressed the entire staff. They gave him loads of fluids and he'll be fine, but he can't drive, so he rang me to fetch him."

"Oh my," I murmured. "Poor guy."

"Silly tosser, more like," Niall laughed. "What can you expect, subjecting yourself to medical experimentation?" I made a noncommittal noise. "Can you believe that next he was going to lie down for three straight days? He was voluntarily electing to waste his muscles so that scientists who wouldn't do it to their own selves could see what happened."

I couldn't think of anything to say to that. My legs started itching worse, as if to support Niall's sentiments. I ignored it. There was an awkward pause. He cleared his throat.

"So, did you enjoy the wedding?" he asked.

"Yes." I was grateful for a new topic. "Very much. You left early," I ventured. "I looked for you later but you'd gone. I guess your date got tired?"

He looked surprised. "Fiona? She's my sister." Then he laughed.

"And you thought my sister was my date? That's rather like an American teenage movie farce, isn't it?" Huh.

I made a noncommittal noise. My legs did not want to be ignored. "Yes, well, I love a wedding. I can't hear First Corinthians too many times."

Niall laughed. "I won't comment on the ambiguity of that phrasing. I'm just sorry I never got that dance." He looked at me intently.

I flushed with pleasure. And I gave in to the strident demands from my calves and rubbed my right leg with my left foot. It felt so good I almost moaned. I rubbed up higher and higher. I forced my attention back to Niall, but as I was putting my foot down, my right leg spasmed and buckled. I tried to correct but my shoe caught on my jeans and I teetered precariously backward. This is it, I thought, windmilling my arms, I'm about to topple into an Oscar-worthy dramatization of The Most Humiliating Moment Of My Life. At least I was already in a hospital.

Suddenly, I was jerked forward against a rock solid chest. I clutched Niall's lapels in relief as he grasped me tightly. I buried my face in his clean-smelling shirt and inhaled his crisp male scent for a long moment. Then I reluctantly pushed back to support myself on wobbly legs. His arms remained around me. It felt really good. I met his eyes.

"Thanks . . ." I stammered. We stared for a long moment.

"Are you okay?" he asked in concern, giving my back a little stroke. Zing.

"Fine, fine." I stepped back reluctantly. "Thanks for saving me."

He quirked a crooked grin at me and dropped his arms. "Any time."

Our eyes caught again and held. He opened his mouth as if to speak . . . and was interrupted by a petulant pout that doused my dreams.

"Niall!" sulked a voice I'd heard before. "I've been sitting in the car *forever*. Where's Simon? We're going to lose our dinner reservations." The willowy brunette from Traci's wedding was walking toward us. She was stunning, with sleek hair and expert makeup I couldn't manage if I had three days, an airbrush and Bobbi Brown at my side. I remembered my cheesy sweater and felt like a prize idiot. Shit. Here I'd been flirting with Niall and forgotten I was dressed like a refugee from *Breakin' 2: Electric Boogaloo*. What an ass I was.

Niall looked away from her and searchingly at me. Did I imagine regret?

"Your other sister?" I asked hopefully.

"No," she cut him off, sliding her arm through his. "His date. Vanessa. And you are?"

"Vi Connelly." I held out a hand. She ignored it. Bitch.

"Charmed." She wasn't. "Nice outfit. Last time I saw something like that, she was in a Camaro, draped over the finest mullet I'd ever seen." She looked around as if expecting Billy Ray Cyrus to pop up and escort me out.

"David Bowie had a mullet, and he was a glam rock icon," Niall interjected gallantly, defending mullets, as if it'd actually been *me* in the Camaro.

"So did Michael Bolton." Vanessa's voice was ice. "Niall, we have to go." To him, she was a cooing dove. To me, I was surprised she didn't lift a leg and pee on Niall to mark her territory. I was crushed I'd misread Niall's flirtation. It was time to flee.

"Well, nice to meet you, but I have to make my Achy Breaky Start toward dinner too." I edged away. "You kids have fun." I was mid-stride toward escape when someone did stop me.

"Vi! You're still here! Why, you ran out in such a hurry, I didn't get a chance to talk about this weekend. And here you are half an hour later!" Evelyn giggled, pouncing from behind.

"Evelyn," I gasped. Good Lord, please don't let the humiliation get worse, I prayed.

"We really need to go over some things for Friday," she admonished me cheerfully. "I guess you forgot in your hurry."

"Yes, yes," I exclaimed, desperate to prevent her from exposing me. Niall showed curiousity, no doubt surprised Braxton was dating a sixty-four-year-old. "I had to dash to make a call. Um, but I'm finished here," I trilled. Vanessa looked on sourly.

"I can bring the forms to you if you want!" She sang. "They're just releases for—"

"Super! Great!" I hastily interrupted. "Actually, let's go right now." I linked an arm through Evelyn's, dragging her away. "No sense in wasting time."

His friend returned then, saying, "I've gotta go, man. I need to lie down."

"Thank God," Vanessa declared.

"Oh, look!" Evelyn chirped, recognizing Niall's friend. "You two are both—"

"'Bye! Great to see you again!" I hollered as I hauled Evelyn away, waving at Niall's surprised face. As I muscled Evelyn around the corner, I realized with regret that Niall had no way to get in touch with me. Then I remembered Vanessa and sighed. Not that he'd want to. I'd totally misread his niceness as interest because that was what I wanted him to feel, not because he did. I pushed back Disappointment resolutely. I was On A Break anyway. Definitely.

"I'm happy just the way things are," I voiced my mantra.

"What dear? That's good. Now let's get you sorted out," said Evelyn.

CHAPTER THIRTY-ONE

Martha's Star Chamber

Dee Marries Jerry, Harrisburg, Pennsylvania, July

From: ViViVooom@gmail.com
To: Ben@siddickens.com
Sent: July 10
Subject: More tiles

Ben,

   I'm off to exciting Harrisburg for another wedding. Can you pick out a tile for me? Have the card say congratulations, blah blah blah, happiness, blah blah blah, best wishes, yadda yadda. Whatever will do.

Have a great weekend!
V.

"Sorry I'm late." I settled into my seat as Charlie came over with a wineglass and a club soda.

"How was the wedding?" asked Mona.

"Unbelievable." I was still in a state of incredulity. "It was sponsored."

There was silence at the table. This doesn't happen often.

"I'm sorry," Ellis said. "But . . . what?"

"Think of a baseball stadium wall," I explained. "Dee and Jerry bartered advertising space to get everything for the wedding donated. There was a banner draped across the aisle proclaiming 'Harrisburg Laser Hair Removal.'"

"Genius," Imogen laughed. "Dum dum de dum, Hair(less) comes the Bride . . ."

"Talk about a marriage of love and money," said Babette.

"All weddings are about money," I pronounced darkly. "The average wedding costs $28,000 and lasts twenty-two minutes. Only bungee jumping has a better cost per minute ratio. I'm convinced there's a Star Chamber comprised of Vera Wang, Kodak, the Wedding Channel, *Town & Country*, Williams-Sonoma, and Uncle Ben. They're led by Martha Stewart."

"I always suspected Martha had a broader agenda." Imogen raised a brow.

"And how did you uncover this ruthless cabal?" Mona cunningly used her wineglass to conceal a suspiciously mocking expression.

"When I was instructed to buy a 'tussy mussy' for Amy's wedding. And no," I cut off a wiggling Imogen, "a tussy mussy is not a rude name for your future mother-in-law. It's a metal bootie for your bouquet. Ranking with the pogo stick as the most outrageously expensive item you'll only use once. They went out with the Victorian era but made a roaring comeback when Oprah named them one of her favorite things. No doubt after a lucrative kickback from the Star Chamber."

"And some cookies from Martha," Mona added.

"Laugh all you want," I continued my rant, "but the insidious workings of Martha's Star Chamber scare me. They make perfectly normal people buy ridiculous stuff they don't really want. Do you know," I told them, "that Radiant Bridal Barbie is included under the 'Essentials' link at the David's Bridal website? Along with a tin filled with personalized pink heart-shaped 'Mint to be Together' mints, a 'Father of the Bride' baseball cap, and a book called *Ten Neat Things About Being a Flower Girl*. Interesting, considering that most flower girls can't yet read, and most fathers would be shot if they showed up at the wedding in a baseball cap."

"Are you also opposed to doves and precocious little kids in miniature grown-up clothes?" she teased.

"Hey," I protested. "My outlook on love is jadedly cynical but irrepressibly hopeful at the same time. I'm a sarcastic optimist."

"She does get teary-eyed at McDonald's commercials," Babette teased. That had happened once, but I'd been home sick and watched way too many episodes of *Little House on the Prairie* for my emotional well-being. Warranty instructions would have moved me to tears.

"Not relevant," I redirected. "My point is that weddings and marriage seem to be increasingly unconnected goals. Hats off to Dee and Jerry for unclouded perspective."

"But getting married is natural," Ellis said.

"Well, so is being devoured by a predator twice your size, but you still fight like hell to avoid it," I countered.

"So you don't want to get married anymore?" Ellis probed. "What about your sheath dress and barefoot on a beach in Charleston?"

"I'm not sure," I replied, knowing I was lying, just as everyone at the table knew I was lying. And they knew that I knew that they knew I was lying. But the beauty of friends is that they let you say ridiculous things without making fun. Until later.

Ellis patted my hand. "Overexposure to anything can put you off it for a while," she said. "Even chocolate. But you'll recover."

"Maybe," I said noncommitally. But secretly I wondered if I wouldn't end up like Dr. Bruce Banner, whose massive overexposure to gamma rays permanently transformed him into the monstrous Incredible Hulk. "Anyway, I've only got five left. I don't know who's happier, me or Ethan." An unnatural silence fell over the table.

Mona cleared her throat. "Imogen," she said. I looked at Imogen. She was studying her hands. "Imogen," Mona repeated sternly. "It's time."

"What?" I said again. Something was up.

"Actually, Vi," Imogen said haltingly, "I was going to mention that Ethan and I have sort of been spending time together."

"Well sure," I said, perplexed. "Of course." The awkward silence reappeared. I was confused. Did Imogen feel left out?

"Um . . ." Imogen scrutinized her hands some more. Then, "For God's sake, Mona, stop kicking me," with a glare. Imogen met my eyes. "Dating," she said with a pained look. "We're dating."

I goggled at her. Imogen and Ethan?? *Dating?* I looked around the table, but everyone looked shifty and wouldn't meet my eyes.

"Whoa. How long has this been going on?" I demanded. This was too weird.

"Um, well, it hasn't been serious . . . until maybe, sort of recently. . . ." She trailed off at my stare. "So, I guess, um, six months?"

Six months?? Was I *blind*? My head was spinning.

"We didn't want to tell you until there was something to tell. We thought it would be weird for you." Imogen looked miserable. "At first it was just a late night smooch once in a while. Then we decided to give it a real go about two months ago. And, well, it's been working."

"Wow," was all I could say. I struggled to get my head around it. I wasn't upset, just slightly uncomfortable. Like my two secret thought and feeling vessels had merged into one, leaving me exposed. But I couldn't love two people more, so I guessed I'd get used to it. Wasn't this *exactly* the situation I'd wished for with Jen? With whom else could I share Imogen? I'd lose my friend a little as I stood waiting on Want To Be There Pier, while she was already safely across Lonely Lake in Union City. But there wasn't much you could do about it.

I looked around the table. Ellis married. Mona dating Brad. Now Imogen with Ethan. And Babette, of course, who had no interest in a committed relationship, yet unremittingly had to evade thronging suitors. "It's down to me," I mused. They were silent. I refused to release the self-piteous "What's wrong with me?" that wanted to wail out of my mouth. I'd recentered since Caleb and was happy. I straightened my shoulders.

"Have I been a rotten friend?" I looked squarely at them. "Completely self-absorbed?"

"Oh honey, no," Babette dismissed me. "You've had a lot going on."

"No more than when I was miserable at work and trying to find a new job." Mona looked at me sympathetically. "All I did was complain and fret, and you all let me rant and cheered me up and e-mailed job listings."

"We were very, very happy when you got your new job." Ellis patted Mona's hand, and Mona made a face. "And I spent most of this year boring you to death about tuxedos and mother-in-laws. But that's what Clyde's is all about."

"The nice thing about your friends is that they love you no matter what," Babette assured me. "You guys saved my life when my dad died, and I'm sure that was no fun for anyone. You flew to France to hold my hand at a funeral, Vi. I can listen to you bitch about oranges until the cows go to heaven." Mona covered a chuckle.

"Besides," Mona shot Imogen a look, "some things were specifically camouflaged from even your keenest, least self-absorbed eye." Imogen hunched in her seat.

"Well, okay then." I paused to slug back my wine. "As of now, I'm officially rejoining the living and promise to be less obsessed with all the wedding stuff." I considered Imogen. "Ethan's a lucky guy. But if you get Ethan, I get to wear your red Prada heels for a month." She wilted in relief. I was happy. They were sharp shoes.

CHAPTER THIRTY-TWO

Turns/Tile

Aurora Marries Laken, Salem, Massachusetts, August

"Sid Dickens, this is Ben speaking. How may I help you?"

"Yo, it's Vi. How's Raincouver?"

"Vi, how delightful. Wet."

I laughed. "Better than too dry. I just got back from Aurora and Laken's wedding in a field outside Salem, Massachusetts, where some ley lines intersect. After a brief crystal ceremony by an inner bonding facilitator, we 'turned in the steps of the ancients,' which basically meant walking in figure-eights in a dusty field and ruining my excellent quality knockoff Christian Louboutins. We were supposed to venerate the mystical veil with reverent silence but everyone started violently sneezing. Seems the ancients hadn't swept their mystical driveways in a while. A case of 'Salem's Snot.'"

"I don't understand what that means." Ben sounded puzzled.

"You need to get hip with American pop culture, Ben. It's a movie."

"I prefer documentaries. So, are they legally married?" he asked.

"Who knows?" I said. "But you know what? It was more mean-ingful than a lot of weddings. The bride and groom were focused on their commitment ritual, not oranges."

"You really need to let the oranges go," Ben chided.

"Are you a-peel-ing to me, Ben? Heh. Anyway, legal or not, they get a gift. I don't want anyone putting Wiccan spells on me."

"Hmmm. Sid designed a new tile that might be just the thing. I'll e-mail an image."

"Thanks, Ben. I'm leaving work early today, so I may get back to you tomorrow."

"I won't ask. Between those harebrained lab tests and the amount of time you spend on the phone with me, I wonder that you get any work done at all."

"Oh, Ben, orange you glad when I call? Heh."

CHAPTER THIRTY-THREE

Not in the Pink

Adele Marries Peter, Washington, D.C., September

"It's the home stretch," Imogen reassured over the phone. "You only have four more."

"I don't think I can take anymore," I answered honestly. "I used to think weddings were wonderful and romantic. Now I'm 'Bored of the Rings.'" I paused. "And, honestly, I feel a little left out. How can you resent something and resent not being a part of it at the same time?"

"Voltaire probably has an answer for that," Imogen said. "My guess is common sense battling societal brainwashing."

"I suppose. It just gets me down. My love life these days consists of zero activity interspersed with dramatic moments of public humiliation." I'd given Imogen the abridged version of my "bump into" Niall, leaving out the NIH part. I thought it best if she didn't know about my little experiments.

"I suspect the almost-tumble was not as humiliating as you make out," Imogen speculated.

"My outfit alone was that humiliating," I corrected her. "Niall

Devlin is the icing on the cake. Not only do I have to repeatedly live the best day of other people's lives, there's also a fun rejection cycle of pratfalls in front of the Irish Dream."

"Having seen how overhyped it is, do you even want a wedding anymore?" she asked.

I reflected. "I want those perfect crystal moments. That second when the groom's eyes fill with tears, the light in the bride's smile as he grips her waist tighter when they dance. I want to relax into someone. To know he's there to catch me." I thought of the crisp smell of Niall's chest.

"Teaching children to read in the sunlight in Africa," Imogen suggested.

"Exactly."

"Maybe you need to lower your standards," she suggested seriously. Maybe it isn't about perfection but about finding a nice person that's good to you.

"You sound like Jen," I said. "But I can't do that. I believe in holding out. It just has to work that way."

"Or what?" Imogen pressed.

"Or none of it was worth it. It has to be worth it. Right?"

"I don't know," she said. "Maybe you can be wrong once, and right later. Look at your parents. We were silent, both aware that Imogen's parents had never been "right." "What time is Mona picking you up?"

I looked at my watch. "Four-thirty. Adele wanted us to come by the church early."

"Jitters?"

"No idea. Wants a gnat swarm, I guess."

"What are you wearing?"

"Adele asked us to wear pink."

"Forget pink. Wear something that feels good. You believe the Holy He is out there. Don't overlook that he could be anyone. Even Niall. There's no rule that the most amazing guy won't also think you're incredible. Everyone who knows you loves you. Remember that."

"That's lovely, Imogen." I was moved.

"It's true. You know he'll be there, so pick a dress that makes you feel pretty and have fun."

"Oh yeah—I can't wait to play with Vindictive Vanessa."

"Point one: You don't know if she'll be there. Niall knows you're coming, right?"

"Adele said my name came up. Peter and Niall are rugby buddies. So is Jennifer's boyfriend, Henry." I named some mutual friends we had with Adele.

"D.C. is so one degree of separation," Imogen observed. "But that's good news about Henry. I like him. He could be a good resource. So, not to hinge too much on it, but what if this guy comes alone? Babette swears he's into you." I snorted to indicate I didn't think it was likely, but felt a crazy hopeful flare.

"Point B: Even if Vanessa is there, you'll be dressed to kill this time. You can take her. Sharpen your claws and channel your goddess powers."

I made a noncommittal noise.

"Thirdly, if he doesn't give you the adoration you deserve, you're better off without him. You don't want to be with someone who makes you feel bad."

That was a good point. I never again wanted to be the nervous wreck I was with Caleb. Though Niall had never been anything but charming. It wasn't a matter of him making me feel bad; it was a matter of wanting what someone can't give you.

"Red's close enough to pink, right?" I asked.

"Perfect," she agreed.

"Do you think it's a problem that I didn't wear pink?" I asked as we entered the church, eyeing Mona's pale pink dress and feeling anxious about my rebellion. I was wearing a fitted red Shelli Segal cocktail dress with high silver sandals. It looked amazing, but I felt a pang of Guilt. The day was supposed to be about making the bride happy, not impressing Niall.

"You're fine," Mona assured me. "Red's just a really strong pink. I bet she doesn't even notice." We followed laughter down the hallway.

"Girls!" Adele called out when we entered. "I'm glad you came early." She saw my dress and her face fell a tiny bit. "Oh. No pink?"

"I'm sorry, Adele. I didn't really have anything," I lied. "But I brought pink champagne!"

"Oooh, yes please!" Adele giggled. There were three other girls in the room, Lori, Jennifer, and Lesley, whom I knew and liked. They were all wearing pink. I felt very, very conspicuous. I didn't see anyone resembling a bridesmaid. Adele kept looking at us and giggling. A few minutes later another pink-clad girl showed up and was introduced as Gabrielle.

"Oh good," Adele bubbled. "Everyone's here."

"I'm so excited for you," Gabrielle beamed.

"And I'm excited for *you*," Adele said. "I have a surprise!" She whipped out a large bag.

"What is it?" Lori asked brightly. I began to have a bad feeling.

"You're all my bridesmaids!" Adele announced with glee. "Surprise!" She handed each girl a jewelry box. Mona looked at me with what can only be described as pure terror. "I didn't want you to buy some dress you'd never wear again," Adele went on, "or feel pressure. But once I knew you were each coming, I wanted to include you, so I thought you could wear the same color and these!" Adele had the grace not to point at me, shrieking spoilsport. Inside the box was a pink choker spelling my name and a shiny pink tube of lip gloss.

"Oh," said Mona.

"Put them on!" clapped Adele. "Perfect!" she enthused as we donned our dog collars. "This will be great. You'll walk in before me like any other wedding. It'll be so fun!" Jennifer caught my eye across the room and blew me a big juicy pink lip gloss kiss.

It dawned on me that I was about to be the Scarlet Letter(s) in a Pink Parade. I closed my eyes in horror at the image of my harlot self, walking like a glaring red STD among flower petals. It was so unfair. It was small comfort that Mona looked like she might self-immolate.

"One bottle of champagne won't be enough for this," muttered Lesley.

"You're in luck," whispered Lori. "Either Jennifer had an erection or she snuck a bottle in too." Jennifer indeed had more champagne, which was soon coming out my nose as we all laughed about the absurdity of our "surprise." Except for Mona, who just looked stricken. At six, a little giggly from champagne, we lined up according to height, which put me behind her.

"This has to be contrary to the Geneva Convention on torture," she moaned.

"At least you're wearing pink. I stand out like David Blaine."

Our surprise processional was particularly inelegant. We just . . . walked, bouquetless hands stiffly graceless, my red dress pulsing like a blood blister. Once Adele had been handed to Peter, we lingered awkwardly, unsure what to do, until the minister urged us to sit. We sat.

"If you don't stop wiggling, I'm going to beat you," Mona snapped out of the side of her mouth after a few minutes, contradicting "love is patient, love is kind" being read at the altar. I was trying to spot Niall without craning. No mean trick when you're in the front row. I also kept fidgeting with my collar, which was driving me crazy.

It was over soon enough, and after some clumsy milling about, Team Surprise Bridesmaid managed a disorganized recessional.

Mona, Lesley, and I were hoofing it to Meridian House for the reception when Adele called after us. "Yoo-hoo . . . girls! Don't forget pictures!" Thwarted, we backtracked. It was another thirty minutes before we were released.

"What do you think of the collar?" Lesley muttered as we beelined to the beautiful stone Meridian House and the open bar therein.

"I'm sorry, I can't talk right now," I said. "I have to find where I buried my bone." A set-faced Mona just snorted.

"Do you see him?" I whispered to Mona as we hit the bar. I was frustrated, having lost a significant portion of my best opportunity to talk to Niall.

"No," she said. "Again." We collected glasses of chardonnay. Mona got one more "for a friend" and tossed the first glass back alarmingly fast.

"Are you okay?" I asked.

"I will be," she said severely, starting in on glass number two.

"How soon can I take this off?" I tugged at my choker.

"You can't," She ground out. "It's an honor."

Team Surprise Bridesmaid grouped together like a giant pink ambulatory brain (with a glaring red hematoma) and surveyed the crowd.

"I kind of like the guy with pineapples on his tie," offered Lori.

"Too beefy," I said. We surveyed some more.

"What about the guy in the purple pants?" Jennifer suggested.

"He's in purple pants," I declined. I was scanning for only one person.

"What about the guy in the seersucker suit?" said Lesley. We looked at the guy in the seersucker suit. He had potential. Someone else thought so too, as she sidled up to him and slipped her arm around his waist. We all sighed in unison.

"Not much out there, ladies. I suppose we should mingle, but I feel like a goof in this collar," I lamented.

"Honey, we all do," Jennifer agreed. Our brain stroked out when Henry joined the group, attaching a charcoal grey tumor.

I didn't see Niall anywhere. I began to be disheartened. Maybe he'd canceled. Maybe he was avoiding me so I wouldn't topple into him again. Maybe he was making out in the cloakroom with Vanessa. Maybe—

"Niall!" called Henry. "Where've you been, mate?" My armpit glands announced their presence as forcefully as a red dress in a pink wedding, producing enough lubricant to ease Jabba the Hut into Nicole Ritchie's miniskirt. I turned and found Niall looking directly at me, tan features striking against a sharp olive suit. We're here! We're here! Exclaimed my sweat glands. "Jesu, Joy of Glands Perspiring."

"Sort of a family emergency," he answered, eyes remaining on me. "I had to dash after the ceremony to ring home before it got too late in Ireland. Anyone need a drink? Vi?"

"I'd love a glass of wine," I said.

"Absolutely. Hello, I'm Niall." He turned to Mona. "Can I get anything for you?"

"Yes." Mona drained her glass. "Definitely."

"Sure and back in an instant." He smiled and walked to the bar.

Mona looked at me. "Oh my."

"I told you," I retorted.

"My, yes," she repeated. "I see."

Jennifer giggled. "If I wasn't taken—"

"What's that?" asked Henry.

"Nothing," we answered in unison.

Niall rejoined the group and handed wine to Mona and me. "Lovely to see you again." He smiled his lopsided grin. "Ourselves seem to have alarming popularity at weddings."

"Too true," I laughed.

"I thought today's performance was particularly inspired," he teased me.

"Yes, well, I left my pink Super Bridesmaid Suit in the telephone booth when I changed to fight crime."

"I've always wanted to meet a superhero," he said. "What's your specialty?"

"I can change sizes with nothing but Häagen-Dazs to aid me, lift a car key with my bare hands, confound with a single phrase, and occasionally be invisible."

"Do you have a Super Identity?"

"My alter ego is Charming. People call me Charm for short. When I get nasty, I drop the C and download some heavy on the forces of evil. Have you got any superpowers?"

"Your man can regularly limit the destructive effects of Stupid Boss by drawing on my powers of Controlling and Disregarding. I'm hoping to develop the additional skills of Promotion and Replacement in due course."

"Drink more vitamin C," I advised. A bell sounded.

"I believe we're seated together," Niall said. Oh heaven, I thought. "May I have the honor?" He crooked his arms, and Mona and I each took one.

There were fifteen tables spread around three sides of a dance floor. The fourth side was occupied by unattended band equipment and a guy with large teeth and a sequined jacket bellowing into a microphone. "C'mon in, folks, c'mon in. Let's get this party started. I love weddings because you can really party *heart*-y, if you know what I mean." He drew a heart in the air with his hands, yukking it up to his own terrible joke. Mona and I were transfixed.

"Did he just say party hearty?" Mona asked.

"Oh yes," said Niall, staring too.

"Party is not a verb," I frowned. My views on the use of nouns as verbs are strong.

Our table was closest to the emcee. Niall held out chairs and then sat next to me. Oh yes. Jennifer, Henry, and Lori were sitting with us as well.

"Well folks, hopefully we'll have some fu-un tonight. People *do* say I have a *sparkly* personality. . . ." He did a twirl holding out his sequined jacket like the Fonz to bludgeon his joke into the one obtuse person who might not have gotten it.

"In your superpower arsenal, do you have the ability to make someone disappear?" Niall asked me hopefully. Only Caleb, but I elected not to mention that.

"Sadly no. I have to rely on garlic, a sliver of the cross, and conversations about my biological clock, but I left all that at home."

He looked taken aback for a second, then laughed. "Yes, I see. Well, I'm not sure whether I'm glad or regretful you don't have your tools of the trade."

"Please take your seats so we can enjoy this lovely dinner. And someone get the groom a map. He keeps getting lost in the bride's eyes . . ."

"Oh God, make it stop," begged Henry. But the emcee kept up a constant stream of the worst and corniest jokes.

"Well folks, I sure am looking forward to entertaining you tonight. Hopefully it'll go better than the last time I had to stand up in front of a room full of people. I was found guilty and fined two hundred dollars . . ." We all groaned.

"It's like he's channeling Rodney Dangerfield . . . on purpose," Mona marveled.

"Last time I listened to anything this inane was conversation with my date to Tim's wedding." Niall spoke to Henry but was looking at me. "I'd hoped I was free of such drivel when I cut that cord." He was talking about Vanessa. I felt a jolt of excitement down the hoo-hah highway. Niall was signaling his interest. I beamed delightedly at him, and he smiled back as he gave a lock of my hair a gentle tug. "She wasn't nice," he said.

They served appetizers but there was no peace from the emcee. It was a blessed moment when Sparkles announced he was taking a short break.

"Silence of the Ham.' Thank God," I said.

"Quite. As much as I hate to miss the peace and quiet, I must excuse myself briefly," said Niall. "Pardon me."

"Of course." The table was at last able to enjoy conversation. Niall returned as I was talking to a skinny guy across from me about Central California wines, but Mona kicked me so repeatedly I feared I'd never walk again if I didn't make her stop by flirting with Niall. As if I wasn't happy to oblige. Cha. It was some time before I noticed the commotion near the stage.

Sparkles was windmilling his arms in an agitated manner to someone resembling a maitre d'. The maitre d' alternated shaking his head with shrugging his shoulders, as the emcee became increasingly irritated looking. Finally the maitre d' walked away mid-windmill. The emcee turned puce.

"What do you suppose that's about?" I asked Niall. He gave me a look of unconvincing innocence, like a child with chocolate-covered fingers.

"I don't know. Perhaps your man's learned that Rodney Dangerfield has copyrights." His expression was one of virtue. I narrowed my eyes suspiciously.

"You know something, don't you?" I demanded.

"I don't know what you're talking about. So, tell me more about your study program in London." I rolled my eyes but let him change the subject. The irate emcee stalked over to Adele and Peter, employing a full range of anger gestures. Adele and Peter looked trapped. Peter said something to Adele, and they stood and walked with the emcee to the table next to them. They paused for a moment, then moved on.

"Something's going on," Mona said, interested. "Here they come."

"The silence was too good to last," groused Henry.

Adele, Peter, and Sparkles approached the table. "Hi, guys,"

Adele said brightly. The emcee stood silently next to her with his arms crossed, looking pissed off.

"Um, listen. George here seems to have misplaced his mike." At the word "misplaced," George looked livid, but restrained himself. "And we were wondering if anyone might have seen it, or, er, accidentally moved it?" Adele looked hopeful. I sneaked a suspicious glance at Niall, who studiously avoided my eyes. There was the hint of a grin hovering around his mouth.

"Okay then." Adele continued awkwardly when the emcee suddenly let out an outraged squawk. He pounced on the flower arrangement in the center of our table. Blossoming from the center like an exotic bloom was the microphone. George plucked his prize, cradled it lovingly for a moment, then rounded on us.

"*Infidels!*" he snapped. Peter made a curious sound between a cough and a snort of laughter.

"Um, okay then," Adele said, relieved. "I'm glad that's resolved." On stage, musicians began to appear at their instruments. She brightened. "Oh look. Just in time to introduce the band!" she pronounced happily, and hurried Peter back to their table.

George generously spread his glares around the table, then stalked off for his last round of torture before retiring. As soon as he was out of earshot we burst out laughing.

"Cheers, mate," Henry toasted Niall.

"I really have no idea what you're talking about," Niall insisted, then gave me a wink.

As we finished dinner, the band took over the entertainment, to everyone's relief. Couples were dancing but I was only interested in talking to Niall. Time flew by.

"I think you're vibrating," Niall said to me.

"What's that?" I laughed up at him. "Vibrant? I'd give myself engaging and clever, maybe, but *vibrant* is probably a stretch," I joked modestly.

"Er, no, not *vibrant*, um *vibrating*," he said. "Your bag." He pointed to my clutch, which was indeed vibrating. My phone.

"Oh." I flushed in embarrassment. "Excuse me." I hastily grabbed the phone without checking the ID. "Hello?"

"Vi? Is that you? Vi?" Caleb's voice came over the line. It sounded loose. I was shocked. I don't know what my face did, but it did something because Mona looked at me in concern. Niall looked curious.

"Are you all right?" Mona asked. I just nodded.

"Vi? It's Caleb. I need to talk you, babe." He was definitely sloppy.

Excuse me, I mouthed, and hurried to the cloak room. "Caleb? What's going on?"

"Oh good, you're there. Where are you?"

"I'm at a wedding. Why are you calling?"

"Vi, I been thinking about you. All day. Miss you."

"Really?" I said in a hard voice.

"Yeah baby. Want to see you."

"Have you been drinking?" I demanded. There was quiet on the phone. "Caleb?"

"Jus' lil' bit," he admitted. "Was with James and Katrina on the boat. Had a few beers." More than a few from the sound of it. "Was missing you. Want to see you. Come over?"

"Are you serious?" I snapped. "No, I will not come over." I was outraged. I was furious. And a lot of it was directed at myself, because a part of me leapt with pleasure at his call. A part of me considered it. The better part of me took charge.

"Caleb, you're drunk and you're acting very disrespectfully to me right now. Sleep it off, and call me tomorrow if you want to see me." I hated myself for the last bit, but my wings of independence were still new and I was too chicken to fly without a net. "I'm hanging up now."

"Vi, wait—" I snapped the phone closed and took a few deep breaths.

"I'm okay," I told myself. "I'm okay." Another deep breath and I returned to the table. I tossed my phone down. Mona looked up in concern.

"Everything all right?" she asked. Niall just watched.

"Yeah," I nodded.

"Come with me to the bathroom." She stood, and I obediently followed her. We went to the ladies' lounge and sat on the love seat.

"It was Caleb," I said. "Booty call."

"No shit?"

"No shit."

Mona observed me for a moment. "How do you feel?"

"Fine! Great!" I stopped. "Um, completely not sure? I feel like I don't know what I'm supposed to feel. What *am* I supposed to feel?"

"What do you *actually* feel?" Mona asked gently.

"Do I have to tell the lame bits?" I whined. She nodded. "Part of me is glad. Glad he still wants me."

"That's normal."

"Is wanting to say yes normal?"

"Sure. Do you? Want to say yes?"

I thought about it. "No. I don't think so. I do but I really don't," I tried to explain. "It's like smoking a cigarette when you've been drinking. It seems like a good idea at the time, but when you actually do it, it isn't very pleasant and leaves a bad taste in your mouth. The next day you regret it. You just forget in the moment."

"That makes sense."

"Yes." I was nodding to myself now. "I want him to want me, but I can't separate him from the bad ways he made me feel anymore. I don't want to go back."

"Good," Mona pronounced. "Because that Niall is smoking hot."

I perked up. "Cha, right, huh?"

"What are we waiting for?" Mona stood. At the table, Lori and Jennifer were giggling and looking tickled. I smiled at Niall as I took my seat, but he didn't smile back. He looked stern.

"Vi . . . guess who just called you? *Three* times?" Lori sing-songed happily. Oh no. I looked for my phone but it was gone. Lori waggled it at me. Mona looked pained.

"Caleb!" Lori blurted triumphantly. "I know you're psyched! We were telling everyone how he's been the love of your life forever." I stared at them in horror. "And sure enough," she giggled, "his caller ID is 'Lure Lover.' "

I closed my eyes in pain. Why oh why had I given him that stupid moniker? Why hadn't I changed it? Why didn't life have rewind? Mona kicked me under the table and I jumped. Right— salvage mode.

"Um, actually . . ." I started, wondering what the hell I was going to say to set Niall straight without looking like an overeager idiot.

"Wait," Lori trilled, clearly delighted. "The phone kept ringing, so after the third time I answered it for you in case it was an emergency, you know. *Anyway,* Caleb said to tell you that you should come right over and he's waiting up for you. He's *pining* for you!" Lori beamed at me. I wanted lasers to shoot from my eyes and vaporize her.

"Actually . . ." I desperately tried to think of damage control measures.

"Actually, I need to go as well," Niall announced, pushing back his chair and standing. "It's been a lovely evening, everyone." No. No! I frantically tried to think of something to fix the situation but my mind was blank.

"You don't really have to go so soon, do you?" I tried to stop him.

"I'm afraid so." He glanced past me, not making eye contact. "Good night everyone." And with that he was gone.

I sat there fish-mouthed. "But . . . but. . . "

"Shit," said Mona.

"What?" Asked Lori.

"Nothing." I slumped in my chair. "Just being invisible."

A week later I was surfing the Internet and found a *Grey's Anat-omy* blog written by the show's producer. She wrote enthusiasti-cally that she had her fingers and toes crossed Meredith and Derek would get back together. I thought about Caleb and knew one thing to be true. You don't want him back, Meredith. Trust me on this one. Once your fundamental trust is breached in a re-lationship, you can never repair it. You'll always be waiting for the axe to fall again. Round two doesn't work. Or three, or four . . . or five.

I clicked into my e-mail and pulled up the message again. And read it for the hundredth time.

To: ViViVooom@gmail.com
From: Caleb.Carter@McKinsey.com
Sent: September 25
Subject:

Vi,

I know you don't want me to call you again. It was stupid to call when I'd been drinking. But I've been doing a lot of thinking and I've figured out that I screwed up monumentally. Since we broke up I've had this loneliness hanging over me, even when I'm surrounded by people, and I realized that it was missing you. I also realized that I have the best times with you because you make me a better person. You help me be the best version of myself. I now know how important that is. And how important you are.

I talked to Audrey last week and told her I couldn't be with her anymore because I was in love with someone else. I think I always have been. I know I've screwed up—a lot—but this time I have my priorities straight. I want to be with you. I'm flying back to DC on Friday for good. My project here is finished. Can we get together as soon as I get back? I want to show just how much you mean to me and make up for the time we lost over my foolishness. And this time I mean it forever.

You are my love.
C.

I stared at the message for a long time. How long had I waited for this? For two days my fingers had itched to reply, filling with thousands of words clamoring to wing their way to Caleb. In the end I wrote just one. Then, smiling, I turned off my computer and went home.

To: Caleb.Carter@McKinsey.com
From: ViViVooom@gmail.com
Sent: September 27
Subject: Re:

Dear Caleb,

Unsubscribe.

Vi

CHAPTER THIRTY-FOUR

There Won't Be Any Weddings in The Movie Starring Me

Lisa Marries David, Washington, D.C., November

I sat in the third pew of St. Matthew's Church of Washington, D.C., trying not to jiggle my leg in impatience. The bride was taking *forever* to get her butt to the altar. It was like watching corn grow. A woman next to me wearing a hat that looked like parts of a pheasant trying to escape a box gave me an irritated look. By focusing on leg-jiggle prevention I'd failed to be vigilant about finger drumming. I stopped and gave her a big fake smile. I wondered what happened to the unlucky half of the pheasant. I turned back to watch the bride syrup her way up the aisle. I'd had speedier visits to the DMV.

It wasn't really the bride that was getting on my nerves. It was my birthday. My twenty-ninth yielded that glorious septennial event of a birthday actually falling on a Saturday, and I was stuck at a wedding. I was sulking and mentally taking it out on Lisa, a perfectly lovely girlfriend who'd committed no offense other than deciding to marry on my birthday and invite me. They'd even given me a plus one, but I couldn't be bothered. It felt weird to take Ethan now that he was dating Imogen. I'd decided to treat the wedding like a big dinner party and go it alone. It'd be over soon enough. *If* the bride would ever reach the groom's side. The bird lady gave me another nasty look, and I realized my leg was jiggling away. Sigh. PETA would take my side if we rumbled.

I thought back to the wish I'd jokingly made a year ago, to survive the next twelve months. I had to smile to myself. I'd made it. I was looking forward to a long break in weddings, though reluctant to jinx myself, as I'd surely done after Jen's wedding. Still, it felt safe. The only person I knew getting married in the next year was my cousin Michelle, and that was months away. I was done with my matrimony marathon. But I felt a long way from where I began.

I thought back to the first wedding of the year, Holly's, and recalled avidly absorbing every ceremony detail, daydreaming the minutiae of my own theoretical wedding. I shuddered at the thought. The idea of planning a wedding made me queasy and averse, like licking congealed bacon fat or seeing my dad naked. I tuned in briefly to the ceremony at hand. We hadn't even reached first base—we were just approaching First Corinthians. I tuned out.

I marveled that brides don't see the joke. First Corinthians at a wedding is like a derby hat in a Magritte painting—so banal it's meaningless. But brides have a total lack of irony when it comes to weddings. The ceremonies evoke a rationality blind spot.

I tuned back in. Lisa and David were rounding second with the lighting of the unity candle. I tuned out. Observing the blind spot on display like a Bearded Lady made me edgy. I couldn't bear the idea that one day I'd be that dupe. A Feeling seized me. It was Conviction.

"I don't want to ever get married," I murmured in astonishment.

My feathered friend looked scandalized. I don't know if she'd heard my words or that I'd whispered in church. Or that I was one of those crazy, jiggling, talking to herself people who needed a bumper of malt liquor in a bag and a shopping cart missing one wheel. I didn't care. I sat marveling at myself. I poked the Feeling with my brain to see if it was genuine, and it became more deeply rooted. I didn't want to get married. I didn't want any of this.

I checked back in on our progress, somewhat in awe of myself for the heretical thoughts I was entertaining. Strains of music rose. I peeked at the program. Was this it? Whoa . . . the pitcher faked and threw back to first, slowing everything down. There was a soloist. We'd be here a while. I returned to my profane thoughts.

Could I be discovering my lesbian destiny? I wondered in anxiety. I scanned the church to see if I viewed the world differently now that the scales had fallen from my eyes. Just some bad hats and . . . oh, *hello* sixth row. He was hot. Right. Not lesbian. I peeped back at the sixth row. He rubbed his neck, wedding band catching the light. I felt Disappointment. Okay, clearly I still wanted a man. Too bad really. I knew plenty of available women.

I checked in. Lisa and David were safe at third, pushing on rings. I sat taller in my seat, feeling like I'd made an important discovery. I genuinely didn't want a wedding—and it wasn't sour grapes. Overexposure had eroded any romantic notions I nurtured about weddings. I felt a little giddy. I couldn't have been prouder of myself than if I'd been Vasco de Gama. I was startled when everyone in the church started to clap. Had I made a pronouncement? I looked around in alarm, but no. The applause was for Lisa and David, who had safely crossed home plate to become Mr. and Mrs. Married. I started to clap too, but I was cheering for myself.

At the Hay Adams, I collected my name card for Table 12 and went to the bar. I was preparing to force myself brightly upon an unsuspecting cluster of nice people who probably genuinely wanted to converse with each other, when my clutch vibrated, granting me a reprieve.

"Hello," I said. In response I got garbled sounds.

"Vi, ids Mona." Her reply was feeble and sounded laden with snot. Not good.

"Mona, what's the matter? Are you crying?" I was concerned.

"Do. Des." She drew in ragged breaths, and then let out a sob.

"What is it? Tell me, please." I could hear her trying to control her breathing.

"Id's Brad," she managed, then issued a string of garbled syllables. I isolated the word "dumped." "Can you come ober?" She cried full-on heartbreaking sobs.

I felt caught. I looked at the reception filling with guests. Lisa and David had arrived. I wondered if I could leave after the main course. Then I shook myself. What was my problem?? I didn't even like weddings anymore. Of *course* I was going to go to Mona. There were two hundred people here. Lisa wouldn't even know I was gone, and if she did, she'd still be my friend tomorrow. I felt more chains fall away, and breathed easier. I didn't have to attend every wedding on earth to prove I was beloved. Mona needed me.

"I think I finally have my priorities right." I spoke my thoughts.

"Whad?" asked Mona.

"Nothing. I'll be right there, honey."

"Tanks," she sniffled.

I found Lisa and David to stage "The Runaway (from the) Bride."

"Vi! So glad you could come," Lisa beamed, and hugged me. I hugged them both.

"You look amazing." I was sincere.

"Thanks!" she bubbled. We burned through the expected wedding exchange, and it occurred to me that it might be as much a relief to Lisa as it was to me when the conversation wrapped up and I slipped away. We'd had, and would have, far more interesting talks at Café Deluxe on an ordinary Thursday. As I strode out I felt like Private Benjamin at the movie's end . . . totally liberated. Except I wouldn't get a perm and die my hair red. Not a good look.

Twenty minutes later I opened Mona's unlocked apartment door and called her name.

"In here," she answered from the living room. She sounded better but the room was dark, which was a bad sign. I crossed the hall and walked in.

"Surprise!!" yelled a chorus of voices as the lights came on.

"Holy shit!!" I yelled in alarm, jumping a mile. My sweat glands went into hyperdrive.

The room was full of people beaming at me. They started to sing "Happy Birthday" as my brain groped for comprehension. There was Brad. And Imogen. And about thirty others.

"Happy Birthday!" said Imogen as she and Mona hugged me.

"You're okay," I said idiotically to Mona. She looked sheepish.

"Sorry about that. We didn't want you to squander your birthday alone at some lame wedding, so we had to make it good." She shrugged. Babette and Ellis joined us.

"I can't believe you dragged me out of a wedding," I marveled. They looked anxious.

"You're not mad, are you?" Ellis asked. I looked at them, so concerned, and then at the room filled with my friends, and smiled. I was *thrilled*.

"No way." They laughed in relief, and I was surrounded by well-wishers giving me hugs. I was the center of people I cared about, and it hadn't required months of planning or anything more complicated than being myself.

"I hear the river, Oh Buddha," I murmured.

"I thought The River was The Boss." Imogen was at my elbow. I poked her. "Having fun?" she asked.

"Definitely," I said. "Thanks. Guess what I realized today?"

"Tell me."

"I never want to get married."

"Have you been watching *Four Weddings and a Funeral* again?" she asked.

"Nope. More Like '400 Weddings and Up Grows the Girl.' I was watching someone get married. And it was nothing much. And I didn't want to be there. And I didn't want to do that to other people. And I don't want a bunch of vases."

"Sounds serious."

"The thing is, it's not. Serious is honest, loving relationships. Not serious is prancing down the aisle in a white dress, or watching someone else do it."

"I think you get your grown-up badge today." She clinked my glass.

"All badged up and no clue what to do with it."

"I might expect you to come to my wedding one day," she said.

"Oh, I'll come," I said. "But I won't give a sheet." She snorted and coughed as her wine went the wrong way. Heh. "Now is that cake over there?"

From: ViViVooom@gmail.com
To: Ben@siddickens.com
Sent: November 24
Subject: Thanks!

Ben,

Thanks for the birthday tile! I was completely surprised. Isn't it funny this is the first Sid Dickens tile of my very own?? It means a lot that you picked it out for me. Say,

when is your birthday? Send me the mm/dd/yy so I know
when it's your turn.

Love,
V.

From: Ben@siddickens.com
To: ViViVooom@gmail.com
Sent: November 25
Subject: Re: Thanks!

Vi,

I am delighted you like the tile. It was certainly my
pleasure. I celebrate my own birthday on January 29
every year.

Best,
Ben

Rats.

CHAPTER THIRTY-FIVE

Rumble At The William Tell

Michelle Marries Steven, LaGrange, Illinois, April

"You know Uncle Tom told me someone was killed here once," Maeve said, getting out of the car at the William Tell Holiday Inn in LaGrange, Illinois, a town rivaling Pittsford in having nothing to recommend it. Our cousin Michelle was getting married at what appreared to be the Mecca of banquet halls. "Apparently two banquets had a brawl and someone got shot. Now they won't serve alcohol after eleven P.M."

Fantastic. I could see my Irish family throwing elbows at 10:45 as they stockpiled before the dread journey into the Heart of Starkness. No more booze. The horror, the horror.

We hurried inside, only to stop dead at an Op Center worthy of a commander played by Dabney Coleman in the made-for-TV movie. The lobby was the hub of a wagon wheel with numerous hallways spoking out, each sprouting multiple banquet rooms in a root system a mangrove tree would envy. There was a large board suspended from the ceiling like Grand Central Station, indicating where receptions were located. Uniformed people with

walkie-talkies scurried about. Years of boiled chicken and un-
funny speeches permeated the air.

"Awesome, you're here." Michelle smiled when we found her.
A source of constant awe to me, Michelle is an auto mechanic. She
fearlessly touches things under the hood that frighten me terribly,
with my conviction that they would blow my eyebrows off. Michelle was marrying her boyfriend Steven, a boat mechanic (more
awe) she'd dated since high school shop class. Steven was tall and
impossibly thin, and had the Basic Mullet, as common in Chicago's west side as saying "pop" for soda and having a Bears flag
outside your house. I knew for a fact that Michelle and Steven had
a Bears flag outside their house, but they didn't drink pop. They
drank Pabst Blue Ribbon.

Our cousins Kate and Alice were also there. Kate was a demure sweater-set-wearing future law student. She was generally
quiet but fiercely loyal, and would rise like a gater for a cat stray-
ing too close to the edge of the lagoon to defend one of her circle.
Alice, from the west side suburb of Glen Ellyn, couldn't have been
raised more vanilla if her last name were Cleaver. But since spending a summer as a camp counselor with a bunch of girls from
Brooklyn, she'd acted like a refugee from *The Warriors*. To her
mother's horror, she returned with a nose ring and a magenta
streak in her hair that made her look like a New Wave badger. We
had to endure lots of "You talkin' to me?"

The dresses were simple, floor-length satin with spaghetti
straps. The only thing extraordinary about them was the color.
After much discussion, Maeve and I'd decided that the gowns
were "yam," a bizarre orangish-brownish shade. Michelle had
snapped them up because the shade was discontinued and they
were half off. As with glass hammers or peep-toe Wellingtons,
there's usually a reason a thing is discontinued.

"These are hideous," Maeve whispered to me as she zipped
me up.

"Oh, grass-hoppah," I mimicked in a sensei Master Splinter voice, "you have much to learn." The dress had a flattering fit, crinolines and all. I smiled fondly at the youngsters who had no idea what a truly dreadful bridesmaid dress was. Cute little tykes hadn't yet encountered their first pouffed sleeve. So sweet.

Michelle was getting married somewhere called Courtyard C. We descended into the nerve center and navigated the labyrinth of party pods. I was about to suggest Tremaux's algorithm of maze solving when we saw light at the end of the warren.

Chicago has been described as an October kind of town, even in the spring. Unprecedented, the weather in middle April was springlike, enabling the outdoor wedding. I had been dubious (read: horrified) when Michelle informed me that we'd been moved *outdoors* (in *April* in *Chicago?*) due to double-booking. Was the entire Mormon church getting married several times each? But fortune was shining on Michelle. Or, as she'd put it, "We're supposed to be in goddamned Disney World by Monday and I'm not going on my goddamned honeymoon until I'm goddamned married. We'll get married that day if we have to snowshoe to the goddamned altar and have paramedics on site with oxygen and IV fluids for hypothermia. God dammit." Can't argue with that logic.

I peeked around the hedge shielding us from view. There was a small courtyard sandwiched between two buildings with a dozen rows of folding chairs in front of a trellis and an anxious-looking Steven jerking nervously at his clip-on bow tie. The shrieks of children and smell of chlorine wafted out of the building on the right. A child wearing water wings was hanging out one of the windows, yelling, "Look, Mommy, that man is dressed like Chilly Willy!" It felt like Michelle was about to get married at the YMCA.

"Who's gettin' hitched?" a nasal midwestern voice asked. I turned. The speaker was short, fat, and bald, and wearing nothing but Hawaiian swim trunks and flip flops, with a belly whose excess overhanging flesh would hold fast an anvil tucked under it. I closed my eyes. When I opened them, the vision was still there. We blinked at him, four yams clumped around a single white stalk.

"Who the hell do you think is getting married?" Michelle voiced our thoughts. "It ain't the fat guy in the bathing suit, so it must be the stunning beauty in the white dress. Jeesh."

Deductive Reasoning from Des Moines shrugged his shoulders and ambled to the courtyard, where he plopped himself into a folding chair.

"In the movie, the wedding crashers were significantly more hot," Maeve muttered.

"This isn't *The Wedding Crashers*, it's 'I Am Yam,'" I whispered back.

"Just so long as he doesn't try to drink my booze," Michelle dismissed him. "Where the hell's the priest? I'm ready."

"Here I am," panted the priest, jogging up. He looked like Droopy the Dog in a clerical collar. "Terribly sorry." He stopped and wiped his spectacles on a handkerchief. "Eighteen weddings here tonight." (pant, pant) "Bit of a fracas at the last one. Bride was nervous, bless her, and dropped the traditional Irish horseshoe on the groom's foot. We had to administer first aid. Then, when the groom tossed gold foil chocolate coins into the audience, there was a bit of a stampede. Apparently some of the relatives hadn't been alerted that the coins were edible." He clicked his tongue. "More first aid." We stared open-mouthed. "So," he briskly clapped his hands, "shall we?" He hurried to join Steven.

As soon as my uncle Leo took his place next to Michelle, the priest pressed a button on the boom box at his feet, and a processional march began. We hit the aisle to the splashes of Pachelbel's Cannon Ball. Twenty minutes later, Michelle and Steven were joined as husband and wife to the romantic cries of "Marco!" "Polo!"

Afterward, we trooped into the banquet room opposite the pool. Without speaking, Maeve and I headed straight for the bar. We'd barely taken a sip when everyone was urged to sit. We went back for seconds instead. You can never be too careful until you know the layout of the bar service. There might be no table service, and nothing would be more embarrassing than having a grandparent shriek across the room, "Is that Vi going to the bar again? Well, I hope she doesn't want *my* organs when she has cirrhosis at her age!!"

After muscling aside six cousins with the same idea, we sat at the head table. A completely unisex person wearing a Holiday Inn-issue grey polyester pantsuit stepped to the courtyard doors. At the push of a button, Van Halen's *"You Really Got Me Now"* began to blare and we were bathed in the twinkling reflections of a disco ball twirling on the ceiling. As the song reached its first big chorus ("you really got me, you really got me . . ."), Michelle and Steven entered the room with rock 'n roll high kicks, jamming the air guitar. They rock-stepped to the center of the room and shook it up to the thumping music ("you got me so I can't sleep at night") before arriving at the head table for the end of the song ("oh, oh, oh"). Flushed and beaming, they dropped into their seats. Some jackass immediately started clinking a glass and the new bride and groom obediently kissed, to raucous laughter from Table 8.

I needn't have worried about standing out as a frequent bar visitor. Mechanics and Irish relatives, it seems, like to drink. I sensed that 10:45 P.M. was going to be ugly. Maeve and I sat at the bar listening to power ballads and watching the dancing until Michelle's mother, aunt Marty, approached, holding a Mr. Microphone. Maeve spotted it from 400 feet.

"Gotta go," she bolted from her barstool faster than a Frenchman from a battlefield. "Bathroom," she called over her shoulder, hustling away.

"Wha . . . ?" I barely articulated, when Marty was upon me.

"Vi! Its time!" She shoved the Mr. Microphone at me. "The Dollar Dance! You have to get everyone to dance with Michelle and collect the money." I have to hand it to Maeve. She can smell unpleasant work better than Paris Hilton can sniff out a photo opportunity. Cursing her, I accepted Mr. Mike.

Ten minutes later I was standing on the dance floor shooting an Extremely Dirty look at Maeve, who gazed innocently from the safety of the door. "Let's get this party started!" I cried with false enthusiasm. Marty pushed a button on the boom box and the sounds of a polka began. I'd soon learn it was the longest, most painful polka in the history of mankind. "Who'll buy a dance?" I hollered, feeling like a mail order bride auctioneer. No one moved. I spied my brother. "Brick Connelly! Fantastic. Step right up! NOW!" Brick started, then shot me a dirty look to rival mine to Maeve.

"You're dead," he smiled brightly as he handed me $20 and prepared to cut in.

"Ski boot!" I smiled brightly back. How long *was* this fucking song? Slowly uncles, cousins, even mechanics from Elgin fell into line under my unremitting torture. The money stacked up, but the song wouldn't end.

"Who's left? Who's left??!!" I was manically pushing dances like Girl Scout cookies. There was a resounding echo to my words. The song had ended. Everyone was looking at me. Marty gently pried away the Mr. Microphone, and Maeve eased me toward a barstool.

"$985 dollars!" I gloated over my, er, Michelle's money, fanning the bills. "Almost $1000! I'm 'The Polka-Dollar Kid,' heh."

"That's great, hon." Maeve patted me just like aunt Marty. She reached for my, er, Michelle's money but I jerked the wad away. "Vi!" She snapped. "Snap out of it!"

Suddenly I recovered myself, and wiped a shaky hand over my face. "Oh God. What happened?" I was woozy.

"Polka overdose," Maeve said. "You'll be all right." She handed me a shot. "Drink this, focus on the power ballad, and call KROQ in the morning," she named her favorite radio station.

"Where's yours?" She looked shifty. "Bartender," I called out. "Wait . . ."

After I forced Maeve to do her shot, which I found extremely satisfying, we stuffed the money in an envelope and shoved it down my bodice. It wasn't going anywhere. My mother ambled up.

"You always were such a good dancer in school," she said.

I sighed. "That was Maeve, Mom. I never danced."

My mother furrowed her brow. "Is that right?"

"Mm-hmm." I was used to being a jumbled set of memories to my mother. She loved me, but probably wouldn't recognize my third grade photo on CNN if I shot up a mall or won the Nobel Prize. My dad joined us.

"Well done, well done," he complimented me.

"Thanks, Dad."

"So," he looked around. "No date?" I felt a pain start behind my left eyeball.

"No, Dad, no date."

"So, no Caleb, then?" In a weak moment I'd told my parents I was seeing him again. I regretted it. Even though I called my mother after we broke up, I hadn't told her much. And I didn't want to explain now. Some things parents don't understand. I think they're biologically incapable of crediting offspring with adult feelings of love, sex, and pain. Maybe this barrier is necessary to ensure survival of the species, as parents might not bear children if they perceived the heartaches in store. Of course, my parents still thought of me as nineteen anyway.

"Nope," I answered with studied casualness.

"No fellow in your life, then?"

"No, Dad."

"C'mon, tell him about the former pro snooker champion turned rubber boot baron," Maeve jumped in, giving me a sympathetic look. "He dotes on Vi."

"Is that the one from your trip to the Grand Canyon?" My dad's question confounded me. To my knowledge, I hadn't been to the Grand Canyon since I was nine.

"No, that's the hip hop mogul with tattooed knuckles." Maeve played the game.

"Ah, I can't tell them apart. They all run together to me," Dad exclaimed jovially, relieved to be back on comfortable ground away from a conversation that hinted at real pain. He tousled my hair then turned to my mother. "Care to dance, my dear?"

"That sucked," Maeve said as they walked away.

"I'm okay," I shrugged. I'd let go of my frustration in trying to force my parents to see me as an adult, just as I'd let go of my idealizing them. To them I was forever nineteen. I'd knock myself out trying to show them how grown-up I was, and just end up knocked out. It was enough that they loved me, even if they didn't know me. As it turned out, I hadn't really known them either, and I didn't love them less. I was okay about Caleb too, though it didn't mean I wanted to probe the wound.

"Oh God." Maeve nudged me and pointed. I looked and wished I hadn't. My parents were dirty dancing to Whitesnake. Brick walked by and followed our gaze.

"My eyes are bleeding now." He winced, and went to sneak cigarettes with our cousin Jimmy.

"Why," I asked Maeve in a pained voice, "can't I have a normal family?"

"Oh please." She rolled her eyes. "All families are screwed up. Normal is the new dysfunctional. Want to crash the wedding next door?"

"We can't do that!"

"Why not? Everyone here drinks Pabst Blue Ribbon, is related to us, or both." I thought about it. Maeve exploited my hesitation. "How about we do a bathroom reconnaissance mission? If it looks clear, we penetrate."

"Surgical strike?"

"I was thinking Shock and Awe." I nodded and clunked fists with her.

In the hallway immediately outside were restrooms shared with the other banquet room in the pod. Maeve and I sauntered out, casually glancing into the other ballroom. People were clustered by the bar, milling about, or dancing. It seemed safe enough. We ducked into the ladies' room.

"Well?" Maeve asked.

"Sure," I said, fixing my lipstick and fluffing my hair. The door opened and a lizard with a poodle perm walked in. Maeve and I were transfixed. The woman was clearly a bridesmaid, and the bride had chosen her colors even more sadistically than Michelle. The dress was a long reptilian green, with sort of a darker green pattern, ruched sides, and a little cape off the shoulders. I dubbed her the "Gremlin." She jostled me from the sink without apology in her determination to acquire pole position to reapply her violet eye shadow. She saw my dress and gave a snort of derision before refocusing on her favorite thing—herself. Maeve and I exchanged incredulous looks that *she* was mocking *our* dresses, and left her spritzing up her high bangs, which I suspected were her pride and joy.

"I'm beginning to reconsider whether there might be any talent in there," I said to Maeve.

"What's not to like about our cold-blooded friends? C'mon." Maeve swanned into the ballroom without hesitation. Connelly Rule—whatever you do, do it confidently so others will think you're supposed to be doing it. I followed her in. Confidently.

The Ryan wedding was in the midst of their Dollar Dance. I tensed at the sound of the polka, but Maeve laid a calming hand on my arm. "You're all better now," she assured me, and wandered off toward the bar. I watched the emcee and rolled my eyes. I was *way* better than that. The bride was a pretty girl, dancing with florid-faced older men, teenage boys, and a young man who was limping. There were a number of Gremlins running around, presumably stuffing their faces before midnight. No handsome men caught my eye. Then a voice behind me shot adrenaline through the top of my head. "We're here! We're here!" cried my armpits.

"Now I *really* think you may be taking this quest for the Guinness Record for wedding attendance a bit too far. Have you got North American tour T-shirts? Next stop Detroit?"

I knew that voice. I *loved* that voice. I turned in shock to see Niall Devlin looking unbelievably sexy in a tuxedo. A zing went right down the highway. For a moment I thought my overheated imagination had conjured a hallucination. I stared open-mouthed at his chocolate eyes and luscious eyelashes, waiting for him to disappear. No more tequila, I thought. A Gremlin coming off the dance floor roughly jostled me, but Niall was still there.

"Niall? What are you doing here?" I marveled. Had I done something really right today and God was rewarding me? I wracked my brain to recall if I'd accidentally cured cancer and forgotten about it.

"My cousin's wedding?" His tone was wry. "I was invited. What are *you* doing here?" He seemed equally surprised. I flushed. I was crashing his cousin's reception. That *was* the question.

"Um. It's my cousin's wedding next door. I just came in to, uh, look for my sister." His laughing eyes told me he wasn't buying it.

"Not to worry. I popped my head into—your cousin did you say?" I nodded. "To check it out as well, but left fairly quickly after seeing some disturbing dirty dancing."

"I can't believe we're both in LaGrange. This is surreal." I'd been fantasizing about the guy for months but never saw him. I had an alarming thought. Maybe I'd cracked up from all the weddings and Niall Devlin only existed as a figment of my imagination, a crutch I invented to help me get by. The one time I'd seen him outside a wedding, I was delusional with a medical experiment gone awry. Had I ever seen him interact with anyone else? In *Sixth Sense* you *thought* you saw Bruce Willis interact with Toni Collete, but later you realize they hadn't. Had I gone so crazy that I even convinced myself that Mona talked to my imaginary friend? Okay, I know it's weird, but I stuck out a finger and poked him. He laughed.

"I was about to do the same thing," he said. "I was starting to wonder if you existed on a parallel plane where we have contact only through a wedding wrinkle in the space-time continuum. Like that movie with Sandra Bullock and Keanu Reeves." He touched me as well, but his contact was a gentle caress, stroking hair off my shoulder.

I shivered at his touch. "*The Lake House*? I was going for *Sixth Sense*."

"Right. Where you think other people see him but you realize later that no one did?" I nodded. He looked at me intently, then smiled in a way that made me go warm all over. "Well, there's really only one cure for it. When we're back in D.C. we'll have to go out for dinner *not* at a wedding, and if they serve us, we know we're real." I felt a little dizzy. Was it a date? Did he just ask me on a date? He winked. "I'll let you pick your own outfit."

"Sold," I agreed. Date? Not date?

Just then a beautiful brunette walked up. "Niall, could you please be responsible for this? It is Penny's Dollar Dance money. You saw what happened over chocolate coins—God knows what would happen over real dosh. "There's over $700 in there." I smirked. Amateur. My conceit faded as I focused on her. Who was she?

"Dollar Dance? Is that the sanctioned prostitution we were just observing as our ears bled from the polka?" Niall asked. She rolled her eyes. He turned suddenly, a furrow between his brows. "Vi, you must let me introduce you."

Uh-oh. He seemed anxious. What did that mean?

"This is Anne. She's a relative. A *related* relative. To me, I mean." He looked embarrassed. Anne regarded him strangely. "Not a sister, but very, very related," he repeated, flustered. I smiled. Anne considered me speculatively

"Did I ever mention it was basically a relative who kept phoning me at Adele's wedding?" I said, and was delighted to see Niall smile. "Now deceased." The smile widened.

Anne got impatient with our mooning and shoved the envelope into Niall's hands. "Don't lose it," she commanded, and walked off.

"I had to emcee our Dollar Dance," I told him. "Got my own stash right here." I patted my bodice. His eyes followed my hand and I blushed again. Curses on my telltale coloring.

"Extraordinary tradition, really. Sort of a 'Pimp My Bride,'" Niall said as he slid the envelope inside his jacket pocket. I gaped at him. Could the man be more perfect? He was sharing *my* love of perverting titles. I could almost hear the air whooshing past me as I tumbled deep, deep into extraordinary extra-super-like. So this is what thunderbolts feel like.

I realized he was talking to me.

"If the Dollar Dance involves paying money to dance with the bride, does this 'Chicken Dance' I've heard of involve paying to dance with a chicken?" Niall looked at me expectantly.

"Only at occult weddings," I answered. "But you have to be careful. What might seem like an innocent polka with a chicken may actually be a voodoo blood curse. I know a girl lost seventeen cousins that way."

"You seem quite well-versed on weddings and wearing extraordinary dresses of a peculiar color. Tell me, are you actually a professional bridesmaid?"

"If only the money flowed in that direction," I lamented. "Alas, no. I'm a wine buyer for Darien & Dodd."

"Oh that's right. Henry told me," he said, then flushed. I was giddy. He'd asked about me! I gracefully pretended I hadn't noticed.

"How about you?"

He pulled a sad moue. "At the moment I'm looking for new employment. I'm a photojournalist with the Washington office of the BBC."

I blinked in surprise. "That sounds pretty great." Photojournalist? Could he be sexier?

"You'd think so," he said, "but it's rather like being the unrelated employee at Roberts, Roberts, Roberts and Sons. The senior journalists will die at their desks rather than retire. So, your man is stuck covering headline-burners like 'Sonny the Squirrel Water-skis for Sick Kids!'"

"Sonny should surf for a proper alliteration," I suggested. "Have you considered ordering extra-large buckets of Kentucky Fried chicken for the office? Then you can sit back, and listen to arteries harden until a senior position becomes 'available.'"

His laugh burst out. "You've formed an alarming affiliation between chickens and death."

"I think I misunderstood *Chicken Soup for the Soul* the first time I saw it." I shot back.

"I don't care for chick lit myself. Hopefully we'll avoid fowl play tonight."

I rolled my eyes. "Very punny. You're poultry in motion."

"Now and hen." His eyes twinkled at me. "Your job sounds interesting."

"Dodging a pullet?" I raised a brow. "Well, if I'm honest, Work treats me just fine and regularly deposits money into my account, thereby holding up its end of the bargain. I, on the other hand, treat Work terribly disrespectfully, telling all my girlfriends how I really don't think it's working out, flirting with other options and openly cheating on Work with Happy Hour, Play, Yahoo!

Games, Travel, and Hangover. But while my relationship with my work is ambivalent, my relationship with my salary is enthusiastic."

He laughed out loud. "Excellent priorities. And speaking of priorities, let's get another drink, shall we, and continue this fascinating discussion," he suggested, holding out his hand.

"Absolutely," I beamed, placing mine in his. I felt a shock of electricity from head to toe when we clasped hands, and he froze. He muttered something under his breath I couldn't make out, but it sounded like, "Christ, so that's what a thunderbolt feels like."

"What?" I breathed.

He just shook his head, then twined his long tapered fingers with mine. Smiling, we threaded our way to the bar, adjacent to the entrance. I turned to say something to Niall but was interrupted by a commotion in the hallway.

"What?" came a high-pitched screech from the direction of the ladies' room.

"I *know* you're not talkin' to me!" I heard the belligerent tones of Alice Does Atlantic Avenue, then saw my cousin face-to-face with a surly Gremlin in the hallway.

"Yeah, I'm talkin' to you, pumpkin." Gremlin smacked her gum in Alice's face. "That's the *ugliest* dress I ever saw. It *almost* makes your face look good." Uh-oh. It was like a bad parody, but Alice's propensity toward temper meant Trouble.

"Did you just call me a squash? Your dress is the color of primordial snot and you called me a vegetable?" Alice's voice went deadly, her squint lethal. I could see demure Kate edging up behind her with a mulish look on her face. Double uh-oh.

"Squash," taunted the gum-smacking Gremlin. Two puce green henchwomen appeared at her back, like raptors hunting in a pack.

"I'll show you squash, you goblin." Alice hurled an entire glass of beer into her face. The Gremlin gasped as her high bangs wilted. Triple uh-oh. Alice turned to Kate, all catty innocence, and said, "Whoopsie. I forgot. You're not supposed to get them wet, are you?"

The Gremlin let out a shriek of rage and launched herself at Alice. Kate leapt on the Gremlin's back with a yell, pulling poodle hair with all her might. Two Gremlin henchwomen went for Kate. There were shouts from both banquet halls as people realized what was happening. Niall stepped in front of me to shield me as someone hurled a drink on the writhing mass of girls, like hosing down dogs to break up a fight.

"This is going to be good," Maeve said, working her way around the fray toward us. A reptilian henchwomen spied Maeve. She took bleary aim and tossed a full drink on her.

"Pumpkin bitch," the girl slurred.

Maeve froze in shock, beer dripping down her face. *Serious* uh-oh. Maeve had a temper too. Since *Oprah*, July 2000, she blamed it on extra testosterone. Whatever it was, you didn't want to piss off Maeve when she had a few drinks in her.

"You fucking whore," she spat out, enraged.

"Maeve, no." I tried to grab her but it was too late. She'd launched herself at her attacker, and the two went rolling down the hallway. The girl-fight was now a full-blown fracas of hair-pulling and petticoats a-flying, green clashing with orange in battle. A ring of stupefied men encircled the girl mosh pit, staring in wonder and titillation. I could see our gender neutral official skirt the melee and hurry toward Op Center. An equally gender neutral official emerged from Niall's wedding and followed the same path.

I was roughly jostled as a big man with a drooping handlebar mustache shoved by me.

"Sanity at last," Niall said over his shoulder. He was still shielding me with his body, arms reaching behind his back to hold me against him. Even distracted by the conflict, I couldn't disregard the tingle I felt where our bodies touched. I stood on tiptoe and peeked over his shoulder. "That's the father of the bride," Niall explained. With his mustache and red face, he looked more like Kaiser Wilhelm to me.

"What the hell's going on here?" the Kaiser shouted. There was a momentary calm as everyone froze comically, mid bitch-slap.

"Uncle Terry, she hit me," lied the treacherous Gremlin, pointing at Alice, Kate still clinging like a monkey to her back.

"Is that true, girl?" he bellowed. "You ruin my little girl's weddin'?"

Just then Michelle charged to the center from "our" side of the hallway. I hoped we were the Jets not the Sharks. They had the better song. "What the hell's going on here?" she shouted, looking around in astonishment.

"I'll tell you what's going on." The Kaiser got in her face. "You people are trouble."

"Well now, let's calm down and discuss this in a civilized way." Michelle tried diplomacy.

"Hell no! Your miscreant family's ruined my baby's wedding. And you're going to pay for it." The Kaiser enunciated his words with several hard jabs at Michelle's chest. I winced.

"Shelley, did that bastard touch you?" came the enraged bellow of my uncle Leo. Leo pushed through the crowd and the hush deepened, if possible. Uncle Leo was a big, beefy man with a neck like a bull and arms like Popeye, proof of his years hustling sides of beef at the Halsted Packing House. More dangerously, he also had the glassy eyes of an Irishman who's been making sweet, sweet love to Paddy's whiskey all night long.

"Did you touch my little girl," he roared. Before the Kaiser could respond, Leo threw a punch and connected dead on. Kaiser reeled, blood spurting from his nose. No midget himself, with a snarl of rage he drove his head into Leo's midsection, barreling him back against the wall with a thud and an oof. Hostile engagement by the so-called hosts released everyone else from decorum and galvanized the brawl to a new pitch. Men started throwing punches; elderly women started throwing elbows. The pile on the floor grew into a many-legged beast.

"Christ, this is insane," Niall expostulated, pressing me deeper into the room for protection. Guests were pushing past us toward the fight, which was expanding into both banquet rooms. Niall looked me over. "You're a freaking bull's-eye in that dress," he stressed, like I was sporting a jaunty crown during the French Revolution. He anxiously pulled off his jacket. "Put this on, and tie your skirt up so you don't get spotted." I did as he said, feeling very *Sound of Music*. My brain was telegraphing joyous thoughts: He's concerned about you! He's taking care of you! He's hiding you like the nuns who disabled the car! Niall's jacket and my lopsided knot didn't hide the yam completely, but it did look different. Stupider, to be precise. Niall pressed me to the back of the room.

"Wait here. Be inconspicuous," he instructed. I huddled in enemy territory trying to look Inconspicuous. I channeled Maria crouching behind the tombstone during the great escape scene. It was all so dramatic. Long minutes passed. It gradually felt less dramatic and began to feel stressful. The heaving mass was slowly creeping toward me. The Movie Starring Me was more like "The Sound of Bruises." Where was Niall? Had he been sucked in? Then I heard the alarming sound of a bullhorn.

"This is the police. Cease and desist all aggression at once!" ordered the mechanically amplified voice. The unpersuaded mob continued to whale on one another with the bloodthirsty aggressiveness of shoppers at the annual Barney's fire sale.

"Good Lord, we're all going to get arrested," I whispered to myself. Suddenly, Niall reappeared. I almost melted in relief.

"Sure and there's nothing for it. We can't get out through the main doors, so we'll find another way. Ready to move fast?" Yes, definitely. I reached down and took off my high heel sandals, unsure what he was planning, but certain it'd be easier in bare feet. I looked nervously at the brawl. Oh my God! Did my cousin Rudi just punch a cop? I shot a terrified look at Niall.

"Whatever it is, let's do it. Now," I said.

"That's my girl." He smiled and took my hand. Tingle down the hoo-hah highway. Inappropriately timed lewd thought. Jesus, Vi, get a grip. It's just a hand. (Cha.)

We hurried to some doors marked EMERGENCY EXIT ONLY. DO NOT OPEN. THIS DOOR IS ALARMED. I couldn't say for sure, but I'd bet I was more alarmed than the door at that point. Niall pushed them open and immediately a strident clanging added to the chaos. We ducked onto the balcony outside. The banquet hall was a level up from the ground. I craned over the edge. Too far to jump. Niall was pressed against the building wall.

"What is it?" I asked, concerned.

"I'm afraid of heights." He looked tense and sheepish at the same time.

"It's not that high," I assured him. "But too far to jump down." He paled at the word "jump," and pressed farther against the wall, looking anxiously around.

"Right," he said through gritted teeth. "Nothing else for it." There was another balcony to the right, separated by a two-foot gap. Niall climbed the divide, somewhat awkwardly, as I noticed that he was juggling a bundle in his free hand. Had he saved his wedding gift? I wondered. How odd. I didn't reflect long because he was urging me over, looking anxious to be off the balcony. I tossed over my shoes and clambered across with his help. I leapt down just as a police officer burst through the doors.

"Hey, you two. Stop right there! No one in this friggin' freak show's going anywhere!"

He sure had that wrong. The effort to shout had caused beads of sweat to pop on his florid face. I was laying odds he'd never make the wall, but didn't wait around to find out. I wanted a rap sheet less than I wanted my sandals. We launched ourselves through the balcony doors and tumbled into another banquet room. This room was off a different feeder hallway, completely insulated from the chaos of the pods we'd escaped. At least it had been until we activated the door alarm during the best man's speech. Two hundred elegant-looking people turned to stare. The best man stood immobile at the microphone, mouth hanging open. Cool as a cucumber, Niall effected a casual saunter.

"Careful mate, you'll catch flies." He winked at the best man then turned to the astonished crowd. "Don't mind us, folks. Filming a remake of *The Graduate*. This is the bit where ourselves hop the bus. Though in our version it's a hot air balloon. Bit more romantic, you know, evoking childhood fantasies of escape from *The Wizard of Oz*. Quite brilliant directorship really. Spielberg, you know. Sorry to disturb. You'll have gotten notice of the filming in your gift bags, of course. And don't you make a lovely bride . . ." He kept up a steady stream as we edged through the room, nonchalantly accelerating our pace toward the door. I looked back anxiously, but Johnny Law hadn't appeared. After an eternity, we hit the door, and with a cheery wave and "Carry on then, look for us in theaters everywhere this summer," dashed through.

The hall was blessedly quiet and mercifully deserted. We paused for a moment, panting. Niall pulled me close with a groan, resting his chin on my head. I leaned against him.

"In theaters everywhere this summer?" I demanded from the folds of his collar.

He gave a snort of laughter and smiled down at me, smoothing my hair. "I'm just glad to be off that balcony." He looked around. "We'd better keep on," he said, and cautiously led me along the hallway. "Best not to hit anywhere public in that dress. They were looking to arrest everyone from both parties." Up the hallway was a battered swinging door.

"Bingo." I recognized access to the hotel underbelly from years of catering, and pushed open the door to reveal a cement hallway lined with wire racks laden with reception implements. We progressed carefully until we reached a break niche. I'd have hurried on but Niall stopped me.

"And voilà," he pointed. Hanging on a hook was a shapeless, grey polyester server's dress. I looked at him aghast. He misinterpreted my look. "Don't think of it as stealing. Think of it as borrowing. We'll bring it back."

"You want me to wear *that*?" I hissed. I could give a damn about the morality of appropriating the dress. "It's horrid." He raised an eyebrow. Okay, it's true. I was wearing a yam-colored prom dress with the crinolines knotted in front like a Daisy Duke halter. "It's *polyester*," I tried again. His expression remained laconic. "It's a size sixteen!"

Ten minutes later I was chafing under the enveloping grey shroud and toting a pillowcase full of yam. Niall had an amused smile lurking around his lips but wisely kept his eyes averted.

Soon, we emerged onto the hotel loading docks. We were facing the parking lot with a hill beyond. I looked at the incline dubiously. I had no shoes.

"Hold this," Niall instructed, handing me his awkward package. I stashed it in the pillowcase. He turned his back to me and leaned forward a bit. "Hop on."

"What?" I asked in surprise.

"Hop on. You can't climb in bare feet. But I bet there's a hell of a view at the top." He smiled a wicked smile. I clambered on his back, holding the pillowcase over my shoulder like Hazel playing Santa Claus. Even with my weight, Niall scrambled to the top in no time. And the view was stupendous.

"It's beautiful," I gasped. I was dazzled by the colored lights of every emergency vehicle in LaGrange and Hinsdale assembled below in full disaster incident glory. We had a perfect view of people the size of beetles dashing about, those in uniform gently palming the heads of those in long satin dresses into the paddy wagons.

We were rapt before the pretty lights. Then Niall spread my gown on the grass, sat, and unbundled his mystery package, which turned out to be a raincoat with sleeves intricately knotted to encase an open and recorked bottle of red wine and two glasses.

At my surprised look, he grinned. "Perhaps you weren't the only one guilty of garment-pinching this evening." He poured two glasses of wine and handed me one. We clinked and leaned our sides contentedly together as we watched the spectacle below. Then he turned to me with a serious look on his face. My insides tensed.

"I have something to say to you," he said gravely. Oh God, I thought. He has a girlfriend. He finds my crush embarrassing. Whatever it is, it's going to suck. He looked back over the bedlam, face somber, and took a deep breath.

" 'Nature's first green is gold, / Her hardest hue to hold. / Her early leaf's a flower, / But only so an hour . . .' "

Halfway through the poem I was laughing so hard I snorted wine though my nose, and he couldn't maintain his earnest facade. But he soldiered on, recreating the exchange between Ponyboy and Cherry after they escaped the rumble in *The Outsiders*, wiggling his eyebrows at me, his voice becoming more theatrical with each verse.

"Then leaf subsides to leaf, / So Eden sank to grief. / So dawn goes down to day . . ."

". . . and Nothing gold can stay!" We shouted in unison, clinking glasses again. Frost would roll in his grave to know his beautiful poem was remembered most for a Coppola movie.

"Here's to you, Ponyboy," I said gravely.

"Back at you, Cherry," he grinned. Our eyes held. Flustered, I looked away.

"Oh look! There's Maeve!" I pointed to my bedraggled sister being escorted out in handcuffs. It looked like she was flirting with the arresting officer. "She always did like men in uniform," I explained.

"And you?" he asked, looking intently at me. "What do you like?" My breath died in my throat and I panicked for a minute. What should I say? Tell the truth and face possible humiliation? Or take a chance? His expression was honest and warm, but guarded. What the hell? I thought. Nothing ventured, nothing gained.

"You," I whispered. "I like you, Niall Devlin." He broke into a relieved smile.

"Well, that is good news," he said. "Because you ruthlessly caused your man to develop an enormous crush on you from the moment I laid eyes on you."

"Really?" I asked in shock.

"Really," he murmured, staring at my mouth. "You were so genuine at Tim's wedding. Everyone else was bitching about wristbands and hoarding drinks, but not you. You just observed what was going on as if you were studying the human race but weren't sure what you thought about it. No airs. It was refreshing. Then we kept meeting at all those weddings and you made me laugh so." He smiled at the recollection.

"I did?" I marveled.

"You did . . . though I'm not sure you intended to. You were, *are,* smart and beautiful, but also so loyal and willing to do any-thing for your friends. The ridiculous things you would do"—here I frowned a bit—"and wear"—well, no argument there—"and al-ways with good humor and grace. And I remember thinking, 'That girl is a genuinely lovely person. And sassy.' It got to be where I wanted to be around you all the time. I actually started to look forward to weddings."

"I had no idea. . . ." I was breathless.

He leaned in toward me slowly, stopping his lips a hairbreadth away from mine, our breaths mingling. "But every time I'd get close to you, you'd bolt. And I kept asking myself," he whispered, "will . . . this . . . kiss . . . ever . . . happen. . . ."

I hung breathless, fainting from anticipation. Please, God, let it happen. Then he covered my lips with his in a pulse-spiking kiss. Skyrockets went off to shame the emergency vehicle light show and my scalp tingled like an electron helmet. The man could kiss. And he did. And did. And did, his hands cupping my face, fingers threading in my hair. And I know it's cheesy, but if I thought I'd been kissed before, I was wrong. This was the Kiss, not from someone else's movie but the one starring me, the Kiss you thought was too amazing to exist in real life. It was the thunderbolt I'd been waiting for.

Niall sat back and smiled his lopsided smile, drawing a deep breath. "That kiss certainly isn't going to help my inability to stop thinking about you," he teased. "You know, when I first saw you tonight, I actually thought my infatuated imagination had conjured up a hallucination."

I sighed happily. He rubbed a gentle thumb over my lips, staring intently at them, then dropped another kiss on them.

"You're a very hard woman not to kiss," he said seriously, kissing me again. And again.

As if I wanted him to stop. Cha. My hands were pressed against his washboard sternum. I clutched the fabric of his shirt and tugged him toward me, open-mouth kissing him like a porn star. The tenderness and anticipation of the first kiss past, we devoured each other. His hands slid to my collarbone, slipping inside my loose size sixteen collar to caress my shoulders, and slowly we tilted over until we were laying on our sides, embracing. I slid my arms around him and buried one hand in his thick curls, running the other along his muscled spine. Christ, his body was hard and flawless. The entire time I was simultaneously rejoicing and marveling. I could barely believe this was happening. It was more surreal than my entire family being arrested. He slid one arm down and around my waist and pulled me so we had complete body contact, his lips wandering down my neck. His mouth returned to mine and I gently bit his lower lip before deepening the kiss. We kissed like we were starving. I gripped his hip bone, my toes curling as he moved to nibble on my earlobe. A Thought nudged me. I sluggishly pondered it, concentrating on the sensations caused by Niall's wandering lips. The Thought was persistent.

"Wait, wait," I gasped. "What . . . about—oooh, that feels good—bail?" I managed. After all, my sister did just get arrested, likely along with my entire family. There was a snuffling in my neck and I realized he was laughing. He rose up on one elbow to look at me. I lay limply on my back, meeting his eyes.

"You're delightful," he murmured, pulling a twig from my hair. "Indeed, as the lone survivors of the Rumble at the William Tell, we'll have to do something about this situation." We sat up and surveyed the dwindling activity below as the vehicles packed up and drove off with our relatives.

"Still got your prostitution money?" Niall asked.

"It's called a 'Dollar Dance,' it wasn't *mine*, and yes." I patted the pillowcase where I'd stashed the envelope. "Do you have yours?" He nodded and tapped his jacket.

"I doubt we have enough. That was a lot of paddy wagons." I started to rise when Niall tugged me back down.

"You know," he looked mischievous, "it'll take time for the station to finish booking everyone."

I wanted to pinch myself. I couldn't believe this dream of a man was mine. I mean, my politically correct self amended, his *own* person of course, but also mine. Mine, mine, mine! I wanted to shout and dance with pure joy. Instead I smiled radiantly at him.

"You're right." My tone was serious as I settled myself against him. "It'll be chaos for a while. I'd better stay here with you."

"Stay with me," he murmured. "I quite like the sound of that." He was looking at me as though I was the soccer World Cup, the lottery, and Christmas all rolled into one.

"Yes, I like the sound of that too," I sighed, allowing him to pull me close for a melting kiss that felt like the beginning of something and the end of all other kisses at the same time.

From: ViViVooom@gmail.com
To: Ben@siddickens.com
Sent: April 27
Subject: Joy! Joy! Joy!

Ben,

You are not going to *believe* what happened at my cousin's wedding! Best day of my life so far . . .

V.

Part Four

Things Fall Apart

CHAPTER THIRTY-SIX

I'm in Love

Something heavy prevented me from rolling over. I fought through sleep and it gradually penetrated that I was pinned by a tanned male arm slung heavily across my waist. I felt the morning shot of joy that hadn't abated in three months of waking up next to Niall. For the first time since Christmas morning when I was seven, I loved waking up. I slyly peeped at him from under my lashes but he was already awake, grinning at me.

"You dog." I laughed and swatted him. "You're always up before me."

"Not hard," he laughed. "I like to watch you sleep." He dropped a kiss on my nose and smoothed my hair away from my face. "And I adore watching you try to wake up."

"Humph," I humphed, but snuggled closer for a proper kiss. And another. And another. Until The Movie Starring Me was definitely *The Firm*.

Yes. I loved mornings now.

"I'm in love," I sang to Traci, still effused with afterglow when I walked into D&D two hours later. She rolled her eyes. I made a face and kept going to my office.

"I'm in love," I said to Giles as I walked in.

"*I'm* in love!" he said excitedly. Giles and Matt had moved in together. It was our favorite new game to happily spend the first half hour of the day exchanging the perfections of Niall and Matt. Sometimes we even forewent pandacam for more time swapping "Did I tell you what Niall said the other day . . ." or "And then Matt surprised me . . ." It never got old. Well, for us, anyway.

We were interrupted by the phone, which caller ID told me was Imogen.

"I'm in love," I sang into the phone in lieu of hello.

"Yes, yes, I'm aware," she said wryly. "But have you told him yet?" I shut up. We hadn't said the L word. I was confident in Niall but terrified to go first.

"What's up?"

"What should I get Ethan for our anniversary?" she asked.

"A gym membership," I snorted.

"Are you trying to get me dumped?" she accused, and hung up. I laughed. As if. Imogen and Ethan were the perfect couple. Next to me and Niall, of course. I dawdled in thoughts of Niall and me teaching children to read in the sunlight in Africa for a moment before turning my attention to work. Which, to be truthful, didn't require much attention. I continued to be au courant with wine, consuming trade rags like they were ABBA reunion tickets. But my passion for D&D was waning. Al deflected most of my proposals, and now that I actually knew what I was doing and wanted to get creative, my job wasn't challenging. Once you get the basics of event planning, it's plug and chug. The same was true for inventory management. Stockwise, D&D was conservative. Though Al had given me some rein to try experimental vineyard productions, for the most part we stuck with the tried and true. I was obsessed with exciting things happening in Northern Virginia. But they weren't happening in the hallowed walls of my store. I was hobbled.

I cranked out my chores for an upcoming in-store tasting and a catered retirement luncheon and was finished by two. Even after poring over trade magazines, I had plenty of time to e-mail Ben and surf the Internet. I was looking for a hook to push Al more, especially with regard to regional wines.

"So what're you up to this weekend?" Giles asked at the end of the day. It was a beautiful July Friday, before D.C. became as hot and humid as the inside of a dog's mouth.

I laughed. "We have a wedding. This will be the first one we actually attend together!" I looked at my watch. "Egads. Speaking of Niall, I've got to dash. I'm meeting him at Obelisk in thirty minutes."

Forty-one minutes on the dot later I walked into the tiny romantic dining room at Obelisk. Niall kissed me hello and the waiter seated us at a cozy candlelit table.

"So how was your day, dear?" He pulled my hand across the table to play with my fingers.

"Okay," I shrugged. "It's hard to get excited about restocking the same wines and organizing indistinguishable events. I try to shake things up, but there's little I can do."

"What about another shop?" Niall suggested.

"I think it'd be more of the same."

The waiter came and asked Niall for our drink order. I cleared my throat. The waiter looked at me, not expecting a female lead. Niall looked amused.

"We enjoy richer red wines from the Umbria and Tuscany region, like the Brunelo or Vino Nobile," I said, "and we're following recent viticultural innovation in Virginia. Do you have local wines that use Sangiovese grapes and reflect a similar palate? I think Barboursville Vineyards just released its Octagon Piedmontese Nebbiolo."

The waiter went glassy-eyed. Niall suppressed a chuckle. "I don't think we have any Virginia wines," he said.

I sighed and glanced at the wine list. "It says you have a Justin. Is that the Isosceles?"

"Um, I'm not sure."

"Could you check?" I gave him my best I'm Just a Sweet Lil' Ol' Thing expression. "And find out what year? Thank you *so* much. . . ."

As the waiter hurried away, Niall couldn't stop from laughing. "Right, that wins deepest Southern accent since your phone conversation with the bank about the lost ATM card."

I smiled back. "Ya'll just come on ovah and set on the porch swing for a mint julep, heavy on the julep, suh. . . ." Then I frowned. "It annoys me how little patronization the Virginia industry gets from local establishments. There are some good wines down there."

"Seriously, Vi, you know your stuff. You've got to get out of D&D and spread your wings. What about a restaurant? You could be a sommelier, and specialize in Virginia wines."

"I've thought about it," I admitted. "But I'm more excited by viticulture than flogging bottles to the masses." I hesitated. "I was toying with the idea of a graduate degree," I confessed I hadn't told anyone else. I was sure I was wholly unqualified.

He lit up. "That's a great idea! At Georgetown?"

"No. That's part of the problem," I said. "The best one is in California at U.C. Davis. I don't think there are any around here, and I don't want to leave the area. It's just an idea." The waiter returned, and indeed the Justin was the Isosceles, so we ordered it.

"Tell me about *your* day." I started a new topic.

He let me drop the subject but his look said it'd be back. Mention of his day brought a frown. "Same old Sonny The Squirrel," he said.

"Have you thought about the *Washington Post* opening my friend mentioned?"

"As an editor of the International Section?" He scoffed. "I'm not qualified for that."

"I think you're qualified," I said stoutly, capturing his hand and squeezing. "I think you can do anything you put your mind to. Besides, you never know if you don't try."

"Perhaps," he said noncommittally. Then he smiled at me, candlelight playing on the masculine planes of his face, and I forgot what we were talking about. "Thanks for your faith."

I just nodded, Astonished anew that this man needed me as much as I needed him.

Middleburg is a Virginia country town geographically just outside D.C. but culturally universes away. It's green and serene, with rolling fields nestled at the base of the Appalachians, fox-hunting, polo matches, vineyards, and Civil War battlefields. If D.C. is the height of preppy, Middleburg is "horse country couture." Think Charles and Camilla without the accents or thrones.

"Did you know a Revolutionary War officer originally bought the land for Middleburg for only $2.50 an acre from a cousin of George Washington," I told Niall as we drove out to Four Fox Vineyards. He grinned at me.

"At least it's one of the close vineyards," he said. "That only took twenty-five minutes."

"Super secret back way," I said smugly, loving him for letting me be the boss of directions. "Oh look, there's the Red Fox Inn. It's the oldest original inn in America, and was a Confederate meeting spot." I pointed as we drove through town.

Four Fox Vineyard was just outside of Middleburg. We stepped from the car and were riveted by the panoramic view.

"It's absolutely gorgeous," Niall said. It was. Acres of vineyards rolled away to meet a lake among gentle green foothills with the blue shadow of mountains behind them. The property had a beautiful new tasting room, a barrelhouse, the wine production facility, and landscaped lawns and gardens for picnics, events, and visitors. Everything was dominated by a majestic white colonial mansion with great columns, black shutters and ironwork, and a central fountain.

"I feel like Thomas Jefferson come home to Monticello," Niall murmured, pulling me against him. Then he murmured sexily in my ear, "By the way, I lied to you about what time the wedding started. Want to do a tasting?" At my look of outrage, he just cocked an eyebrow. "What? I didn't want to be late." Damn, I envied that eyebrow trick.

We found the tasting room empty but for a jovial man in his seventies wearing red suspenders. He reminded me of Wilford Brimley, but when he was doing *Our House*, not flogging diabetes medicine.

"Hello, hello, come have a taste," he beckoned, setting out glasses. "Name's Chester and I own the joint." We joined him at the counter and soon were engaged in a lively discussion about the Virginia wine trade, developments in grape cultivation, and inventive avenues for vineyard revenue generation. Well, Chester and I were engaged in a lively discussion. Niall just sipped his wine and admired.

"My goodness," Chester said after a bit. "You know your wines, young lady. And so enthusiastic about the local business, bless you! I wish I had someone like you working for me."

Niall and I both went still.

"Work for you?" I parroted, trying not to imagine myself sallying through the halls of Mansion-O-Perfection with an authoritative clipboard in hands as I discussed our recent wine awards with an avid journalist from *Wine Spectator*.

"Well, I'm lookin' to retire in a year or two," Chester said, "and I want to find a young person to take over managing the operations. We've got events and we've got wine production and we've got wine distribution, we've got all the on-the-ground operations here, and to top it all we just got busier than Santa in December with the Supreme Court ruling we can ship wine over state lines." He winked at Niall. "I joined that suit, lad. I like to stir things up."

"What, um, what are you looking for?" I ventured.

"I have a passel of managers all good at one thing, and I need someone who knows a bit about everything to coordinate 'em all and make the decisions. It's a full-time job."

"What sort of qualifications might that person need?" Niall asked, giving me a kick under the counter for being struck mute.

"Someone whose neck I don't want to wring who has common sense, enthusiasm, and will love the job. I haven't commenced aggressively searching—I'm not dead yet!" He laughed. "But I've always got my beady eye open for the right person."

"Oh," I managed faintly, trying not to swoon from Desire.

"Vi's actually looking for something in viticulture," Niall jumped in.

"Zat so?" Chester looked at me. We heard a string quartet begin to play outside. "You here for the wedding?" We nodded. "Tell you what, young lady. You come back and have lunch with me. We'll see what skills you got and figure if there might be a match."

I couldn't talk so I just nodded idiotically. It was Niall who pumped Chester's hand promising, "You'll be glad, sir. She'll blow you away." Then he guided me out.

I walked down the hill until Niall redirected me from my course into the lake.

"My, my, my, I don't think I've ever seen herself speechless," he teased.

"Oh, Niall," I breathed. "It would be a dream come true." I was giddy.

He looked into my eyes. "You can do this—"

We were pounced on by three athletic-looking boys. "Oi, mate! We're all sitting together so we can Huzzah! when the deed's done." They marshaled us to what was definitely going to be a rugby wedding, at least on the groom's side, while I daydreamed about Niall smiling proudly at me as I eloquently accepted Four Fox's Decanter World Wine Award gold medal.

Later that night we cuddled on the sofa in Niall's apartment.

"It was a nice wedding," I said. What'd been nice was being there with Niall. I'd lost the anxious adrift feeling. I could feel my rock's chest rising and falling steadily beneath me.

"What's nice is my mates think I have the best girlfriend in the world," he said smugly. "How'd you know it was going to be twenty-two minutes?"

Like it was rocket science.

"One hundred and sixty-two bucks," he crowed. "That's the biggest pool from any rugby mate's wedding. And *my girl* won." He kissed the top of my head and chuckled. "Don't worry, love. I won't let them get up to any pool shenanigans at our wedding."

I laughed. "Too right," I said. "We're not having one."

"What?" He sounded surprised.

"I don't want to get married," I told him. "I had this epiphany after my gazillionth wedding. You're off the hook."

"You mean you don't want to get married right now," he corrected.

"Not ever," I said firmly. He gave me a funny look, but I was too excited to probe. I bounced to face him on the sofa, wiggling in excitement. "Niall, can you imagine if I got that job?"

He chuckled. "I quite liked your man Chester."

"He was great! And the place was gorgeous. Just think what you could do! There'd be tastings and events and tours. And I could learn all about growing the grapes and making the wine, and maybe even have a hand in it. Oh, and I could start a wine club." I was starry-eyed. "And a concert series on the lawn! You know Virginia's known as the birthplace of country music, thanks to the Original Carter Family. I could incorporate local music history—"

Niall cut me off with a rich laugh and pulled me close for a kiss. "God I love you," he said. Everything froze. Then the neurons went crazy.

"What?" I was breathless. I had to hear it again. I hadn't been ready the first time.

"I love you." He smiled deep into my eyes, tucking a strand of hair behind my ear.

"You do?"

"Insanely, I'm afraid."

My heart choked my throat with Happiness and for a minute I couldn't speak, I could only look at him with teary eyes. Then, "Oh God, oh definitely, I love you too. I love you. I'm so in love!"

I fell on him, kissing him, and we stopped talking at all.

"Hellllooooo." Babette snapped her fingers in front of her eyes.

"What?" Startled, I jerked my attention back to the present. It was Sunday night. Oh, right. I was at Clyde's with the girls. I'd been late because Niall had—

"There she goes again," said Ellis in fascination.

"It's fantastic," Babette marveled.

"I've never seen it quite like this." Mona smiled. "It's about time."

This time even Imogen was beaming. "So I take it 'something happened'?" she probed.

I glowed at them all. "He said the L word. He said it first and he said it twice. Then he proved it." A zing shot down my hoo-hah highway at the recollection.

"There she goes again," said Mona.

"It's like she's in outer space," said Ellis. "Let's get her to sign a bunch of legally binding documents. Mona, write something up."

I looked up at them and sighed. "I'm in love."

CHAPTER THIRTY-SEVEN

Fear of Heights

From: ViViVooom@gmail.com
To: Ben@siddickens.com
Sent: August 24
Subject: Suit or DVF?

Ben,

 Can you send a tile to Kathryn Fisher at 1112 Belmont Street, NW, Washington DC, 20009? Niall says to pick whichever you want and put it on his credit card (the one I gave you for the wedding last month). He liked talking to you the other day.
 So you really think I should wear the brown Donna Karan suit instead of the DVF wrap dress? I told you how informal Chester seemed. But maybe you're right. I want to look professional.

V.

From: Ben@siddickens.com
To: ViViVooom@gmail.com
Sent: August 24
Subject: Re: Suit or DVF?

Vi,

Definitely the suit. And I don't think carrying a clipboard
will make you seem "more authoritative," as you suggest.
Perhaps just a nice leather portfolio.
Best of luck. I know you will be sure to impress.

Yours,
Ben

"You have another wedding?" Ellis asked in astonishment. It was
Friday and we were having happy hour at Zaytinya. D.C. had
reached its sticky late August best, and the humidity was wilting,
making patio cocktails impossible.

I groaned. "Martha's Star Chamber thrives. As a couple, we
have doubled exposure. I *was* able to persuade Niall that according to my OFW system we should decline the on-board Odyssey
river cruise reception for a coworker he doesn't particularly like.
He agreed if we did something decadent instead, so we skived off
to Hershey Chocolate Spa for a ridiculously silly weekend of co-
coa baths and chocolate facials. The cats stalked me for days."

"Haven't you been to four weddings already this summer?"
asked Mona.

I looked a little shifty and Imogen snorted. "Three and a half?"
she offered.

"Niall and I sort of slept through the last one," I admitted
sheepishly, "but we made the reception!" Ellis just shook her

head, laughing. "Hey," I defended, "it was the couple's fault, over-serving at the rehearsal dinner. Niall felt terrible about it, but honestly, the bride and groom were none the wiser. I was only disappointed to miss the excitement. Contrary to all reason, the bride dressed her bridesmaids in velvet for an outdoor ceremony at high noon in August. One of them fainted dead away."

"You've become quite cynical," Ellis ventured.

I just shrugged. Since my epiphany, I felt like a missionary of the mind, but I stayed quiet about it in front of married friends.

"Who is it this weekend?" Imogen asked.

"A friend of Niall's. Niall actually enjoys weddings," I marveled. I paused, then said casually, "We're thinking of moving in together." I'd barely been able to contain the news.

"What? When?" They burst into excited chatter.

I laughed. "It's just talk right now. But both of our leases are up soon and Niall has a realtor friend Dale who's really good. So we're casually seeing what's out there."

"Are you looking to buy something?" Imogen asked in surprise.

"Maybe," I shrugged. "We're keeping our options open."

Ellis laughed. "You won't get married, but you'll buy a house together? Let me tell you, a house is a much bigger commitment, time suck, and relationship trial." Ellis and Jack were unendingly involved in renovations on their house.

"It's just talk." I laughed with them but couldn't stop from smiling. I'd been collapsed on Niall's chest, spent from stupendous lovemaking and the mind-blowing multiple orgasm he'd delivered, when he brought it up. We got so excited that we stayed up all night decorating our imaginary future place, until we made ice cream sundaes, then of course the whipped cream was right there, and . . . "Sundae In The Dark with Engorged." I ended up collapsed and sweaty on Niall's chest, exactly where I'd begun.

"I'm so happy for you!" Mona hugged me.

"Thanks." I hugged her back. "I have to admit, I never thought I'd be this happy. I feel like nothing can go wrong since I met Niall."

A person should know better than to say foolish things like that.

"Are you ready?" Niall stood by the door, car keys in hand.

"Um, just using the toilet real quick," I called as I slipped into his office. I slid the *Washington Post* job application in his computer bag next to his laptop where he couldn't miss it, then hurried to join him.

"You look stunning." He kissed me. I was wearing a floor-length black dress with a plunging V-neck, and high strappy silver sandals. Niall looked devastating in his tuxedo.

As we drove to the Hotel Washington, I asked, "How was rugby today?" as I wiggled uncontrollably in my seat.

"As if," Niall chuckled, reaching for my hand and shooting me a wry glance. "The face on you! Tell me."

"Oh, Niall," the words burst out of me. "It's *perfect*. Chester is so sharp and the vineyard is seriously about to break onto the national scene. And he really needs someone. This job would be a dream come true. Lunch went really well."

"So will you get it?"

"I think I've got a shot. I'm not the most qualified, but Chester seems interested in someone willing to work hard to gain experience under him. But I'd have to go back to school for a graduate degree in Viticulture and Enology."

"Viti-what and what?" Niall laughed. "Did yourself say something dirty?"

"No," I giggled. "It's basically a graduate degree in grapes and winemaking."

"I would have thought after all the Sunday nights at Clyde's you'd have that already." He quirked his lopsided smile at me.

"That's just extra credit." I became thoughtful. "I'll have to look into course work. Most of the programs, understandably, are out West. But if I can find a good distance learning program, or maybe something at Maryland, I think I can make a case that by the time Chester wants to retire, I'll have both the degree and the hands-on knowledge under him that I need."

Niall looked at me. "And this is what you want?"

"Yes." I was emphatic. "You know, I fell into my job, but I find it fascinating. And this position would be about what I've discovered I like best—innovation at the vine." I was quiet a minute. "I have a Feeling—it's Awakening. Like I'm finally waking up to my own life. For years I've lived with what happened *to* me. I kept running over old ground with Caleb when he'd present himself, I went to my college because it was the highest ranked one I got into, I moved to D.C. because it was the biggest city between Charlotte and New York, I fell into my job because it found me. It's like I've been afraid to actually want anything of my own so I wouldn't feel Disappointment if I didn't get it." I reached out and touched his cheek. "I almost let you get away." He gave my hand a quick kiss but just listened.

"I want to figure out what *I* want now and go after it with both hands. You know, I've been frustrated with my parents for not 'seeing me,' but I wonder now what there was to see. I was just rolling with everyone else's flow. Not anymore. I'm going to get this job," I finished confidently. "I'm going to *act*, not *react*."

We pulled up at the Hotel Washington and the valet took the car. As we walked in the door, Niall put his arm around my waist, pulling me close to kiss my temple.

"You're going to knock them barmy. I know you will. You impress the hell out of me." My heart gave a happy beat. "Maybe you're right. I dismissed that *Washington Post* job because I didn't think I was qualified, but what's there to lose? Maybe I'll give it a shot."

After a twenty-six-minute ceremony we took the elevator to the roof deck for the cocktail reception. Niall tensed as we stepped onto the patio.

"Are you okay?" I was concerned.

"Fine," he said tightly. "Er, I don't suppose you'd fetch the drinks?" He swallowed. I glanced at the balcony bar, with a stunning view of the Mall and the White House.

"Oh, Niall, it's the balcony, isn't it?" His curt nod conveyed both embarrassment and frustration over his weakness. I hugged him. "We don't have to stay. We can go downstairs until dinner."

"No, I'll be fine. I'll stay away from the edge. It's silly, I know, but I feel like the ground and all that space between will reach out and pull me off."

"I'll get drinks." I gave him lots of pats and hurried to return to him.

When I walked back he was talking to Vanessa the Vixen. I froze, hands dangerously clenching the glass stems. Then I calmed myself. Niall wasn't Caleb. Unnoticed, I observed. He wasn't talking to her. *She* was talking to *him*. Relaxed, I strolled to join them.

"Here you go, darling." I handed him a drink. "It was much easier to get these than the ones you sneaked to me at Traci and Tim's wedding. Oh, hello, Vanessa." Just because I wasn't worried didn't mean I couldn't have some fun.

"How sweet, Niall," Vanessa meowed. "She fetches." I had to admit, she looked stunning. Dammit.

"Well that's a bit rude, then, isn't it?" Niall shocked us both by saying. Vanessa was shocked at the rebuke. I was shocked because Caleb had made me think all men savored a catfight. Instead, Niall put his arm around my shoulders and pulled me tight. "Vi certainly doesn't fetch. But she's expert at the little kindnesses that make her the perfect girlfriend." He smiled into my eyes at that. "If I have a complaint, it's that she doesn't let me spoil her more rotten with bonbons and foot rubbing and the like."

"Bonbons make you fat," I explained.

"Oh," Vanessa deflated. "Well." She pulled herself together. "It was really lovely to see *you*." Ah. Down but not out—she'd gone to the Dani School of Singular Pronunciation.

"That was really lovely," I said to Niall as she sauntered off.

"I don't have time for nonsense like herself," he dismissed. I looked at him closely.

"She really bothered you," I marveled.

He blew air through his lips. "She's a one, isn't she? I feel a fool for dating her at all. She was one of the first girls after Gwendolyn and I was still a bit of a mess." I palpitated with desire to hear more. Gwendolyn had been Niall's serious ex-girlfriend. He caught sight of my expectant face and gave a little chuckle. "Poor darling. I never talk about it, do I? And you have every right to know. Gwendolyn and I met our first year at Oxford University. We dated all four years of school and moved to London together afterward. I was working for the BBC then, and after a while was offered a job in Budapest. The position was only for a year and Gwendolyn urged me to take it, so I did. She came with me but left within a month. We were constantly losing electricity and hot water and she couldn't handle the deprivations. I urged her to go back to London, planning to return as soon as I could. I thought it was quite clear we would marry eventually." He stopped talking and drank some wine.

"And?" I prompted. I was drooling to know.

"Same old sad story, really. I came home to surprise her one weekend and walked in to find herself living in my flat with a mate from school. I was flabbergasted, but Gwendolyn coolly explained that as I hadn't put a ring on her finger she couldn't be expected to limit herself, could she? Seven years together and she needed a diamond to feel that we had a commitment." His smile was bitter.

"Do you miss her?" I ventured.

"Lord no!" He set down his wine and cupped my face. "I was mad to think it would've worked in the first place. She's not a wicked girl, she's focused only on what's best for Gwendolyn. But we were so young, and I was quite romantic and fancied myself in love."

He grinned. "As it turns out, life had a plan. Instead of returning to London, I took this job in America. I was sort of frozen off dating for ages. Then I was introduced to Vanessa. It was never serious but she was refreshingly transparent and very, very American. Gwendolyn pretended to be something she wasn't. Vanessa is blatant in every way, and it felt quite safe to be with her because I knew I'd never be deceived, or become attached. And then I met you." Here he smiled at me. "You were without guile and you made me want to trust a genuine woman again. I'd missed having a real connection with an intelligent sentient being. I'm not really a dating man. I prefer to spend quality time with one woman." He tapped me on the nose. "One *particular* woman, as it turns out. With you, I've learned what it means to truly fall in love. I'd only been practicing before." He kissed me so sweetly I wanted to cry. Instead, we responded like Pavlov's dogs, following the waiter ringing a triangle down to dinner.

After dinner Niall and I were the first on the dance floor. After several songs we took a break and Niall excused himself to "visit the loo." Surprisingly, all the women from our table were seated when I returned, but none of the men. I surveyed the room, and oddly, each table presented a similar picture—women sprouted like mushrooms, but men were absent. The dance floor was almost empty. It was a little spooky.

"Where's Dan?" I asked his wife, Janelle, whom we'd met at dinner.

"He went to the bathroom half an hour ago and I haven't seen him since," she puzzled.

"So did Juan," said Laney, another woman at our table.

"Lee's been gone for almost forty-five minutes," bitched a woman named Christelle. From her expression, Lee wasn't going to cherish his homecoming.

"Weird," I said, wanting Niall to return in case it was a mass alien abduction. No one probes *my* man. I was Relieved to spot him crossing the ballroom, an odd look on his face.

"What—" I started to ask him, but he cut me off.

"Dance with me." He held out his hand, upset. As he pulled me into his arms, I opened my mouth to ask what was wrong. I was stopped by an inhuman screech, and an enraged bride streaked from the ballroom, trailed by an anxious groom. Niall looked pained.

"What's going on?" I demanded.

"Oh, it's dreadful," he said. "How she could do this?"

"What? Do what?"

"Apparently, the groom's ex-wife slipped into the men's loo and placed large photographs of the bride and groom in each urinal."

"What?" I gasped. "Seriously?"

"That's not all. Your woman left a keg so the male guests would hang around in the loos and urinate more." He winced. "The priest is in there singing Scottish drinking songs."

"Good Lord! She's an evil genius." I had to chuckle.

Niall frowned at me. "I don't think it's funny at all. It's wretched. This is Kathryn and Eric's wedding, and she's made it a travesty."

"Most weddings are a travesty to start with," I dismissed. "Eric and Kathryn made it one when they forced a four-year-old kid sobbing and terrified down the aisle in a miniature tuxedo with a blue satin pillow. And for what? It's not even the real ring. It's a fake so the real one isn't lost. Kid'll need therapy over a fake ring."

"You can't be serious." Niall looked astonished.

"I'm deadly serious," I assured him. "And it's all to venerate marriage—an institution that makes no sense."

"But getting married is natural," Niall protested.

"Why does everyone say that? Is it natural? No other animals mate for life—not even the Emperor penguins. It's mythology—they only mate for one breeding season. Only death is natural, and we fight like hell to avoid that."

"You don't believe in mating for life?" The astonishment was back. He had me there.

"Well, okay, I do," I relented. "Of course."

"Then I don't see the distinction. Why wouldn't you marry?"

"Because I can have the life relationship without the marriage. I'm resistant to unquestioning acceptance that I *should* marry just because 'they' told me so. *Why* should I marry?"

"Because marriage is the way we sanctify commitment to another."

"The commitment should sanctify itself," I countered. "I think marriage is harmful to commitment because it makes people lazy."

Niall's face hardened a bit. "It doesn't work that way."

"Look, since I was a kid, I've been taught to dream about marriage and the BDOYL, the wedding as Best Day Of Your Life. It's a fishhook in women's mouths that drags them willy-nilly into a huge princessy wedding if they can muscle some guy to the altar. I think the obsession leads women to poor decisions. By removing myself from the race, I'm preserving clear judgment."

"I think marriage is meaningful. As you say, it's the judgment in choosing that matters."

"Well, we may have to agree to disagree on this." I was eager to get off the topic.

"But how can we, when we're in a long-term relationship?" He paused and looked guarded. "I assume we both believe this is a long-term relationship?"

"Of course." I was surprised he would question that.

"Thus eventually we would marry."

"Niall—"

Another hysterical screech interrupted us. I remembered "Flush Hour" going on in the men's room but suppressed my giggle from a perturbed Niall.

"Darling." I put my hand on his cheek. "We're not going to resolve all the issues of matrimony tonight." I kissed him. "But I know I'm where I want to be with you now." He kissed me back. And again. Until hysterical yelling again sliced through the romantic dance.

"Let's get out of here," he suggested. "I believe I'd like to take you home and ravish you." His eyes smiled but a small frown wrinkle remained on his forehead.

"I don't see why he doesn't get it," I said to Giles over coffee Monday morning. "Oooh look, he's moving." Tai Shan wobbled toward some eucalyptus.

"A*dor*able! Well, darling, I have to say, I'm with Niall on this one."

I looked at Giles in surprise. "What?"

"I'm all for marriage," Giles said to me. "I think its terribly moving that a person would organize a big event to tell the whole world they love you for life."

"You do?" I goggled at him.

"Absolutely. I want to get married."

"You do?" I was completely Flabbergasted. "But I would've thought you'd be more pissed off at marriage than anyone, because it discriminates against gays."

"Darling, it's the assholes in Congress that discriminate against the gays. Marriage is nothing more than a union between two people."

"A *legal* union."

"On a literal level, perhaps. But on a romantic level, it's saying 'I Choose.' I've definitely chosen Matt and would give my eye-teeth to have him marry me. I'm working up the courage."

"But—"

"Vi, darling, you are wonderful and bright and my best friend, but you're a bit daft about the whole wedding thing. You've evolved into a reverse obsession against it, and sometimes I wonder if you can really untangle what you believe anymore."

"Of course I can," I defended stoutly. Giles patted me on the knee indulgently.

"Just be careful with Niall," he warned. "You can't dictate what a man thinks just because it makes sense to you. If you could, I'd have Armani make salmon-colored satin suits.

CHAPTER THIRTY-EIGHT

Two Separations, a Divorce, and a Civil Ceremony

"I'm in love," I jokingly sang to Traci for the millionth time when I walked into work several weeks later. To my horror, she burst into tears.

"Traci! What's wrong?" I hurried over. She just sobbed, and I awkwardly put my arms around her. Despite having gone to her wedding, I barely knew the girl. I did have a soft spot because that's where I'd met Niall. After a few minutes she stepped back and blew her nose. I noticed an accumulation of crumpled tissues on the floor near her register.

"What is it?"

"It's Tim. He le-e-e-e-eft. . . ." she wailed. Oh dear.

"He left? What happened?"

"He said I didn't 'get' him, that I only got his bank account," she managed. "He thinks I'm not sma-a-a-a-rt. . . ." Here, she burst into fresh sobs and I soothed her as best I could. When I could reasonably escape to my office, I pondered her news. It seemed to me that Tim should've had a pretty good bead on Traci's intentions and intellect before they married. They'd dated twice as long as the year they'd been married. Though to be sure, the entire second year they dated was consumed with wedding planning. And, as I recalled, the entire first year had been consumed with Traci doing whatever it took to get Tim to propose so she could move into his "gorgeous" Bethesda house.

"Another case of wanting it without figuring out whether you really should," I muttered as I hurried to grab my ringing telephone. I chose not to dwell on my conversation with Giles.

"Hello?"

"Vi? It's Lila."

"Lila!" Since her wedding, I could count the times I'd seen Lila on one hand. And those times, she'd been withdrawn and edgy. She'd stopped drinking and rarely went out. "Great to hear from you. How's—"

"I'm getting a divorce," she announced flatly.

I was flabbergasted. "What?"

"I've left Hart. My divorce is almost final." She gave a laugh that sounded like a bark. "I've finally come to my senses."

"What happened?"

"You saw what happened. I stopped being me. I stopped talking first—Hart said my chatter made his head spin. Then I stopped going out with friends or drinking wine—Hart didn't approve. Then I stopped laughing—Hart scared me. When I stopped breathing, I realized it was leave or die."

"Oh God. I'm so sorry." I felt horrible Guilt. "I wasn't there for you. I'm so sorry."

She barked again. "You can't be there for someone who's not there for herself, can you? Don't you dare take on blame for this, Vi. I went into my cave and stopped calling you or anyone. And Hart cut me off from everyone else so he'd have total control."

"What did you mean he scared you?" I was Afraid of the answer.

She was quiet. "He never hit me or anything like that. Yet. But he got crazier and crazier. He forbid me to use the phone. When I was at work, I had to check in every few hours. He made me refuse out-of-town business trips, and when he'd travel, he forbid me to leave the house. He got really crazy." Her voice got small. "What's crazy is that I put up with it."

I was quiet a moment, then said, "They say if you put a frog in boiling water, he jumps right out. But if you put a frog in temperate water and turn up the heat slowly, he'll sit there until he boils to death. Hart was a different man when you married him."

"Was he? Who knows. He had all the check marks I was looking for. I don't know if I ever really found out who he was beyond that he was the *sort* of person I was supposed to pick."

"I'm sorry I let you down. Not pressing you more before you married him," I lamented.

"Honey, I let *myself* down."

We hung up with my heart aching for Lila and another Feeling lurking. Fear. A part of me anxiously dreaded similar calls from Jen and Amy. Knowing it had happened to my parents made me feel that nothing about marriage was safe. I hadn't moved when Giles arrived.

"I'm in *love*," he sang as he pranced in. He seemed surprised at my silence, but obviously couldn't wait because he barreled on. "And I'm getting *married*!"

"What?!" I exclaimed.

He bounded over, practically hopping up and down in excitement. "I did it! I proposed! Oh, I was so *nervous*. . . . I was a total goof! Then he said yes!"

"But—"

"Oh I love that man. And he's going to *marry* me!" He did a little dance.

I didn't want to burst his bubble but . . . "Um . . ."

He caught sight of my expression and swatted me lightly.

"Nitwit. I know we can't *legally* get married, but we don't care. We're having a Commitment Ceremony at All Soul's Church. And you're my best man. Oh, and you should see my *ring* . . ."

I let his excitement wash over me. Despite Giles's belief in marriage, unbidden on my score chart it got another black mark. Giles and Matt had a nurturing, committed relationship—everything that marriage *should* embody—and they were legally prohibited as pariah. Yet marriage for filial duty (Lila) or social advancement (Traci) was encouraged. I was more convinced than ever that marriage was artificial. It was so clear. Thank God I had Niall. I ignored the little voice whispering in my brain that Niall didn't agree. . . .

". . . so you'll stand up with me Saturday?" Giles asked me anxiously.

"Saturday," I repeated in surprise. "So soon!"

"Why wait?" warbled my giddy officemate, then The Movie Starring Me was "Big Stat Queen Wedding" as he sucked me into frenetic planning so he could have it in a week.

I was Exhausted when I let myself into Niall's apartment that night.

"Honey, I'm home," I tossed my keys on the hall table.

"In here," he called, sounding tired and flat. I walked into the living room and found him on the couch with no lights on.

"It's dark." I sat next to him and put my head on his shoulder.

"Mmm." He absently stroked my hair. "You smell good."

I giggled. "You always say that."

"And you always do." He kissed me, but distractedly.

"What's going on?" I pushed away to look at him. He sighed.

"It's my sister."

"Fiona?" I'd grown to love his sister.

"No, my other sister, in Ireland, Nora. She and her husband are getting separated."

I peered at him in the semidark in astonishment, trying to

make out his features. His voice sounded heavy. "Are you serious? Because Traci and Tim just got separated, and Lila told me today she's divorcing Hart."

"Really?" Now he sounded surprised. "What's wrong with everybody?"

"What's wrong with everybody? Inflated expectations of marriage is what's wrong," I pronounced with a snort. "Marriage isn't panacea, yet people expect it to deflect all trauma."

I felt Niall scrutinizing me. "You're quite serious," he said slowly. "You won't marry me." I felt a stab through the heart and knew I was on very, very careful ground. Was he asking?

"I always told you I didn't want to marry or have a big hoopla," I said hesitantly. "That doesn't mean I don't love you and want to stay with you forever."

"But if you wanted to stay with me forever, you'd marry me," he countered. "It doesn't have to be a 'big hoopla.'"

"It's not that simple. . . ."

"I think it is. In my family, people marry because they want to spend their lives together."

"Not your sister." The low blow was out before I could stop myself.

"That's different. She got pregnant. It was Ireland. She didn't want to marry him and she didn't love him but it was what you did. You and I love each other. Or I thought we did."

"We do! Yes," I agreed fervently, glad to be on positive ground.

"Then there's no reason not to marry unless you're hedging your bets. Unless you think you might not want to be with me down the road." He sounded painfully vulnerable, and if Gwendolyn had been within my reach at that moment I'd have slain her on the spot.

"It's not hedging bets!" I was desperate to reassure him. "Our relationship is perfect."

"Our *relationship* is nothing more than one day to the next unless we take the next step. And apparently you don't trust me enough to even consider making a real commitment."

"That's not it." I was practically gasping with Panic. "I'm afraid marriage does the opposite. Like if you marry someone, you've done all the investment you need to do. You've shown the world and now you're done. It doesn't cure problems or change people, except to maybe make them more complacent. I believe in real commitment. But I don't see marriage as a necessary or meaningful way to have that."

"I do," he said quietly, and heaved himself off the sofa. "Excuse me. I'm quite tired and am going to read and turn in."

I sat alone in the now full dark, desperately trying to breathe and wondering if this was how Lila had felt.

Five days later I stood on the altar of All Soul's to Giles's left. He'd been bouncing around all day like a bipolar Ping-Pong ball, alternately weeping and laughing. Matt was a complete waterworks. Imogen kept rolling her eyes and passing out tissues. She stood next to me. Ethan and Niall sat in the front pew, Ethan looking amused, Niall inscrutable.

"What's going on?" Imogen had whispered to me earlier. I'd only shaken my head. I wasn't ready to talk about it. After our fight, we'd rigidly lain in bed side by side until Niall rolled over with a groan and we made desperate love. In the five days since, we hadn't seen each other. Giles had hijacked me full-time, and Niall worked late each night. I was still having trouble breathing, but I knew Niall would see reason eventually. Though Giles and Matt certainly weren't helping, wearing their joyous emotions on their sleeves. I'd outlawed First Corinthians and Mona was reading The Owl And The Pussycat. I glanced at Niall. Our eyes caught and held. Then he looked away.

After the ceremony we walked to Perry's for the reception. Giles and Matt had a first dance and cut the cake. Then Giles produced a ridiculous bouquet of bright red poppies.

"I always wanted to throw the bouquet," he proclaimed. "Now all the single ladies—and 'ladies' too—get together. . . ." I allowed myself to be reluctantly herded to the front of the group, between Imogen and Mona. Giles beamed at everyone. The gleam in his eye as he looked at me gave me a bad Feeling. As if on cue, he turned and hurled the bouquet directly at me. My arms were paralyzed and the flowers bounced off me and landed with a thud on the floor. I stared at the garish red blooms, then lifted my eyes very slowly, afraid to meet Niall's gaze over the corpse of the bouquet. I needn't have worried. He wouldn't look at me either.

CHAPTER THIRTY-NINE

Packing Baggage

I sat on the bed watching him pack things into a duffel bag. I fought to hold it together until he was gone before I fell completely apart. "Saving Private Crying." It was slow going, as he frequently excused himself to the bathroom. He'd return with eyes as red-rimmed as mine.

"That's it, then." He zipped the bag. "If I've missed anything, just give me a ring, right?"

"Niall . . ." My throat closed and I couldn't manage any more.

He looked at me, exhausted and worn. We'd talked through the night, me trying to explain, him uncompromising.

"I can't—" His voice cracked. He closed his eyes and cleared his throat. Then he went on. "Vi, I can't talk anymore. I just can't. We want different things. We view relationships differently. It's better we know this now, before . . ."

I didn't see how it could feel worse than this. I desperately tried one last time.

"Remember when we were talking about your fear of heights? It's like that for me. I'm afraid of marriage. I'm not afraid of commitment. I want that, with you. But I see partnership as needing fierce protection, and I'm afraid marriage cheapens it. It's more often a logical next step that elevates unworthy relationships for all kinds of wrong reasons. The 'Oh, we've been dating a year' benchmark, now it's time to get married." I looked pleadingly at him. "I don't want to wonder why you married me. If we aren't married and nothing else binds you to me, I'll always know you're here because you love me and want to be with me. And if we have problems we'll work harder to fix them."

"I would hope you'd know that regardless," he said quietly.

"Like you 'know' that the ground can't reach out and pull you off a balcony?" I tried to make him see. "Marriage makes relationships *more* vulnerable. It lulls people into thinking they don't have to work at the day-to-day anymore. You assume that because you're married your relationship is secure, and you take it for granted. I don't want that to happen to us. Niall, *I love you*. Please understand." I was begging. I was also struggling. It was hard to articulate being for commitment but against marriage, and I knew I wasn't doing it well. It was something I felt deep in my gut. It wasn't just that weddings were distasteful to me. It was that wanting them endangered something pure, something important. It made you take your eye off the ball, and if you did that you could lose it all. But I wasn't saying it right.

His look reflected the agony I felt. I thought he might waver, but he shook his head.

"I'm a simple man, Vi. To me, marriage means you've found the one person you want to spend your life with and you proclaim that commitment before God, the law, your friends and family. It means you trust that person enough to join your lives in every sense." He sighed heavily. "Call me old-fashioned, but I want to know the woman at my side loves me above all else and isn't afraid to declare it to the world." It was the echo of Giles's "I Choose." I Felt something struggling in my chest.

He picked up his duffel bag and walked to the bedroom door.

"Niall . . ." A strangled sound escaped my throat.

He paused and looked back. "I wish you happiness, Vi," he said in a quiet voice. His beautiful brown eyes were sorrowful. And then he was gone.

I gingerly walked my eggshell self downstairs and tried to stave off the inevitable collapse with the mundane. Niall was being unreasonable. I'd just feed the cats. He'd come around. I'd just hang up last night's clothes. He hadn't seen the blind choices I'd seen. I'd just get the mail. It was when I opened the envelope from University of California, Davis, and saw the application for their distance degree program that Niall must've ordered to surprise me that I lay down on the floor and sobbed. That's when I learned what it meant to truly feel your heart break. I'd only been practicing before.

Part Five

ROUND TWO

CHAPTER FORTY

Broken Up

From: Ben@siddickens.com
To: ViViVooom@gmail.com
Sent: September 20
Subject: Where are you?

Vi,

I'm becoming quite concerned over your lack of
response to my voice messages. I know this is a terrible
time for you, but I'm worried sick. Please, please get back
to me and let me know what's going on, and if there is
anything I can do.

love,
Ben

"This can't go on," Imogen said, sweeping her arms about. I
looked at her dully. "You haven't left the house in two weeks, you
won't return calls, you're not eating, you live in pj's. When was

the last time you bathed? For heaven's sake, it looks like it's been at least a week."

"I'm fine," I muttered.

"You're not fine," said Ethan.

"What's this, an intervention?" I replied crossly.

"Yes!" said Imogen and Mona in unison. "See all the people sitting around trying not to smell you?" Imogen, Mona, Ellis, Babette, Ethan, and Giles were crowded into my living room.

Imogen's voice softened. "Sweetie, I know how much it hurts." She rubbed my back. "But you have to pull it together now. It's been two weeks. You can't star in 'Lie-Low & Ditch' forever. It's a documentary short. 'A Star Reborn' is waiting for you."

I doubted I could do anything but lie low. I was flattened. I couldn't think about next week without gasping in panic at the idea of no Niall. The future yawned like a black hole of crushing pain. My brain backed away from the chasm like Niall from a balcony. Niall . . . The intrusive comparison caused a shot of pain, but I was too exhausted to cry anymore.

"Vi, please," Mona pleaded. "Please go back to work. Or at least leave the apartment."

"Can't," I said. I couldn't face the world.

"What *can* you do?" Ellis asked gently.

I stared at her. "Watch movies." Burying myself in someone else's fantasy and forgetting my life was the only thing that gave me temporary relief.

"How about a Chipotle burrito in Dupont Circle?" Mona coaxed me with one of my favorite things. "It's beautiful out."

I looked out the window at the indifferent sunshine that'd been offending me all week. How could it keep shining like that? Didn't it know I was dying? I'd see people walking outside my window and marvel that they could just go about their ordinary lives like nothing happened.

"You're going to have to go out soon because I called Pizza

Mart and told them not to deliver to this address anymore," Ethan said. I suspected he was serious.

Imogen sat next to me, practically pulling me onto her lap. "What happened to my Kevin? I want her back. Where's my best friend who's tough enough to think for herself and act on those beliefs, huh? Who's survived other knocks and will survive this one too? Who teaches me how to live like every day is an unopened gift?" I looked at her helplessly. I didn't know what had happened to that person.

Mona sat on the other side of me. "Vi, you did what you had to do based on what you believe. It sucks that it didn't work out with Niall, but don't abandon the Awakening."

"Maybe the story isn't finished," ventured Ellis. "Fiona told Jack that Niall's a complete mess." Something sharp and hard shot through me. I stared at Ellis, who shrugged.

"No matter what, *we* love you. *We* need you back. *I* need you back." Imogen hugged me hard.

"Me too." Mona hugged from the other side, echoed by a chorus of "me toos." Tears welled, but for the first time in weeks they were good tears. I felt a flicker of life.

"Me especially," stressed Giles. "I don't think Al's going to buy the pneumonia thing anymore since it's eighty-five degrees outside, and I can't keep holding down the fort—I need to plan my honeymoon, Tai Shan misses you, messages are piling up. Ben calls every day, and someone named Chester's called five times. I can't keep covering much longer." That got a reaction.

"What did you say?" I stared at Giles. "Who called?"

"Ben, relentlessly. Eh."

"No, the other."

"Someone named Chester. Said you knew what it was about. Didn't want anyone else."

The flicker flared. All attention was on me. I shook off hugging bodies and got to my feet. There *was* one thing I wanted besides

Niall. Suddenly it became urgently important. It's my life, I thought. I'd better take it back.

"I'm going to take a shower." I really did smell. And suddenly I was starving. "Then I want a burrito. Oh, and Imogen," I threw over my shoulder, "its not 'Lie-Low & Ditch.' It's 'Parader of the Lost Heart.' "

Everyone's mouth dropped open in comic harmony.

"Are you having an affair with someone named Chester?" Imogen demanded of my back.

CHAPTER FORTY-ONE

Round Two

"We're going to miss you terribly," Al said, looking truly sad. I hugged him.

"I'll miss you too, but I'm not going far. I'll come see everyone. Especially when D&D sponsors Four Fox wine tastings," I teased. It was hard to conceal my exuberance from Al. I was over the moon about my new job, though I still felt dreadful about Niall.

He laughed. "You're on." I was staying a few more weeks at D&D to hand over the reins, and then I was officially a full-time employee of Four Fox Vineyards. I'd already started classes in the Davis program. I'd persuaded the school to let me start though two weeks of the fall quarter had elapsed, and I'd been working my butt off to catch up. The Movie Starring Me was "The Days of Wine and Quizzes." I was grateful to be busy. It made it easier to keep my mind away from the black hole.

After Al went back to his office, Giles resumed swanning about as he had for days, carrying on theatrically. "I just can't *bear* it. What will I *do*? Whoever replaces you will be wretched," he moaned. "You *can't* go."

"I'll ask them about showtunes in the interview," I promised.

He perked up. "Are you coming with me and Matt Monday night?"

I looked doubtful. I hadn't been going out. I wasn't ready to face the world. Most nights I spent studying and trying not to think. "I don't think I can," I hedged. "So much to do . . ."

"Oh, I can't *bear* it," Giles wailed. "I'll *never* see you again. I must get a latte for strength. Want one?"

"Sure," I laughed. "Skim."

"Back in a jif."

When Giles was gone, I sighed and picked up the phone.

"When exactly does it get easier?" I asked Lila when she answered.

"I don't know," she said. "Somewhere between zero and two years, three months." I'd been talking with Lila regularly in the month since Niall and I broke up. She got it.

"There's no greeting card for this. What do you mean two years, three months? That's rather precise."

Lila laughed. It was good to hear her laughing again. "You're not going to believe it. My brother Guy's getting remarried. It's like we're passing the baton back and forth."

"What?" I was genuinely shocked. "He swore he'd never marry again."

"Well, that was until he met Kimberly."

"Wow. So you couldn't talk him out of it?"

"Talk him out of it? Are you kidding? I've never seen him happier!"

"No, I don't mean Kimberly. I mean getting married," I clarified.

Lila sounded puzzled. "Why would I talk him out of getting married?"

"Well," I was confused, "don't you think marriage corrupts? After your experience?"

"I don't think there's anything wrong with getting married if you're not an idiot about who you marry," she said. "I did it for the wrong reasons, so I ended up with the wrong guy. I thought getting married would show the world someone picked me, and increase my value as a person. The seduction of the shiny white wedding didn't help. I overlooked Hart's obvious flaws, and stayed in an emotionally abusive relationship, because I was frightened I was worth less if no one wanted me. Marriage didn't fail me—I failed myself."

Something panicky danced in my chest. I was starting to lose my grasp on the nuances between getting hitched, getting hoodwinked, and getting hurt. It had been clear once. "So, you'd remarry?" I pressed. "Even though the first one was a bait and switch?"

"Absolutely," Lila said. "It's too bad I had to make a colossal mistake to figure it out. But I have every intention of marrying again. Next time I'll be smarter about who I choose. And I'll have a much smaller wedding."

"You know, my friend Paula called last week to invite me to a dinner party. She's having a 'do-over' of her wedding. She said the first one was a big pain in the ass, and she and Mark had no fun, were stressed out, and never focused on what was important. So, they're doing it over with only twenty friends."

"That sounds nice," Lila said. "I wish I could do a complete do-over and erase Hart. Your friend has no regrets on the marriage?"

I shook my head slowly. "None at all. They're more in love now than when they got married." I felt confused. I forced a laugh. "Maybe people should only have second marriages."

"Maybe," Lila laughed. "Vi, it's about the person, not the institution. My experience didn't put me off marriage . . . just Hart. I look at my brother—who took a blood vow with Satan not to remarry—and have no doubt he's doing the right thing."

"Oh," I said.

I was pensive when I answered the phone again some time later. I was surprised to hear my mother's voice. My mother wasn't fond of the telephone.

"What's up?"

"Well, dear, I was calling to congratulate you on your new job."

"Thanks, Mom."

She paused. I felt like she was trying to figure out how to say something. Finally, she said, "Maeve told me about Niall." Oh. "I'm terribly sorry, dear."

"I'll be okay, Mom," I lied. I didn't feel like I'd ever be okay.

Another pause. "Did your father and I turn you completely off marriage, Kevin? I know we aren't the most traditional family but—"

"Oh, Mom, no!" I interrupted her anxiously. "Don't think that!" I felt terrible. I'd punished my parents for not being perfect because I badly wanted to believe perfection was possible. I still wanted the easy answer. I'd transformed Caleb into a white knight fantasy that was laughably one-dimensional. It took a realistic relationship of my own to recognize the genuine article and open my eyes to the fact that there is no easy answer.

Pause. "I know how much it upset you to learn I was married before I met your father. There never seemed to be a way to talk about it with you."

"Mom, I'm so sorry. I'm totally ashamed of myself. I was so rigid. I don't know what happened to me." Whatever happened before they met, my parents had an enviable relationship. They each had space to be their own (grantedly odd) self. They had a lot more than I had.

"Part of the fault is mine, Vi. We expect you children to act like grown-ups and understand things, but then we treat you like children and don't tell you things you need to know. I didn't trust you to understand about Daniel when you were younger, so I never shared. It was unreasonable for me to think you'd instantly be fine hearing about it as an adult just because more years had passed."

I felt better. "Tell me about it," I asked her. I was desperate for answers.

She gave a little laugh. "Oh my, I was young! It wasn't only Jackie who was eager to marry and get out of our house."

"What happened?" I asked.

"Oh, I wanted out of my parents' house and I found someone to help me do it. It lasted less than a year. I realized immediately I'd made a terrible mistake. Daniel wasn't a bad man, but he wasn't the man for me. We divorced quickly. I had no idea what happened to him or where he is now. That's why it was such a shock when he found me after Maggie died." She was quiet.

"Do you miss him?" I was afraid of the answer.

"Oh no. Not like that. I miss the idealism I had back then. But the girl who married Daniel was pretty silly, to be honest." Like me with Caleb, I thought. "After I left him, I spent some time figuring out who I was. I realized too late that I could've gotten myself out of the house whenever I'd decided to grow up. But when we're young . . .

"When I met your father, I was actually capable of being in a relationship because I knew myself and a little about reality. And I *liked* myself much better than before, which really helps. My second marriage has been everything I hoped it would be. I've never regretted a thing." Pause. "I think I would've regretted not marrying him," she said significantly.

"Why does it have be marry or not marry? There are other options." I was frustrated.

"Well, people aren't all as thoughtful as you are. Kevin, I know you're quite cynical about weddings, and that's understandable. It's a terribly exploited event and girls are taught to covet one before they know what a tampon is. Sometimes I think Martha

Stewart has a conspiracy or something." I laughed. Maybe my mother had more clarity than I thought. "But the wedding is a very small part of the equation. Marriage can be wonderful."

"Don't you take Dad for granted since you know he has to stick around?" I asked.

"Good Lord, yes!" She laughed. "I defy anyone married or not to truthfully tell you differently after thirty-five years. But what happens in any relationship is within your control. Love doesn't spring fully formed and perfect. It involves missteps and false starts before you build something with the right person. But it does happen."

"Mom?"

"Yes?"

"Thanks."

"We can't make life easy for you, Vi, because life isn't an easy thing. But your father and I love you. Even when you're a pain."

"I love you too, Mom."

I dialed the phone again as soon as my mother hung up. I needed my shrink.

"Sid Dickens, this is Ben speaking."

"Ben, do you think I made a mistake?" I demanded without preamble.

There was a brief silence. "Vi, there's no answer for that. I know you love Niall, and it seemed like he loved you. To me that means there should be a way to work things out."

"Even if it means I get married when I'm not sure I believe in it?'

"That's the hard question," Ben answered. "I don't think any-one can answer that for you." He was quiet. "Did something hap-pen?"

"Only that I feel sick whenever I think of life without him. And suddenly everyone is remarrying or would like to be remarrying, even to their own spouse. It's like a conspiracy."

"How does it make you feel?" asked my faithful therapist.

"Partly Panicky that I made a mistake, and partly Angry that no one sees my point of view, and mostly like I'm losing sight of my point of view. It got all blurry."

"Walk me through it."

"First it was Desire for a wedding like any other girl. Then it was Dismay as I saw people so driven toward having a wedding and getting married that they didn't choose for love. Then it was Distaste over how commercial and artificial weddings are. Then it was Distress because it seemed like marriage was actually bad for the kind of love I want."

"What makes you afraid?"

"That Niall . . . um." I swallowed. "I mean that a husband would forget to love you and would only be there out of obligation. You'd become Nice Wife and you'd lose your identity and delight in knowing the person loved you." My voice fell to a whisper. "That because getting married is so expected, it has no meaning. That maybe they never loved you at all but just took the bridal path because they thought they were supposed to."

"Vi, you're an extremely thoughtful lady. I'd imagine you'd be hard not to love. This isn't an easy question, but I trust you'll work it out. You know I'm always here to listen."

"Thanks, Ben, eh?"

I hung up the phone, thoughtful. Then I dialed again. "Meet me for a shot of schnapps."

"You want schnapps?" Imogen was incredulous. "Right now? And gross."

"It worked once. Meet me at Local 16 in half an hour. Bring Ethan."

I left a note for Giles and headed out. There was an elusive Thought I was chasing and I didn't want to let it get away from me. I was so preoccupied I nearly waltzed into a torrential cloudburst. I halted my momentum, clutching the door frame. It was raining so hard I could barely see twenty feet. I was about to go back inside for an umbrella when a blurry figure caught my eye. Standing motionless across the street was a body that, even shrouded in a raincoat, accelerated my heart, telling me I knew it well. I squinted but couldn't see clearly. The figure turned and hurried down the street. I ached to cry after him but knew I couldn't. Tiredly, I went back inside to get an umbrella.

CHAPTER FORTY-TWO

A Pea Grows into a Walnut

My chest felt tight as I stared at Mona's engagement ring a week later. It was no surprise, certainly. And I no longer feared losing my friend. Things would change, of course, but I'd learned that the mettle of true friendships isn't altered by marriage. So I couldn't explain the constricting band of panic encircling my lungs.

"It's gorgeous," Babette gushed. Mona flushed with happiness.

"Was it romantic?" demanded Ellis.

"I thought so," Mona said. "Brad took Moxie for a walk so I could sleep in. Afterward they both got on the bed and he slid the ring to me down Moxie's leash. I cried." She looked ready to cry again, her happy tears different from the ones I was holding back. "You want to know the best part? He proposed on a Sunday so I could tell you all right away."

Imogen nodded in satisfaction. "Excellent. He knows he's marrying all of us."

"I'll give him Jack's number," Ellis laughed.

Charlie brought champagne on the house and I managed inadequate oohs and ahs over the ring, and everyone had the grace to cover my silence. I felt the terrible black hole inside me and feared anything coming out of my mouth would corrode like poison.

I forced a smile until Mona turned to me.

"Vi, please relax. I know you're unhappy, but it's not like you'll poison me." I gaped, startled out of my self-absorption. She squeezed my hand. "Don't be so hard on yourself."

"Mona, aren't you leery that somewhere along the way someone put blinders on us?" I asked. "That getting married takes the focus away from the relationship?"

"No. I feel like Brad and I see each other pretty clearly, flaws and all. I'm not worried there'll be any nasty surprises. And I can't wait to keep discovering more of him every day." A Feeling in my chest wiggled. It was Doubt. I had an image of Niall laughing at me as I bossily unpacked and repacked his suitcase because I thought he'd done it poorly, or his saying, "I love your brain," as I bored him to tears with my trivia. Was that seeing clearly? I thought of the Performer who had danced for Caleb, and knew with clarity that the Performer had never set foot in two sacred places—in Clyde's and with Niall. I sucked in my breath, fearing a terrible mistake.

"Imogen, what about you and Ethan? You must talk about it." I was desperate for an answer.

Imogen was thoughtful. "Marriage simply means a union of two people, and Ethan and I have that already. I'm indifferent to whether we have a wedding or make it legal. Funnily enough, Vi, I think you've been right all along about the wedding stuff. Too many people rely on the wedding to make the marriage, rather than the relationship, like some badge of proof."

My pea-sized brain stretched, recalling Niall's words. "But maybe there has to be something more," I said slowly. "You can't just be there the next day. If you want to build a real partnership, you need to demonstrate that you're committed to a life partnership. Something that moves 'just dating' to 'marriage,' legal or not."

Imogen smiled at me. "I think we did that when we told you we were a couple. It was the scariest thing we could do because we were both risking what was most valuable to us—your friendship." Her words went into my heart like an arrow. "It forged our trust in each other because we were willing to take that risk."

"So now you're all three married," joked Babette.

"Maybe it's time to stop the 'Wedding Bashers,'" Mona suggested gently. "And figure out what you really want."

Mona and Imogen were right. Getting married wasn't the problem. Fear was the problem. "I was emotionally lazy my whole life," I admitted. "I never wanted to be responsible for my choices. Even after Caleb, I clung to this idea that falling in love would be like walking along a path and find a shiny, golden chalice. I'd pick it up, and voila, done. No work, and no risk, just destiny. I needed to believe that, because I was afraid of making the wrong choices."

"And now?" Imogen asked.

"I want Niall. But I equate marriage with that earlier laziness. Like believing in destiny. Getting the ring on your finger is like picking up the chalice—the hard work is done, and nothing else has to happen. Even if you don't intend it, marriage can make you inert with false security. I don't want to go back to being passive and directionless. I want to live each day as a choice. With Niall."

They waited.

"But I relapsed into lazy anyway." I was aghast. "I made a terrible mistake. Instead of fighting for Niall, and finding a compromise, I did nothing. He thinks I wasn't willing to take a risk for him. But it was the opposite."

"There's no mistake that can't be fixed," Ellis said. "From what I hear, Niall's been a lost cause since you split."

"Honey, don't forget he couldn't see your point of view either," Imogen reminded me. "You have good reasons for your position, and wisdom to dig in your heels rather than let the dominant culture put a bit in your mouth."

I nodded slowly. "I want Niall. But I don't want a wedding. I want the trust, clarity and commitment marriage is supposed to represent—the Holy 'I Choose.' And I'm willing to give him something that means those things to him in return, even if it scares me. I trust him that much. Because I love him." My eyes welled up, and I was nearly pushed under the table with loving pats from all the girls. A phone rang and we all jumped for our purses.

"It's Brad!" Mona, the winner, glowed and stepped away.

Charlie brought another bottle of champagne and whispered something to Ellis. I wasn't paying attention. How could I fix this? Ellis announced she had to go home right then. She gave me a kiss good-bye and whispered something to Imogen.

"I've got to go to the bathroom." Imogen disappeared faster than Maeve spotting a Mr. Microphone.

"Walk me to my car," Ellis said in a funny voice to Babette, who looked confused.

"Why? Ow! You kicked me!" she protested. I tuned them out right before Babette's eyes caught on something and she jumped to her feet. "Yes, yes, of course," and they scurried away. I was so lost in my reverie it was a long moment before I realized I was alone. I looked over my shoulder to see where they'd all gone. And I froze.

Unshaven, haggard and thinner, Niall in a badly wrinkled suit was standing, arms limply at his sides as if he didn't know what to do with them, looking longingly at me. My breath died. We sat frozen for a long moment.

And then I ran to him.

"I'm sorry," he whispered against my hair as he swept me tight. "I know it's girls' night but I couldn't bear it a moment longer. God, you smell good."

"I'm sorry, I'm sorry, I didn't trust you," I sobbed.

"No, I didn't trust *you*," he whispered back, repeatedly kissing my wet cheeks and eyelids and lips. "And I didn't listen. At least not with my brain. I was a great girlie swot and I almost made a poxy whore's melt of it. Christ, you have no idea how I've been torturing myself." He rained more kisses on my face. "Vi, I've made a mistake. I thought I was being traditional, but I was being rigid. I made exactly the snap judgments I despise in others. Whether or not you marry me is no way to measure love. It wasn't because she had no ring that Gwendolyn left. It was because she didn't love me. I want to know that you're next to me every day because you *want* to be there, not because everyone expects it or you're bound. Marriage won't protect me from losing you. Only loving you the best I can will. Your man can do that. I beg you to let me try again."

"Really?" I breathed, staring into his beautiful brown eyes and wicked long lashes.

"Really." He kissed my nose, the first hint of a light returning to his eyes. "I got the job. You're looking at one of the new International Section editors of the *Washington Post*." I squeaked in happiness and he chuckled. "I never would've applied but for you. You made me believe in myself. When I got the job, it was this dreadful pain, because I had no one to tell. And it hit me that relationships aren't about the grandiose declarations, they're about each day." He gazed at me. "I miss you so much. Please come back and promise not to marry me every day?"

"Yes," I laughed. "Yes, yes, yes. But I've been blind too. Marriage doesn't have to be a bad thing. I just think the lure of the security it offers distracts from figuring out what we really want. But love needs trust and a willingness to take risks. I never want you to doubt that I'll be there, truly there. For me, that meant *not* being married. But for you, I should have tried harder to work it out."

"I don't think we have to resolve all the issues of matrimony tonight," he teased me with my own words. Then he got serious. "I love you," he said.

I looked at him for a long minute. "And I might marry you," I smiled. "Someday."

"Not a chance," he murmured before covering my lips with his. Even the sound of the girls' raucous cheering didn't pull us apart.

Part Six

BDOYL

CHAPTER FORTY-THREE

B DOYL

Something was tickling my face. I brushed it away. It retreated then returned. I reluctantly opened my eyes to identify the assailant, and saw the beautiful white rose Niall was caressing against my cheek. He was propped on one elbow watching me, curls tousled and scratchy stubble on his chin. He looked dazzling. I smiled beatifically at him.

"Is that your wild Irish rose?" I teased. We were in an enchanting bed and breakfast in County Wicklow, Ireland, sleeping on rich white cotton sheets and plump pillows amidst rolling green downs and wild tangled rosebushes. It was like being in a fairy tale.

"Two of them, I reckon." He tugged my nose.

"I love you," I said.

"You take my breath away," he answered. "Every day for the past year I can't believe my good luck when I wake up next to you."

"I'm not going anywhere." I ran a hand down the side of his face. "I Choose."

He smiled. "Are you ready for today?"

"Not quite," I teased, and sighed into his kiss as he pulled me into his arms.

Later, I dressed in a simple white dress with spaghetti straps and sandals. Niall was devastating in his crisp white shirt open at the collar, revealing his strong tanned neck. He turned me to face the dressing table mirror, and meeting my eyes in the glass, he laid a stunning David Yurman choker across my collarbone and fastened it behind my neck.

"Just because," he said. My breath fled. How had I gotten so lucky as to deserve this man? I turned to face him but couldn't get out any words for fear of crying. He kissed me seriously, brushing a thumb across my cheek, then took my hand and led me out.

We walked hand in hand along the lanes of Glendalough until we arrived at the Glendalough Monastery, originally founded by St. Kevin in the sixth century. We'd been in Galway for a week, and I'd met all of Niall's family. Now we were in the seat of my family tree and the home of my namesake.

"Let's walk through the cemetery first," I suggested. "Under Celtic monastic traditions, the graveyard was the place where you'd cross from one world to the next." We paused among the ancient consecrated stones to take in the beauty of the ruins, situated in a valley between two lakes and embraced by lush green grass and blooming flowers.

"Did you know the name Glendalough means 'the glen of the two lakes'?" I told Niall.

He brushed a kiss across my knuckles. "I love your brain," he grinned.

He stopped me before we crossed the threshold. "My favorite story about St. Kevin," he said seriously, "says that one day he was meditating in a tree when a bird came to sit on his outstretched hand. The bird laid an egg there and the saint took it as a sign from God. He remained with his hand outstretched until the egg safely hatched and the hatchling bird flew away." He looked deep into my eyes. "My hand will always be there for you, Vi. I'd wait patiently at your side forever just to see you wake each day. We may not be legally bound, but I'm bound by something much stronger."

I nodded. "I know," I whispered. And I did. "Me too." He kissed me again, and we stepped into the ancient cathedral whose roof had long since fallen, leaving it open to clear blue skies. I shrieked when a bird startled me, and Niall caught me up and swung me in circles, my dress fluttering in the air as I clung to him, laughing. After, he carried me over the threshold.

We held hands and began walking the trail around the Upper Lake. "Look, love. There's St. Kevin's cave." Niall pointed to a rocky spur high across Upper Lake. "It's called St. Kevin's Bed." We paused and gazed at our destination, then continued. Below the cave, we looked up the trail we'd have to clamber over for the view. I saw a light sweat break out on Niall's forehead.

"Niall . . ." I laid a hand on his arm.

"We go," he said firmly. He tucked my shoes into his jacket pocket and began to climb. Twenty minutes later and gasping, we crested the plateau of St. Kevin's Bed. Niall hauled me safely onto the ledge, then flattened himself against the rock wall to catch his breath. I laid fully against him, kissing him hard and deeply. He kissed me back, and calmed.

"I love the way you smell." He managed a smile. Then clenching my hand, and with a set jaw, he stepped away from the rock wall to take in the view. If possible he went more pale.

"Are you scared?" I whispered.

He looked at me, lips quirking into a smile. "I'd be scared to death if I was alone. But when we're together, there's nothing I can't do."

"Hey, this is a moment," I grinned. "Want me to say First Corinthians or something?"

He laughed and clutched my hands. "Well, this is lovely, but . . ."

"The greatest of these is love . . . of the ground." I smiled. "Let's go down."

We clambered back down, Niall wilting in relief. Then he took my hand and we returned to the path around the lake.

"This was a good day," he said, squeezing my hand.

"It was the best day," I agreed.

"What should we do tomorrow?" he asked, pulling me close and kissing my temple.

"Whatever we want," I smiled. "Let's see what we feel like tomorrow."

From: ViViVooom@gmail.com
To: Ben@siddickens.com
Sent: September 21
Subject: You Are the Best

Ben! We just got back from Ireland and got the tiles. I'm not sure what merits an "Unwedding Gift" but we're delighted. It was so generous—and of course you remembered my favorites. They'll look beautiful in our new house. You must come visit. We're near the zoo. I'll introduce you to Tai Shan.

I'm about to fall over from exhaustion and Niall's starting to tickle me so I have to go, but I'll call you tomorrow. Thank you and Sid again for the beautiful tiles. I've never been happier than I am right now. Hmmm . . . I've been saying that a lot lately. Guess there's no such thing as a BDOYL—you can have as many as you want, each one better than the last.

Love, V.

Epilogue

From: ViViVooom@gmail.com
To: Ben@siddickens.com
Sent: April 1
Subject: What???

Ben!

   Did we _really_ just get an invitation to your wedding??!!
Call me immediately . . . Vi.

(P.S. Good lord, what will we get you???? I'll actually
have to shop. . . .)

A⁺

AUTHOR INSIGHTS, EXTRAS, & MORE...

FROM
KERRY REICHS

AND

AVON A

The scary thing about this book is that most of the wedding stories, outrageous as they are, are true. I've been accused of being a professional wedding guest—I think I've attended over one hundred. This year is a slow year—I only have six, and am only in one. I've attended weddings on four continents, ranging from Ecuador to Australia. And let's not even get into the tropical islands. Visit my website at www.harpercollins.com/AvonAuthors to see some pictures of me in rather unfortunate updos with some of my brides. What can I say? I was trying to make them look good.

It would be hard to pick my most extraordinary wedding moment, though Clark the Turtle would come close. The groom insisted on including his beloved pet turtle in the ceremony . . . as the best man. I suspect the bride was hoping Clark the turtle would smell sweet, sweet freedom and make a break for it. She was always bitching that he made the apartment stink.

So there was Clark, on a stool next to the groom. Or Clark's shell, I should say. Clark was having none of his miniature bow tie, and the Best Man was a headless, legless shell radiating an I'd-rather-be-laying-on-a-highway-in-Mexico vibe. He stayed that way the whole time until the maid of honor had to "escort" him out. Then the bride almost got her wish. Pictures took forever as they tried to coax Clark out of his seemingly uninhabited shell with lettuce, radishes and kind words—to no avail. After the pictures, everyone stampeded to the bar and Clark accidentally got left behind. The groom realized later and after a frenzied search,

Clark was scooped up determinedly plodding into the sunset, presumably to the Cayman Islands or wherever turtles dream of living.

I think all girls and women fantasize about what their own wedding might be like. I know I have, though my vision has changed dramatically over the years. I used to think I'd want to pack the house with all my friends. But I actually think Vi, and writing this book, has had an effect on me. I'm not sure I'd do that anymore.

It didn't make the book, but one night all the gals from Clyde's sat around and talked about the wedding they would like to have. I thought you might like to take a peek, so I've included the scene below. It's especially appropriate because it is snowing in D.C. as I am writing this.

Oh, and meet Rosie. The first draft of my book was "overpopulated" as my editor told me gently. Poor Rosie didn't make it, but she used to be part of the gang. Rosie was what my mother would call "a pistol." She was born and bred in Manhattan and didn't put up with any shit. She had a funky New York vintage style that stood out in conservative D.C. That and her hair, which was thick, dark, and curly and fell to her waist. It could take two days for Rosie's hair to dry. Mine took twelve minutes, max. After years of training as a dancer, Rosie had, logically, gone to medical school at NYU. She had moved to D.C. to do AIDS research at the National Institute of Health. One day Vi was walking across Dupont Circle, and, passing her, threw out an innocuous "Hey." She immediately whirled around, demanding "What? What? What is it?" Vi was baffled. As you know, where Vi comes from, "hey" was simply the Southern equivalent of "hi." And, naturally, in the South, if you are sharing the sidewalk with anyone, even if they were a stranger, you *always* called out a friendly "hey there." To Rosie, on the other hand, "hey" meant "HEY!", as "HEY WATCH OUT THERE IS A LOCOMOTIVE ABOUT TO FLATTEN YOU!" And one did *not* talk to strangers on the street unless it was critical ("move your ass") or your statement was a variation of "What the fuck you lookin' at?" She still tries to dissuade Vi from saying "hey" to strangers.

Enjoy girls night in!

It was one of those days in January where it is cruel to go outside. Washington, which normally remains tolerable even in the dead of winter, was in the throes of the cold snap that had started New Year's Eve. We were now facing more snow and a looming ice storm. Immediately upon leaving the D&D building I felt icy cold fingers navigate the minute gaps between my scarf, collar, and bare neck to lance cold right through to my bones. I shuddered miserably, and pulled my scarf more tightly around me. I hated winter. And I loathed the cold. My hands were freezing. Unfortunately, I hated gloves. I had gotten a case of sun-poisoning on my face and hands once in college, and ever since then I was convinced that the backs of my hands tingled and itched whenever I wore gloves. It was only the occasional lightweight pair that wouldn't bother me. Mittens were intolerable. So, I mostly went without and my hands were chapped and miserable most of the winter, especially when it got really cold.

I stepped to the curb to try to hail a cab home. It was barely 5:30 P.M. and already darkening rapidly. Fortunately, work had been absolutely dead. In the face of impending bad weather, absolute paranoia overtook D.C. Offices closed early, the government shut down, and the good citizens of town raced to the store to stockpile bottled water, batteries, and canned goods. Lactose intolerant people would buy gallons of milk in preparation for the looming Armageddon. God forbid you were running low on toilet paper when a storm was predicted to hit because the hoarding masses would have cleared the shelves to squirrel away a year's supply, just in case. Three flakes of snow created chaos. And, usually, despite dire forecasts, only three flakes of snow would fall. But schools would be closed for a week.

Having spent four years in Ohio during college, I was adept at driving in snow and ice. D.C. residents, deplorable drivers to begin with, were simply shocking in bad weather. It was like wet or slippery conditions caused their minds to shut down completely. Maybe they were preoccupied with making rations lists for commando shopping. Either way, as my mother used to always say, it is not you, it is the other driver I worry about. Therefore, with predictions of icy rain and snow, I had wisely elected to take the bus to work this morning. Now, it was too cold to wait for the bus and then trudge to my apartment from the stop, so I held my arm out to flag a taxi, painfully exposing the vulnerable bit of skin at the back of my neck. Numerous cabs passed by without pause. Another charming D.C. peculiarity was the total failure of taxi drivers to use their cab call sign lights to indicate their availability for a fare. A cab was either a "Light On" guy or a "Light Off" guy. None of this switching between the two to indicate vacancy. Instead you had to hang your arm out there for every passing cab, squinting to see if you could make out the second head of an existing passenger in the car. It drove Rosie, the New Yorker, insane.

After about ten minutes of going numb, I gave a snort of disgust and pulled out my cell phone with hands so frozen I could barely dial.

"Babette?"

"Yes, sweetie?"

"No cabs. I am freezing my ass off."

"Good. I need to stop working. I'll leave the front door open."

"See you in ten. Anything?"

"Hmmmm. Usual?"

"Done."

I went back inside and grabbed three bottles of Fess Parker

Cabernet, a carton of raspberries (Babette's favorite), a box of Ferrero-Rocher chocolates, some foie gras and a wedge of Manchego. As an afterthought, I grabbed a chicken potpie and some pasta salad in case we wanted real food. My phone rang.

"Hello."

"Where are you?" demanded Rosie. "I just had a meeting with the folks at Lombardi Cancer Center. I cannot find a cab and I am stuck in Georgetown. Want to grab a drink and see if it calms down after rush hour?"

"I am on my way to Babette's."

"Excellent. See you there. Did you get raspberries already?"

"Yep."

"Hmmmm. Okay, I'll think of something else." Rosie hung up.

I paused to stick my head in my office and hopefully scanned the room for a forgotten extra layer of clothes but was disappointed. I peeked on Giles's side to see if he had left anything warm, but he hadn't either. Darn fastidious gay men. So, I wrapped my scarf around me as tightly as possible and set out the five painful blocks to Babette's house on N Street. I paused halfway for some warmth and a breather in Booeymongers before forging back into the cold. Then I decided to get some sandwiches too. You never knew how long the city would shut down. My phone rang in the deli.

"Where are you? If there is going to be a snowstorm tonight I want to get snowed in at your place in Dupont. There is nothing out here on T Street. I could starve to death."

"How about Georgetown? I am on my way to Babette's."

"I'll call her. I have Netflix."

"Tell her Rosie is coming," I remembered.

"Natch." She hung up.

True to her word, Babette's door was open.

"I'm here," I hollered out.

"Be right down," floated from upstairs. I went into the kitchen and put the chocolates out. I rinsed the raspberries and put them in a bowl. Then I set out the cheese and fois gras on a small cutting board. I put the sandwiches and real food in the fridge. I was scrabbling through the kitchen drawers for a bottle opener when Babette came down.

"Poor sweetie," she took my hands and rubbed them between hers. "You really need to learn to wear gloves."

"I'm glad you were home." I kissed her cheek.

"Who goes out in this weather?" she asked. "You know how people drive in D.C. And I am a terrible driver to begin with. Besides," she laughed, "you aren't the only one descending."

"Oh yeah, sorry," I said sheepishly.

"Don't be silly," she dismissed me. "I am happy. Ooooo, is that for me?" She spotted the snacks.

"Yes ma'am. Who knows how long we will be holed up here. There is some other stuff in the fridge."

"This looks good to start with. I'll also get out this one cheese I have that you like. I am pretty sure you told me once." My face lit up.

"Reblochon?" I asked, excited.

"That's the one," she answered happily, rummaging in the fridge.

"I love the French," I enthused. "You always have wine and cheese in the house. And you don't even drink wine."

"Oh, but I eat enough cheese to float the French economy," she countered.

"Quick, get it out before Imogen gets here. She likes it too."

The door opened and Rosie walked in. She had some flakes in her hair.

"Damn, it's a bitch out there," she pronounced, stamping her feet on the doormat. "I hate cold weather. And the snow is starting. Hope no one needs toilet paper." Rosie had a true New Yorker's scorn for the way Washington wilted in the face of sleet or its brethren.

"Did you walk all the way from Lombardi?" I looked at my watch, astonished. Even cutting through campus, that was quick.

"Nah. This doctor was walking out as I got off the phone with you and he gave a ride to the lady in distress. It was only a mile." Rosie pulled off what seemed like thirteen layers of outerwear and was hanging them up in Babette's closet.

"Oh, how nice. How did you know him?" asked Babette, adding more cheeses to the food tray.

"I didn't. Never seen him before. But I needed a ride, so I sort of presented him with a question that didn't have a no answer. Along the lines of 'please kind sir, without you conveying me a mere ten blocks I will be stranded to turn into a frozen corpse in this godforsaken part of town, leaving you to lament the loss of your soul every night for the rest of your life over the simple steps not taken to save my life. So would you?' You know. New York charm. It was only a mile. And there is *nothing* out by the Lombardi."

Babette shook her head chuckling in disbelief. "You are something else." As soon as she set out a knife and crackers I pounced on the cheese.

"Yeah, well, you should have seen Vi in action on New Year's Eve. I learned it from her."

"Mmmmmmm. . . ." The cheese was delicious.

"Ugh, I don't know how you eat that stuff," Rosie wrinkled her nose. "It smells like feet. I can only imagine what it tastes like."

"Good. More for me." I savored another cracker. I was actually pretty hungry.

"Oh, hey, I brought something." Rosie picked up a bag at her feet and pulled out two pints of Ben & Jerry's. "Coffee Heath Bar Crunch for Vi, and New York Super Fudge Chunk for me and Babette."

"How did you get that?" I marveled. "Do they sell ice cream at the hospital?"

"Nope," she shrugged nonchalantly. "I got my good Samaritan to stop at the corner market on the way so I could dash in."

"I should be so talented," ruminated Babette. Rosie and I looked at each other and snorted. Men would hew down a tree with their teeth to make firewood for Babette if she looked a tad chilly. We carried the tray and snacks into the living room and settled onto the couch. I inhaled some more Reblochon. Imogen would be here soon.

As if on cue the door popped open and Imogen bounced in, with Mona behind her.

"We're heeeree," Imogen sang.

"Just like the ghouls in *Poltergeist*," I retorted.

"Mwah," she blew a kiss at me. Then she looked closer. "Is that Reblochon?"

"Back off," I threatened, pulling the plate closer, and shoveling another crackerful in my mouth. The small portion of cheese was history once Imogen descended on it.

"Sorry for invading, Babette," Mona said. "I was kidnapped."

"Don't be silly—the more the merrier," welcomed Babette.

"Vi, where is the wine?" asked Rosie, looking around.

"Oh, I forgot—I left it in the kitchen." Babette, Rosie, and Mona looked at me in surprise.

"How unlike you," exclaimed Rosie.

"Very funny. Mona, will you . . . ?" Mona was already heading to the kitchen.

"We have Netflix," Imogen waved around six red envelopes. "*Legally Blonde, Bourne Identity, Four Weddings and a Funeral*—that is for you Vi, I was going to save it until later but inclement weather calls—the newest *Harry Potter, The Thin Man*, and *Grey's Anatomy* Season One.

I laughed. "How long do you expect the storm to last?"

"How did you get so many at once?" asked Babette.

"Mona had some too. And I brought pj's. We both did. Please can we stay Babette, please, please, please? Can we? Huh? Huh? Huh?" Babette laughed.

"Of course. Vi, you can stay in with me, Imogen and Mona you get the guest room, and Rosie you can have the couch."

"And Babette, can we . . ."

"If you get the wood," Babette consented. "It is in the shed in the garden, and I promised myself that I wouldn't set foot outside today."

"Yay!" Imogen gave a little hop and clapped her hands. "I'll get it. Now give me some of that cheese." Satisfied that I had consumed three quarters of it, I yielded the plate.

"Babette, can I . . ."

"Your favorite red ones are on top of the dryer." Babette's ability to anticipate our needs was uncanny. It was also inversely related to her ability to pick out appropriate dates for us—the one skill excellent, the other abominable.

"Awesome." I hopped up and went down to the laundry room to change into some comfy yoga pants. I also found a big, enveloping sweatshirt that I swapped my work shirt for. I scraped my hair back into a goofy short ponytail and sighed in well-being. I padded back to the living room in some thick wool socks I had rooted out. Rosie was helping Imogen start a fire, bickering over the challenge, as do any two people trying to accomplish a feat of skill that has no objective criterion. I looked hopefully toward the cheese, but the Reblochon was gone. Mona was making inroads into the Manchego. She held out a glass of wine for me and I went to sit beside her.

"Cheers," Mona and I tinged glasses. Imogen and Rosie succeeded in starting the fire. They high-fived each other triumphantly.

"Not that it was hard," Mona said to me dryly under her breath. "They just had to pile the real wood on top of Babette's Duraflame log and light the paper." I grinned. Babette came down from upstairs now in her sweats and we all settled around the coffee table in front of the fire.

"This is perfect for a snow day," announced Imogen. We had to agree. We were quiet a minute.

"So, who brought the Mad Libs?" demanded Imogen. "Should we crank call Billy White from sixth grade, or 867-5309? We could put our hair in curlers and paint each other's toes. And talk about boys. Has anyone done 'it' yet?" We laughed.

"What *do* you do on grown-up sleepovers?" Rosie asked. "Besides drink. Trivial Pursuit?"

"Talk about boys," Mona offered. "And doing it."

"Plan weddings," I declared.

"Well, that sort of goes hand in hand," suggested Babette. "Who would you marry and how would you do it?" Mona rolled her eyes, but it had been so much on my brain that I liked the idea of hearing the other girls. I couldn't be the only one that was semi-meticulously planning my own eventual wedding. Could I?

Imogen looked thoughtful. "I have no idea who," she reflected. "But I always thought I'd have a destination wedding. I don't want to have it back home. And I like the idea of all my close friends being with me for more than just one night. Instead, we would all go somewhere for a week, like a group honeymoon, only before the wedding. So it would be small, no more than thirty people. And in a really cool place where we would all be together, like an island. Capri would be perfect—sophisticated town, beautiful nature, fabulous food and wine. For the ceremony I want it to be just my husband and me at the altar. I don't want anyone walking me down the aisle. I can get there myself." We all knew that Imogen was not close with her parents.

"I like that," said Babette. "Dress?"

"I don't know. Not white. That would be silly. Maybe pale blue. And maybe a sapphire ring instead of a diamond. I don't really care for diamonds—they seem cold and impersonal to me. I like flowers, so I would want lots of flowers everywhere. And candles. I think I'd like to get married outdoors, even if it is risky. I don't care about the nature of the service or who performs it or anything like that. I just really want an intimate experience where all the attendees feel involved. I'd like the whole thing to seem like a big Thanksgiving dinner." We were quiet, thinking about it. It seemed nice. But, when I got married I thought I would want everybody I liked to be there to celebrate with me. I couldn't imagine only having thirty people. It would not be possible. More like three hundred. Imogen shook herself from her musings and turned to Rosie.

"Your turn, Rosie."

"Well, for me I think it is more about the man than the wedding. If I find the right guy, I don't really care if we get married or if we perform a Zulu fire dance. More important to me is finding someone who respects my work and my strength, and who himself is committed to a career of his own. I think it would be nice to meet someone who also was involved with medical research. It is such a unique field that I would like someone who could understand what I do, and get me when I deal with the tough parts. Bonus if he also shared my passion for medicine and for trying to eventually make a discovery that will improve lives. He needs to be athletic enough to exercise with me, preferably a squash player. And he needs to be funny and want to have a dog. Then, we would live together before getting married and get the dog."

"It sounds like you want the dog more than the guy," teased Babette.

"Well, it would be sort of a litmus test. I would watch how he handled the dog and dog-related issues, like the dog ruining his most expensive shoes, or the responsibility the dog demands —compromising our personal whims to adjust our schedules for the dog. Let's call him Rex. If it worked, having Rex together, I'd marry him. Oh, and I'd want Rex to be a part of the wedding. And I guess I'd get married here in D.C. because I wouldn't let my parents pay for it, so we would have to manage on our budgets. It would be easier to organize in the place where we lived. But not at a hotel. I hate hotel weddings."

"Why?" asked Mona, curiously.

"It is just this feeling that hotels are the opposite of home. Temporary, transitive, based on the idea that you can buy whatever you need. It seems inappropriate to celebrate a wedding in that environment. Also, guests can be all over—the reception, their rooms, various bars, and so on. Plus, there are all these transient people there too, you know, other guests. I'd like a place where everyone there is a wedding guest and is gathered in a single location." Rosie thought about it. "Except for a boat. The idea of being trapped on a boat for a wedding reception is horrifying."

"I agree with that," I said. "Plus someone would no doubt ralph over the side, ruining the ambience."

"I hadn't thought about the hotel thing, but I see what you mean," Mona reflected. "I think I agree with you. I'd like to marry someone who is Catholic like me. And also liberal. As I get older, and as politics and politicians seem to become more corrupt, it has become important to me to be with someone who shares my political bent. For a wedding I would like to have a Catholic ceremony that lasts over half an hour. It seems like something as important as getting married should be done with reflection and consideration. It shouldn't take less than twenty minutes. I would invite a moderate number of people outside of family to attend, but I wouldn't involve a bunch of people in the ceremony. Just for some readings. There might be around a hundred total, assuming his family is the same size as mine. I guess I'd have a typical reception with a nice dinner and dancing." I was immensely relieved that Mona had put sincere forethought into a future wedding. It made me feel less childish for doing it myself.

"And now, for the traditional wedding. . . ." Mona gestured to me.

"Well, I guess it will be," I conceded. "I've always thought about what it would be like. I want all the people I like to be there with me, and the people that matter the most to be a part of it. I worry that I won't have enough positions to include everyone I want, between bridesmaids and readers and maybe a soloist and so on.

"And so on?" asked Rosie. "There's more?"

"Well, yes. There are guest book attendants and honorary bridesmaids and gift coordinators. I am sure I am even forgetting some. I want to try to include as many people as possible and just pray my future Mr. Connelly doesn't have a sister. I'll probably max out on readings and musical pieces. I also agree with Mona that the ceremony should be longer than a half hour."

"Vi, given the number of people you are friends with, if you invite them all, your wedding will be huge. You won't even have time to talk to everyone there," Mona predicted. It was true that if I invited everyone I remained in friendly touch with over the years, the wedding could easily be over four hundred people. But, at the same time I craved the idea of having all the people I knew there for my big day. It was like wanting everyone to see you at your diva performance, when you were looking your absolute best. Naturally, I wanted to pack the house.

"Maybe. I want a simple sheath dress, straight to the floor, maybe with a slit. Nothing pouffy. Similar for the bridesmaids, something simple and straight, probably cocktail length, probably in a wine-red color. I'd like to get married at a destination too, probably Charleston, South Carolina. It is beautiful down there."

"Any thought as to who will be the groom?" Imogen asked. I immediately thought of Caleb.

"No," I lied. "Just as long as he can walk and put on a tuxedo by himself, he will do."

"Actually, there won't be room for him in the church given all the wedding guests," Mona teased.

"Ha, ha. What about you, Babette?" I asked.

"Oh, I am not getting married." Babette replied airily, helping herself to some foie gras. We all groaned.

"Cheater," I accused.

"Cop out!" Imogen threw a cracker at her. "Lame." Babette ducked the cracker, laughing.

"What? It is true. I do not think I'll ever marry. But, if I do, I suppose we would just go to the courthouse and have a judge do the legal requirements. Nothing more. But marriage isn't really my thing. I don't know if I would be with just one person my whole life."

"The male population at large is breathing an enormous sigh of relief right now," I teased. "Mona, pour me some wine. I think we need another log on the fire." Imogen tossed a log on.

"So," she said after she had poked up a flame. "Shall we watch *The Thin Man* and drink every time Nick and Nora do, or should we watch *Four Weddings and a Funeral* for additional wedding ideas? Vi, you can work on your toast," Imogen wiggled her eyebrows at me.

"If I drank every time Nick and Nora do in *The Thin Man,* I'd have alcohol poisoning and a ruined liver halfway through the film," I declared. "And I do *not* want to talk or think about the toast right now. That is *work.* And the weddings are over four months away. I'd rather watch *Grey's Anatomy,* because I am going to marry Dr. McDreamy."

"Oh, me too!" exclaimed Rosie, nearly spilling the wine she was pouring in all of our glasses. "I said doctor, right? He counts."

"Vote," Imogen said. "*Grey's Anatomy*?" Everyone raised their hands, and Imogen went to get the DVDs. I snuggled in the couch between Mona and Babette.

"You know what?" I said. "I am glad all the wedding talk is theoretical. I mean, I want to get married some day and I want you all to get married too . . . if you want, that is, Babette. But, I am seeing how planning a wedding becomes this obsessive quest. And also, you give up so much of your life to another person when you marry. I kind of like being my own person right now. That we can decide on the spur of the moment to have a slumber party, and I can make decisions like that on my own without it impacting anyone else. I am not ready to give up that freedom."

"To being single and happy," Mona approved. "Because you know no guy would sit through several hours of *Grey's Anatomy* in a row. Except maybe Giles."

KERRY REICHS graduated from Oberlin College and Duke University School of Law and Institute of Public Policy. She practiced law in Washington, D.C., for several years until she took a sabbatical and discovered that sabbaticals agree with her. She now writes full time, splitting her time between Washington, D.C., and Los Angeles, and is still trying to convince her two cats that driving across country is fun. Kerry has been in twelve weddings, has never married, and has never worn any of those dresses again. This is her first novel. Visit her at *www.kerryreichs.com*.

Kerry Reichs